EVES
OF
DESTRUCTION

ISBN: 1-4392-5593-8
EAN13: 9781439255933

Visit www.booksurge.com to order additional copies.

EVES

OF

DESTRUCTION

Roy
Berelowitz

ACKNOWLEDGEMENTS

A LOT OF PEOPLE helped me with this novel. My wife is an excellent sounding board to discuss ideas and provide objective and wise criticism, and my parents for always being a source of encouragement and inspiration. My sisters, Dr. Jo-Anne Berelowitz and Susan Berelowitz and many good friends took the time to read early drafts and provide excellent feedback and more importantly, encouragement to keep writing, including John Murphy, Robert Frackelton and Dr. Curt Condon. Mary Kuli and Marty Ortegon provided outstanding help with editing. Dr. Madonna Fernandez was an excellent source of medical expertise as was my brother, Dr. Mark Berelowitz who provided the initial suggestion that made this story possible.

Dedicated to the ones I love.
Michelle, Adam and Michael.

Something wicked this way comes.

<u>Macbeth</u>
William Shakespeare

The nation calls upon the FBI to protect its citizens.
We at the FBI will always answer that call.
We remain committed to accomplishing that mission.

John S. Pistole
Deputy Director
Federal Bureau of Investigation

BEFORE THE BEGINNING

THE LARGE WOMAN stood impassively in the doorway, her fat fleshy arms folded across her ample bosom. Her body was covered in an ill-fitting faded blue uniform that stretched uncomfortably across her chest and hung below her knees. She stared absentmindedly into the distance, until her eyes focused on a cloud of dust gathering behind the black sedan speeding towards her along the dirt road. She tensed, and then shuddered slightly, involuntarily.

The sedan bounced along the dirt road and skidded to a stop outside the doorway. The uniformed driver climbed out and quickly ran around the car to open the rear door for his passenger. The passenger climbed out, strode directly towards the doorway and stopped in front of the woman beneath a faded sign with Cyrillic writing that said: 'Orphanage 132'.

"Welcome Comrade-" the woman began, affecting the best gapped toothed smile she could.

"Where is she?" the man asked, brusquely.

"This way, Comrade," she said, pointing a fat finger down a corridor.

The corridor was long and dark. The floor was covered in black linoleum, shiny once perhaps, but now well worn and ripped in places exposing the gray concrete floor below. At the end of the corridor, diffused sunlight struggled through a dirty window; the only other illumination was provided by the few light bulbs still working. The paint on the walls and ceiling, once white, had turned yellow, and large patches of paint were cracking and flaking. A small dark entrance hall separated the two wings of the long building. One wing, on the eastern side of the building, was comprised of classrooms with rows of wooden desks. If the visitor had cared to look inside, he would have seen that behind the desks sat young children, most of them between five and twelve years of age. They were quiet, the kind of unnatural quiet that comes from strict and harshly applied discipline.

But the visitor did not look. He did not even notice that outside one of the classrooms a small boy stood facing the wall, his face and the wall barely an inch apart. The boy's back was straight, his thin arms held stiffly by his side. He was slowly clenching and unclenching his hands, but he was careful not to move his arms or feet. Large tears slowly rolled down his cheeks, wetting his upper lip.

The west wing was made up of large dormitories closer to the center of the building, and a few offices at the far end. The dormitories were sparse and stark. Each bed was perfectly aligned, blankets neatly folded. The walls in the dormitories were completely bare save for one large picture above each row of beds in every dormitory. The eyes of the personage in the picture were dark and without warmth, although the mustache that split his face slightly softened his appearance.

The man strode purposefully down the west wing in the direction the matron pointed. His beige suit looked as if he wore it everyday, which he did. It was crumpled with large sweat stains under both armpits, the cloth thinning around the pockets. He moved down the corridor at a speed that belied his girth, shoes squeaking with every step. Behind him, the fat pasty-faced woman followed anxiously, skipping every few steps to keep up.

"Is this the room?" the man said, stopping at the last doorway in the corridor. The sign on the door said 'Director'.

"Yes, Comrade," the woman said heavily, panting.

The man turned the handle and pushed the door open. The room was an office, utilitarian and sparsely furnished with one metal frame desk and one upright office chair behind the desk. Two rusty filing cabinets lined one wall. In the middle of the room was a faded, thin rug covering some of the black linoleum. Above, a single unshielded light bulb hung from the ceiling on a long black cord.

Two small children stood in the middle of the room, a strong handsome little boy of about eight or nine and behind him, a little blond girl, about three years his junior. The boy was dressed in dark washed out shorts, a long sleeved shirt missing its breast pocket, and shoes at least two sizes too large for him. His socks did not match.

The little girl wore a dress with faded flowers, one side of which hung, apparently unnoticed, off her shoulder.

The boy stood firmly, eyes fixed on the man in the doorway. The little girl whimpered, barely audible, behind him.

"What is this?" said the man, turning to the woman. "I told you we are just taking the girl."

"Yes, yes," said the women anxiously affirming his statement. "I thought I would have them both ready for you... in case-"

"In case what?" said the man, cutting her off.

"Myda!" he shouted out, looking past the boy at the little girl. The child did not reply.

"Myda?" the man said again, turning questioningly to the woman.

"Is this the girl?" he asked.

"Yes," said the woman. "Come here, child," she said harshly, directing her small, unpleasant eyes at the little girl, and beckoning with a fat index finger.

"No," said the boy. "She stays with me."

"Come here now," the woman shouted, as she reached towards the little girl.

The boy took a step back, avoiding the fat woman's hands, shielding the little girl.

"No," he said again. "She stays with me."

The man stepped forward and roughly pushed the boy aside, knocking him to the ground. The little girl cried out as the man grabbed her right hand in his and then swung her into his arms.

"No," the boy shouted as he jumped to his feet. "No, she stays with me."

But the man had already turned and begun to walk out of the room into the corridor. The boy rushed towards him, but the fat woman blocked his path with her large rear end as she too turned towards the door.

The little girl struggled in the man's arms and called out to her brother, "Vladi." "Vladi please...," as her crying made her words indistinct.

The man continued to walk down the corridor, striding purposefully, ignoring the girl's plaintive cries. The woman skipped behind him, blocking the boy's efforts to get around her. The man reached the entrance hall and kicked the door open with his foot, stepping quickly outside.

The boy pushed past the fat woman and stumbled through the doorway. By now the man had moved towards the large black sedan. The uniformed driver held open the back door and the man climbed swiftly in, pushing the little girl before him. The driver closed the door, rushed around the car, and climbed in. He started the car and immediately pressed the gas pedal, causing the tires to squeal as they bit the dry earth, sending up a cloud of dust and gravel.

The boy stood still, ignoring the pebbles bouncing off him, his face and body slumping dejectedly. The woman stood behind him, a smug and satisfied look on her face, her fat arms resting on her wide hips. As the car drove off, the little girl stood up in the back and looked out through the rear window, crying out to her brother. He could not hear her, but he could see her, her sad despairing face.

"Now get back inside," said the fat woman to the boy. "You will never see her again, so you might as well forget about her."

The boy ignored the woman, his eyes focused on the rapidly disappearing car. She grabbed at him, but he ducked quickly away and turned back towards the building.

CHAPTER I

I T WAS A TRAP. She was sure of it.

There were five of them standing in the hot dusty courtyard, four men and one woman, each in combat boots, khaki pants, standard issue side arms, and an assortment of T-shirts and hats. Two of the men were wearing ankle holsters with small 38 caliber pistols hidden under the cuffs of their trousers. The woman was tall with a strong athletic frame, her blond hair pulled into a short and tight pony tail beneath her cap. Despite the expensive wrap around sunglasses she and most of the other civilians and soldiers in the camp wore, she squinted slightly against the harsh glare of the noon sun.

Surrounding the courtyard was a series of mud brick buildings common in the rural areas of Afghanistan. The buildings and courtyard were in turn surrounded by a five foot high wall, also built of mud bricks and straw. The wall was generally intact except for a few gaps where it had obviously been shattered by explosives. The exterior of the wall was stacked with rows upon rows of sandbags. Beyond the sandbags was a huge sand berm rising almost ten feet high, covered with deep coils of barbed wire stretched out ten feet beyond its base. The compound had the air of a fortress under siege which it was; it had been attacked on numerous occasions sometimes with drive by shootings, occasionally by small mortar rounds and often by snipers. Each successive base commander had ordered additional hardening features to provide added security to the forces stationed there.

The compound, which sat in a vast open plain close to the mountains of eastern Afghanistan had once been the domain of a minor Afghan warlord and his extended family, surrounded by lush orchards of pomegranates and grapes, but when the Soviet army had dropped napalm and seeded his fields from the air with thousands of batwing shaped landmines, injury, death and then starvation had forced them to escape to Pakistan. The landmines remained a danger to US troops and at least two soldiers had been injured not far from the compound in the last week. Strict orders were issued to keep soldiers from walking into unsafe areas.

Loosely arranged around the courtyard was a range of military equipment and vehicles including a large mobile water tank, two Humvees, one tracked troop carrier and two small pickup trucks. About fifty yards beyond the perimeter wall, two UH-60 Black Hawk helicopters sat squat on the ground with their rotors tied down and engine panels removed. One group of mechanics was huddled around one of the Black Hawks while the other was unattended. Both helicopters were also surrounded by huge walls of sand almost ten feet high and dense rows of concertina wire with one small gap to allow access to and from the aircraft.

On top of every building was a sandbagged guard tower with two mounted machine guns, one high powered search light and two army Rangers. In front of one of the guard towers was a crude and faded hand painted sign that said, 'Welcome to Camp Doug Hughes.' No one in the camp ever knew who Doug Hughes was; the first Army Ranger to die at the compound early in the Afghan war. The current set of soldiers had rotated into Afghanistan long after his battalion rotated out and now everyone referred to the outpost as Camp Huge, a name very popular with the young troopers.

"Look," said Casey, the woman in the group. "We really need to follow protocol here. The rest of the team is already out conducting a search mission, so we only have the five of us. The Ranger escort is with them and we can't take the remaining Rangers with us because that will leave this position unprotected. Anyway, how are we going to get there? Both Black Hawks are out of service and the rest are with the Rangers."

"No, you look," said the man directly opposite her, jabbing his forefinger in the air at her. "We have a bona fide lead here from a local that a senior Al Qaeda leader is in the vicinity. If we just sit around on our candy asses waiting for the others to get back, he could be fucking who knows where by then. I say we go and we go now!"

Peter Mulos, the temporary Special Agent in Charge or SAC glared at Casey. He was a chartered public accountant who, despite his best efforts to toughen up his appearance, still looked like a stereotypical desk jockey approaching middle-age. He wore thick glasses, had soft hands and a slight paunch which he endeavored to hide as much as possible. He had arrived in Afghanistan only three weeks prior and his pasty white skin had quickly burned bright red and was only beginning to deepen to the dark farmer's tan common to everyone else in the camp.

Mulos had spent most of his career in the FBI achieving moderate success chasing down white color criminals, but had finally arranged a transfer to a unit tasked with finding Al Qaeda terrorists. He knew, and everyone around him knew, he was completely out of his element. He had neither the experience nor aptitude to be assigned to investigative work in Afghanistan except for one unusual talent: he spoke Pashto fluently. His father had been an official stationed in Afghanistan with USAID, an independent federal government agency tasked with helping disadvantaged countries. Mulos and his family had lived in Kabul for almost seven years until he was fourteen years old and although he had attended an American school, at his father's urging he had learned to speak fluent Pashto, a fact he had kept mostly to himself until the attacks on the World Trade Center. He quickly realized his special language skill could land him better assignments and more promotional opportunity but despite his language skills, his lack of field experience had kept him out of the best assignments. Only a lack of qualified resources at the FBI had finally brought him to Afghanistan and he had been left temporarily in charge of this group due to his seniority in the FBI. He was absolutely determined to demonstrate he merited the assignment.

Casey lowered her voice just slightly, trying to ease the tension as she responded. "If we go now, we go in with no backup, no extraction team and no air transport so we're going to have to hump the last bit to even get there. Shit, by the time we get there it will be way after dark."

There was a pause as the four men said nothing and then Mulos responded, his mouth curling into a sneer, voice dripping with sarcasm.

"Are you afraid of the dark little girl? Fine, then you can stay here with the rest of the Rangers. We," he said as he pointed to the other three men, "are going now."

Even as he uttered the words, he realized he had made a mistake. His eyes widened and his mouth opened almost as if to retract his comment but it was too late and the words hung uncomfortably in the air.

The color drained from Casey's face as she glared at him. There was a brief moment of silence as the three other men either looked down at the ground or shuffled their feet nervously. Her face set and lips tightly pursed, Casey tore off her sunglasses and stepped forward, leaning into his face, their noses barely six inches apart.

"I don't know what rock you just recently climbed out from under but don't you ever presume to talk to me like that again. Do you understand me?"

She remained in place, her face filling his field of vision and paused for a moment before repeating the question louder, almost shouting.

Peter Mulos tried to hold her gaze, but blinking rapidly he turned slightly and then looked away. He found most women intimidating and Casey in particular made him feel more uncomfortable than most.

"Whatever," he mumbled as he tried to square his shoulders and pretended to ignore her challenge. He could not think of anything to say and realized what he had said was completely inappropriate. He noticed one of the other agents was slowly shaking his head and looking at him with an unsympathetic smirk.

Casey glared at him for a few more seconds then stepped back and, placing her hands on her hips, said calmly, "If you're going, I'm coming with you. I'm just saying I think it's a bad idea."

"Duly noted," Mulos responded unconvincingly. "Now gear up. We go in five minutes."

They set out in two vehicles, the Hummer in the lead, the pickup truck trailing behind with the local Pushtun who had given them the lead sitting in the back. Riding with Casey who was driving the pickup, was Agent Michael Cole while the other two men were in the Hummer with Peter Mulos.

The going was difficult, the road little more than dirt trails. Mulos who was driving the lead vehicle pushed the pace pretty hard, making it difficult for Casey to keep up. There had been very little rain in the area and the wheels of the leading vehicle kicked up dry choking dust. The pickup lacked an air conditioner so they had to choose between stifling heat in the closed cab or thick dust. Cole kept his window open and Casey kept hers closed. The pickup danced around in the pitted path, bouncing them up and down in the small cab.

"You know this is fucked up," Casey said to her colleague as she kept her eyes focused on the path. "We don't know where we're going and we have absolutely no idea what we are going to find when we get there. Why didn't you say something?"

Cole shrugged his shoulders. "Mulos is a dick and a moron but he is also the SAC and he gets to make the decisions," he said somewhat defensively.

"He's only the SAC because everybody else is out. If the rest of the team were here, this wouldn't be his call."

"I know," Cole replied, "but hey, you know the pressure to capture Al Qaeda right now is huge. If we have a lead, we have to pursue it."

"And I'm not suggesting we let this go. I'm just saying we should do it properly. We either wait till the rest of the team gets back so we have the right resources or we call in for support. Rushing out like this is just... well... fucked up."

Cole nodded slowly but did not say anything.

Casey turned her eyes from the road and glared at him for a second. She had no issue being the only woman in the fort among all Rangers and FBI agents, but sometimes she definitely felt like the odd one out. The SAC had insisted despite her protestation that she bunk in her own room forcing the other FBI agents to double up in the quarters with some of the Rangers. When she arrived on post, the military commander on site had banned the practice of open showers which the Rangers used to keep clean; one man pouring water on a naked buddy while he soaped up and then one more bucketful to get the soap off. Casey could have cared less but it took a week to get a couple of covered showers built which caused some mumblings about having a woman in camp. Ironically the young rangers seemed most comfortable with her in camp and were very friendly. She recognized that their generation was already used to having women in positions of authority or in roles previously considered unfit for women and, to them, her presence was not unusual. It was the older men in their late thirties and early forties who seemed to struggle with it. She could really care less what people thought. She was completely confident of her skills and would back down from no-one.

But Cole was right about the pressure to capture or kill Al Qaeda terrorists as quickly as possible. There was increasing frustration in Washington that for so long after the attacks of 9/11, Osama bin Laden was still at large and sending radio and video messages to the world via the Al Jazeera Arab news channel seemingly at will. It was hoped that by pairing up the FBI's analytical skills in the field with US Special Forces, they would increase pressure on bin Laden and flush him out of his suspected hiding place in eastern Afghanistan along the border with Pakistan. Casey's team had been in the country for almost two months and had been hard at work trying to coordinate a new strategy. So far they had achieved very little.

They drove on in silence, Casey fighting the steering wheel trying to keep the truck from breaking an axle on the rough road. The sun was setting behind the high mountains off in the distance, the long shadows making it even harder to see the trail.

Up ahead, the Hummer slowed down as the trail narrowed. Casey slowed down as well, keeping her distance — better to make two targets instead of one she thought to herself.

Suddenly her partner shouted at her. "Casey, our guide just jumped out the back of the pickup. Where the fuck is he going?"

Cole turned in his seat trying to find the fleeing Afghan who was now running back down the trail.

"Oh shit," Casey shouted, "we're in a fucking ambush."

She pushed hard on the horn trying to get the attention of the vehicle up ahead. Just then, out of the corner of her eye she saw a streak of light arcing towards them. Before she could shout a warning to her colleagues, the rocket propelled grenade struck the Hummer just below an open window and the vehicle exploded with a large flash.

"Get out of the car — get out, get out," she screamed to Cole as she grabbed her weapon and rolled out of the moving truck, landing hard on the rough ground. She bounced up, running away from the still rolling truck, screaming for Cole to get out. She saw him roll clear of the truck's cab and then winced as she felt the flash of heat as a second grenade hit the front of the pickup truck, ripping it apart and upending it on its side. Legs driving hard, she could hear small arms fire cackling around her as she ran towards a group of large boulders just beyond the trail, diving behind them as bullets bit into the earth near her feet. A moment later, Cole dove in beside her. Both agents quickly assumed firing position between the rocks.

"Are you hit?" Cole hissed at her, as he fought to catch his breath.

"No," Casey whispered back. "Are you?"

Cole shook his head. "What the fuck happened?" he asked as wiped the sweat off his brow.

"It was a fucking setup. We drove right into a fucking trap." Casey shook her head in disgust.

Slowly she raised her head and peaked over one of the rocks trying to see what had happened to the Hummer. It was still burning and she could make out two bodies lying next to it.

"Do you think they're all-?"

Cole never did finish his question. The bullet struck him in the left temple, the other side of his head exploding in a flash of brains, bone and blood splattering Casey's face and chest. She stifled a scream as his body collapsed at her feet. She ducked her head down and reached for him and then recoiled at the sight of his smashed skull. She closed her eyes and tried to control her breathing, fighting off panic.

Voices from just beyond her hiding place snapped her quickly back to reality. In the gathering darkness she allowed herself a quick glance over the rocks and could vaguely make out at least four men advancing towards her position. She ducked back down and did a quick assessment of her situation. It was bad. She was outnumbered and knew any attempt to fight her way out was suicidal. She was all alone in an unfamiliar location with no means of communication. Darkness was her only protection if she could hide until the last light of the day disappeared. She squeezed between the narrow boulders behind her and as quietly and quickly as she could, she crawled away from the approaching attackers.

Their voices grew louder as they found the body of her colleague and paused to abuse his corpse and rifle through his pockets. She gritted her teeth in anger at the sounds of rocks smashing his already broken skull, but used their distraction to find a better hiding spot. As the last vestiges of light disappeared, she tucked herself into a wedge of large boulders, pulling her legs to her chest to form as small a target as possible and placed her weapon across her waist. She could feel her heart pounding in her chest and struggled to calm her breathing.

For what seemed like an eternity she sat there not moving. She wondered what time it was but did not dare press the light button on her digital watch. She could hear voices that seemed quite close but could not make out any figures moving around. Her body grew stiff but she was afraid to move. As she sat in her hiding spot she made a quiet resolution with herself; she would go down fighting. Under no circumstances would she let herself be captured alive. She had seen what the Taliban had done to American men they had captured and she could just imagine what they would do to a woman. She would not let it happen.

As darkness enveloped her, Casey shivered against the desert cold. Dressed only in a T-shirt and fatigues, she had little protection from the cold night air. Her throat was dry from the dusty road and the stress of the attack. Her body was stiff from sitting still in a confined space but despite her discomfort, she stayed still. She did a quick mental inventory of her equipment. Rolling out of the truck so quickly, she had not noticed that her camel pack, a large backpack water pouch carried by most of the troopers and field agents had by some good fortune, snagged on her rifle and was now still dangling from the weapon. As quietly as she could, she untangled the backpack and slowly took a couple of quick sips to quench her thirst. Fortunately, the pouch was full and held almost two liters of water, good enough to sustain her for a day or so even in Afghanistan's brutal daytime summer heat. She also had her M4 carbine, a shortened version of the M16 rifle, two spare ammunition clips in her trouser pockets, a standard issue FBI semi-automatic handgun in a holster on her hip, a six inch bowie knife in a sheath attached to her belt, and a small pack of sucking sweets in another pocket. She ached to reach for one of those sweets, to feel its flavor in her mouth, but she resisted the temptation.

A burst of gunfire snapped her out of her reverie and she winced before realizing the Taliban were just firing at shadows. She could still hear voices not far away and it was obvious they were searching for her. She assumed they had seen her jump out of the truck before it was hit and were intent on finding her. A captured American soldier would make a great prize. When they realized she was a woman and an FBI agent, her value would only increase.

Fortunately, when the waning moon rose late in the evening it was just a thin sliver in the sky, proving little illumination to her pursuers. Gradually, after what felt like an eternity, their voices trailed off and then there was silence. Casey fought to stifle her shivering body, straining to hear any hint of movement. At first she was afraid they might be tricking her into revealing her position, but after what seemed like a very long time, she was certain they were gone. Slowly, she uncoiled herself from the narrow wedge of boulders that had been her hiding place and carefully stood up, weapon at the ready. Peering into the dense desert darkness, she could make out very little. She briefly illuminated her watch to the check the time. It was close to midnight.

She pondered her situation. They had driven for almost two hours before the ambush and despite the difficult road conditions, had probably averaged about thirty miles per hour. That would put her at least sixty miles from camp. Even worse, they had left without providing a time certain when they would return so it might be some time before someone even raised the alarm that they were missing. They had had satellite phones in each vehicle but communication was notoriously bad in the mountains and valleys of Afghanistan so even if they did not have contact with their base, it was unlikely their failure to return would cause anyone to raise an immediate alarm.

Casey shook her head in disgust. Self pity was a luxury in which she never engaged. Since joining the agency almost nine years prior she had worked hard to establish a reputation of excellence in all her work. She had been a nationally ranked collegiate athlete, was a quick study, a diligent student and good at her work. Each year she received glowing reviews from her supervisors and anticipated a steady upward career in the Agency. But at some point, she was not quite sure when, she hit the glass ceiling. Men who had served less time than her were promoted. Choice assignments went to others. She could not really recall any overt sexist comments other than the natural flirtatious ribbing among the younger FBI agents which never bothered her, but slowly she began to resent the overt fraternal nature of the Agency. Most of the agents were men. A disproportionate number of managers were also men. There were an increasing number of women in management but they seemed to have the least prestigious jobs.

When teams were being selected to go to Afghanistan to accelerate the capture of Bin Laden and top Al Qaeda leaders, she campaigned hard to be included and despite her low expectations, was one of only two female agents chosen for the mission. She knew there was some grumbling among agents not chosen that her selection was more political than deserved but Casey just ignored the sniping. At thirty-eight years old, she knew her capabilities and was confident in her ability to perform as well or even better than any man on the team.

Carefully, she began climbing through the rocks back to the dirt road. For a moment she considered going back to the burnt out vehicles up ahead but quickly dismissed the idea: they were all dead, if not from the first missile then certainly from the shots fired by the attackers. She was equally certain the equipment inside the vehicles had already been looted or destroyed in the attack.

She reached the road and, after pausing briefly to look carefully in each direction and listen for any sounds, she struck out back to Camp Huge. She hoped to cover at least thirty miles before sunrise.

She started out at a fast walk, startled to hear how loud her steps sounded. If anyone was nearby they would hear her for sure. But after covering about a mile, she gained confidence that she was alone. Slinging her rifle into a more comfortable position across her back, she broke into a run. Running had always been a sort of solace: an escape from the rigors of school or college or even FBI training. A solitary run in a park or forest had always lifted her spirits. Now, as she settled into a comfortable pace, she felt stronger and emotionally uplifted as she began her long trek back to base. She was not naïve about her circumstances: a lone woman in hostile territory with limited water and sixty hard miles to safety. She wondered how long it would take before her water ran out and her thirst became unbearable, probably two days if she kept out of the sun during the day. The trick was not to deny herself water, but to try to keep what she had for as long as possible. Two days would be tough, more than that and her kidneys would start to fail. Worst of all, her faculties would decline at the moment she needed them the most. She shrugged off the negative thoughts and just focused on keeping her pace steady and her breathing regular.

As a land locked country, Afghanistan has big differences between day and night temperatures. Even as she ran, Casey could feel the temperature rapidly fall and she noticed she was barely sweating. Her mouth was very dry and after two hours of running, she took a break and allowed herself a couple sips of water and one of the sucking sweets in her pocket. The sucking action created saliva in her mouth and at least temporarily, she felt the thick dryness in her throat ameliorated. It felt good while it lasted and before the sweet had been reduced to nothing in her mouth, she resumed her run.

Before dawn she began to hallucinate. A large rock up ahead suddenly looked like an old Russian tank and she scrambled down to the side of the road before she realized her error. On another occasion she thought her college roommate was running beside her and imagined they were having a conversation. It had been a pleasant distraction from her actual circumstances.

She was exhausted and began to feel the first effects of dehydration, a drumbeat in her head constantly demanding that she stop and quench her thirst. Sparingly, she sipped the water and twice she had fallen asleep on her feet and stumbled as she startled awake. Still, she drove herself on recognizing even in her muddled state that her survival depended on getting back to base as soon as possible. Daylight would force her to stop and seek cover from the blazing Afghan summer sun and Taliban fighters who might still be looking for her, but every step she could run now would bring her closer to safety.

Just before dawn broke in the mountains behind her, she finally stopped running and began to walk slowly for a while, cooling her body down before seeking some shelter to hide during the day. Casey understood she needed to harbor her strength and expected to cramp up from the hard run and rationed water supply. She stepped off the road and slowly began to climb the small hill to her right looking for shelter. The land was barren of trees and almost bare of vegetation. Her best hope was to find a large rock that would give her shelter from the sun and protection from searching eyes. She moved off the road almost one hundred yards to the crest of the hill, weapon at the ready and settled on a large cluster of rocks covering a small, tunnel-like narrow patch of dirt. She started to climb in headfirst and then reversed herself, working her feet in first, keeping her head oriented towards the road. She laid her weapon down directly in front of her and tried to stay alert. A cluster of rocks in front of her would keep her hidden from road but still allow her to see anyone approaching, at least so she hoped.

She rested for half an hour and, drank a little more water and rewarded herself with another sucking sweet. Just as she was about to doze off, she was suddenly startled by the sound of voices from the road. Her heart was pounding and she struggled to listen but it was unmistakable; someone was coming down the road. She could not make out the voices but they sounded uncomfortably close but because of the way sound echoes between the hills and gullies of Afghanistan, she could not be sure.

She moved lower into her hiding place and watched as a group of heavily armed Afghan men came walking around the corner. She quickly counted eight men and noticed that they were walking purposefully at a quick pace. But they were also walking carefully, spread out to avoid a surprise attack, and weapons at the ready. Casey slunk down lower behind the small boulder and watched them walk past her.

She was not sure who these men were but it was likely they were part of the same group of Taliban fighters that had ambushed them the night before. She was surprised at how quickly they had caught up with her, disappointed she had not been able to put more distance between herself and her attackers.

Peering cautiously from her hiding place as the men disappeared down the road, she realized that her situation had quickly worsened. Now the Taliban were between her and the road back to Camp Huge. If she continued on the road she might run into them or of they turned back up the road, they might see her first. Either way the road was no longer an option. Pondering her situation, she decided to remain in place until the sun set and then consider her options.

She woke with a pounding painful headache and then groaned as her body quickly cramped up as she tried to move. He eyes were almost completely gummed shut and her tongue felt swollen in her mouth and her breath sounded thick and congested. Her lower back hurt and she knew her kidneys were probably shutting down, shriveling up due to the lack of hydration. She lay still for a moment, gritting her teeth against the pounding in her head and tried to calm her aching body.

Slowly she reached up to her eyes and, squinting against the bright sunlight penetrating her little shelter, gently rubbed them to clear her sight. Every movement felt painful and her throat felt so dry that swallowing seemed to absorb all her energy.

She allowed herself a deep refreshing drink of water and then another sip which she first sloshed around her mouth and then swallowed. Wiping the spittle of her mouth with the back of her hand, she drew in a deep breath, trying to clear her mind and force herself to think rationally. Thankfully, she seemed to have slept most of the day with the late afternoon sunlight finally striking her hiding place and waking her up. She glanced at her watch and was grateful sunset was less than an hour away. She took a quick inventory of her water supply and realized she had drunk almost half her supply. For the distance she had covered, she had drunk very little but at this rate of consumption, she would be out of water by the next day. She resolved to manage her consumption more carefully.

Cautiously, she peered out her hiding place and for almost five minutes she watched the road in both directions, listening carefully. She could see and hear no-one. Slowly she crawled out of her hiding place, rubbing her legs to fight the cramp and fatigue as she glanced down at the road, badly tempted to use it to return to Camp Huge, but knowing at the same time this was not an option. She turned and walked up the short distance to the top of the hill. Her only option now was to try and find a route parallel to the road for navigation purposes, but that kept her far enough away so as not to encounter the Taliban. If she strayed too far from the road, she ran the risk of getting lost among the hills and gullies.

She crested the hill and carefully picked her way through the rocks to the gully below. It was much harder and slower to walk off the path and she had to be careful not to fall and injure herself in the diminishing light. She decided to put a little more distance between herself and the Taliban so she walked up and over another small hill that put her about half a mile from the road. Then, using the last rays of sunlight on the distant mountains as her guide, she turned west and began to walk as quickly as she could through the uneven terrain.

Casey's second night alone had been much more difficult than the first. She had fallen more times than she could recall and once cut her hand on a sharp rock. She had torn off a piece of her T-shirt to wrap the wound, but she found it difficult to protect the injured hand and to stop falling on the uneven terrain. She was constantly thirsty but was adamant about limiting herself to one small sip of water every two hours. She tried hard to keep a fast pace but darkness and the terrain were making her work harder and go slower than she wanted. As she felt the first flush of dawn's light behind her, she guessed she probably had only been able to walk about fifteen miles the entire night. At this pace she would need at least one more night of hard walking before reaching the camp.

As the sun rose she was less cautious about stopping because she felt more secure from Taliban fighters this far from the road, but suddenly she came upon a narrow but well worn path. It caught her by surprise and she quickly dropped down to one knee and glanced up and down the path which ran perpendicular to her route. A path implied the presence of people and now she might be more vulnerable than ever. If there was someone walking in either direction towards her, she would have no time to run and hide.

Looking up the path to the north, she could see it wind its way for almost half a mile and to the south it disappeared out of her view in a few hundred yards but not before turning west. Looking carefully in both directions and not seeing anyone, she picked the route appearing to go west.

Walking along the path in daylight was much easier and Casey quickened her pace, but on the barren landscape she felt terribly exposed. She kept checking behind her to see if anyone was approaching but as the path continued in a westerly direction, she saw no-one.

The sun rose higher into the sky behind her and she began to feel the intense heat of the day and an overwhelming sense of exhaustion from her difficult walk the previous night. Her body was very fatigued and cramps were developing in her legs and back as she continued to minimize her water consumption. She knew she could not continue walking on the exposed path through the day but she could see no place to hide.

Casey realized her exhaustion was limiting her vigilance and she caught herself walking with her head down focusing on her feet and the ground a few paces ahead. She jerked her head up to look around, shocked to see she had almost walked directly into a large compound.

Scrambling to find cover she ducked beneath a low stone wall surrounding the compound and held her gun in the ready position, her body tensing up as she expected to be challenged, but she heard nothing. Carefully, she slowly rose and peered over the low exterior wall surrounding the compound. There was one long building in the compound but it was mostly in ruins with the roof caved in and the walls collapsed. After pausing for a moment, Casey carefully rolled her body over the wall and into a low crouch as she landed on the other side. Weapon sweeping the compound in conjunction with her eyes she heard and saw nothing. The place was deserted. She walked to the building and peered inside. The floor was covered with debris of the collapsed ceiling and there was no sign of human habitation. She stepped inside and carefully walked through the building to the open court-yard on the other side. The courtyard was quite large, almost as big as football field and surprisingly flat and clean. It was obvious someone or a group of people had worked hard to clear it of rocks and flatten it.

Still shaken by her unexpected discovery of the de-serted compound, she found a shaded spot and sat down with her back resting against the wall, her weapon laid across her lap. She allowed herself two small sips of wa-ter and one more sucking sweet. She was running low on both but needed the water and sugar to help keep her mind clear.

As she rested against the wall trying to catch her breath, she carefully scanned the courtyard. The only ev-idence of human presence she could see were three large metal drums typically used by remote Afghan villages to store water. But these drums were peppered with holes and one of them was completely crushed.

At the far end of the courtyard she noticed a single wooden pole standing upright. She stared at it for a mo-ment and then despite her exhaustion, slowly stood up and walked towards it. As she got closer she noticed it was actually a square piece of wood about four inches thick and eight feet tall, embedded very securely in the ground. About one foot from the top of the post, a hinged and thick metal ring was bolted on.

Casey looked closer at the post and noticed it was badly nicked and scared, with large chunks of wood missing, mostly in the lower half of the post. The ground around the post was dusty like the rest of the courtyard but there were also dark spots where the sand had seemed to congeal. As Casey kneeled down to look at one of the dark spots, she noticed a small piece of metal, no bigger than tip of her finger. She picked it up and examined it but could not determine what it was. Then she noticed another similar piece of metal and as she scratched the ground around her, she saw buried in the sand numerous pieces, all similar in size. She stared at them in the palm of her hand and then without really considering why, dropped them into a pocket in her pants, walked back to the dilapidated building and found a sheltered spot to lie down.

Casey awoke to a pounding headache and for a moment was completely disoriented and panicked. She quickly recognized her surroundings and, fighting the pain in her head, and the ache and fatigue in her body, she slowly got up and walked out of the building. It was the late afternoon and already there were long shadows cast by the huge mountains to the west. She checked her water supply and guessed she was down to just a couple of sips. She allowed herself one small sip which she held in her mouth as long as possible before swallowing. She knew she would not be able to survive another day alone and had to reach the camp tonight. She decided to try and head back to the road, assuming if she did not run into the Taliban, that would be the quickest way to get back. Checking her orientation to make sure she was heading in the right direction, she started to climb the hill to her left, carefully picking her way through the rocks. The terrain was flattening out which she knew was a good sign because it meant she was finally getting out of the foothills of the mountain range they had been ambushed in and was approaching the open plain where Camp Huge was located.

She walked for about an hour in the direction of the road going up and down two small hills and just as she was starting to worry she might be lost, she crested a third hill and saw the road just below her. She knelt down and looked cautiously in both directions and not seeing anything, began to walk down the hill. She had barely gone ten paces before she heard voices. She scrambled back up the hill and lay down just below the crest, anxiously peering over.

Her heart quickened as she slowly peered between a gap in rocks back to the road and saw a group of men about five hundred yards down the road from her position. She could not be certain but they looked like the same men she had seen the day before. This time however, they were walking back up the road and at a more leisurely pace than the last time she had seen them.

Instinctively she pulled her weapon close and tried to think. Her head was pounding in pain and her lips were so cracked and dry she could barely move them. It was so difficult to maintain rational a thought she was briefly tempted to succumb to the desire just to put her head down and ease the pain when suddenly another more familiar sound caught her attention.

Two Black Hawk helicopters were approaching her position flying low and fast. She was tempted to jump up and catch their attention but with the Taliban so close, she did not dare. She glanced back at the road and could not see anyone. Panicking for moment, she thought they had left the road and snuck up on her but then she spotted a couple of men hiding among the rocks. They had heard the helicopter before her and had quickly sought cover.

The helicopters passed by in a few seconds, the familiar sound of their rotors beating the air faded away. As the sounds of rescue wafted away, she glanced back at the road and saw the men emerge from their rocky hiding places. Squinting through the rocks, she counted eight men, all armed with Kalashnikovs and two of them were also carrying rocket-propelled grenades. They were standing together in the road in what looked like animated almost angry conversation.

They were moving again, walking up the road past her. Finally it seemed luck was on her side. If she just waited patiently until they disappeared up the road, she could scramble down the hill and run down the road to the camp. She closed her eyes and briefly contemplated what would have happened if she had been a few minutes earlier and was already on the road when they came by. She shook her head and pushed the thought from her mind.

Just then she heard the men shouting at the same time she heard the sounds of helicopters again. At first she thought it was the Black Hawks she had seen earlier returning but now the sound was louder. She looked towards the noise and saw two CH-53 Sea Stallions approaching. The big troop carriers were flying in the same direction as the previous two helicopters but higher and slower and again she ached to jump up and wave her arms at them but stifled the impulse. She glanced back at the road again and spotted the Taliban soldiers hiding in the rocks. One of the men carrying the RPG appeared to be aiming at the helicopters but he held his fire and they passed without incident.

Again the men reassembled in the road but this time they quickly resumed their walk up the road and out of her field of vision. Casey laid her head down and tried to relax her body. Her heart was pounding and she felt faint. Sucking in big gulps of air, she tried at once to calm herself and get ready to move again. Slowly, she climbed to her feet, picked up and slung her M16 over her neck, holding it in the ready position.

Gently rubbing her thighs she glanced back up the dirt road but saw nothing. She needed to start moving right away, but instead sat on a large rock to rest and take stock of her situation. She reached in to her pocket and pulled out her packet of sucking sweets; she had only one left. She could not recall sucking them as she stumbled through the rocks during the night but she must have been reaching for them quite often, enough to almost empty the pack. She placed it back into her pocket and checked her water pouch and was not surprised to see it was almost dry. She sighed deeply, and then shrugging off a momentary flash of self pity she stood up and scanned the road. Certain there was no movement, she carefully climbed over the rocks back to the road. It was not yet dark but she was determined to get moving. The Taliban could return at any time. She paused once more before stepping on to the road and then confident there was no-one around, positioned her rifle more comfortably across her back and began to run.

For the first hour, she was able to maintain a reasonable pace, but as night fell she struggled. Her discomfort was intense and she had to constantly fight the urge just to stop and lay down. Images of her parents, friends and even strangers she had seen just once flashed in and out of her mind. Sometimes they were indistinct and other times they were so real she thought they were with her. At one point she saw her father standing at the side of the road and he seemed so real she started talking to him, asking him what he was doing there. The most painful image was of her late husband, forever young and vibrant, smiling at her with that grin he always got when he was about to pay her the sweetest compliment. Most of the time she was cognizant enough to clear her mind at least for awhile, but after thinking about her late husband, she became quite weepy and emotional. She stopped running and collapsed onto her haunches and just cried.

She was moving again when a light suddenly appeared up above. It was glowing quite brightly and casting a broad canopy of light above her. She stopped and swayed in place, trying to make out what it was. Then, from a distance a very bright light was shone directly at her and she squinted as it penetrated her dry eyes. She stood blinking against the light and thought she heard voices. She was spent; she could run no further or even protect herself. Fumbling at her holster, she struggled to pull out her sidearm and put an end to her misery, but even that was beyond her. She sunk to her knees and rolled over on to her side, unconscious.

CHAPTER 2

THE REAL PHILIPPE MÉTIER would have been the same age as the man who had taken over his identity if he had lived past his first birthday. Instead, only his name and identity had survived, providing cover to his alter ego who had lived under deep cover for the past nine years. His real name was Abd Al Rahman. Sitting alone at a small coffee table with his back to the wall outside a Parisian bistro alternately sipping strong coffee and inhaling deeply from the cigarette he held delicately between the forefingers of his left hand, he looked like an average middle-aged Frenchman. His right hand he kept obscured, occasionally resting it in his lap or slipping it into his trouser pocket.

This was one of his pastimes; sitting away the day at a small outdoor bistro or café on a late summer afternoon with a newspaper or magazine. It had never been his custom to be gregarious so, other than an occasional brusque *bon jour* or *au revoir*, he rarely spoke to anyone. He was not interested in making friends. In fact his instructions so many years before had been very clear; hide in plain view, blend in, assimilate completely, become one of them.

Forget who you were, he was told. Give up cultural associations, even old mannerisms to suggest the past, surrender yourself to the local temptations and don't feel guilty about it.

To serve us best you must become one of them.

By all measures, he had done well but it had been a struggle. His real name meant *Servant of the Merciful* and giving it up for his *nom de guerre* was difficult because it spoke to him about his faith, his commitment and obedience to God. He despised his assumed name, false identity and seemly pointless assumed life but saw them as a test of his faith. At first he had struggled to abandon the culture of his birth which had always felt like a warm embrace and a path of piety, but after some time he rationalized that the greatest test of a man's faith is not his ability to practice openly and fervently but to pretend to abandon it completely without actually doing so; to maintain his love, his loyalty and devotion without ever expressing it. How much stronger was his faith now that he lived this false life for so many years with no contacts from the old days, no promise of contact in the future, just the promise that when the time came, he would be summoned to the cause and well used.

No one who knew Abd Al Rahman from the old days in Afghanistan when he fought against the infidels and godless communists would ever have accused him of weakness. He was still in his late teens when he arrived from Lebanon and was treated with suspicion at first because he was lighter skinned than the other Arab volunteers and spoke both French and Arabic fluently, that is, when he did speak. He was so taciturn that sometimes it would seem that days went by with him not speaking at all, but he was pious and his reputation as a fearless and merciless warrior was quickly established, particularly his capacity to endure the unendurable. Neither bone numbing cold in the mountains of or incapacitating heat in the deserts seemed to deter him from his sworn mission to kill every Soviet invader of Afghanistan.

One of his many storied attacks took place at the Salang Tunnel north of Kabul. Originally built by the Soviets for the Afghanistan government starting in 1955, the tunnel and highway were completed in 1964 and at the time, the Salang Tunnel was the highest in the world at over ten thousand feet. The highway and tunnel were vital conduits for the Soviet army in Afghanistan and the site of constant and fierce fighting between Soviet forces trying to keep it open and mujihadin who sought to close it and use it to capture Soviet army equipment.

After numerous losses, including the deaths of over two thousand people in one attack in 1982, the Soviets decided to maximize the use of the tunnel in winter when conditions would be so severe the mujahideen could not mount a serious attack, or at least so they believed. When Pakistani intelligence, who worked closely with the mujihadin, reported that a very large Soviet Army convoy planned to pass through the Salang in the next few days, Abd Al Rahman organized an attack force that spent seven days at an altitude of over ten thousand feet, sometimes in a freezing snowstorm waiting for the Soviets. When two of his men froze to death, half the

men abandoned the mission and escaped to a lower el-
evation, but Abd Al Rahman never left nor allowed himself any quarter. He maintained his vigil, encouraged
and helped the remaining mujahideen soldiers to survive
and attack the Soviets when they passed by. He led the
destruction of over fifty vehicles in the convoy and killed
over 100 Soviet soldiers and officers.

When he found two of his mujahideen trying to rape
a captured female Russian officer he personally executed
both rapists by slitting their throats and then shot the
Russian woman as she begged for her life.

But his most legendary success was how he dealt with
the Russians when they captured him. He had become
a marked man, known for staging bloody attacks on
Russian convoys on lonely highways and later for even
more blatant attacks on senior Soviet officers in Kabul.

In desperation the Soviets brought in a *Spetsnaz* unit,
Special Forces from the KGB comprised of elite troops to
hunt him down. The *Spetsnaz* soldiers were extremely
well trained and unlike their regular army comrades,
could fight the mujihadin on their own terms in the
toughest terrain and the most brutal conditions. For
months they played a deadly game of cat and mouse with
some close calls, but Abd Al Rahman always managed
to elude them while still tormenting them with periodic
attacks and bombings. The Soviets applied increasingly
brutal methods, torturing captured mujihadin for information on his whereabouts, indiscriminate shelling of
villages in which he was suspected to be hiding, but all
to no avail. One commanding officer of the search team
was killed in action and anther removed from command

because of his inability to complete the mission. Finally, a young KGB major was brought in. He was much like the man he was chasing; methodical, relentless and fearless in his pursuit of his quarry. When the KGB team finally tracked Al Rahman to an area in the mountains near Kabul, they began a weeklong running pursuit that cost the lives of fifteen Soviet elite soldiers and an unknown numbers of mujihadin fighters.

Abd Al Rahman realized the noose was tightening but he embraced the idea of dying in a holy war against the infidel invaders. He did his best to be killed rather than captured in the final fire fight when his hideout was attacked, but he was knocked unconscious and injured in his right leg when a shell exploded nearby and the Soviet Special Forces dragged him out alive.

He was given perfunctory medical treatment to fix his wounded leg but the torture had begun almost immediately. An expert was brought in directly from Moscow to quickly get any current information about the disposition of the mujihadin fighters. The expert was systematic and unashamedly sadistic and even seasoned KGB officers stepped away as the intensity of the torture was ratcheted higher and higher, beyond what they were able to witness. But despite the expert's best efforts with beatings, sleep deprivation, electric shock and repeated dunking in cold water, he gave them nothing. He would just stare back at his torturer's face, blinking slowly against the pain and give himself to Allah, his faith and fortitude carrying him through.

Finally, his torturer began the harshest and most painful attack that Al Rahman knew he could not withstand indefinitely. With garden shears, he systematically began cutting off the fingers of his right hand joint by joint. Over a period of two days, he started with his thumb and quickly worked it down to a small raw stub and then moved on to his index finger. When it too was a just a raw bleeding stub, he started cutting off his other fingers, piece by bloody piece.

The pain was unspeakable. He cried in anger and rage against his tortures and to Allah to have mercy on him, to take him to heaven. He bit his lips and tongue raw as his hand was mutilated and shattered two molars as he clenched his jaw against the pain.

But suddenly, for reasons never explained to him, the torture stopped. His hand was treated, not well, but just enough that he would not die of infection, and late one night he and a few other captive mujihadin were flown to Moscow. He never learned why the torture ended or why he had been taken from Afghanistan but he later assumed it was because the Soviets had decided to abandon Afghanistan and did not to want to leave obvious evidence of their mistreatment of Arabs.

For six years he languished in a variety of Russian jails. He received additional treatment for his mangled right hand and his leg injury but for the first year of his incarceration he suffered from severe pain in his hand. The conditions in the jails were primitive and harsh and at first the Russian prisoners treated him roughly but over time his natural leadership and fortitude won them over. He learned to speak good Russian and encouraged the few other Moslems incarcerated with him to maintain their faith.

In 1996, without warning or explanation he was released from prison, transported to the most eastern border of Russia, provided with a small amount of money and pushed over the border into Kazakhstan. He was no longer the young fit man he had been and the injury to his leg limited his mobility but his mind was clear and there was no question in his mind where he was going and who he would seek out when he got there. He was picked up by police or paramilitary groups on a number of occasions but always somehow managed to get away. Food was sometimes plentiful but more often it was meager and he struggled on his journey, but he always kept his faith, embracing his struggle as a catharsis. Traveling mostly on foot, occasionally in the backs of trucks and once by train, it took him three months to reach the Afghan border. Avoiding the border crossing, he found an unprotected and sparsely patrolled area and crossed into Afghanistan late one night.

By the time Al Rahman returned to Afghanistan he was disconnected from the events of the past six years. He knew nothing of the current state of affairs in Afghanistan since the Soviets had been defeated by the mujihadin and that another war had broken out between the Taliban, a radical Sunni Islamist group, and the Northern Alliance, a group of warring factions united to fight the Taliban. What Abd Al Rahman also did not know was that his mentor and friend, Osama bin Laden had also just returned to Afghanistan after being deported from the Sudan. Soon after his arrival in Afghanistan, Al Rahman was picked up and quickly recognized by seasoned Taliban fighters who knew him from the old days. Within a week he was reunited with his old friend, a meeting both men immediately understood was by the providence of Allah.

The two old warriors spent days together, praying and reminiscing only briefly about their struggle against the Soviet Union but focusing on their desire to attack America, destroy Israel, return all of Jerusalem to Arab control, expel all non-Muslims from the middle-east, returning Arabia to the days of the Caliphate when all Arabs lived by the rules and tenets of the Koran. It was never stated between them but Al Rahman was quite certain Bin Laden was a true Caliph and he sometimes referred to him as *Amir al-Mu'minin* or Commander of the Faithful.

Al Rahman attentively listened to his old friend describe his plans to wage war against the despotic Arab regimes and their western sponsors. With the increasing power of the Taliban in Afghanistan, Bin Laden was confident they could operate almost in the open, recruiting and training young fighters who were committed to the cause.

Abd Al Rahman considered his reunion with Osama bin Laden one of the greatest moments of his life. His allegiance to Bin Laden was absolute and he agreed without reservation with his friend's declaration of *jihad* against the tyrannical and despotic Arab leaders and their western supporters. Despite his age and injuries he asked his former commander to assign him a mission, another opportunity to achieve martyrdom denied to him so many years before on the battlefield with the Russians.

Weeks passed before Bin Laden responded to his request and when he did, Al Rahman was disappointed. He wanted to fight the enemy directly, but instead he was told, "To serve us best you must become one of them. Adopt their lifestyle," Bin Laden directed him in his soft, almost monotone voice.

"Live openly in their secular world, cut off all ties to Islam and live amongst the infidels. When the time is right, we will call on you to our struggle."

He was directed to live in Paris, a relatively easy place for an Arab to blend in among the large Muslim pollution but even that was not allowed him. Fluent in French from his childhood in Lebanon, he made no contact at all with his fellow Muslims and followed his orders explicitly. He lived as a Frenchman in Paris, but during his first year there he felt adrift and without purpose. During the Afghan war against the Soviets, his purpose had been clear; to kill as many Russians as possible, and later in Russian prison his goal had been to survive while keeping his faith and spirit intact.

After some time in his forced exile, he began to explore, first only in France then later on, other countries on the continent; Italy, Germany and Holland. He regarded these trips as intelligence gathering, an opportunity to identify possible targets to attack, to learn more about security in each country so when the time came and he was called upon, he would be ready. His trips gave him purpose, made him feel as if he was still part of the struggle, ready to act when called.

In the summer of 2000 he crossed the Channel and spent a week in England, mostly in London visiting tourist sites, learning about the subway system, riding with the huge crowds that descend in to the London subway every weekday morning and evening on their way to and from work. He imagined what would happen if a bomb or series of bombs exploded in the subway. The death toll would be huge but he believed the psychological impact of the attack would be diminished because the destruction would take place in an area not easily seen. Al Rahman understood that the power of the terrorist was to create a sense of vulnerability in the common man, to give him a perpetual sense of insecurity. He understood that the threat of terror was much more powerful than any real action. But, he also understood that for the threat to be perceived, there had to be occasional and direct action to remind the populace they were not safe.

He took a boat tour of the Thames and stood on the open deck as the boat motored past the British Houses of Parliament. He could hear the tour guide droning on about the history of British democracy but all he could think of is what the building would look like as a shattered and burned out shell. In his mind's eye he could see the bombs exploding; great big sheets of fire leaping high into the air as the walls came crashing down. It was a satisfying daydream and he prayed silently that one day he would be called on to do something like that.

His trip to England reminded him that his English language skills were very limited and upon his return to Paris he immediately began to study. As the common international language, he felt that learning English was a necessary part of his preparation for whatever mission he was given. Unwilling to expose himself to too many questions he decided against signing up for a class, instead buying language tapes and renting English language films so after a year he felt confident enough to return to England to test his skills. He was pleasantly surprised he could easily manage simple conversations and even read the local newspapers.

Despite the years spent living in France and traveling the continent, his hatred for the infidels was not in the least bit diminished by living in their midst. On the contrary, he was revolted by their filthy lifestyles, the disgusting way in which they dressed in public, the open displays of affection between men and women and even people of the same sex. But his greatest hatred he reserved for the Americans. Every time he saw them flooding into Paris in the summer with their backpacks and their loud insistent voices he just wanted to smash their faces, to rip out their beating hearts and feed them to the dogs. The Jews were the enemy of all Arabs for the illegal occupation of Arab land but the Americans were the ones that created and then supported the despotic and tyrannical Arab regimes in countries like Jordan and Egypt where the Muslim brotherhood were suppressed and massacred. He considered the Saudi royal family just as bad despite their adherence to the faith and to Sharia, the Muslim law, because they aided and abetted the activities of the Americans by allowing the infidels to defile the land of the Prophet by inviting in their army.

The Americans played them against each other first equipping the Iraqis and helping them fight the Iranians and then turning on their former allies as if they were just animals to be manipulated and abused. And all just so they could keep the flow of oil pumping out of the ground and then making sure the oil revenues were never equitably distributed for all Arabs but kept for the wealthy elite and then repatriated back to America. If he had any doubt about America's intentions, they were erased after the invasion of Iraq in 2003. He understood what it meant; hegemony over Arab and Muslim lands and peoples and natural resources. Next would be Iran and then Syria. He was quite certain it was just a matter of time.

On September 11th 2001, he had been sitting in a small café sipping coffee and reading a book in the late afternoon. He noticed people gathering around television sets in the cafés and restaurants nearby and wondered what had happened. He joined one small group and stared in disbelief first at the site of the Twin Towers burning, then felt utter joy as first one then the other collapsed. He hurried back to his apartment and watched on his small television as the chaos unfolded in Manhattan and knew without a doubt that his mentor, his friend, his brother in arms could be the only one who could have arranged and carried out such a bold and daring attack.

He closed all the curtains in his small apartment, carefully washed his hands and feet and for the first time in many years, turned to face the holy city of Mecca. He stood quietly chanting a prayer and then threw himself to the ground, prostrating himself before the prophet and God almighty.

First he prayed for the souls of his dead comrades who had with so much courage, turned their planes into guided missiles. Then he prayed for the souls of his dead parents and dead comrades from the wars in Afghanistan and Lebanon. And finally he prayed for himself, that Allah the all merciful would find a use for him, a poor servant of God to avenge the crimes of the Jews and Americans and the British against his people.

"Send me," he intoned repeatedly. "Send me."

In 2004 he decided to visit America. He applied for a new passport, concerned his false identity would be revealed but in a few days the passport was issued and he booked a three week trip starting in New York.

Despite his recent urbanization in Paris, he found New York quite staggering in its size and pace. He walked around lower Manhattan and spent time staring at the pit where the World Trade towers had once stood. There were many other tourists looking over the site with him, mostly Americans and he was struck by the almost religious significance and reverence they gave to the place. While he celebrated the attack and was awed by its audacity, he had witnessed so much death and destruction in his life that the response of weeping Americans seemed irrational to him but it also strengthened his belief that their very lifestyle, their expectation that life should be predictable and secure made them so vulnerable.

He traveled to Las Vegas for one night and as he walked up one side of the strip early in the evening, he was confounded by the huge crowds wandering from hotel to hotel to throw their money away gambling. Even after years of living in Paris, he still found the blatant use of course sexual themes in giant billboard advertising attached to the top of taxis confounding. Every few minutes as he walked on the sidewalk, he was handed pictures and cards of mostly naked young women in suggestive posses advertising their services. He found the city and people incongruous with the image of America he carried in his mind; a militaristic and nationalistic society, but here it just seemed that all it cared about was hedonism. Could a society so openly blasphemous really survive he wondered. Would it fall under the weight of its own sin or would Allah intercede to show the people the true path of faith and devotion.

He stopped in front of one of the giant hotels on the strip and again imagined the terror and destruction possible with a well placed bomb.

His last stop was in San Francisco, a city that at first reminded him a little of Paris; lots of tourists, fancy shops and endless numbers of restaurants. But the open display of affection between men as they walked hand-in-hand or kissed openly in public was completely repugnant. When he saw two transvestites walk by he lost his normal reserve and stared at them with open disgust.

He studied the City, rode the cable cars, walked the crowded streets and was fascinated by its location on a peninsula on the Bay, hemmed in on three sides by water with just three bridges allowing people in or out, and imagined how a large attack could create panic, trapping people in the City with limited means of escape. He stood across the road from the Transamerica Building, a towering white skyscraper designed to resemble a Pyramid. He laughed to himself at an image of the building, itself an homage to Arab architecture, lying smashed across the City, not collapsed on itself like the World Trade Centers, but fallen like a giant scythe smashing other buildings as it fell.

Upon his return to Paris, the attacks in Madrid and London inspired him and helped him keep the faith and, the ongoing violence against the Americans in Iraq made him even more certain of the cause but, as the time passed he felt increasingly disconnected from the fight. His trips to England and America had proven to him how vulnerable they were and he wished he could act on what he had learned. He yearned to visit a mosque, talk with like-minded people, and share with them his faith and his passion.

At one point he briefly considered going to Syria and then finding a way into Iraq to participate in the battle against the American occupation but he quickly dismissed the idea. He had been given his assignment and faithfully carried it out all these years. But he continued to pray to be called upon.

"Send me," he intoned to himself repeatedly. It became his mantra, a soothing thought that briefly cooled his passion and desire for action.

Now as he sat alone at the café, his ardor had not cooled, his faith undiminished but the pain of his martyrdom denied weighed ever heavier on his mind. He was lost in thought when an unfamiliar middle-aged man dressed in a neat double breasted suit seated at the next table leaned over and handed him a small package.

"Monsieur, I believe you dropped this package," said the elegant stranger.

Al Rahman glanced at the man and then at the package, shaking his head he said, "No, that is not mine."

The elegant man stared hard at Abd Al Rahman, paused for a moment before leaning closer to him and whispering in Arabic, "The Prophet says otherwise."

Abd Al Rahman's eyes widened briefly and then he quickly replied in French, "Oh yes, thank you. It must have fallen from my coat."

The man just smiled but said nothing and then tossed a few Euros onto his table and walked off not looking back.

Abd Al Rahman remained in his seat watching the stranger walk away until he could no longer see him among the other pedestrians on the broad sidewalk. He glanced around to see if anyone was watching him and not seeing anyone, stared at the brown manila envelope in his lap. It had a large bulge in the bottom and he thought for a moment it might be a letter bomb but he felt no fear. He had faced death so many times he had complete control of his emotions as he picked up the package and sniffed it briefly. If it contained cordite, he might be able to smell it but there was no identifying odor. He was anxious to open and examine the contents of the package, but he counseled himself to wait a little while before returning to his apartment.

Verifying first that the door to his apartment had not been opened since his departure earlier in the day, Al Rahman locked the door behind him as he stepped into the small and sparsely furnished apartment and placed the package on the kitchen table and just stared at it for a few moments. Then very deliberately, he felt around the edges looking for a trip wire or some indication it might be dangerous, but felt nothing. Reaching for a sharp kitchen knife he carefully sliced open the package and peered inside. Wrapped in layers of plastic wrap were a single DVD disk and a small clamshell shaped cell phone. He pulled them out with some difficulty because of the limited capacity of his right hand, and unwrapped the plastic until both items were completely exposed. He picked up the cell phone and turned it over in his hands for a moment and then set it back down on the table; he had never used one and was not sure what to do with it. Looking at the disk, he observed that other than the manufacturer's label, it was unmarked. He reexamined the package and found no note or instructions. He inserted the disk into the cheap DVD player and pushed play. He stood back from the television as the images came to the screen and then sat down on the worn-out couch opposite the small television.

The video camera was filming from a fixed point, probably a tripod. He heard sounds and voices, distant but still quite clear.

"Is it on?" an unseen figure asked in Arabic.

"Yes, yes it's on. We are ready," another unseen figure replied, louder and much closer to the camera.

"Bring her out." The voice was commanding and authoritative. "Stand her in front of the camera. Is she too close? Can you see her clearly?"

The camera angle widened so three individuals came in to clear view in the middle of the screen. There were two armed men, both in long flowing robes and jackets typical of the Afghan Taliban, with their faces entirely covered, only their eyes showing through narrow slits. Between them and supported under each arm by both men stood a figure completely covered from head to toe in a dirty blue burqa, a full body veil commonly worn by women in Afghanistan and required dress before the collapse of the Taliban. The figure under the burqa seemed to sway uncertainly on her feet.

Another large man stepped into the picture with his back to the camera and roughly pulled the burqa up and over the woman's head and then he stepped out of the frame.

Abd Al Rahman drew in a short sharp breath and his eyes widened as he stared at the nearly naked woman. It was immediately obvious she was neither an Afghan nor Arab woman; her skin color was very pale like a northern or eastern European. Her breasts were exposed but she had on a pair of dirty underpants. She was quite tall and thin but he could not guess her age. Her head hung forward as if she lacked the energy to hold it up and her disheveled blond hair hung over her eyes. Her mouth was agape and Abd Al Rahman could see a trace of blood on her lips, but her body seemed unmarked.

"Take her over to the post," the first voice barked again.

The two men walked or rather dragged the semi conscious woman over the dusty courtyard to a large wooden post. One man held her while the other looped a rope around one of her wrists and then ran the rope through a metal ring attached high on the post. He tied the end of the rope to her other wrist so she hung uncomfortably by her wrists, feet barely touching the bare ground.

Someone barked out an order that Abd Al Rahman could not hear but two men quickly ran into his view and wrapped two flack jackets around the lower part of the wooden post. Then all the men stepped out of the frame. The cameraman opened the angle of the shot so the woman appeared in the distance but he could still see her quite clearly as she hung almost limp from the post.

"Is the camera ready?" he heard a muffled voice asked.

"Yes, it is ready. I am filming right now."

There was some shouting in the background that was hard to make out but it sounded as if people were being admonished to stand back. Then a moment of silence followed by a flash as the woman's body exploded. Abd Al Rahman jumped slightly in reflex to the explosion and then squinted at the image as he tried to make out what had happened. As the smoke cleared, he could see the lower half of woman's mangled body lying on the ground in front of the post while her shattered upper body swung slowly from the post. For another moment the camera held steady on the woman's upper body as it swung slightly from side to side and then abruptly the filming ended the recording faded to black.

The sound of the cell phone ringing on the table jerked him out of his reverie. He picked it up and for a moment was unsure how to answer it but then opened it and placed it to his ear saying nothing. Then he heard the familiar voice of the man who had handed him the package.

"Did you watch it?" he was asked in French.

"Yes," Abd Al Rahman answered. He started to ask a question but the caller quickly cut him off.

"Listen to me carefully. Go back to the café where we met and take the phone with you. In about one hour the phone will ring and a man will give you a location nearby to meet him. Go there and watch what he does. Do you understand?"

"Who are you?" Abd Al Rahman demanded. "How do I know I can trust you?"

There was a pause before the caller responded.

"I will explain later. But there is one more thing." The caller paused briefly. "When you meet this man, you will recognize him from the old days at Pul-e-Charkhi." At the mention of the notorious Afghan prison located outside Kabul, Al Rahman tensed, momentarily flashing back to the pain and horror he had endured there.

"You will recognize him not as a friend but an enemy. Do not act on your impulse. He is expecting you." The stranger's voice was strong and emphatic. "This man, this Russian, is a gift to us from Allah. When the thing is done go to the park nearby where the children play on the carousel. Do you know the one I mean?"

"Yes," Al Rahman replied.

"Good, I will see you there." The phone was disconnected.

Abd Al Rahman slowly closed the phone shut and stared at it absentmindedly for a moment, his eyes narrowed, brow furrowed. Then, casting aside a few lingering doubts, he quickly threw on his jacket, scooped up the phone and put it in his pocket and walked out of his apartment to await the call.

CHAPTER 3

Michael Devskoy sat in the dark bar slowly nursing his drink. He longed to drain the glass and quickly order another to quell the discomfort in his stomach and calm his nerves, but not today. Today he was doing his best to temper his behavior because he knew they would be meeting soon and if he was drunk, there would be repercussions. He shuddered involuntarily at the thought.

Today was the big day, the day of days, the day on which his goals, his dreams, his aspirations would all finally come true. He chuckled briefly to himself and in a moment of weakness reached for the half empty glass in front of him and drained it. It hit his stomach with a sharp burning sensation and then quickly dissolved into his system giving him the momentary calm he craved. He slowly wiped his mouth on his sleeve and then, muttering under his breath, admonished himself to stop. Not today, today there could be no mistakes.

He giggled into his empty glass at the anticipation of what would happen and at the extraordinary good luck that had literally dropped this incredible opportunity into his lap. Eight months earlier he had been one of the old guard, a former KGB agent with skills more suited to the Cold War between the Soviet Union and the United States, barely hanging on to his job in the new *Federal'naya Sluzhba Bezopasnosti,* commonly referred to as the FSB.

He needed to survive for six more months to qualify for his full pension, not that it was much money, but for a man with very little, it was important. He watched as other colleagues found high paying jobs with private security firms or big corporations needing experienced field agents, but he doubted anyone would call him. Once a successful operative, today he was essentially a broken man, an alcoholic just filling space, retained only because of his past service. Earlier in his career he had earned a measure of respect from his colleagues for his tenacity on assignments but he had been told, quite bluntly, if it was not for his heroic service in Lebanon many years prior, he would have been thrown out of the service long ago.

Officially he was assigned to an analyst's position, monitoring internal threat levels from Muslim agitators within Russia, but his boss had not spoken with him for four months and really did not expect him to produce anything. He actually found him quite repugnant and preferred not to have any contact with him.

He had been assigned a small cubicle in a section of the building that was mostly unused. There was no-one sitting near him although there were a few other men on the floor in similar circumstances to himself also whiling away their time to retirement. Mostly he just sat at his desk surfing the internet. Conversant in French, English and fluent in Arabic, he had plenty of websites and blogs to visit, but he had spent most of his time looking at pornography until a colleague warned him they were tracking internet usage and firing people who accessed pornographic websites. That left him with little or nothing to do.

One day as he sat at his desk in a stupor from too many vodkas consumed at lunch, a young delivery clerk stopped by with a small cart on wheels carrying a number of boxes and mail items. The clerk was loudly chewing on gum and silently mouthing some song he was hearing from the headphones he was wearing, which were connected to an MP3 player on his belt. He picked up one of the dusty boxes off the cart and without saying anything, handed it to Devskoy.

Devskoy just blinked at him, wondering why anyone would bother to send him anything. He took the box, stared at it for a moment and then placed it on his desk.

The clerk stuck a clipboard with a single form on it in his face and tapped on it loudly with a pen.

Devskoy glanced around the sheet for a place to sign and finally just scrawled his name on the sheet and then glanced unhappily at the box assuming it contained work files he would have to review. The idea he would actually have to do real work was disconcerting and he ignored the box for the next two hours until the day was done and he could escape from work.

The next morning he reluctantly sliced open the tape on the box and peered inside. As he expected the box did contain some old files and three identical objects he could not identify; tubes about five inches long with a thin red wire attached at one end and a red button on the other. A small safety switch was located just below the button. He turned one of the tubes around in his hand wondering what it was, released the safety and pushed the button a few times but nothing happened. He put the tubes back in the box. He pushed the box to the side and played games on the internet until lunch.

In the afternoon out of shear boredom he pulled one of the folders out of the box and began to read through it. At first he just scanned the pages not really seeing anything interesting until he became across a folder about the 1980 Moscow Olympics.

That's when he found gold.

A set of classified documents staggering in its content had been literally dropped in his lap. At first he did not believe what he was reading, but as he carefully read and re-read the documents he became convinced it was real. He reached into the dusty box again and pulled out one of the tubes. He unscrewed the top and look down the tube realizing there were no batteries. He re-read one of the documents and then sat back in his chair shaking his head in wonder.

That night he was surprised at his lack of desire to drink. He felt excited and energized for the first time in years and lay in bed in his small drab apartment thinking about what he had found. It was absolute gold he could easily sell to an interested party.

In a panic he realized he had left everything back in his office. What if someone realized it had been sent to him by mistake, and then it would be lost to him for ever? He lay awake in bed until the dawn feeling both anxious and excited then quickly dressed and went to work early half expecting to find the box and all its contents gone, but it was exactly where he had left it.

He decided he had to move the documents. Making copies would be too obvious and simply carrying out the box might also attract attention so he had to carry out the contents within his clothes or a small bag. Fortunately, a lot of the documents were background information, the pertinent data limited to the names of the five hundred and four women listed.

The data provided on each woman was very detailed; date of birth, height, weight, work assignments, special training, even sexual orientation. But as he read through the contact information his heart sunk realizing the list was dated from August of 1992. So many years had passed; it was unlikely the data would be accurate. Without recent and accurate contact information, the information was worthless.

He sat slumped in his chair crestfallen for a moment but then turned to the computer on his desk. He pulled up the FSB intranet, an internal organizational site just for FSB employees he had used only a couple of times to verify his pension status and official retirement date. He looked at some of the links and nothing seemed promising until he found a link to a registry of employees. He clicked on the link, entered his own name and found himself listed with his current job status, office phone, home phone and home address with an 'as-of-date' listed for just one month earlier. Clearly the data in his profile was current.

He typed in the name of the first woman on the list of five hundred and four names. He held his breath as he pressed enter hoping to get some current data returned. He seemed to be in luck; her status was listed as operational and her contact data also seemed current. He checked the next name on the list and got the same result. The third and fourth names were more disconcerting. The third name listed status as 'deceased' while the fourth name was listed as 'furloughed'.

As he continued working down the first twenty names the results seemed to be consistent; most of women were listed as furloughed, a few as operational and a number as deceased. He decided to call one listed as furloughed and briefly considered leaving the building to use a public payphone but he dismissed the idea and dialed the number. The phone rang twice and a woman's voice answered. He was momentarily unsure what to say and so just asked for the woman by name. She confirmed her identity and he quickly hung up. He tried three more numbers and successfully reached one more woman while other two numbers rang unanswered.

Sitting alone in his cubicle, Devskoy pondered his options. Not once did he consider the extraordinary act of betrayal he was considering. The only thoughts that came to mind were about feasibility and getting away with it; could he take what had been given to him, by obvious error, and capitalize on it. The risk was huge but the decision ultimately was easy and he had made it quickly.

Three weeks later, having closed his small bank account and sold practically everything he owned, Devskoy was in Beirut, Lebanon late at night lying on dirty sheets in his cheap hotel room, sleeping off a night of despondent inebriation, drunk to dull his failure to find the former Syrian intelligence agent he had worked with when the Soviet Union and Syria were allies. He had not quit his job or announced his departure; he had just left, guessing it would be some time before someone missed him.

Now he had spent all his money desperately and unsuccessfully looking for the one man he thought could help him. He passed the word on the streets and in the bars, paying bribes with the little money he had, trying to make a connection, but to no avail. He was met with either dull stares or sometimes angry dismissals; the Syrians were unpopular in Lebanon since their participation in the death of Lebanon's Prime Minster and much of their security apparatus had been dismantled. He knew it had been a long shot he might actually find his old associate and by the tenth day in Beirut he was completely broke without even enough money to get home. He drank himself into a stupor.

He awoke to the unmistakable sensation of the cold hard metal of a gun barrel shoved into his mouth, almost breaking his teeth. A bright light shone in his eyes and he blinked in terror as he tried to catch his breath.

He lay as still as possible trying to control his bowels which threatened to release uncontrollably. He could feel the weight of the gun pressing down on his tongue and gagged just as he felt a sharp blow to his stomach.

He doubled over in pain and then was harshly pushed off the bed and crashed hard onto the floor. Strong hands reached for his shoulders and pushed him into a sitting position against the wall.

The gun was now pressed hard to his forehead driving the back of his head uncomfortably against the wall. The bright light was still shinning in his eyes and he could not make out the face of the figure hovering over him.

"Why are you here?" a voice barked out at him in guttural English.

"Uh...I am looking for someone," Devskoy answered, grunting out the words uncomfortably.

"Yes, I know, but why?" The man pressed the gun a bit harder to punctuate his sentence.

Devskoy gritted his teeth fighting the pressure on his forehead and the discomfort from the back of his head against the wall.

"I have an offer...something to offer him... an opportunity." He was having trouble speaking.

The figure hovered above him for a moment then stepped back releasing the pressure on his head with the gun. "Get up and sit on the bed."

Devskoy rolled awkwardly to his feet and sat heavily on the edge of the bed holding his head. The bedroom light flicked on and he looked up at the familiar but older man he remembered from years before.

"Rifiat Ali," he said with some relief as he recognized the Syrian, "don't you remember me?" he asked plaintively looking at the impassive figure still pointing the gun directly at him.

The man nodded silently for a moment. "Yes, many people around here remember you Devskoy. I am surprised you dared to come back."

"I had to come... I needed help – your help to make some contacts."

The Syrian eyed him suspiciously.

"Who do you wish to contact and why?"

A conspiratorial smile crossed Devskoy's face as he looked up the Syrian. "I have a very good story to tell you my friend. When I am finished you will be very happy that I came back and found you."

After many hours of conversation, the Syrian had not disappointed him. It took another two months, some days of uncertainty and a few moments of terror but as he hoped, dared to hope, the deal was done and money changed hands, at least enough to get started. The real money would come after today's final test.

Standing at the bar, Devskoy contemplated his empty glass one more time, checked his watch again, tossed a couple of Euros on the bar counter and walked out. He blinked against the sunlight as he stood outside on the broad sidewalk and subconsciously looked at his watch once more. It was nearly time. It was a short walk to make sure they were in place and then a quick phone call. In a moment of panic he patted his inside jacket pocket to make sure the cell phone was still there. He wiped the sweat beading up on his bald forehead with his hand and then wiped his hand on his trousers. He had to hitch up his trousers constantly as they kept slipping below his fat stomach.

His confidence ebbed and flowed and he was surprised at how nervous he felt. He had done things much more risky, been in places and situations much more dangerous but that was a long time ago and this was the first time he was doing it all alone. Worst of all was the person they were forcing him to meet with. It made him ill just thinking about it but they had insisted. He knew he would have to be wary, careful not to show fear and careful to control the situation. He had all the power but they had the money. He needed to be smart to keep the power and get the money.

Today was vital. It was the second test but the first test in a real setting. If it failed, if the test did not work, they would kill him. Of that he was certain. They had invested so much money and worked hard to make this happen. He was tempted to step back into the bar for one more drink but it was time to go.

He hoped she was there on time, just like they planned. He had considered following her to make sure she was doing as she was told, but he no longer trusted his own skills to follow her without being noticed. By force of habit he glanced around to see if anyone was watching him and when he did not spot anyone, strode off purposely to his rendezvous.

* * *

The Russian was late. Abd Al Rahman had been told to wait an hour but almost twice that time had passed. He worried the phone was not working properly or that he had inadvertently turned it off. He closed his eyes in momentary frustration and then forced himself to relax and be patient. His curiosity and craving for action was getting the better of him despite his best efforts to remain calm. He lifted the small coffee cup to his lips and took one last sip just as the phone rang. He let it ring once more before picking it up and flipping it open.

"Yes," he said.

"Sorry I'm late," the caller said panting slightly and in heavily accented but fluent English. "It took longer to set up than I expected."

The voice and the accent — he recognized them both immediately. Despite the warmth of the summer sun, he felt a chill go up his back. His hand tightened on the phone, as he involuntarily tensed at the voice he would forever associate only with pain.

"Rue 15, sixth floor, room 616," the caller said. "And hurry. They will be starting soon." The phone went dead.

Starting what? Al Rahman was not sure what the man was talking about but he assumed it was related to the video he has just watched. He snapped the phone shut and as quickly as he could with his awkward gait, started walking. He knew the general area of the address and after walking for about fifteen minutes, he arrived at a non-descript looking pension. He glanced up and down the narrow street and, other than a couple walking hand in hand some distance away, he saw no one. He stepped in to the lobby and then slipped unnoticed past the old attendant and rode the rickety and very small elevator to the top floor. Exiting the elevator into the empty corridor, he looked for the room number and when he got to it, knocked twice.

As the door swung open, Abd Al Rahman steeled himself to remain calm. He stared at the man framed in the doorway, fat now and completely bald but the Russian still had the same ugly beady-eyed appearance he recalled from those dark days.

The Russian looked afraid, terrified at the site of Abd Al Rahman in front of him, but he managed a weak smile as he welcomed his visitor.

"Please come in." The pitch in his voice conveyed his anxiety.

Peering past the Russian, Abd Al Rahman could barely see into the room; the lights were off, heavy curtains drawn. He stepped cautiously inside and forced a smile at his former torturer trying to put the man at ease.

The Russian locked the door behind them and then beckoned Al Rahman to follow him across the room to the heavy curtains. Still feeling uncertain of his circumstance, Al Rahman followed him and then peered cautiously through the gap in the curtains as the Russian parted them slightly just enough so both men could look beyond them to a similar hotel across the narrow road.

The Russian nervously checked his watch.

"They should be starting about now," he said peering anxiously from behind the curtains.

As Abd Al Rahman lit a cigarette, he regarded his former nemesis with a combination of hate and disdain. There was a pungent odor of sweat and alcohol about the man and even in the dim light he could see that the Russian's face was soft and pasty, his nose bulbous and laced with red veins. He wore an open collar shirt, slacks cinched up tight below his stomach, and a dark blue jacket which had long ago lost its capacity to hide any more stains. Sweat was beading up on his bald pate, which he would wipe away with his hand and run along his pants to dry. When he spoke, it sounded like he was panting to keep his breath.

"Look," said the Russian interrupting his reverie while offering him a small set of binoculars to Al Rahman. "They're starting."

CHAPTER 4

THE LARGE HOTEL room was cool and dark, diffuse late afternoon sun the only illumination. A lacy white curtain billowed lazily in and out of the open window as a gentle breeze swept into the room, carrying with it the city noises.

The room was plain and functional with only a large bed, supported by a garish metal frame and two chairs, one of which was in need of new upholstery. On it a woman's clothes had been carelessly dropped: bra, panties, and a flowery summer dress. On the other were a general's uniform, jacket and pants, neatly folded. A thin colored bar, about four inches long, was pinned above the jacket's breast pocket. White boxer shorts draped over one chair arm, a pair of highly polished black shoes below. Inside each shoe was a black sock, neatly folded.

On the bed a large, naked, middle aged man lay on his back, hands kneading the breasts of the woman sitting astride him. His mouth was agape, a dull expression on his face as he watched her moving slowly, rhythmically, methodically on him. Small beads of sweat hung above his upper lip and on his brow and he grunted as her weight pressed down upon him.

Though younger than her partner, the woman was not young. Her body was firm and toned, legs long and strong, but her face, although still attractive, was creased by age. She rested her arms on his shoulders, supporting herself as she moved back and forth. He reached down and placed his hands on either side of her hips. His right thumb settled just below a large thin scar on her left hip, but he did not notice it.

She took his hands off her hips, moved them back to her breasts and leaned her head back as she shook her hair out of her eyes. She stayed like that for a few seconds, holding his hands on her chest.

Then she leaned forward again and began watching his face, noticing his breathing, measuring his responses to her movements. She observed that his breathing had quickened and she let his hands drop from her breasts. She began to move faster, lifting her pelvis up and down, up and down. Then she leaned closer to him, kissing him, wrapping her arms around his neck, still moving her hips rhythmically. Suddenly he grabbed her, pulling her towards him as he climaxed.

* * *

Across the road in a similar hotel room, the two men stood at the window, listening and waiting. Both men were careful to stand a half step back and to the side in the shadow of the open window, but their eyes were focused on the room in the building across the street and two levels below them. Although they could not see the details of the activities in the room, they could make out the vague outline of the woman and knew what position she was in.

The Russian carefully withdrew from his left pocket a thin tube, about five inches long and about the thickness of a man's thumb. On top of it was a red button and just below it, a small safety lock. A thin red wire, about six inches long, hung from the base of the tube.

Al Rahman watched carefully as the Russian, moving very deliberately, removed the safety lock from the tube, licked his lips in nervous anticipation and then squinted as the sun emerged from a cloud and the bright summer sun made it more difficult to see into the darkened room across the narrow street.

"What is that?" Al Rahman began to ask, but the Russian ignored him. He was concentrating, staring through the binoculars at the two lovers, anxious to make sure he got his timing just right. This was a free test, the final proof and he did not want to waste it by making a mistake.

In the dim light of the distant room, he could vaguely make out the women's upright form and at that moment she leaned forward and disappeared below the rim of the distant window and out of his view. He quickly placed his thumb over the red button and pressed it down hard. He stiffened briefly at the flash of the explosion from across the way, while his companion showed very little expression and calmly raised his left hand to his thin lips and took a long hard draw on his cigarette. He turned his face up to blow the smoke from his lungs as the muffled explosive sound slowly rolled across the street towards them over the city noise. As he watched, a small puff of smoke rose out of the open window in the building opposite and wafted into the city air and a smile briefly creased his lips, but was quickly erased as the Russian turned towards him with a triumphant look on his face.

"I told them it would work," he blurted out. His companion briefly closed his eyes and muttered something under his breath, nodded slowly and then with a jerk of his head indicated it was time to go. They left the building about ten minutes apart, the Russian staying behind briefly to make sure no evidence of his brief occupation of the room remained.

Across the way, the two lovers lay in a twisted mess of commingled body parts, indistinguishable and inseparable from each other. The explosion had killed the woman instantly, shrapnel shredding her lungs and destroying her midriff. The man lingered on for a few moments, unable to assimilate the incongruity of his situation, but feeling his life ebb away, his blood mixing with the woman's as he quickly bled to death.

CHAPTER 5

A BD AL RAHMAN walked as quickly to the park as
his damaged right leg would allow. His gait was
unbalanced because he had to throw the dead
weight of his right leg forward with his hip to get it in
front of his body. The motion was tiring and made his
back ache, but the anticipation of a call to action, to the
meeting to discuss what he had just witnessed was strong
motivation and he ignored his discomfort.

He reached the park and slowed his pace, and almost
as an after thought, he looked around cautiously to see
if he was being watched or followed but noticed nothing
untoward. It was quite late in the day and mothers were
gathering up their children to leave the park and a few
older people were strolling along the path. He considered taking a seat on one of the park benches but decided
to keep walking through the park. For some reason he
felt it was better to keep moving rather than sit and wait
for his contact. As it turned out, he did not have to wait
long. A hand slipped inside his left arm and a now familiar voice spoke to him in French.

"I see your wounds from the old days are still with you," the stranger said. "Does it pain you to walk? Would you rather sit down?"

Abd Al Rahman turned to look at his companion and shook his head. "No, I am fine. We can keep walking."

The two men walked in silence for a few a minutes accompanied only by the sounds of their feet on the gravel and the noise of distant traffic wafting over them.

Abd Al Rahman broke the silence. "Who are you?" he asked.

"Who I am is not important but what I am is very important," the stranger answered cryptically.

"I don't understand," Al Rahman responded with a quizzical tone in his voice.

"Osama sends his regards and prays you still walk with Allah."

"Osama? You have seen him and spoken to him?" Abd Al Rahman asked with surprise in voice.

"Not directly but we have exchanged ideas and plans."

"How is my brother? It has been so long since I have seen him or spoken with him. Is he well?"

The stranger smiled briefly and ignoring the question stopped walking and turned to face Abd Al Rahman. He stared hard at him for a few moments and then asked, "Is Allah still in your heart and soul, Abd Al Rahman? Are you still with us or has your life here in Paris made you soft and feeble?"

Abd Al Rahman stared back at the stranger, a hard fixed stare, his face flushed, his jaw clenched tight, his eyes narrowed to small slits. When he replied his voice was strong and resolute.

"I have lived among these infidels, these weak, self indulgent French pigs and their filthy whores for more than nine years. I have idled away the best years of my life for a cause in which I was not permitted to participate and I have denied myself the comfort of my faith and the companionship of fellow Muslims. And you dare ask me if I have maintained the faith."

He pulled his mutilated right hand out of his pocket and held it in front of the stranger's face. "I thought this was the greatest test of my faith, but living here doing nothing, just waiting to be called, to have no purpose, has been worse."

The two men remained staring at each other a for a moment after Abd Al Rahman finished speaking and then, with a smile, the stranger leaned forward and gently pulled Abd Al Rahman's mangled hand to his lips and tenderly kissed it.

"You have served us well Abd Al Rahman," he said. "First in war and now you will serve us again. Osama has named you to lead the next battle against the infidel."

"*Inshalla*," Abd Al Rahman said under his breath. Eyes closed, he repeated the mantra three times, as for the first time in years, he felt a sense of peace and fulfillment briefly overcome him as he intoned God's greatness.

"*Inshalla*," the stranger repeated as he again took Abd Al Rahman's arm and guided him down the path. He led him to a park bench in a relatively secluded spot that still had a clear view of the path. The two men sat and the stranger began to speak.

"The meeting with the Russian, it went well." The stranger said it more as a statement than a question.

"Yes, I think so," he replied. "I'm not exactly sure what I saw but I think it was similar to the woman in the video."

The stranger nodded. "That woman in the video, what did she look like to you? Did she look like an Arab?"

Abd Al Rahman shook his head. "No, she looked northern European, white with blond hair."

"Exactly," the stranger replied. "She looked like them," he said as he nodded his head at the direction of a couple young women walking down the path. "They all look like them."

Abd Al Rahman glanced at the two women and back at the stranger. He did not quite grasp what he was being told. "What do you mean all? Are there more like her?"

"Seventy," the stranger replied slowly and then repeated. "Seventy."

The stranger stopped briefly and then continued. "We are now in the next phase of our operation and with the guidance of Allah and the wisdom of Osama we — you Abd Al Rahman, in the name of Allah the almighty shall strike again."

He smiled briefly, conspiratorially and then said, "We only have about an hour and I have a lot to tell you so please listen carefully."

For the next sixty minutes Abd Al Rahman sat and listened very carefully while his companion spoke clearly and deliberately. What he heard was so extraordinary he found himself in disbelief. He wanted to interrupt, to challenge what he was hearing but he kept his thoughts to himself.

The stranger stopped speaking and sat back on the bench looking at Abd Al Rahman expectantly. "You understand everything I have told you, yes?"

Al Rahman slowly nodded in response.

The stranger withdrew an envelope from the inside pocket of his jacket and slid it across the park bench to Al Rahman who quickly put it out of sight. "These are the banks and account numbers where the money will be. You will need to memorize them. Don't carry them around with you."

"If I need more money, how do I ask for it?" Al Rahman asked.

"Don't worry," replied the stranger. "Each account will always have a minimum balance of close to one million dollars. As you withdraw funds, they will be replenished."

"How much can I spend?"

The stranger shrugged his shoulders. "No more than you have to but as much as you need. Use your best judgment."

The two men sat silently for a moment.

"And Devskoy?" Al Rahman asked, referring to the Russian.

"This evening you will meet with him to negotiate the terms. He is afraid of you and was very reluctant to work with you but we insisted. It is good he is afraid, but you will need to put him at ease. We have spent almost a million dollars getting these women into position but only he knows exactly where they are and how to contact them. He is suspicious of us, and you can't blame him, but the money we gave him is all spent now and he wants money, lots of money."

"What do I offer him?"

"I told you, whatever it takes. Do the deal, get access to the women's locations and contact information and then when you are certain you have it, get rid of him. He is a drunken fool and will only be a liability."

"Where will you be?" Al Rahman asked the stranger.

"In a few minutes I will be gone and we shall not meet again."

"You are not going to work with me?" Al Rahman asked, surprised.

"No, I told you, this is your mission, your task. My role in this is done. If they capture me I can't even tell them what you will be doing or when because I won't know and I don't need to know."

"When does it begin? When do I start? How do I start?" The questions poured out in quick succession.

The stranger smiled at him. "It has already started. Today you watched Devskoy kill an American General. Tomorrow, it's up to you."

CHAPTER 6

ABD AL RAHMAN carefully watched the Russian through the window of the smoky bistro from across the street. He had arrived at their meeting place a few minutes early and had waited in the shadows watching as the Russian arrived late, walking as fast as he could with his heavy swinging gait. He could see the Russian briefly look for him and then take a seat at a small table and quickly order drinks. Abd Al Rahman would keep him waiting for a few more minutes, happy to let the man get more anxious, sweat a little and consume a few glasses of vodka. Finally, Abd Al Rahman stepped into the bistro and took the unoccupied seat at the Russian's table.

The Russian quickly gulped down the remnants of his glass as he saw Abd Al Rahman and wiped his month with his sleeve.

"Worked perfectly, didn't it?" he said, the words spilling out quickly, the pitch of his voice exposing his anxiety.

They spoke in Russian, just one of the languages common to both of them but one Abd Al Rahman insisted be their only language.

Abd Al Rahman nodded with a small smile on his lips. "Yes, it worked. It was very impressive."

"Impressive! It was fucking incredible, you know, fucking incredible."

The Russian was very excited, loud and slightly inebriated but Al Rahman was not concerned about who might overhear their conversation. The bistro was loud and crowded and they were less likely to get noticed here than at some secluded spot. But right now he needed the Russian to relax, think more clearly so they could negotiate the deal. First the video and now the final live test had confirmed with certainty the plan would work. The participants were ready. Only the details had to be worked out.

"What do you want?" he asked Devskoy directly.

The Russian waved at a nearby waitress and signaled for her to deliver two more drinks. As she set them down, the Russian put one glass to his mouth and downed the alcohol in one gulp and again wiped the residue off his lips with his sleeve. He stared at his companion for moment and then speaking quickly said, "one hundred thousand dollars each."

When the Arab did not respond, he continued speaking, nervous about asking for the money.

"I have seventy ready to go. You will pay me one hundred thousand for each one, payable before delivery."

The Arab sat impassively for a moment his face revealing nothing. His demeanor did not reveal his intense discomfort at sitting across from a man he hated and looked forward to killing, but he also felt awkward negotiating the transaction. His time as warrior, prisoner and the recent years of hermetic existence had left him ill prepared to negotiate terms.

"Where are they?" he asked after a moment.

"You mean the women?" Devskoy replied stating the obvious.

"Yes."

The Russian shrugged. "Here, there, everywhere," he replied with a smirk.

The two men stared at each other saying nothing. The Arab broke the silence.

"So, I give you seven million dollars and you give me all their names, contact information and locations."

The Russian shook his head vigorously. "No no no, we exchange them ten at a time. You give me a million dollars and I give you ten names. When you are done with them, I will give you ten more."

The Arab's expression changed and showed his displeasure.

"Why play games?" Abd Al Rahman asked. "Give me all the names now and walk away a very rich man. You can go anywhere, do anything..." His voice trailed off.

Devskoy grabbed at the second glass on the table and drained it again in one gulp. The warm liquid hit his stomach quickly and he felt his confidence grow.

"I am not so stupid to think the past is just forgotten," he said. "What I did to you, what you did to us..." He stared up at the Arab with red eyes, a trace of spittle on his lips. "If I give you what you want right now, I won't live long enough to enjoy any of it. No," he said as he pounded on the small table with his fist. "We will do it just like I said. You give me one million dollars and I give you ten names."

Abd Al Rahman said nothing for a moment wondering if he should bargain, try to negotiate a better deal but he just said, "Very well. We shall do as you say. But," he continued as he pointed a finger at Devskoy, "you will deploy the women as I instruct you, not just the ten you give me, but all of them. They will move with your instructions, yes?"

The Russian nodded. "Of course, I can send them anywhere you need. It will take time of course, and money, but moving them is no problem." He smiled showing yellowing teeth and the same malevolence Abd Al Rahman had witnessed many years before. "Where shall we begin? Who would you like your first target to be?"

Abd Al Rahman did not answer for a few moments. All this had happened so quickly he had not had a chance to make a plan or strategy for most effectively using his weapons. The stranger had been very specific about the mission when they spoke in the park. Whereas the attack on the World Trade Center in New York was designed to create shock and awe, these new small attacks were to create fear, uncertainty and doubt.

"Do you have any more assets here in Paris?"

Devskoy shook his head. "No, I was told to concentrate them in London and America."

"How many do you have in London?"

Devskoy paused for a moment and then replied, "Nine more."

"Where are they?"

"I have them staying in various hotels in London."

"How quickly can you reach them?"

Devskoy pulled his cell phone out of his pocket and tapped on it a couple of times. "I can reach them right away."

Abd Al Rahman sat impassive for a moment, oblivious to the sounds of people talking around him trying to think of a good strategy. "Very well," he said. "We will start in London. You will give me the names and contact information for each of the uh..." he paused looking for the right word, *"istishhadiyah"*.

The Arabic word for female martyr elicited a coarse laugh from Devskoy. "These women are not *istishhadiyah*, they're whores," he said as he continued to laugh. "They're a bunch of worthless whores who have been fucking all kinds of American and European pigs for years just so we could steal information from them." He leaned back in his chair as he continued to laugh, and then stopped suddenly as he saw the angry stare from Al Rahman.

He leaned forward and took another gulp from his drink. "Ok, call them what you want. Do you want me to do it with you?"

"Yes," Abd Al Rahman answered, his face softening slightly. "At least the first one or two, after that I will work on my own."

"And the money," Devskoy asked.

Abd Al Rahman considered for a moment it might be best to offer to pay half the total for nine women but he wanted Devskoy to trust him and so he simply replied, "Where do you wish me to deposit it?"

The Russian licked his lips and looked around anxiously. This was the part he was most worried about. Large transfers of cash would attract attention and he wanted to avoid attracting any to himself. He reached in to his breast pocket and pulled out a small folded piece of paper.

"On this sheet you will find a list of twenty bank names located throughout Europe. You will transfer an equal amount to each account listed over the next few days, not all at once you understand. That will be dangerous. Do it slowly and no-one will notice."

"How will I reach you after the transfers are complete?"

Devskoy thought for a moment and then his expression brightened as he said, "The Dorchester Hotel in London. Do you know it?"

Abd Al Rahman shook his head.

"Well, it's only the best and most expensive hotel in London. You will feel at home there – it is full of Arabs. Meet me there at the tea room next Friday at four o'clock. That should give you enough time to complete the transfer."

Devskoy stood up, his confidence swelling as the Arab had appeared to accept his terms. "I will start checking the balances in a few days. If the money is there by next Friday, you will see me at the hotel. If not..." his voice tapered off.

CHAPTER 7

ICHAEL DEVSKOY SAT in the bar at The Dorchester Hotel in London feeling very pleased with himself. The Arab had done as he had been instructed: the money had been transferred to all the banks on the list. Devskoy had quickly moved the money again, transferring large and small amounts to banks all over the world. That was the one benefit of being in London. In the City of London, the financial capital of Europe, almost every major international bank in the world maintained an office. Opening accounts in banks in Europe, Asia, America and Australia had been quite straight forward.

He ordered a glass of Vodka and despite his usual habit of drinking the glass in one gulp, slowly nursed the exquisite smooth taste of the best Vodka he had ever drunk. This was *Stolichnaya Gold*, a premium Russian brand unlike the usual rot gut he normally drank. He licked his lips savoring the flavor and smiled to himself as he slowly rotated the glass in his hand, watching the clear liquid spin in the glass. The bill would probably be ten pounds per glass but he did not care. This was how he intended to live the rest of his life, indulging every pleasure he could think of, denying himself nothing. With millions of dollars in cash, he could go anywhere, become anyone, and do anything. He almost giggled out loud at the thought.

He had two more days before the Arab showed up. He felt a pang of anxiety about something happening to Abd Al Rahman and the entire enterprise collapsing but quickly put the negative thought out of his mind. He glanced around the bar and noticed a tall, well dressed and quite handsome man walk in to the bar. The man paused as he glanced around the room and then selected a spot at the bar a few stools away from Devskoy. The man nodded to the barman and ordered a drink and Devskoy immediately recognized the New York accent. Trying not to be obvious, he watched the American in the mirror behind the bar, envious of his good looks and obvious self confidence. The thought of the American soured his good mood and he tipped the glass to his lips and swallowed the remaining alcohol in one gulp. As he set the glass back down on the counter, out of the corner of his eye he caught the American staring at him with a look of obvious disdain. Devskoy turned to face the American with a hard stare and the man looked away.

Swearing under his breath, Devskoy tossed a twenty pound note on to the counter, stood up and walked out of the bar. He spotted a house phone near the restrooms and walked to it quickly. Picking up the receiver, he heard the operator's voice on the phone.

"Room 412," he said quickly.

* * *

Katia Molensk stood before the full length mirror with a large white towel wrapped around her body just above her breasts and another smaller towel wrapped turban-like around her head. She let the towel around her body drop to the lush carpet and stood in the mirror staring at her body. Despite approaching middle age, her body still retained the look of an athlete: legs long and lean, stomach flat and slightly muscled. Her breasts were small, and slightly drooped but still firm for a woman of her age.

As she stared at herself in the mirror her mind wandered, pondering what might have been and the strange circumstances that had brought her to this elegant hotel room. In 1979, at the age of twenty one, she was nationally recognized in the Soviet Union as one of the best volleyball players in the country. A serve and set specialist, her serve had a topspin which made it almost impossible to return and her ability to dig out the hardest slams was almost legendary.

From the age of twelve, her life had been focused around volleyball. A standout player at her local school, her athletic abilities had garnered the notice of the Soviet sports machine intent on finding and grooming outstanding athletes for every Olympic event. She was quickly removed from her school and enrolled at an elite residential school and sports academy where the best young athletes were groomed for success. The new school was not far from her home but in terms of lifestyle and privileges, it was another world. The food was excellent and plentiful. The training facilities were outstanding and the athletes who survived the rigorous training were well rewarded with perks and privileges not afforded to most Soviet citizens. The separation from her family was most difficult for her mother but she had quickly acquiesced, realizing it was probably best for her daughter.

As the Soviet Union geared up for the 1980 Moscow Olympics every effort was made to prove the superiority of the Soviet system by dominating in as many athletic events as possible. Trainers and doctors analyzed every player's strength and weakness, altering training regimes to maximize each athlete's performance. Every aspect of their lives was regimented from hours of sleep to weight lifting and cardiovascular workouts to food and performance supplements. Katia's upper body developed a musculature that would have seemed unusual to most women but to her appeared quite normal compared to her peers. She was a little embarrassed about the facial hair that had suddenly appeared on her chin and was surprised on a number of occasions when her mother did not recognize her voice on the phone because, as her mother claimed, it sounded so much deeper than before.

In late 1979 just before the final twenty five women were to be selected for the national Olympic team, she felt a sharp pain in her left hip. As first she tried to ignore the pain and play through it, but as the pain persisted, she could not hide her discomfort from her trainers. They put her on a regime of rest and rehabilitation but after a few weeks it became clear that her situation was not improving. There was obviously something seriously wrong with her hip and just like that, her athletic career and all her dreams and aspirations seemed to evaporate.

For the first time in her life she had to contemplate a life outside of sports. She sunk into a depression when she returned home to her family's drab and bare apartment, a far cry from the luxurious accommodations she had grown accustomed to at the athlete's academy. She pondered her future with bleak anticipation until one day soon after coming home she was summoned back to the training academy and told to report to the onsite hospital facility. Her spirits lifted thinking they found the cause of her discomfort and were going to treat her and return her to the team. She was ushered into a small examining room with a doctor she knew and two other men she could not identify. The doctor had her remove her pants and lay on her back on the examining table while he methodically examined her hip joint, testing her flexibility and pain point. After completing a rigorous physical examination, the doctor huddled with the other two men and whispered between them in conversation she could not hear. Then the doctor turned back to her and instructed her to stand up and remove all her clothes. She hesitated for a moment, unwilling to be naked in front of the strangers but the doctor repeated his instructions forcefully.

She did as she was told and stood before the three men as they stared at her naked body. For a moment nobody said a word and then one of the strangers told her to slowly turn around which she did. The men huddled together again for some more hushed comments and then the doctor told her to get dressed and wait in the waiting room.

After some time a nurse came up to her and gave her a folded piece of paper which she unfolded and read. The message was brief. She was instructed to be at an address the next morning in Moscow at 9:00 o'clock. There was no explanation as to the purpose of the meeting.

She arrived the next morning at the address in downtown Moscow as instructed. The building, an office complex built just after the Second World War, was squat and stark and quite foreboding. With some trepidation she went inside and reported to the receptionist who curtly instructed her to take a seat in the lobby. She did not have to wait long; soon after she arrived she was taken to a small windowless room furnished with one small well-worn Formica table and four metal chairs. An attendant handed her an aptitude test and she spent the next hour carefully answering each question. As she completed the test, a man in a white coat entered and told her he was a psychiatrist. He interviewed her for about half an hour and when he was done, he left her alone in the room and she sat there nervously wondering what was happening when the two strangers from the previous day's medical exam stepped in. This time they introduced themselves and explained very briefly that they were members of the Soviet Security Service but they did not specify which agency.

For a terrifying moment, Katia thought she or someone in her family was in trouble. As a valued athletic asset she had been protected from the heavy hand of the

Soviet internal security system but was still well aware of the capricious nature of Soviet justice. One of the men realized her discomfort and put her at rest.

"You are not in trouble," he said gruffly as if putting people at ease did not come easily to him. "Don't worry. We just need to learn more about you, to ask you certain questions. You just answer as best you can. Do you understand?"

The color which had drained from Katia's face slowly returned and she nodded quickly that she understood.

For the next two hours the men interviewed her about every aspect of her life, her academic record, her friends, her older brother, her parents, her grandparents, and even her grandfather's service in the Second World War The questions became increasingly personal focusing on her sexual history, her sexual orientation, different sex acts she had engaged in, even pressing her on homosexual encounters with other women, which had never happened. They already seemed to know a great deal about her life but insisted she tell them everything, sparing no small detail.

When the session finally ended, she felt drained. It had been humiliating to speak about oneself in so open a manner with two complete strangers but, as a product of the paternalistic Soviet system, she had simply complied as instructed.

The next few weeks after the interview had been a rush of unexpected activity. She was scheduled for surgery and her hopes rose again she might be able to return to her teammates but the doctor explained that due to a serious deterioration of her hip joint she would to have hip replacement surgery to alleviate the pain and allow her to walk normally. But he was very explicit; her sports career was over. Following surgery she would have to be very careful to avoid further injuring her hip by running or jumping.

Within a few months of her injury Katia found herself in a new career, as unlikely as anything she could have imagined. Even before she was off crutches from the surgery she was informed she had been selected to join the *Komitet Gosudarstvennoi Bezopasnost,* or Committee for State Security more commonly known as the KGB. She immediately had to report for training which, in the beginning consisted mainly of full emersion in the English language. All the students, a few young women like her, a number of young military officers and other civilians became residents of an English only dormitory. Any conversations in Russian were strictly outlawed and the few students who disobeyed lost privileges. Katia found it difficult at first while her knowledge of the language was quite rudimentary, but she was a diligent student and as the weeks and months past, her conversational and comprehension skills improved rapidly. By the sixth month she was easily conversing in English and by the time she completed the first full year, she found herself even thinking in English.

Additional training classes in standard espionage skills followed and by the end of her third year she was sent on her first foreign assignment; the Soviet embassy in Norway. Her job was to read and translate documents and intelligence related to the North Atlantic Treaty Organization or NATO. The Soviets had learned that

Norway was the easiest way to get access to confidential English language NATO documents and Katia was assigned to read through and select documents for translation based on their value.

The job was quite tedious but life in Norway with its open society and warm friendly people more than made up for the tedium of her job. The Embassy staff was encouraged to meet and mingle with the local people and report back to their superiors on what people were saying or thinking. On a number of occasions she was sent on missions to other European countries, at first as part of a surveillance team and later on her own. Most of her assignments during these missions were innocuous but everything changed one day when she was summoned directly into the Ambassadors office. There were two senior KGB officers in the room with him.

"Do you know who this man is?" one of the KGB officers asked her, laying a picture of a smiling middle aged man on the table in front of her.

"Yes," she answered quickly. "He is the deputy Minister of Defense here in Norway."

"Have you met him?" the same officer asked.

"Um.. yes," she replied. "I think we met last year at our embassies New Year's Eve party."

There was a brief silence as the two KGB officers glanced at each other. The ambassador stood by saying nothing.

"Would he recognize you if he saw you again?"

Katia shrugged. She knew that as a tall athletic blond, most men remembered meeting her but she responded cautiously.

"We spoke for some time. He seemed very interested in my sports background."

The two agents looked over at the Ambassador as if this was his cue to speak. The Ambassador cleared his throat and pulled his chair closer to Katia's. He seemed uncomfortable with what he was about to say.

"This man, he could be very useful to us." He cleared his throat again and dropped his eyes from Katia for a moment.

"We need someone to uh... become friends with him. Get to know him, gain his trust, you understand. He is coming here tomorrow for an embassy dinner. You will be seated next to him, while his wife will be seated elsewhere."

The Ambassador stopped speaking and stared in to Katia's eyes.

"Make him like you, want to see you again. Be suggestive. We know he has had some affairs outside of his marriage. Do you understand?"

Katia glanced around the room at each man, a quizzical look on her face. "Am I supposed to have an affair with this man, to sleep with him? Is that what you are asking me?"

One of the KGB officers answered brusquely. "This is a very important assignment. You should be grateful we have chosen you for this undertaking." His words and tone left Katia no doubt that refusing was not an option.

Nor was it the next time nor the time after that. She became a reluctant expert at sexual seduction and manipulation. She did as she was told and seduced men so they became enamored with her, desperate for her affection until the KGB milked them for their secrets or blackmailed them into spying for the Soviet Union, but for Katia, it came at great personal cost. Her life descended into a spiral of alcohol and self loathing. She began to hate men for what they made her do and what they did to her. After six increasingly miserable years, she was no longer useful and she was returned to Moscow for a desk job in translation.

Unable to have normal relations with men, she lived a lonely and occasionally drunken life, her once magnificent athletic body deteriorating to the point where she no longer recognized herself in the mirror. But in an ironic twist, as the Soviet Union collapsed in the early 1990s, her situation improved. She and thousands of other government employees were furloughed as the new Russian government was unable to pay its bills. Katia quickly sobered up and got a job with a Norwegian company in Russia working on improving Russia's crude oil drilling operations. Her language skills in Russian, English and Norwegian were considered very valuable and the management at the Norwegian company was pleased with her work. She joined a fitness club and while carefully avoiding any exercise that would hurt her hip, became fit and strong by lifting weights, swimming and riding a stationary bicycle. For the first time in many years she felt good about herself and began a healthy relationship with a Norwegian man stationed at the Moscow office. She kept her past a secret and rejoiced in her new life until a surprise phone call at work. She answered by saying just her first name.

"Katia Molensk?" said the man's voice on the phone.

"Yes," she replied.

"Your personal ID number is 38374747," he said. It came out more as a statement than a question. Katia paused before responding. She had not used her KGB identification number for a number of years.

"Who is this?" she asked with some uncertainty in her voice.

"It does not matter who I am," the voice on the phone replied. "You have been recalled to service. You will need to take a leave of absence from your work immediately."

"But...but I was fired years ago," she stammered in response. "I don't work for the KGB-"

The caller cut her off in mid-sentence.

"You were not fired. You were furloughed, temporarily released from service. You are now being recalled."

She said nothing and sat ashen faced with the phone gripped tightly in her hand. After a moment of silence she replied, "What if I refuse?"

There was a snort of laughter on the phone before the man replied. "I know your history Katia Molesk. I, uh... we have pictures of you, compromising pictures which we will be happy to send to your colleagues at work."

Katia swallowed hard. She was angry and afraid, a feeling of nausea welled up in her throat.

"A package will arrive for you at your office. Inside will be a safe deposit key. Now listen carefully and write down these instructions."

The next few days were a whirlwind of activity. She never met the man on the phone but he directed her to a safe deposit box which contained traveler's checks, a newly issued Russian passport, a slightly worn Norwegian passport with her name and picture and instructions to fly to Norway on her Russian passport, stay there a few days then make her way to England via France, using only ground transportation. A cell phone was provided as well with strict instructions never to call anyone but to make sure it was fully charged and close by at all times. Within three weeks she was in a cheap hotel in London, waiting for instructions.

For days she had no communication and wondered what she was supposed to do. She had been provided with almost fifteen thousand dollars in traveler's checks but felt awkward about spending too much money without authorization. Finally after idling away her time for more than a week, she received a call with instructions to move into a room reserved in the named on her Norwegian passport at the Dorchester Hotel and stay in her room until instructed otherwise.

The sound of the phone ringing jarred her out of her reverie in front of the mirror.

"Hello," she said.

"You know who this is?" the voice on the phone said in Russian.

She stiffened slightly as she responded.

"Yes."

"Good. Now listen carefully. Do exactly as I say." The man spoke for a few minutes and then said, "Do you understand?"

"Yes," she replied again.

"Very good," the voice responded. "Now listen to me, do this job well and I'll send you home and you will be done. Now get moving. I want you down here in ten minutes."

She hung up the phone and starred at it for a second and then quickly crossed the room to the large closet and began to get dressed. She had her assignment with a promise this would be her only assignment and she did not want to be late.

CHAPTER 8

GERALD RIFKIN WAS bored. This was only his second visit to England in fifteen years, and the place still felt exactly the same. On the first trip, he had come over during summer vacation with a backpack and a few dollars in his pocket and seen all the typical tourist sights. All he could remember was that London seemed to alternate between cold and rainy or hot and muggy. He had been bored then, was sorry he had not remained in Greece where the weather was decidedly better and more importantly, the vacationing Northern European girls were both pretty and friendly — his favorite combination.

Now he had been in London for four days, this time as a businessman. His company had arranged accommodations for him at one of London's best and most expensive hotels. He appreciated the luxury and convenience of The Dorchester, but he was getting tired of the bowing and scraping by the staff, and the prices were just ridiculous. One afternoon he paid almost thirty dollars for a cup of tea and a few cucumber sandwiches. Not that the money came out of his pocket, but even so, a cup of tea served in expensive china by a man in coat tails tastes no different than tea in less auspicious surroundings. His fellow residents, the Arabs and Asians, seemed to enjoy the obsequious service, but to him it was just another reminder of what he disliked most about England, the emphasis on class and breeding. He was a New York City College boy, having worked his way up through hard work and guile. Most frustrating of all, he was having trouble getting his English customers to commit to the deal he had assumed was all wrapped up. This was a multi million dollar contract and most of the details for this deal had been worked out weeks before in New York. He could not understand the delays.

The first two days, he couldn't even get the executives to talk about the deal. They started late again this morning, and then decided to take an early lunch which finished at around two. Like an idiot, he followed their example and drank a couple of warm beers with his food. He was not used to drinking at lunch and felt uncomfortable afterwards, unable to follow the conversation, which was compounded even more by his inability to decipher their accents. After lunch, the meeting ended, still with no resolution, and he went back to his hotel.

Now he sat in the bar at the Dorchester Hotel, refreshed and hungry after a two hour nap and a shower. He ordered a drink and then glanced up at the mirror behind the bar and spotted an overweight and remarkably ugly man nursing a drink in his hand. The man seemed to be mumbling to himself and then he watched him place the large glass to his mouth and swallow the contents in one gulp. He turned to stare at the man, wondering how someone like that could be staying at the Dorchester and then turned quickly away as the man returned his stare with a look that made him feel uncomfortable.

Turning around on the stool, he glanced around the bar and was disappointed to find it so empty. A few tables were occupied, mostly men drinking together and a few women also in the company of the other men. He was really looking forward to some female companionship but doubted he would find it this evening. He slowly drank the wine in his glass, chatted with the bartender for a few minutes and then ordered another. Glancing up at the mirror, he noticed one attractive woman walk in and take a seat not far from his. She looked like she might be in her late thirties or early forties, blonde, slender, and although seated, she appeared tall, with long strong legs. She was looking at her watch when he noticed her and appeared to be waiting for someone.

He sighed and looked away, realizing the evening might end up with him in bed alone watching boring English television. Just then, he felt a tap on his shoulder.

"Excuse me, but have you had dinner yet this evening." It was the tall blonde.

"No, no," he said, rising out of his seat, trying to keep the surprise out of his voice.

"Well, it seems I have been stood up. I noticed you were drinking alone. I thought you might like some company."

"Well, yes," said Rifkin, barely able to conceal his enthusiasm. "Please, won't you sit down. I am here on business. I don't really know anybody."

"Oh, me too," said the blonde. "I am here from Norway on business. By the way, my name is Greta Franz," she said extending her hand.

"Oh, I'm Rifkin, Gerald Rifkin," he said taking her hand and shaking it. "Most of my friends just call me Jerry." The woman let her hand linger in the American's grasp, and then slowly withdrew it.

"Well, Jerry, now that we have been introduced, let's go and eat. What's your fancy?

* * *

Dinner lasted over two hours and had been fantastic — the company, that is. She was funny, attentive, entertaining. She was so comfortable talking with him, and casually let her hand touch his, or their feet touch and linger together under the table. In the taxi on the way back to the hotel, he wanted to kiss her desperately, but did not know how she would respond. He had no idea what was expected, but he was hoping, praying she would spend the night with him.

"I take it you are staying here," she said as the taxi stopped back at the hotel. "Oh yes, of course," he replied. "Great," she replied happily, taking his hand in hers, "then we can have a night cap together in your room."

He wanted to kiss her in the elevator as they rode up but the Dorchester had elevator operators in each elevator so he just reached for her hand and was rewarded as she took his and let her hand rub against his inner thigh. As they entered his room, he grabbed her and kissed her. She responded until he began to undress her, fingers fumbling at her buttons. She stopped him and then undressed him, kissing his face, his neck and then his chest she slowly removed his clothes. He was passive, watching her, feeling her, head numb with alcohol, food, and pleasure. Then she gently made him sit on the edge of the bed and stood in front of him, while she methodically removed her own clothes. She watched his face carefully, making sure she kept his interest, touching herself here and there to maintain his focus. But it was unnecessary; he was focused and very interested. Her body was firm and full. She had strong legs and a flat belly. As she removed her panties, his eyes focused on her pubic hairs and he did not notice the long thin scar above her right thigh.

Finally, she pushed him back on the bed and climbed on top of him and they began to make love. After a few minutes of kissing and caressing, she sat up, turned her face towards his penis and straddled his face with her legs, her vagina inches above his mouth.

Outside the hotel room, Michael Devskoy stood close to the door, but not too close to be obvious. Had anybody walked by, they would have thought he was waiting for someone. He was waiting, but only for the sounds from within the room telling him that the man and woman inside were intimate, locked in a lovers embrace.

Satisfied with what he had heard, he began to walk away from the room, slowly withdrawing a long tube like object with a short trailing wire from his left pocket. As he turned towards the elevators, he flipped off the safety switch on the tube and put his thumb firmly on the top of a small, button-sized plunger at the very top of the tube. As the elevator doors opened in front of him, he pressed the plunger and stepped into the elevator. Behind him he heard a dull explosive thud and as the elevator started down, he smiled.

CHAPTER 9

V LADIMIR KOSNAR STOOD before the heavy upright punching bag with his feet shoulder width apart, arms bent at the elbows, fists clenched and tight to his sides. His left hand shot out and his fist struck the bag hard. He pulled back on his left and simultaneously punched with his right. He settled into a quick cadence – left, right, left, right. As each punch made contact with the bag, he exhaled, pushing the air out of his lungs, tightening his stomach muscles, driving all his energy and focus into the point of contact between his fist and the bag.

Of moderate height and a slight frame, his stature belied his strength; each punch rocked the heavy bag back on its stand. After fifty punches with each hand he stopped, adjusted his stance, moving his left leg in front, his right leg behind, feet still shoulder width apart, arms raised defensively in front of his face and chest – the classic karate fighting stance. In one fluid motion he kicked the bag, curling his toes back and making contact with the ball of his foot. His leg snapped back from the bag as it rocked back on its wide base. As soon as his leg returned to its starting position, he kicked again. He began to alternate his kicks using different techniques in his repertoire; front kick, round house, jumping round house, crescent kick designed to snap a mans jaw, spinning butterfly kick. His movements were controlled, deliberate and fluid, each strike evolving naturally into the next. After a few minutes he stopped and dropped to the ground and did twenty quick pushups. Jumping back up, he continued his routine, sweat pouring down his face and neck and soaking through his thick karate uniform.

He was in the middle of another punching drill when a commotion at the front of the dojo caught his eye. He stopped and peered around the large punching bag, eyeing the three men standing in the doorway. The one in front was tall and immaculately dressed in the uniform of an officer of the *Federal'naya Sluzhba Bezopasnosti*, the Russian Federal Security Service, commonly referred to as the FSB. The two men behind him were younger and dressed in full combat dress, Kalashnikov rifles slung in the typical Russian military style across their chests.

Vladimir's eyes narrowed as he watched the three men walk confidently into the dojo. It was fairly common to see members of the FSB in Moscow. Chechnyan terrorists struck Moscow with sickening regularity and the Russian authorities maintained an extraordinary high level of visible security forces in their major cities. But as an elite protective force, their police functions were limited, making Vladimir wonder what or who could have brought them to this dojo. As he watched, the officer turned back to his subordinates and barked something at them and they immediately turned and blocked the entrance. The officer then looked around the large dojo and noticed that most of the students and instructors who were training had stopped to watch him. He fixed his gaze on one young instructor and beckoned him towards him with his index finger. Vladimir was too far away to hear their conversation but he quickly knew who they were talking about when the instructor pointed directly to him. The officer turned from the instructor and strode purposefully across the padded floor. The rules against wearing shoes on the training floor were usually strictly enforced but no-one stepped forward to stop the officer.

"Vladimir Kosnar?" the officer said as he stood before him.

Vladimir did not reply. He turned and picked up a small towel hanging on a nearby railing and wiped the sweat off his face and neck.

"Colonel Vladimir Kosnar?" the officer said more emphatically.

"I am Kosnar," Vladimir replied softly.

"I have been sent by General Siminov to collect you and take you to his office immediately."

Siminov was Deputy Director of Counter Intelligence and was Vladimir's last commander at the FSB. It had been more than a year since they had seen each other. Their last parting had not been very pleasant.

"I am busy right now as you can see," Vladimir replied. "Tomorrow will be better, I will have more time."

It was obvious the FSB officer was not used to being rebuffed. He stared at Vladimir for a moment then said: "You have five minutes to get showered and dressed."

He paused briefly and with a smile that did not convey any warmth he said: "Or if you like, we can go as you are. Either way, you are coming with me." He was not smiling when he finished talking.

Vladimir stared at him for a moment, his eyes cold and unblinking and then he turned towards the locker room.

The short drive from the dojo to their destination was done in silence. Vladimir knew quite well that despite his arrogance, the officer who had come to collect him was merely a glorified errand boy without any knowledge of who he was instructed to pick up or why. Asking him any questions would be pointless. The car slowed as they approached the guardhouse, a uniformed guard stepping slowly towards the vehicle as they approached. The main office of the FSB was one of the most secure buildings in Moscow, but even they had suffered at the hands of Chechnyan suicide bombers who twice had blown up cars at the entrance to the building. Now every approaching car had to run a gauntlet of checks before being allowed to enter the inner courtyard of the old building.

Vladimir's escort presented his credentials and they were waived through. The car stopped in the courtyard and the FSB officer turned to Vladimir.

"Out," he said brusquely, pointing at the door.

Vladimir looked at him and then reached for the door handle. He stepped out of the car and waited for the officer to climb out after him.

"This way," said the officer as he walked off without breaking his stride.

Vladimir walked slightly behind him as the officer lead him into the familiar building, up one flight of stairs to an office door. The officer stopped in front of General Siminov's office and opened the door. There was a large interior room, staffed by two female secretaries. Both of them looked up at Vladimir as the officer ushered him through the doorway.

"Hello, Olga," said Vladimir. She had worked for General Siminov as long as he could remember. He did not recognize the other much younger woman.

"Hello, Colonel Kosnar," said Olga with a warm smile. "It is good to see you again. General Siminov is expecting you. Please go in."

Vladimir opened the door to the General's office.

"Vladimir," said the General in a loud voice with exaggerated warmth as he got up and walked around his large desk. "It is good to see you. Please, come inside and sit down."

Vladimir took Siminov's out reached hand and gave it a perfunctory shake. "I'm not sure I am so glad to be here," he said. "I must say I was perturbed by the invitation to meet with you this morning," he continued giving the word invitation a little extra inflection.

"Yes, I'm sorry," said Siminov, ushering Vladimir towards the couch. "But you are here now, so please, sit down and make yourself comfortable. Can I offer you anything — coffee or tea perhaps?"

"No, thank you. I am fine. Now General, you did not go to all this trouble to bring me here to drink tea or coffee. What is it you want?"

The General's face lost it warmth and turned serious. A conspiratorial tone crept into his voice. "I need you to do something for me," he said. "Something very secret and very important."

"General," said Vladimir shaking his head, "I'm retired. You know -"

"I know, I know," said the General, cutting him off with a vigorous nod of his head and wave of his hand. "You are retired, but this assignment is imperative. It must be done at all costs. And," the General said as he sighed, "you are probably the only man who can do this."

Vladimir looked at his former commander with dispassion and a small measure of antipathy. He had to admit to himself that sitting here with his old boss rekindled an old passion for a job he had excelled at, but still he was not inclined to make any changes, and in fact could really care less. His commitment to the Communist Party and the service to the country had long diminished and he had become disillusioned. In rare moments of introspection he sometimes wondered if his life had had any meaning or if he had done anything redeeming at all. A little flattery would get his former commander nowhere.

"I'm sorry, General," he said. "Those days are behind me. I am sure there are plenty of good men, younger men in the new service who can help you."

"Yes, you are probably correct," the General replied unconvincingly as he threw his hands up in an expansive motion. "There are many good men. But I tell you what, I have here a dossier I would like you to read. It will only take you about an hour. If the assignment still does not interest you after reading it, then we will have vodka to celebrate old times and you will be on your way. Is it a deal?"

Vladimir paused for a moment and then said "All right. Give me the dossier. I will read it and then I will leave."

The General rose and walked back to his desk. He picked up a large folder, tucked it under his arm, and walked to the door, motioning to Vladimir to follow.

"Olga," he said to his secretary. "Please show Mr. Kosnar to an empty private office." He turned and gave Vladimir the dossier.

"Yes, General," said his secretary as she rose from her seat. "Please follow me, Colonel Kosnar."

* * *

Vladimir did not know how much time passed since he began reading the dossier. The contents were shocking, even disgusting, but for someone with his background and experience, not very surprising. Working in the KGB for so many years, he had gotten used to strange plots and ill-conceived plans. According to the dossier, in the early 1980s the KGB had created an unlikely team of killers, assassins who could deliver death in a method unique and so secret even they were not aware of it. As he read the dossier it reminded him of a book he had read once called *The Manchurian Candidate* in which a captured American soldier is hypnotized into becoming an assassin.

He was also not surprised they had never been used as assassins. It was common for upper level officers to concoct bizarre plans the senior intelligence management never implemented or the old Politburo reviewed, and then stopped. Vladimir surmised that by the time these assassins were operational, Gorbachev had come to power and the Cold War was ending. Maybe it had been decided not to make use of their special capabilities. There was one strange note, however, in the dossier. Apparently, a lot of the assassins in the program were already dead, many having died in the last three years. If the program had never been implemented, why were so many dead and why so recently? The information in front of him contained no explanation.

Now, it seemed the assassination program had been implemented. A significant number of these women had been activated by someone in the FSB and sent to Europe and America. The exact number was unknown but it was thought to be between fifty and one hundred. At least one and possibly even two had already been used. The remainder were believed to be in contact with their handler, under strict orders not to contact headquarters or their embassy. They were walking time bombs, out of touch and out of contact. The worst part was they were not even aware of their own lethality.

Closing the dossier, he returned to General Siminov's office suite. Ignoring the secretaries, and without knocking, he opened the door to General Siminov's office.

"Well?" said the General.

Vladimir put the dossier back on the General's desk, looked up his former commander and shaking his head said, "I don't see how I can help you."

The General stared at him for a few moments and then said, "Are you curious to know who is doing this?"

As Vladimir shrugged his shoulders with indifference, the General reached into another file folder on his desk and withdrew a small black and white picture. He slid it across the desk to his former subordinate. Vladimir glanced at it briefly and then with a gasp of surprise, he picked up the picture and stared at it. He glanced back at the General and then back at the picture.

"Devskoy, that drunken sadistic bastard, it can't be." His voice was incredulous.

Siminov nodded slowly as he retrieved the picture and placed it back on top of his desk. "I am afraid so," he replied.

"But how," Vladimir responded. "Was Devskoy involved in this project?"

General Siminov sighed loudly as he sat down heavily and slumped in his chair.

"No," the General answered emphatically. "He had nothing to do with this. A year ago he was a fall down drunk just trying to stay in the service long enough to get to his pension. He was going to be dismissed, but he contacted me and based on his record, I stupidly agreed to allow him to be placed on a minimum security task and assigned a small office to work until his retirement date. Mostly he just sat there and looked at pornography on the internet. By some stupid mistake, a box containing all the relevant information about this program was delivered to him. So Devskoy looks inside the box, sees all these files and starts reading through them, obviously realizing he is sitting on a potential goldmine if only he can find a willing buyer."

The General paused for a moment before continuing. "Who and how we don't know but about nine months ago he disappeared without a trace. Then purely by chance, someone noticed that a substantial number of these women in the program had left the country. How he got the money and means to get them out, again we don't know but I am assuming Al Qaeda or Hamas or maybe the Iranians. It could even be the North Koreans but I suspect it is someone on the Arab side because that is where he had most of his experience and some contacts. Regardless, someone gave him money."

"Well I can see why you are so anxious to have someone take care of this," replied Kosnar, his voice slightly mocking and derisive in its tone. "But, like I said before, why me?"

"There are two reasons to use you," the General replied as he leaned forward in his chair. "The first reason is you actually know Devskoy which is not true for many of my younger agents. Also, you are very effective at hunting people down as you showed in Afghanistan."

Vladimir shrugged off the Generals ham handed attempt at a compliment.

"So?" Kosnar replied. "That was a long time ago. At best it would give me a slight advantage but not a very significant one."

The General looked back at him, his lower lip quivering almost imperceptibly, eyes blinking rapidly. He would never admit it but he was intimidated by Vladimir Kosnar, particularly now. The information he had to share was his trump card, but he was not sure what kind of response it would illicit. He cleared his throat and was about to speak when there was a sharp knock at his door and, before he could answer, the door opened and a man stepped in. At the sight of him Siminov rose quickly out of his chair and stood at attention.

The man who entered the room was tall with perfectly groomed hair and a well tailored expensive dark blue suit. His dark red tie was perfectly tied and hung just below his belt line. Vladimir immediately recognized him although they had never met before. Victor Chenko had been appointed head of the FSB eighteen months earlier. He had no background in security or espionage but was a protégé of the current Russian President. Chenko had been one of the first Russians in the post Soviet era to attend Harvard's MBA program and returned to Russia to make a small fortune as the country stumbled its way to a free market economy. Unlike some of the other early capitalists in Russia, Chenko worked hard to maintain good relations with the Russian political elite and was brought in to government by the current President to help modernize Russia's oil distribution system so the country could better capitalize on its vast oil resources. His success at that had led to him being appointed head of the FSB in order to modernize its role in the new Russia. Many people believed he was being groomed to be a future or even next president of Russia.

Chenko completely ignored General Siminov who was still standing at attention behind his desk but focused on Vladimir who was standing in front of him.

"Colonel Kosnar," he said warmly as he grasped Vladimir's hand in a strong grip. "It is an honor to meet you. I have heard many of stories about your exploits in the past."

Vladimir said nothing but smiled briefly to acknowledge the compliment.

Chenko turned to the General who was now standing in a slightly more relaxed stance and said, "So have you told the Colonel our sorry tale?"

"Uh...Yes Sir," Siminov stammered as he replied. "I have explained to him the uh...situation."

Chenko roughly pushed aside a couple of folders on Siminov's desk and assumed a half seated position on the desk with right leg dangling and his left leg on the floor. He picked up the picture of Devskoy lying on Siminov's desk and stared at it for a moment.

"I understand you know this man?" Chenko said looking up at Vladimir.

"Yes, I know who he is," Vladimir replied without much enthusiasm in his voice.

"When was the last time you saw him?"

Vladimir shrugged his shoulders. "Maybe six or seven years ago. I'm not really sure."

"Would you recognize him if you saw him again?"

Vladimir nodded and said, "Yes, probably."

Chenko glanced at the picture again. "He is an unpleasant looking human being isn't he," he said with a brief laugh.

Vladimir remained silent. Chenko stared at him for a moment and then asked, "So, are you going to help us with this little problem?"

Vladimir sighed and said, "As I explained to General Siminov, I am no longer in service. I have other obligations and responsibilities now and I am quite sure there are younger, more able men who can do this."

Chenko said nothing but slowly nodded his head while staring hard at Vladimir. He rose to his feet as he spoke. "Colonel Kosnar, you do know that all retired KGB and FSB agents can be recalled to service at the discretion of the Director. You do understand that, right?"

Vladimir just nodded in response.

"But," Chenko continued, his voice softening slightly, "under those circumstances, your uh... motivation might be limited, shall we say, if I ordered you back into service."

Vladimir remained silent. For a moment no one spoke.

Chenko turned to General Siminov. "Do you have the folder?"

Siminov stared back at him for a moment not knowing exactly what folder Chenko was referring to and then quickly made the connection and reached for a single thin brown folder on his desk. Chenko took the folder and very deliberately opened it up and glanced at it contents. He looked up at Kosnar and then snapped the folder shut, quickly handing it back to General Siminov as if he did not want to touch it for too long.

"Colonel Kosnar," he said as he stuck out his hand towards Vladimir and gave him a quick almost perfunctory handshake, "It was a pleasure to meet you. I am going to leave now and after I go Siminov is going to share the contents of the folder with you and then you can make your decision. I will not order you back into service but I am hoping we can help you make the decision yourself."

As Chenko closed the door behind him General Siminov sighed deeply and slumped back into his chair. He pulled a small handkerchief out of his pocket and patted his damp brow. He glanced up at Vladimir who had remained standing after Chenko had left the room.

"Here," he said holding up the brown folder, "read this."

The folder contained one single spaced typed page and a number of small black and white photographs. Vladimir picked up the typed page and began to read it. As he read his face grew ashen and without realizing it he backed into a chair and sat down. After reading the entire page he began to pick through the photographs in the folder. Some were quite old and fading to yellow, others were more recent. He looked at them again and again in disbelief and then suddenly stood up and leaned over the desk and glared at the General Siminov.

"You fucking son of bitch," he said, his face now flush with anger.

The General threw up his hands as if to fend off Vladimir's fury.

"Don't blame me. I had nothing to do with this-"

Vladimir cut him off. "How long have you known about this?"

"Not long," the General replied.

"How long?" he shouted, demanding an answer.

"I told you, not long. I have only learned about this whole thing recently and it was just this week I finally got all the details including that information." He nodded his head towards the pictures in Vladimir hands.

Vladimir sat back down in the office chair facing the General's desk, face expressionless, eyes staring at the man across from him.

"Well?" Siminov repeated, breaking the uncomfortable silence.

Vladimir took a deep breath. "You knew if I read the dossier, I would accept the assignment."

"Yes," answered the General.

"And you are going to help me," Vladimir quickly responded. He rose out of his seat again and pointed his finger at the General. "Money, information, support, resources, whatever I need you will give me."

"Money and information, yes, whatever you need," the General replied. "Support, resources, no I'm sorry. You have to do this yourself."

"What?" Vladimir exploded. "How can I do this by my-"

The General cut him off. "You can because you are skilled at these things and you will because you have to. Those are my orders. You have to do this alone." His last words hung in the air.

* * *

Less than ten minutes after Vladimir Kosnar had left the FSB headquarters building, the phone rang in General Siminov's outer office. His secretary patched the call through to her boss immediately.

"Good morning," said Siminov, trying to sound pleasant. Chenko did not respond with pleasantries.

"Well, will he do it? Did he accept the assignment?"

"Yes, I think he will help us," Siminov replied, trying to sound upbeat.

"You mean he will help you, you idiot," Chenko responded, shouting into the phone. "You're the fucking idiot who allowed this mess to get out of hand. Now, you better make damn sure you finish it."

"But Sir," Siminov responded, "How could I have known Devskoy would-"

Chenko cut him off. "Devskoy is a fucking idiot and a sadistic bastard. You should have fired him years ago. Instead you kept him around for your own purposes. Now look how he has returned the favor."

The caller paused for a moment, and then asked, "Have you had any success in bringing him back in?"

"Uh, no, Sir. I'm afraid he's not responding. We have had no contact with him now for almost nine months. There have been no sightings of him since he was spotted in Syria although we do believe he might be in Pakistan."

"I'm warning you, Siminov, this had better get resolved and soon."

"Yes Sir, I understand. Kosnar is a good man, well motivated. He'll get it done."

"Well, for your sake, I damn well hope so. If this is ever connected back to me, you will wish you were dead, you fucking idiot. Do you understand?"

There was a click as the phone disconnected before Siminov could respond. Slowly, gently, he replaced the handset and let out a long slow breath. He wiped the sweat off his brow, slumped back in his chair. He hoped he was right about Kosnar.

CHAPTER 10

S*HE WAS RUNNING, legs driving hard into the dry earth fighting for traction and speed. She could hear the bullets whistle past her head and see the puffs of dirt as bullets struck the ground around her and she tensed up, anticipating to be hit any second. Up ahead large rocks offered cover and she ran hard to reach them but seemed to make no progress. She felt like she was running in place and as she fought against conflicting emotions of panic and resignation to her fate, the sound of cruel and jarring laughter began to envelop her as she struggled to get to safety.*

The sound of the phone ringing jarred her awake. She sat up in bed, heart racing, sweat beading up on her forehead. She glanced at her bedside clock: it was just after four-thirty in the morning. She took a couple of quick breaths and reached for the phone.

"Hello," she said her voice thick and unclear.

"Casey, can you hear me?" She recognized the voice of her immediate supervisor, Gordon Lewis. He did not wait for her answer.

"I'm sorry to bother you at home this early but I need you to come in to the office right now please."

"What's up Gordon? What's happened?" She was wide awake now, the urgency in his voice quickly dissipating the lingering affects of her dream.

"I can't discuss it now. Just get dressed, nothing formal and meet me in my office. No, wait a second…" There was a pause as she heard him conferring with someone else. "Meet me in conference room 22B down from my office. Quick as you can please."

Casey was already out of bed and moving towards the shower as Gordon hung up. She took five minutes to shower, throw on some casual clothes grab her computer bag and run out of her apartment to the elevators. She pushed the buttons but then quickly turned and chose to run down the stairs. Within fifteen minutes of Gordon's call she was in her car heading towards the office. Without the typical early morning D.C traffic she would be there in another fifteen minutes.

It had been almost a year since Casey Jenning's plane had landed at Reagan International Airport in Washington D.C. on a flight that took her from Afghanistan to Ramstein Air Base in Germany and then to America. By the time she landed, her name was a household word. A nervous young ranger had almost shot her when he saw her stumbling in the dark and then collapsing near the entrance to Camp Huge but fortunately, he had held his fire and she had quickly been identified and carried back into camp.

Her condition had been critical and only a medic was available in the camp to treat her. Her skin pallor was ashen, pulse rapid but weak, eyes sunken and when he tried to provide intravenous fluids, he could barely find a vein; her veins had contracted so far beneath her skin. The medic had quickly applied standard first aid but he was afraid that without quick treatment by a doctor she might die. A helicopter had been summoned which arrived in short order with a doctor on board and she was transferred to a large medical facility at Kabul's airport and within a few days her medical condition had stabilized and she was out of danger.

The story of her encounter with the Taliban and incredible escape to safety had been leaked to the press only hours after she had provided the first of many depositions to the FBI. She was stunned to find out how quickly her story had became public, but with four agents killed in an ambush, the FBI and the administration were anxious to put some positive spin on the loss. She was quickly elevated to the status of hero, with almost every television station leading their news report with updates about her condition and whereabouts. Her life and life story quickly became public and people she barely remembered from high school and college were interviewed and talked endlessly about her. She could not stand to watch television and studiously avoided reading about herself in the newspaper.

Requests for interviews, offers of movies and ticker tape parades flooded the FBI's media relations office but Casey declined them all. The only public meeting she could not avoid was an invitation to the White House to meet the President. As she was escorted to the Oval office, staffers lined either side of each corridor and cheered her as she walked by. It was an uncomfortable moment but she handled herself graciously, smiling at every one and making small talk with the President, posing for endless number of pictures with him and the Director of the FBI.

Finally, after a week, the press found new topics to cover and her story faded into memory. Casey understood that people need to find and celebrate heroes and she was also cognizant what had happened to her was not trivial, but she also knew her survival was also due to a lot of luck; luck she had not been shot during the ambush, or worse yet, captured by the Taliban. Despite her outward appearance of a full physical recovery, it took longer than she cared to admit to put the loss of her colleagues and the three lonely and trying days in Afghanistan behind her.

The most surprising aspect of her mental state she had not anticipated was her response to coming home to an empty house. She had been married for five years, widowed for almost four years and despite the passage of time since her late husband's tragic death in a car accident, missed him more than ever upon her return. On some days, she found herself grieving as if he had just died and on other occasions, she had trouble remembering what he had looked like. She could rationalize that her state of mind was as result of her escape from Afghanistan, but it made the pain no easier to bear. She had not had a significant relationship since his death and was somewhat resigned to the fact she might never. She had given up dating colleagues from the FBI: it seemed every conversation revolved around the Agency and internal politics and she did not care to bring that home with her. Conversely, men she dated from outside the agency seemed unable to relate to her job and seemed to be intimidated by her. Her sense of loneliness was disconcerting and it was a dependent emotional state that made her feel uncomfortable. She tried to put it behind her by returning to work as soon as possible.

A few months after her return, she had been promoted to a group working on risk assessment, reporting directly to the Executive Assistant Director for Counter Terrorism and Counter Intelligence, Gordon Lewis. She had no staff assigned directly to her but operated on behalf of Lewis to coordinate the reporting process for risk assessment. Practically every federal agency had created their own risk assessment group trying to sift through the voluminous amount of data flowing into the government from different intelligence agencies. The FBI's threat assessment team worked closely with the Department of Homeland Security, the National Security Agency and the Central Intelligence Agency to try and coordinate and assess each risk scenario as it filtered in from the different government agencies. Most of Casey's colleagues were highly trained academics, many with doctoral degrees spanning specialties from nuclear and chemical engineering to political science and psychology. At first Casey felt as if she was insufficiently trained to be a part of this group but, she soon realized that as a highly trained and experienced field agent, she knew a great deal more about how to collect and verify threat information than her more educated associates. She found her new job very interesting although she did miss the opportunity to get out of the office and do field work.

There were always some cars in the parking lot at the Hoover building regardless of the time of day but at this early hour she quickly went through the security check points and found a parking spot. She jogged up to the building and took the elevator to conference room. The door was open as she walked in and she quickly recognized three of the six people in the room; her boss Gordon Lewis, his chief of staff Doug Pruett, and Jane Phillips, an expert on the Russian intelligence services assigned to the National Security Agency.

Casey had attended two seminars conducted by Dr. Phillips at the NSA as part of an interagency educational process to foster great cooperation between federal security bureaucracies after the attacks on September 11th 2001. Casey recalled being very impressed with her broad knowledge as well as specific issues related to Islamic Fundamentalism and efforts to counter it by the Russians. Her first presentation had focused on the various Russian provinces with Muslim majorities or large minorities and what their push for independence or autonomy would mean to Russia and neighboring countries. Dr. Phillips' second presentation, which Casey had found even more interesting, focused directly on the Russian intelligence services since the collapse of the Soviet Union.

The windowless conference room was dominated by a large wooden table and surrounded by twelve chairs. A small credenza, which lined one wall was stacked with Styrofoam cups, an assortment of sweeteners and a pot of coffee. On the ceiling above the table a projector was mounted and the unit was powered up, filling the large screen at the end of the wall with the image of someone's computer desktop.

Gordon Lewis, who was holding a cell phone to his ear, waved Casey over to him and he quickly shook her hand and thanked her for coming in so quickly.

"We are just waiting for one other person from the Bureau and we'll get started," Gordon whispered to her. "Grab yourself a coffee while we wait."

A few minutes later Gordon Lewis finished his phone call and called the group to order. "Please take your seats folks, we need to get started. We are waiting for one other person to join us but we can start without him."

He stepped up the small podium to the left of a large screen hanging down on the far side of the wall. He launched into his presentation directly without making any pleasantries.

"Two weeks ago this man, General Bill Cafery, was killed by an explosion in a hotel room in Paris." The screen filled with a portrait picture of a smiling and plump middle-aged man in dress uniform with numerous ribbons and decorations on his chest. "He was killed in the company of a woman, not his wife." Gordon paused for a moment. "Now I am about to show you pictures of the death scene and I have to warn you they are gruesome."

He pushed another button on the computer and a horrific image filled the screen. Casey's eyes narrowed at the picture, a naked woman lying on top of an overweight man. The woman's body was shattered, apparently having caught the brunt of the explosion. Her upper torso from below the breasts was mostly intact, but below, the body was barely recognizable. The man was a bloody mess where his pelvis had been pierced by what appeared to be shrapnel from her bones and from the explosive device itself. Gordon cycled through another couple pictures of the dead couple from different angles and then back to the portrait of General Cafrey.

Gordon began to describe what had happened immediately after the explosion was reported to the French police. "The death of the General lead to notification of the US Military Attaché attached to our embassy in Paris who arrived at the hotel and death scene soon after he was informed. The nature of the deaths was so unusual the military attaché immediately requested the FBI be summoned. As you can imagine the French police had not been pleased, but did agree and a London based Special Agent named David Green who is a forensic specialist was quickly dispatched to Paris. He got there within a few hours and was present as the French crime scene investigators were finishing up their work. The pictures I just showed you were taken by David Green."

He held up a thin manila folder and said, "This contains David Green's report. Some of you have already had a chance to review the report yesterday and I am going to distribute it the rest of you to review right after this meeting."

Gordon paused for moment. "Now, General Cafrey had been stationed in Germany working on an ordinance project with NATO, specifically to supervise the inventory on aging artillery. It was a low level job and he was scheduled to retire at the end of this year. Unfortunately, he had been warned twice about engaging in behavior unbecoming an officer for having relationships in Europe with prostitutes. We have determined he was not visiting Paris on official business and in fact was not on leave to be away from his assignment."

Gordon paused briefly. "Now, as I said I am going to let you read the details in David Green's report later but there are a couple items in it I need to bring to your immediate attention and quite frankly why I felt it necessary to call this meeting early this morning."

He shuffled through his notes for a moment before continuing. "Firstly, the placement of the bomb is still a mystery. As the pictures indicate, both individuals were clearly naked so it is unlikely one of them was wearing the bomb but according to Green's report, the explosive definitely seemed to come from between them. Green suspected at first that perhaps a hand grenade had been placed between them but, shrapnel from a hand grenade is very specific and no such shrapnel was found."

Gordon paused for a minute to take a sip of water.

"Secondly, we have already identified the dead woman to be Sophia Zlotnic."

He turned to Jane Philips, the Russian specialist. "Dr. Philips I understand you have details on Ms. Zlotnic?"

"Yes, thank you Mr. Lewis," Dr Phillips responded. She glanced around the room before she continued. "Sophia Zlotnic has been known to us since Operation Marked Glass which some of you might remember from the early 1980's. To refresh your memory, OMG was a program designed to try and identify and finger print if possible, every known KGB agent operating in Europe. Suspected agents were followed, photographed and then some object they had touched such as a moist glass was quickly dusted for prints and sent back here. It was a very burdensome program and discontinued after two years but not until a few thousand suspected agents had been identified."

She glanced up at Gordon Lewis.

"Mr. Lewis, I believe Ms. Zlotnic is on the next slide."

Gordon pushed a key on his computer and the picture of a young attractive blond woman filled the screen.

"This," the young woman continued "was Zlotnic in 1983 when we believe she was about twenty six or twenty seven years old. We know for sure at that time she was an agent in the former Soviet Committee for State Security, or *Komitet Gosudarsvtvennoi Bezopasnosti* more commonly known as the KGB. We believe her principle job had been an angel, a woman selected for her good looks and alluring personality to seduce men and sometimes women, to gather information or to compromise them. As you all know, they were also occasionally used by the KGB to kill people or set them up for killing."

The older woman in the group, whom Casey did not recognize spoke up. "So if this woman was actually twenty six in 1983 that would make her over fifty years old right now. No offense to anyone but doesn't that seem a bit old to be engaged in this sort of activity."

"Exactly," Lewis responded. "So..." he paused again briefly. "Here are the open questions. What was she doing with this man, this American General and why now? He had limited operational knowledge that could be useful to anyone. And how did they die? Was her death a suicide or accidental?"

"Sir," Dr. Phillips interrupted him. "I am sorry to interrupt you but there are two more things I discovered late last night that might be pertinent. Number one, in 1979 Zlotnic was ranked the fastest women in the Soviet Union in the 100 meter dash and had posted the second best time in the world that year." She paused as she glanced around the room.

"And yet," she continued, "she did not compete in the Olympic games that summer in Moscow and despite a pretty thorough search I could not find any evidence of her ever competing again after 1979. It was as if she went from being the Soviet's best prospect for winning a gold medal in the most prestigious woman's race in the summer Olympics to oblivion."

Just then there was a knock on the door to the conference room and a young man in a dark suit, white shirt and dark red tie stepped into the room carrying a large brown envelope in his hand. Gordon Lewis waived him into the room and quickly introduced him.

"This is Special Agent Michael Franks. Michael has been chasing down some new developments for me which we will get to in a few moments."

As the young agent nodded a quick hello and sat down at the conference table, Gordon Lewis looked over at Casey.

"All of you know Casey Jennings or at least you know who she is," he said with a quick smile.

Casey nodded once briefly as everyone glanced over at her.

"I know you have all read Casey's detailed report about the unfortunate events in Afghanistan last year, but I would like you to hear a direct description from her of the abandoned courtyard she stumbled into, specifically the tall wooden post with the metal ring attached. Casey, please go ahead."

Casey leaned forward in her chair, unsure why she was being asked to describe something so disconnected from the present conversation but cleared her throat and described what she recalled.

"The courtyard was about the size of a football field, flat and had obviously been carefully cleared and leveled. My guess is it had been used as some sort of parade ground or training facility, although I have no specific evidence to back that up." She paused for a moment, glanced around the room and then continued.

"At the far end of the courtyard was a single wooden post embedded in the ground. As Gordon said it had a metal ring bracketed near the top of the post and was quite nicked and damaged near the bottom. It looked as if someone had made a token effort to clean up the area near the base of the post but there were dark spots in the dirt that looked to me like oil or congealed blood. I did scratch around in the dirt for a few minutes and found a number of metal fragments, which I put into my pocket. They were returned to me with a package of my personal affects soon after I returned to the States, at which time I turned them over to the forensic laboratory, but I never heard back if they were significant or not."

Casey glanced up at the screen and was surprised to see a picture of the metal fragments she had collected arrayed on a white piece of paper.

As she paused, Gordon Lewis spoke up. "This is a picture of the metal fragments Casey found. As she said they were submitted to our forensics lab which quickly determined that the fragments were made of titanium but no credible explanation could be found for them and quite frankly, they were quickly forgotten. Until last week that is, when one of our lab technicians started reviewing the material collected from General Cafery's murder."

Another picture flashed on the screen, this time with a lot more fragments and some pieces slightly larger than the pieces Casey had found. There was an audible gasp from some people assembled in the room.

Gordon said nothing for a moment and then as he nodded slowly he said, "I think most of you have already made the connection. We have a former or perhaps current Russian agent found dead with an American General in Paris whose deaths were somehow caused by a device with identical properties to fragments found in what was probably a Taliban or possibly Al Qaeda training ground in Afghanistan."

He paused for a moment and then with his left hand he gestured to the man who had joined the meeting late. "As I said earlier, this is Special Agent Michael Franks. Mike, I believe you have some current information for us."

Michael Franks pulled a small notepad out of his jacket's interior pocket and glanced at his notes.

"Last night at approximately two fifty eastern standard time or nine fifty Greenwich Mean Time, an American businessman named Gerald Rifkin was killed in London at the Dorchester, a very uh...exclusive hotel located near Hyde Park. He was killed in the company of a woman whose identity has not yet been established. The English detective assigned to the case, Mr. Ian Campbell, described her to me as European, probably northern or eastern European."

He paused as he reached into the large envelope in front of him on the conference table.

"The cause of death has definitely been established as an explosive device. Detective Campbell was kind enough to email me a few pictures of the death scene, copies of which I have here."

He waited as a set of pictures was handed around the room to each person.

"If you look at the picture with the yellow forensic number pad marked #14 you can clearly see a group of metal fragments identical in nature to the ones on the screen."

He paused while everyone in the group paged through the pictures he had just handed out.

"There is one more thing." Everyone looked back up at him. "Ian Campbell has been a Scotland Yard detective for almost twenty five years. He told me has seen numerous criminal killings by explosives and a number of bomb attacks conducted by the Irish Republican Army. He said this one was particularly strange because it seemed the woman had the bomb on her person during coitus, while they were actually having sex."

Michael Franks glanced around the room and shrugged his shoulders. "People's sexual behavior is hard to predict but, it just seems unreasonable to me that a man would make love to a woman who was wearing a suicide bomb."

He closed his notepad and sat back in his chair. There was silence in the room for a moment as everyone tried to absorb what they had just heard. Gordon Lewis cleared his throat.

"If you connect these dots, it certainly gives you pause," he said. "Two Americans are killed in Europe by explosives, delivery method unknown. Fragments, possibly bomb fragments of the identical type, are found at each murder site in Europe and at a deserted training camp in Afghanistan."

He smiled briefly, but the smile did not reach his eyes.

"Ladies and Gentlemen, as I said earlier we have a set of unanswered questions but there is one fact we do know that is quite frankly giving me real heartburn. If these women do turn out to be some kind of suicide bombers, and it certainly appears they are, they would be the first case of non-Muslim woman engaging in this kind of attack. We all know about the few women used by Islamic Militants in Israel and the Black Widows of Chechnya who have conducted numerous attacks against the Russians, but we have had only one incident of a European woman actually being used as a suicide bomber and she was a Muslim convert."

He paused and shook his head. "Officially we don't do any kind of profiling of potential terrorists and

I completely endorse that philosophy. However, let's be frank; it does make it a lot easier if your enemy does not look exactly like you. If suicide bombers start looking like middle-aged Anglo Saxon women and they have found a way to conceal their bombs so even their lovers seem unaware of them, well it seems like we have a whole new challenge on our hands."

Lewis leaned forward and placed both elbows on to the podium, his body language conveying a sense of urgency. "We don't know if these killings are directly related or if this is something big or small but, I do know we need to get ahead of this. Homeland Security has obviously been informed but I'm not ready to tell them my hair is on fire about a new threat until we have more information but, I can tell you the hairs on the back on my neck are standing up. If my instincts on this stuff are any good and they had better be after twenty five years on the job, something tells me we might have a serious problem on our hands."

He turned to the young expert on Russia. "Dr. Phillips, we need whatever information you have on this Zlotnic woman. I also would ask you to get directly involved in helping to identify this second woman who died with the American businessman... what was his name again – Rifkin. Is she also a Russian? Did she work for the KGB or the new FSB? Whatever you can give us."

"Well Sir," Dr. Phillips said, "there is something else that may or may not be related but I think you all need to hear it."

She opened up a folder in front of her and pulled out a small black and white picture. "I'm sorry I didn't have time to make copies of this picture for everyone but this man," she said as she held up the picture, "is Vladimir Kosnar. He was one of the KGB's senior agents during the late seventies and eighties. He is fluent in a number of languages including French and English. We believe that on many occasions he was used for security details, protecting Soviet diplomats, but he was mostly engaged in clandestine activities with KGB's elite First Directorate in Afghanistan, where he was involved in suppressing the attacks by the Mujihadin against Soviet troops. We do know he was quite effective and there was actually some discussion about the US Army hiring him as a consultant for our current efforts in Afghanistan. It was for that reason we have been paying attention to him lately, but right after he visited the FSB he suddenly quit his well paying security job with one of the very rich Russian oligarchs and left for London."

"Why do we think his departure is significant or related to these explosions?" Gordon Lewis asked.

"Well, we don't have any direct knowledge it is related to the explosions, but once we saw the report David Green had put together, we suspected his presence in Paris might not be coincidental. However, it is my opinion, and I feel pretty confident about this, Kosnar has not been sent to aid this program but to stop it."

"What do you mean, Dr. Phillips?"

"Well, I believe and let me be clear," she said as she delicately brushed her shoulder length hair behind her ears, "this is just pure conjecture on my part now, but I believe one or more people within the Russian security services has activated this program. Who and for what purpose I cannot begin to guess but if I am correct, then I am quite certain that given our current relations with the Russians, it is not being done with any high level sanction. On the contrary if my conjecture is correct, then this is part of an unsanctioned rogue program."

As Dr. Phillips stopped speaking, Gordon Lewis sighed briefly and then rubbed his forehead as if he was fighting off a bad headache.

"Are you saying there might be some cooperation between Al Qaeda and Russian intelligence?" he asked, a note of disbelief in his voice and face.

"Nothing formal," Dr Phillips responded, "but it certainly would not be the first time rogue elements of the former KGB worked with terrorist organizations. As you all recall there was some evidence during the early 1990's's that former and even current KGB agents were trying to smuggle uranium out of the former Soviet Union."

As Dr. Phillips stopped speaking, Gordon Lewis turned to Casey Jennings.

"Casey, this is going to be your primary assignment for now. In fact, I want you on a plane for London today. I need an experienced field agent, to give me a personal analysis of what we are dealing with. Get over there, hook up with David Green, get hold of the autopsy documents, better yet go the to morgue and learn what you can, check out the hotel room, talk with this English detective... uh Campbell and get his take on things and then come back here right away."

He turned to Michael Franks. "Mike, please give Casey the contact information for Detective Campbell and then give him a heads up call that Casey is flying in.

Ask him if can't arrange some professional courtesies for Casey on my behalf, transportation and the like. Scotland Yard is usually pretty accommodating to us so I'm sure it will be no problem."

He turned to face Dr. Phillips shaking his head slightly as he faced her. "This Russian agent, what's his name again...Kosnar. I don't know but it sounds like a bit of leap to me." He paused for a moment and then continued. "Look, stay on it and see what else you can find. See if there is any kind of buzz coming out of Moscow on this thing and keep me posted."

He glanced around the room making eye contact with each person. "Any questions? Great, OK. Let's go folks."

CHAPTER 11

V LADIMIR KOSNAR SAT in the back of the limousine staring blankly out of the window, looking out but seeing nothing. He blinked slowly and sighed once deeply as a wave of anger washed over him. He was angry at General Siminov and the old corrupt and malevolent Soviet System of which he was both a product and a part, but which now felt so alien. He was disgusted with what he had learned today, the abject disregard in which the KGB had held its own citizens, former elite athletes that it simply decided to 're-use' in the cause of communism. It was an example of absolute power exercised in the most brutal manner possible.

Next to him was a letter sized manila envelope Siminov had given him as he left the office. He glanced down at it for a moment and then picked it up, untying the red string that secured the envelope and slid the pages out, tossing the envelope back on to the seat. The document consisted of five pages, held together by a single staple on the top left corner. On each page, arranged in rows of four were twenty portrait pictures of women, some in color and distinct, others in black and white and less clear. Beneath each picture was a name and approximate current age of each of the women.

Placing his index finger on the first picture, he slowly scanned them one by one as he moved his hand across and down the page. After reaching the last picture on the first page, he flipped the page and did the same thing again until he stopped towards the middle of the forth page. He lifted the page up to his face, turning the document slightly towards the window to capture the light and stared hard at the picture in the third row. Then he pulled his wallet out of his back pocket and carefully withdrew from it a picture encased in a small plastic sleeve. He looked first at one picture and then the other for a few moments until the sound of a cell phone ringing interrupted him. The young officer riding in the front seat answered the call and then quickly turned around and handed it to him. Vladimir took the phone and put it to his ear.

"Kosnar," he said.

General Siminov got directly to the subject without engaging in pleasantries. "Devskoy is in London. We have just heard that another bomb has gone off in a hotel in London and the characteristics of the bombing seem to be his handy work."

"How long ago?" Kosnar asked.

"Probably within the last twelve hours. Not much more than that based on the intercepts."

"Which hotel?" Kosnar responded.

"A place called the Dorchester somewhere near Hyde Park. Do you know it?"

"Yes," Kosnar replied.

"Good," said the General. I am making arrangements for you right now. When you get to the airport, there will be a seat reserved for you on the next flight to London.

CHAPTER 12

C ASEY STRODE BRISKLY up the gangway into Heathrow airport. She could feel the effects of the flight and lack of sleep, but the bright morning sunlight streaming through the large windows tricked her body into feeling awake. As she exited, she saw a uniformed officer and another man wearing a navy blue sports coat and gray slacks just to the right of the exit way. Typically, passengers could only be met after passport control and customs, but Inspector Campbell had told her he would meet her as she got off the plane.

"Ms. Jennings," Inspector Campbell said as he approached her, easily recognizing her from the pictures published around the world after her escape from the Taliban.

"Hi," she replied as she dropped her shoulder bag and shook his hand. "Please call me Casey."

"Very well. But only if you call me Ian." She smiled in agreement.

"This is Officer Ronald Cole," he said as he turned to the uniformed policeman next to him.

"Good to meet you, Madam," said Cole.

"Good to meet you too, Officer," said Casey, amused by the officer's formality.

"Please let me take your bag, Ma'am," he said and swept it up. Casey hated the word 'Ma'am', but she just replied, "Thank you," as Ian Campbell began to guide her to the exit. "Do you have any other luggage?" he asked.

"No," said Casey, "that's it."

"Traveling light, are you?"

"I don't really expect to be here long," she replied with a quick smile. "If we get through it all today, I might go back as soon as tomorrow."

"Ok. Well, we'll try to fit it all in, then."

Once Inspector Campbell had expedited her passage through immigration and passport control, they were quickly on their way towards London.

"How long is the drive?" Casey asked.

"Oh, about an hour, Ma'am," said Officer Cole.

"Casey, why don't we take you to your hotel to freshen up. Then Officer Cole and I can take you over to the Dorchester Hotel to show you the room and the damage."

"Great," said Casey. "Actually, I would like to see the bodies before I see the room. Would that be possible?"

"Absolutely," said Ian. "In fact, I planned to visit the coroner's office again today myself. They assured me they will have completed both autopsies. You're welcome to join me, but I must warn you it's not a pleasant sight. Bloody awful, really."

"I'm sure," said Casey. "I've seen the pictures of the other bombing. They were gruesome."

"What are you looking for exactly, Casey?" Ian asked.

"Well, for one, we need to know how the bombs are being delivered. Also, how are they activated? It's unlikely the women are activating the bombs themselves. If they are, why go to all that trouble just to kill their targets during intercourse? If they were alone with these men, then they would have plenty of opportunity to kill them without actually initiating coitus. The other issue is that even if we can determine how the bombs are being delivered, we still cannot quantify the problem. For all we know, there could be five or fifty or, God forbid, five hundred of these women out there." Casey sighed, brushing her hair away from her face. She was starting to feel the effects of the flight.

They rode in silence for a while and then Ian pointed out a few of the famous sites as they approached London. Casey had not been to England before; she would have liked to have visited, but under different circumstances.

They arrived at Casey's hotel, The Holiday Inn, close to the American Embassy and the standard location for visiting FBI agents. Ian went off to find out if the autopsies were complete, while Casey checked in and took a quick shower. She was back downstairs in the hotel lobby within half an hour.

"Righto, then," said Ian as Casey walked up to him. "The coroner, Doctor Bellamy, will be there to meet with us. I also contacted your associate, David Green. He said he would meet us over there as well."

"OK, very good," said Casey.

* * *

The coroner's building had an old grimy facade with a surprisingly modern interior. David Green was waiting in the lobby when they arrived. Officer Cole remained with the car while the Inspector led the two American agents into the building, down a long corridor to a room marked in large red letters: 'Entrance Restricted. Authorized Personnel Only.' The English detective pushed the door open and ushered Casey and David before him.

The smell hit them immediately. As law enforcement professionals, they were all familiar with the inside of coroner's laboratory, but the odor and bodies on open display was still disconcerting. The room was a very large rectangle. Every ten feet or so was a large flat metal frame. The frames were slightly elevated at one end with a large drain at the lower end to catch the bodily fluids. Some were bare, others occupied by bodies in various stages of dissection. Above each metal frame a microphone hung down so the coroners could dictate their findings as they worked. The walls of the room were lined with desks and various medical and analytical tools such as microscopes and blood centrifuges. Technicians in laboratory coats wandered about, assisting the different coroners as they worked.

Ian spotted Dr. Bellamy and pointed her out. She was easy to spot, a very tall woman, large all around, although not heavy or fat. The threesome moved down the row of beds until they stopped where Dr. Bellamy was working. She looked up at them and recognized Ian.

"Campbell," she said in a loud, self-confident voice. "Welcome to the dungeon." She grinned, revealing a not-so-straight set of teeth. On the drive over Ian had warned Casey that Dr. Bellamy had a slightly odd personality and an even stranger sense of humor. But she was one of the best forensic coroners in England.

"Hello," said Ian. "This is Casey Jennings and David Green. As I mentioned on the phone, they are with the American Federal Bureau of Investigation, investigating the death of Gerald Rifkin."

"Hello," said the doctor. "G'men hey," she said using the old nickname for FBI agents. "Although I guess in your case, we would have to say G'woman." She laughed heartily as she looked over at Casey. Then she said, "Welcome to England. Sorry I won't shake your hand," she said waving a bloody glove in the air.

"It is very nice to meet you," said Casey. "Thank you for seeing us on such short notice."

"Short notice, hmm…" said Dr. Bellamy. "Speaking of short things, why don't we wander over to your severely shortened Mr. Rifkin. Follow me, please." She pulled off her rubber gloves, tossed them into a nearby trashcan, and quickly washed her hands. Then she turned and walked out of the dissection room through a door stamped 'Refrigeration and Storage'. The two FBI agents and Inspector Campbell followed closely behind.

Dr. Bellamy stopped in front of a large bank of what appeared to be oversized file cabinet drawers. "Ah, lets see…Oh yes, here it is," she said as she moved towards one of the drawers and with an exaggerated motion, pulled one open. "May I present the abbreviated Mr. Rifkin."

Casey looked over at Dr. Bellamy and quickly realized she was staring, her mouth ajar. She had heard that people in forensics often developed a strange sense of humor, usually just to counteract the morbidity of their profession, but Dr. Bellamy seemed to relish her gruesome environment. Closing her mouth, Casey moved to stand opposite the doctor, across the open drawer. Through the opaque sheet, the remains of a man's body were quite obvious. Before Casey had a moment to adjust to the covered corpse in front of her, Dr. Bellamy pulled back the sheet revealing the shattered upper torso of a man's body. There was no blood and the torso was milky white, ending in a mass of broken bones and shattered flesh at the shoulders. The right arm was disconnected from the body and placed incongruously between his legs, hand resting between the feet. Casey starred at the hand, using the curious relationship between it and the feet to help her fight the bile rising in her chest.

"...as you can see..." Dr. Bellamy was saying, catching Casey unaware. "Mr. Rifkin suffered massive trauma to the upper extremities. As the pictures from the crime scene show, his head was directly below and between her thighs. The blast came from the right side of her body, and her left leg acted as a sort of funnel, directing and driving the force directly at Mr. Rifkin's neck. Death for him was absolutely instantaneous, although I'm not sure we can say the same for the poor woman."

"What do you mean?" said Casey

"Well, my best guess, and I think it's quite a good guess, is the woman actually moved a few seconds after the blast."

"She survived the blast?" asked Casey, incredulously.

"Very briefly, but I think she was probably alive a few moments, perhaps as long as a minute."

Though David Green had been quiet up to now he looked over at the doctor and said, "Wouldn't the force of the blast have destroyed her lower extremities as well?"

Without answering, Dr. Bellamy walked around the open drawer to directly behind Casey and pulled open another drawer. "Voila," she said. "Ms. Jane Doe," and quickly pulled the sheet off the woman's body. Casey's eyes first settled on the dead woman's face. At first glance, she looked pretty, peaceful and undisturbed, almost as if she was sleeping, but the dead woman's body had the same alabaster color as Gerald Rifkin's. She was obviously dead, a point made even more evident as Casey's eyes dropped to the bottom half of her body. The hip joints and pelvic bones were completely severed, lower portions of the shattered legs unattached on the slab below her torso. The right leg and hip were noticeably more damaged than the left, but the entire lower half of her body had been mostly destroyed.

"Are you saying she survived this level of damage?" said Casey, almost grateful for the opportunity to speak about something, anything to distract her from the carnage. David Green was next to her, peering at the body, apparently not suffering the queasiness gripping Casey, or more able to conceal it if he was.

Dr. Bellamy's voice lost its jovial tone. "As you can see, the head, heart and even lungs were not severely damaged by the explosion. To be sure, blood loss and shock were massive, but her death was only indirectly related to the blast. She basically bled to death."

"Do you think she was aware of what happened?" Casey asked.

The coroner shook her head. "Maybe. I don't know. How does the brain respond when a trauma like this occurs to the body? I'd like to believe shock prevented her from comprehending her situation, but who knows," she said as she shrugged.

"Dr. Bellamy, do you have any idea where the bomb was located. Was it attached to her body somehow...?" Casey's voice trailed off.

"Well, there I do have some good news for you," the coroner replied, her voice regaining its jovial tone. "I know where the bomb was located and no, it was not attached to her body. It was inside her body."

"What?" Casey and Ian replied, almost in unison. "Did you say the bomb was inside the woman's body?" Casey asked, voice and face conveying disbelief.

Dr. Bellamy did not answer directly. She walked over to a cabinet marked with the sign 'Evidence' and opened it with a key she withdrew from her pocket. She removed a container about the size of a shoebox, and then closed the cabinet, carefully locking it. As she walked back towards the waiting threesome, she opened the box, removed the lid, and placed it in her hand directly underneath the box. Then they all huddled together, peering down. Inside were about fifteen small plastic bags, each numbered and labeled.

"This is what we pulled out of both bodies. Small titanium fragments, most no larger than the nail on your pinkie finger, some a little larger. Any guess as to the source?" she asked, looking at each of them, a grin forming on her lips.

For a moment nobody answered. Then Casey said, "From an artificial hip joint? Isn't that what they're made of?"

"Bingo! Yes, quite right. Jane Doe back there had an artificial hip joint in her right leg. That's where the explosion came from." She paused and then handed the box over to Ian. "You will need to sign for the evidence on your way out."

"Dr. Bellamy, are you quite sure this woman had an artificial titanium hip joint?" Casey asked.

"Oh absolutely. American made actually. It was an older model, discontinued a few years ago. Good product, very durable, but there are better versions on the market today."

"And you can tell this just by these fragments?" David Green asked.

Dr. Bellamy grinned. "If you look carefully at one of those fragments you will find a manufacturer's product code. The number survived the blast. It made identification quite easy."

"How much explosive material could you place in an artificial hip joint," Casey asked.

"Well, I'm not sure," Dr. Bellamy said shrugging her shoulders. "Obviously enough to do this," she said as she nodded her head towards the two corpses.

"And you're sure that's the source of the explosion?"

"Yes, quite sure, Ms. Jennings." She paused for a moment, then said, "There is one other item that will interest you," as she rifled through the small evidence bags. "Ah, yes, here it is." She withdrew one bag and held it up.

"May I?" asked Casey. The coroner passed the bag to her.

Casey peered through the plastic at the small item located inside; a one-inch long opaque tube. One end was broken, but the other appeared intact. Casey passed the bag to Ian Campbell.

"What do you think?" Casey asked, looking first at Dr. Bellamy and then at the Inspector.

"Well, I don't know for sure, but one of the fellows in our lab thinks it is part of a receiver of some kind. I pulled it out of Mr. Rifkin's right shoulder. I suggest you have it looked at by a communications engineer, someone who understands miniature receivers can probably help you." Dr. Bellamy stood quietly for a moment as the threesome stared at the small item in the bag, then turned away.

There was a loud bang as she slammed Gerald Rifkin's drawer closed. "We can't have Mr. Rifkin melting all over the place, can we now," she said, laughing. "Do you need to look at Jane Doe's body any more or can we put her away as well?"

"No, thank you, Doctor," said Casey. "I have seen all I wanted to see. A lot more actually. You have been extremely helpful. Thank you very much."

"Yes, thank you very much, Doctor, we appreciate your time," said David Green.

"Not at all. Nice to meet you both. Ian, you can find your way out, can't you. Don't forget to sign for the evidence. I'm just going to putter around here for a few more minutes."

As Casey said good-bye, Dr. Bellamy had already turned away and was pulling on a pair of rubber gloves. The two FBI agents followed the English police officer out of the building.

CHAPTER 13

ITTING IN THE car riding from the coroner's office
to the hotel, Casey sat quietly, lost in her thoughts.
She stared out the window, not seeing anything, a
hard frown creasing her brow. She was furious and getting
angrier by the moment. What had happened to these
women was rape and murder, nothing less. Actually it was
worse than that. They had been raped and *predestined*
for murder. They were not suicide bombers or Japanese
Kamikaze pilots, but more like battlefield victims, a
modern version of cannon fodder chosen to die for some
ill-conceived goal by unscrupulous commanders. These
women had been *used*, used to death. They reminded
Casey of a story she once read about Soviet officers
clearing minefields during the Second World War by
having soldiers walk through them. The Soviets regarded
this as a more cost-effective solution than the American
method of shelling minefields with artillery. She was just
wondering how the women had been selected when she
heard her name.

"Casey, are you all right?" asked the Inspector. He was touching her shoulder.

"What? Oh yes, I'm fine thank you." Casey looked over at her English escort and noticed that he had a concerned look.

"Are you sure you're all right? The visit to the coroners' office was not too upsetting I hope."

Casey dismissed his concerns with a flick of her hand. "No, I'm fine thank you. Just thinking about what I saw, trying to understand it," she said with a reassuring smile.

During the remainder of the drive, she chatted with Ian and David about investigative techniques used by Scotland Yard. She was making small talk, not really worried about the material collected by the English detectives. Reading the analysis done by the British police after the bombing of PAN AM 103 over Lockerbie, Scotland, Casey knew they had techniques as good as the FBI. In that case, detectives assisted by hundreds of police officers and police cadets found a remnant of the bomb no larger than a fingernail. With just that evidence, they had traced the bomb particle back to its manufacturer, and then used that information to determine that two Libyan Intelligence officers had built and deployed the bomb. It was an extraordinary effort, which culminated in the conviction of at least one of the two Libyans.

When Officer Cole pulled the car directly in front of the Dorchester Hotel, the Inspector quickly escorted the two Americans inside. As the group stepped into the elevator, Ian Campbell withdrew a key from his pocket and inserted it into a slot in the elevator's control panel. "At our insistence and until the investigation is complete, the floor on which the attack took place is closed," said Ian. "All the guests were moved out and relocated to different rooms or even different hotels," he continued. "The guests at this hotel pay a small fortune to stay here and are used to being treated extra special if you know what I mean, and I understand some of them were quite upset," he said looking at Casey and David and smiling.

When the elevator arrived at the floor, Ian Campbell walked ahead. A yellow tape with the words 'POLICE' stenciled on it was taped across the doorway. A large sign was also taped to the door. 'BIO HAZARD. ENTRANCE STRICTLY FORBIDDEN'.

"When the police and the ambulance men arrived soon after the incident, it was immediately decided by the senior officer to declare a biological hazard," Ian said as the group stood in front of the doorway. "There was so much blood on the floor, the walls and the bed, it was regarded as too dangerous to enter without the right protective equipment," he continued.

"How long did it take for the equipment to arrive?" Casey asked as Ian removed the yellow tape from the door.

"Actually, not long," said Ian. "Ever since the nerve gas attacks in Nagoya, Japan and then our subway bombings, we have maintained a standby unit ready to move at any time for just such an event. They were here in minutes."

"Did their presence affect the quality of the early investigation?" asked Casey.

"By that I take it you mean, did they go in and clean up before the detectives could investigate?" replied Ian.

"Yes," said Casey.

"No," said Ian, a little defensively. He was getting tired of Casey's probing regarding the quality of police investigative techniques in Great Britain. "The standard procedure is to have trained officers participate in the biohazard cleanup. They were simply provided with appropriate protection. The investigation proceeded normally, although a little slower than usual."

Turning to unlock the door Ian said, "The biohazard is actually no longer in effect, so you are free to move about the room."

Pushing the door open, Campbell then stepped back, letting Casey enter. David Green followed her. He had already been in the room twice, and knew what to expect. The group spent almost ninety minutes in the room. Ian showed Casey how the bodies were found, what position they were in, where remnants of the bomb had been collected. Casey walked around the room slowly. She really was not expecting to uncover anything the British police had not already found, so she tried to get a sense of what had happened. David Green's notes and documentation on the incident, which she had read before she flew out, were excellent. He had described the room and the damage almost perfectly, but she was still surprised by the amount of damage. The bed frame was visibly bent and there were dark spots from the blood and body parts still visible on the walls, ceilings, and even on a curtain more than ten feet away. This was a revelation to her. There had been discussion about the use of such a bomb to destroy an airliner in flight, or something similar. Now she was sure not only was that possible, but also likely that such a bomb, correctly placed, could badly damage an aircraft, perhaps making it lose structural integrity.

"Ian," she said turning to him, "was any check done on the hotel guests who were staying here to see if they might have been involved?"

"You mean in terms of activating the bomb?" Ian asked. Casey nodded. "Yes, of course, we checked the name and passport of every guest who was a resident that night. We focused a lot of attention on all the residents of rooms above, next to and below Mr. Rifkin's. Most of the people who stay here are typically foreign businessmen and wealthy individuals. None of them appeared to be suspicious. We also interviewed the hotel staff, showed a picture of the dead woman's face to every staff member. She was very pretty so some of the male staff members did remember her. The bartender actually thinks he saw her with Mr. Rifkin the night of the incident, but he is not absolutely sure. Anyway, we are certain she was booked into the hotel."

"And no suspicious individuals were discovered in your search," asked Casey.

"Well, I would not go as far as to say that," said Ian smiling. "One hotel guest was actually deported during our investigation, but on a completely unrelated item. No," he said shaking his head. "We did not come up with anyone who appeared to be associated with this attack."

"Well, thank you for bringing us here, Ian. I appreciate the time you have spent with us today."

"You're quite welcome," said Ian.

"I'm glad we have finally discovered how the bombs were delivered, but I am curious to learn more about the little receiver device they found. If that's what it is, then it will confirm the explosions are triggered remotely." Casey paused for a moment and then continued. "How soon do you think you can get it analyzed?"

"It's a bit late to get started on it today," Campbell replied glancing at his watch, "but first thing tomorrow we will track down a communications engineer. I'll get back to you as soon as we learn anything."

"Thank you, Inspector."

The group rode the elevator back down in silence. When they reached the lobby, Casey thanked the Inspector again for his time. "How far are we from my hotel?" she asked

"Oh, about thirty minutes by car and about the same walking, actually," said David Green alluding to London's notoriously slow traffic.

"I'm quite tired," said Casey, "but it would be nice to walk back."

"I'll show you the way," said David.

"Are you sure you don't mind?"

"Not at all. Actually the quickest way is through Hyde Park. I think I'd enjoy that myself."

"I am going to turn Mr. Rifkin's room back over to the hotel now," said Ian. "I know they have been quite anxious to reclaim it. Casey," he said putting out his right hand, "it was a pleasure to meet you, although I wish the circumstances had been more pleasant."

"Yes," said Casey, "I agree. Thank you again for all your assistance. I expect I'll be returning to Washington tomorrow. Please contact me as soon as you have information about the receiver."

"Of course."

"Shall we go?" Casey asked David.

The two Americans walked towards the exit and stepped into the late afternoon London sunlight.

* * *

It was a stroke of luck. Vladimir Kosnar had rushed from the airport to his hotel in London and then after dropping off his bags, immediately took a taxi to the Dorchester Hotel. Finding a seat that afforded him the clearest view of the entrance and the lobby, he had ordered a drink and settled in for what he expected to be long and probably fruitless wait. But in less than twenty minutes, he spotted the two Americans as they followed the British detective out of the elevator into the hotel lobby. He was certain they were American agents and equally sure they were here investigating the latest bombing. Peering from behind a newspaper, he watched them as they chatted in the lobby and then slowly got up from his chair and followed Casey Jennings and David Green out through the revolving door. The two agents were about twenty yards ahead of him, walking at a comfortable pace. He was surprised to see them on foot, but pleased because it would make his task easier. Since the sidewalk was not very crowded, Vladimir let the distance between them increase to about thirty yards. He was curious to see how long it would take before they spotted him.

CHAPTER 14

ICHAEL DEVSKOY WAS on the verge of panic. He felt like he had just seen a ghost, someone completely unexpected but who could absolutely destroy his plans. Vladimir Kosnar had just walked right past him in the lobby of the Dorchester Hotel. He instinctively knew Kosnar was here for him, sent to hunt him down and stop him. He had expected something like this to happen, that his disappearance and the sudden activation of the assassin program would eventually be linked. Of course they would send someone, maybe a whole team to find him and stop him but not this soon and not Kosnar. He had not anticipated Kosnar.

Fortunately, Devskoy had seen him first and was able to quickly grab a newspaper and hold it up to his face, hiding his identity. But it was just past two o'clock and he was expecting Abd Al Rahman in a few minutes and if he walked into the hotel now, Kosnar would certainly recognize him from Pul-e-Charkhi, the old prison in Afghanistan. He had to get out of the hotel without Kosnar seeing him and then intercept Al Rahman as he came in.

Glancing over the top of the newspaper he could see that Kosnar had crossed to the far side of the lobby and was looking around. Then he saw Kosnar take a seat in the Tea Room just off lobby that gave him a clear view of the lobby and the elevators. Stealing furtive glances, Devskoy saw Kosnar withdraw a rolled up magazine from his pocket and begin to read it.

He turned and looked around to see if he could see anyone else that was familiar. Was Kosnar operating alone or was he part of a team? The lobby was quite crowded with guests showing up for the Dorchester's famous afternoon tea but no-one else looked familiar. He wondered for a moment if he was being paranoid, that Kosnar's sudden appearance was just a coincidence, but just as quickly rejected that idea. He knew why he was here and he would have to deal with him. First however, he had to find Abd Al Rahman.

Devskoy glanced at Kosnar again and then just as a large group of Japanese tourists passed between them he quickly stood up and moved towards the hotel exit. A uniformed doorman held the door for him and he exited the building, glancing behind him to see if Kosnar was following him.

The front entrance to the Dorchester is quite small and inauspicious for such a grand hotel. With a prime location across the road from Hyde Park, London's premier park, there is limited parking and most guests are dropped off or picked up by taxis. The hotel's clientele is generally not the type to use public transport so the lack of a nearby bus stop or underground station was not regarded as an inconvenience. A long row of black cabs were parked just in front of the hotel waiting for fares and a constant flow of taxis were arriving to drop off passengers.

Devskoy had no idea how Al Rahman would arrive but guessed he would get there by taxi as well. He could not remain standing at the entrance to the hotel because Kosnar could suddenly come up from behind him. He needed to find a spot that allowed him a good perspective and yet also gave him some cover, so he looked for a spot far enough away from the hotel that he could see Kosnar approaching and at the same time see Al Rahman drive up in a cab. He walked along the short hotel driveway and turned off on to the sidewalk where he had a good view of taxis entering the hotel.

He was lucky. A few minutes after situating himself, he saw Al Rahman sitting in the back of a taxi as it turned on the hotel driveway. Devskoy scrambled back towards the location where passengers were dropped off and managed to get there just as Al Rahman stepped out of the cab. He said nothing as the Arab paid the taxi driver and then quickly brushed past him hissing "follow me," as he passed by.

Al Rahman looked around in surprise, noticing the Russian walking up ahead but staring back at him wide eyed and gesturing almost wildly at Al Rahman to follow him. Not a man easily rattled, Al Rahman casually but carefully looked away from the Russian and surveyed his surroundings. He had expected to meet Devskoy inside the hotel and obviously something had rattled the

Russian, but he wanted to be sure he was not walking into a trap or circumstance that might blow his cover. He looked around once more and then followed the Russian away from the hotel.

The two men walked for about five minutes, twenty paces apart. The Russian was walking quickly and Al Rahman had to work hard on his lame leg to keep up. Devskoy led them along the sidewalk to a subterranean tunnel that took them under the road and directly into Hyde Park. The tunnel was poorly lit and had a dank smell of urine and disinfectant. The two men were the only ones in the tunnel and their footsteps echoed loudly on the tile floor. Al Rahman followed the Russian as he ascended the steps out of the tunnel, paused to look around, then quickly walked over to a nearby bench and sat down. The Arab approached cautiously and then sat down beside him.

Devskoy was breathing heavily and both men sat quietly for a moment not saying anything.

"What's wrong?" Al Rahman asked looking at Devskoy's sweaty and anxious face.

"Do you remember the man who captured you, brought you to Pul-e-Charkhi? Do you remember him?" Devskoy was speaking quickly and panting slightly, his words running into each other and Al Rahman was having difficulty understanding him.

"What do you mean?" Al Rahman asked.

"The KGB officer, Kosnar," Devskoy replied almost shouting out. "Colonel Vladimir Kosnar. I think he was a Major then." He was speaking slower now, trying to regain his composure. "Kosnar captured you, delivered you to Pul-e-Charkhi. Do you remember him?"

Al Rahman nodded slowly. "Of course, how could I forget him or any of you." It was a statement, not a question.

"He's here!"

"Kosnar's here?"

"Yes, that's what I am trying to tell you. He's right here at the hotel."

"What do you think he is doing here and why at this particular hotel?"

"He's here for me, don't you get it!" Devskoy's voice was high pitched, his entire demeanor completely unsettled.

Abd Al Rahman said nothing, trying to comprehend what he had just heard. He understood the Russians had sent someone after Devskoy. He had been warned about this during his meeting in the park with the stranger in Paris. It was inevitable the Russians would attempt to find Devskoy and stop him but he had not anticipated this would happen so soon just after one killing.

"But why here, at the Dorchester? How did he know to come to this hotel?"

Devskoy said nothing, not sure how to explain to the Arab what he had done. He had not had a drink all day and wished he had been able to order one at the hotel before Kosnar showed up.

"He must have heard about what happened here yesterday," the Russian mumbled.

"What do you mean?" Al Rahman asked.

Devskoy quickly explained what he had done, target-
ing the American, setting him up with one of the women,
killing them in their hotel room. He was nervous as he
spoke, worried about the Arab's reaction. At the time
it had seemed like such a good idea, but right now as he
shared the park bench with his client, he wondered about
his judgment.

"You mean one of women I paid for, you used?" Al
Rahman asked, the anger in his voice unmistakable.

Devskoy tried to flash a confident smile but it looked
more like a grimace. "Don't worry about it. I won't
charge you for that one. I'll give you the next one for
free. Anyway, we got an American so you should be
pleased."

Abd Al Rahman said nothing. He stared at Devskoy
for a moment, his expression revealing little about what
he was thinking. The Russian looked pale, sweat kept
beading up on his forehead and above his upper lip despite his constant efforts to wipe it away with the sleeve
of his jacket. The thin red veins on his face and bulbous
nose appeared more obvious against the pallor of his skin
and Al Rahman could see a small but constant tremor in
the man's hands.

Al Rahman had to think what to do. Getting angry at
the filthy Russian would achieve nothing. He needed the
man stable and cooperative and could not afford to alien-
ate him despite his stupid behavior. But first he had to
deal with Kosnar. He remembered the Soviet KGB agent
very well, how they had fought a long running battle in
the mountains of Afghanistan that most other soldiers
would have long given up. Kosnar, although he did not

know his identity at the time, was relentless, an equal match to his own endurance. Kosnar had persevered and captured him denying Al Rahman's desire to die a martyr. Despite the passage of time Al Rahman understood that he was dealing with a serious adversary who would stop at nothing to ruin his plan.

Suddenly, the Russian grabbed his arm and hissed in his ear. "Look, over there. He's coming this way." Al Rahman glanced over towards the entrance to the park where Devskoy was staring and saw a man and woman walking and behind them, about thirty paces back, Kosnar. He recognized him immediately. He stood, grabbing Devskoy's arm as he rose and steered the Russian away from the path. The two men walked slowly away from the park entrance as Kosnar proceeded up the path away from them. When he was certain Kosnar had passed them, Al Rahman stopped and turned, glancing up and down the path to make sure no-one was following Kosnar.

"Come on," he said to Devskoy as he steered the man back to the path. As distasteful as it was, he kept his hand inside Devskoy's sleeve both to guide the Russian and maintain the appearance of two friends walking through the park.

"Do you have one of the women nearby," he asked somewhat casually.

"Uh, yes of course," Devskoy replied, pleased to be off the subject of the unplanned attack but nervous about being quite so close to Kosnar who he could clearly see up ahead.

"Can you reach her now?"

"Yes, I think so. They all have cell phones with instructions to keep them charged and on at all times."

"Good. Call the closest one. Tell her to come to Hyde Park right now." He glanced around looking for an obvious location he could direct the woman to, but his lack of familiarity with the area left him uncertain. "Just have her come to the park and wait near this lake," he said as they walked past the Serpentine, the small lake in the center of the park.

Devskoy stopped walking and pulled a small notebook out of his pocket and turning away from Abd Al Rahman, consulted it for a moment. He had the names of each London based woman's hotel listed but he could not remember which one was closest to the park. He picked the second name on the list, Sasha Donitz and dialed the number on his cell phone, glancing furtively over at Al Rahman who was standing next to him and then up the path as Kosnar disappeared from view. The phone rang four times before his call was answered.

* * *

Sasha Donitz's phone started ringing as she stepped out of a London subway station near her hotel. She had become ill a few days after arriving in London and after days cooped up in her small hotel room she had finally felt better and left to explore the area near her hotel. Now she struggled to find the ringing phone in her large handbag but finally found it and answered.

"Hello," she said, and listened to the voice on the phone, her body involuntarily stiffening as she recognized it.

She stepped into a nearby doorway to avoid some of the loud traffic noise.

"No, but I think I am nearby," she replied to a question about her location.

"Yes," she said and was quiet again. She listened for almost five minutes, her mind focused, paying close attention.

"Yes," she said again and snapped the clamshell shaped phone shut. She quickly stepped back into the station to confirm the directions to Hyde Park and then set out walking as fast as she could to get to her assignment.

She was relieved to finally have an assignment. She had been in Europe for almost six weeks since being re-activated to field service a week before that. Her last field assignment had been almost five years previous and she really did not expect to be activated as a field agent again. Her current job at the FSB was mostly clerical, helping to translate documents from English into Russian. The work was often boring, but she was happy to have a job. Many of her peers at the former KGB had lost their jobs after the collapse of the Soviet Union, but for some reason she had been retained.

While the phone call at her desk six weeks prior had been unexpected, the seniority of the caller had been unmistakable, his instructions very clear. She was not to report to work the next morning, but to meet him in Gorky Park. She was directed to a bench in a well-trafficked area of the park and arrived there early. She sat on the bench, doing her best to appear nonchalant, but carefully watching the people passing by. She had not been engaged in clandestine activities for a while and was quite nervous.

A man sat down on the bench, not next to her but a few feet away. He opened up a newspaper and began to read, ignoring her. She watched him for a few moments, but did not recognize him and then turned back to look at the pedestrian traffic. After a few minutes, the man closed his paper, stood up, and walked past her. Her eyes followed him as he moved away, then she again began to watch the crowd. As she turned her head, she noticed a small blue bag on the bench almost next to her. She looked at it for a moment, peering at the nametag attached to the handle, and when she read it she was momentarily surprised to see her own name. As casually as she could, she picked up the bag, slung it over her shoulder, and walked back to her apartment.

Inside the bag were plane tickets to Rome, twelve thousand dollars in American Express traveler's checks, hotel reservations, and a cell phone and charger. She was directed to leave for Rome immediately and not to tell anyone, including her mother, with whom she lived, where she was going. The orders were also explicit: absolutely no communication with anyone in Rome. Her handler would contact her. She was to stay close to her hotel, and to be in her room every night by ten and to make sure the cell phone was charged and with her at all times. Her cover was similar to what she had used in the past: she was to tell anyone who asked that she was a Swedish fashion consultant spending the late summer reviewing fall fashions. Sasha's English was perfect, and a slight accent only added to her allure.

She spent three weeks in Rome, reading and doing a little sight seeing. She knew Rome having visited the city on assignments before but usually her job had been a small part of a larger team. Mostly she had been required to target men for furtive liaisons, typically one night affairs, occasionally a brief 'relationship' would last a few days and then when the target had been compromised her task was done and she left. She had never had a situation like this with no specific task, no support team and no contacts. Finally, at the end of the third week, the phone rang and she was instructed to immediately check out of the hotel and catch a ferry to London. Once in London she was to check into a hotel near Hyde Park Corner. Reservations had been made in her name. Her cover was to remain unchanged. Her stay in London became an extension of her time in Rome: no calls, no instructions: plenty of time to wander.

Now the caller had marked a target. She hoped that meant she would be done soon and could return home. She could see the park up ahead and glanced at her watch. She guessed she would be at the Serpentine in about five minutes.

CHAPTER 15

Casey and David walked along without speaking for a minute or two, David leading them to an underground passage under the busy traffic directly to the entrance to the Park. There were quite a few people in the park, adults relaxing in the sun, young children kicking soccer balls and a couple of middle-aged men sitting on a park bench. Casey enjoyed the fresh air, the sunlight on her face. She felt exhausted by the flight and by what she had seen in the morgue. She needed a decent meal and a good nights sleep.

On the path leading them towards the Serpentine, a small lake in the middle of the park, the two special agents discussed the case, pondering their next step. They had no leads, but the information provided by Dr. Bellamy was somewhat helpful. At least they knew the source of the bombs. Given that Gordon Lewis was expecting her to call him in the evening, she was anxious to pass on the coroner's discovery.

"What do you think, David?" she asked turning to look at him.

"At this point, I really have no idea," he replied. "We are searching for the proverbial needle in a haystack. Whoever is masterminding this program has left no trail other than two dead bodies. We know it originates from somewhere inside the FSB, but that gives us little to go on." He paused a second, then continued. "Has there been any consideration to contacting the Russian government?"

"I don't know," said Casey. "That decision is above my grade level," she continued with a quick laugh. "I do know there seems to be great sensitivity to all things Russian these days at the Agency and at State in particular. Russia's commitment to democracy seems a bit uncertain right now but we need the Russians to help us deal with the Iranians, so my guess is the administration is going to treat them with kid gloves. Anyway, at least for now, I think we are pretending to the Russians that this has nothing to do with them."

They walked in silence for a few minutes and Casey noticed that David had begun to increase his pace. She kept up with him, not saying anything, but wishing he would slow down. She was really tired.

David abruptly stopped. "I have to tie my laces," he said, bending down and fiddling with his shoes, then slowly stood up. He began to walk again, now very slowly.

"We are being followed," he said to Casey, his voice even, calm. "I noticed him about ten minutes ago."

Casey's fatigue quickly disappeared. "Are you sure?" she asked, voice pitched slightly higher than usual.

"Yes," said David. "Actually, he is being so obvious, it seems he wants us to know he is there. When we walked faster, he sped up and when I stopped to tie my shoes, he stopped also. Not very professional, whoever he is."

"He didn't look familiar?"

"No, but I didn't get a good look at him," said David.

"Let's turn around and walk back towards him. If we recognize him, we can decide what to do.

"Okay," said David, "but let's do it in such a way that he knows we are on to him. I don't think he is more than twenty feet away from us right now. All right, ready — turn now!"

The two agents quickly turned and began retracing their steps. Vladimir stopped. He was momentarily surprised by their actions, but of course it was exactly what he wanted. His eyes met Casey's and he saw immediately that she recognized him.

"That's Vladimir Kosnar," Casey hissed.

"You're right," David exclaimed. "What do you want to do?"

By way of response, Casey stepped forward, moving directly towards Vladimir. She knew his reputation, instinctively understood that if he allowed himself to be identified so easily, it was because he wanted it to be so.

She stopped about five feet away from Vladimir, who was standing still, hands by his side, doing his best to look non-threatening. David Green took up a position to Casey's far right, keeping himself far enough away from her to create two distinct targets for Vladimir. Neither FBI agent was armed, as required by British law, and

Green did not really anticipate that Kosnar was armed either, but it was better to be careful.

Vladimir's eyes were locked onto Casey's face.

"Vladimir Kosnar?" said Casey, responding to his stare.

"Yes," he replied. "I am Kosnar."

The meeting in the park in London between two FBI agents and one former, and now reactivated Russian agent was certainly bizarre. In past times, during the Cold War, both sides would have been very reluctant to make such contact; it would call into question the loyalty of both sets of agents. But now, circumstances had changed. The enemy was common. Vladimir and Casey needed each other to solve the problem. He knew who was controlling the killers and how many there were; she had access to the resources that could stop it.

Their first words were awkward, both sides loath to appear too anxious. Vladimir focused on Casey, instantly recognizing her as the FBI agent who had survived the ambush in Afghanistan.

"My name is Vladimir Kosnar," he repeated. "I am currently on special assignment for the Russian Federal Security Services. I need to talk to an authorized American agent." He paused. "Are you Casey Jennings?"

"Yes," Casey replied, a little nonplussed to be so easily recognized. "I am Casey Jennings and this is David Green. We are special agents with the Federal Bureau of Investigation. Why do you need to talk to us?" She was not going to give any information unless sure they were working towards the same end.

"Perhaps we can find a more comfortable place to talk," said Vladimir, looking around as a young woman roller-bladed past them. "I have important information to give you, but it will take some time to discuss."

"We can go back to our local headquarters in the embassy," said David, anxious to move this meeting out of the public. "That way you will be secure and we will be alone."

Vladimir was not ready to get so close to the FBI. At this point, he was only assuming Casey and David were investigating the use of the women to assassinate the general and the unfortunate American businessman. If he went to the American embassy and he was wrong, they might detain him or have the British police deport him. He needed to establish some kind of relationship with these agents first before he could trust them and, perhaps, convince them to trust him. But he did not have a lot of time.

"Why don't we find a coffee shop where we can talk? I will explain to you why I need to speak with you."

Casey understood Vladimir's reluctance. She too preferred to stay out of the office for now. Taking Vladimir in would create a bureaucratic nightmare as special agents and supervisors argued about who should conduct the interrogation. She could get a lot more information from him directly.

Before David could respond, she quickly said, "Good idea. David, can you suggest a place around here somewhere?"

"Yes," said David slowly, his voice and face conveying reluctance. He paused a second, then said, "We can continue across the park. There are a number of places near Kensington Palace."

The threesome began to walk, Vladimir in the middle, Casey to his immediate left and David to his right, although David maintained his defensive posture, hanging back a couple of feet behind Vladimir. No-one spoke as they walked in awkward silence.

They reached the coffee shop in less than ten minutes. It had a small outdoor section that was part of the sidewalk in the French café style. Separating the customers from pedestrians were a series of large flower boxes standing on waist-high metal frames. The café was a tribute to British optimism that the rain would hold off long enough during the summer to allow guests to eat a meal outdoors without getting wet. David directed Vladimir to an outside table away from the other patrons; he wanted the group out in the open, preferably where they could be seen but not heard. They chose a table right next to one of the flowerpots, Casey in the middle, David and Vladimir on either side.

As soon as they were seated, Vladimir began to tell them his story.

CHAPTER 16

SPECIAL AGENT DAVID Green sat rigid in his chair, eyes locked on the Russian, his face barely concealing his discomfort. Casey sat on Vladimir's right, her expression mostly impassive, her attention focused.

"What is it you wish to discuss with us, Mr. Kosnar?" she asked.

"Am I correct in assuming you are here in London investigating the murder of the American in the Dorchester Hotel?" When neither agent responded, he continued, speaking deliberately. "I also believe you are investigating the death of an American General in Paris." He stopped again, looking at them, creating an awkward moment, waiting, and trying to force one of the Americans to confirm his statements. After a brief pause, Casey responded.

"Mr. Kosnar, you can understand that we cannot discuss our assignments with you. However, if you have some information on these murders, then we would be very appreciative."

"All right," said Vladimir, shrugging his shoulders. This was the part of his old job he did not miss, the instinct not to trust anyone, the circuitous approach to everything. He had no time for this type of gamesmanship anymore. He would just tell them what he knew and hope for the best. Ultimately, it was all he could do.

"I cannot tell you the precise reasons for the killings because I do not have that information, but I can tell you how they are being carried out and who the perpetrator is." He took a deep breath and continued.

"The two women who died with the General and the American civilian are part of an old, officially discontinued, assassination team. In fact, the whole program was cancelled before it could become operational. The bombs that killed these women and their victims were surrounded by titanium, something you probably already know. More specifically, they were located in artificial hips in the women's bodies. The bombs were set off by a remote transmitter located no more than a few hundred feet away."

"How many women were set up like this?" David asked.

"Five hundred."

The words hung in the air for a second as the FBI agents glanced at each wide eyed.

"Five hundred women?" Casey asked, turning back to Kosnar, her voice incredulous.

"Mostly women," the Russian answered. "They tested the system on a couple men, political prisoners probably."

"Mr. Kosnar, are you saying the Soviet government took five hundred healthy women and turned them into living bombs?" Casey's voice was harsh, indignant in its tone.

"Not exactly, Ms. Jennings," said Vladimir, with a quick shake of his head. "These women all needed to have their hip joints replaced. That was going to happen anyway."

"I don't understand-" Casey began, stopping in mid sentence as a waitress approached their table.

"Would you like to order?" she asked.

"Yes," Casey replied quickly. "Just three coffees, please."

"Is that all you want?"

"Yes, thank you," Casey replied, anxious for her to go away. The waitress turned on her heel and walked away.

"You see," Vladimir continued, "these women were part of the Soviet athletic elite. They had been specially selected at very young ages from all over the country for their athletic ability. Since very early childhood they had been groomed and trained to participate in the Olympic Games. The focus was the 1980 and the 1984 Olympic Games, which, you will remember were held first in Moscow and then in Los Angeles. Of course in the end you boycotted ours and we boycotted yours but the Soviet government had decided to spend every effort to make sure our athletes won the most medals. No effort was spared, no expense was too great."

"I think I know where this is heading," said Casey, her lips pursed in disgust. "Steroids, right?"

"Yes," said Vladimir with a look of mild surprise, "correct. How did you make that connection?"

Casey shook her head. "It's no big leap. The Russians and East Germans were infamous for their use of anabolic steroids to improve athletic performance. They were quite successful at it, but at enormous expense to some of their athletes."

"I'm afraid you've lost me," said David Green. "How does the use of steroids require these women to have their hips joints replaced?"

"Among other ugly side effects of steroids is decay in the hip joints, which results in a loss of mobility and severe pain," Casey answered. "I know because I've seen it. In college, a couple of football players I knew got into steroids in a big way. One of them was almost crippled by the side effects of the drugs. He was the lucky one. The other one committed suicide."

"But surely if these women had their hips replaced, they would not be able to perform as assassins," David Green responded.

"Not so," said Casey. "Do you remember Bo Jackson, the famous football and baseball player? He had a hip joint replaced, then played two more years of professional baseball." Casey turned her gaze back to the Russian. "So now we have five hundred women, unknowingly walking around with these bombs in their bodies. My God, this is unbelievable

"Yes, well, I'm afraid in that regard I have good news and bad news," said Vladimir without any hint of humor. "Of the five hundred original women in the assassination program, only about half are still alive, and of those-"

Casey cut him off. "But you said the program was never operational, that it was cancelled."

"Yes, Ms. Jennings. However, for reasons not provided to me, during the past four years, a lot of these women have died."

"Why, from what?" David Green asked, his voice insistent.

"As I said, I don't know," Vladimir responded, shaking his head. "These women were all athletes whose dreams were destroyed and then they found themselves often coerced into new careers not always suited to their abilities. I am sure some died by natural causes, some by accident, some by suicide. All I do know is they were not operational. Of that I am certain."

"So according to your numbers Mr. Kosnar," said Casey, "we have about two hundred and fifty of these unfortunate women at large and operational?"

"No, we believe that about one hundred have been deployed. A few are unaccounted for, no-one is quite sure of their situation. The rest are in Russia," Vladimir answered, pausing as the waitress arrived with their coffees.

"Anything else?" the waitress asked.

"No, thank you," said Casey with a quick shake of her head.

As the waitress walked away, Casey absent-mindedly poured cream into her coffee and stirred it slowly. Her mind was racing with the information the Russian had passed on. She came out of her reverie as her partner was asking the Russian another question.

"...must be quite an expensive operation," he was say-ing. "Where did the money come from?"

Vladimir sat back in his chair and shrugged.

"I don't know where the money is coming from but my guess is the women have been sold to a terrorist or-ganization. Probably Al Qaeda, but I really don't know. It must have cost a lot of money and required a lot of sophisticated management to get the necessary papers to get them out of Russia into Europe and probably Ameri-ca and deploying one hundred people would also be very expensive."

The two men and one woman sat silently for a mo-ment at the coffee shop, the Americans digesting the in-formation the Russian had just provided. Then, for the next fifteen minutes, the two Americans continued to ask questions. Vladimir answered as best he could, but he was not ready to be completely forthcoming. There was still no guarantee they would not simply turn him over to the British police. He was going to withhold the final details until he thought he was assured of their cooperation.

* * *

Devskoy and Al Rahman followed the threesome out of the park onto Kensington High Street walking on the opposite side of the street, and about twenty feet be-hind the group. The streets were crowded with typical London traffic and the sidewalks were also quite busy, just enough to keep their presence unknown but clear enough to give them a good view of their quarry. As the threesome stopped at the café, the two men kept walking up the road another fifty feet, stopping next to a busy newspaper stand.

Devskoy stared across the road, his face growing darker and more malevolent with each passing moment. Finally, he had enough.

"We need to do it now!" he hissed into Al Rahman's ear. He pressed the send button on his phone and quickly gave Sasha Donitz instructions to continue past the Serpentine and onto Kensington High Street and then hung up.

Abd Al Rahman slowly glanced around. He was an expert at setting up ambushes. This dense urban location was a bit unusual for him but he felt his confidence return and he quickly thought through a plan. This was a perfect spot. Lots of people to cause panic and confusion, a stationary target and seated in the open. He just wished he could find a way to exploit the bomb even more. He glanced around at the stores nearby. There was a small stationary store on the corner.

Standing close to Devskoy, he said, "Call her again. Tell her to go in to that stationary store on the corner to buy two boxes of staples and put them in her bag."

Devskoy stared at the Arab for a moment and then grinned at him with an ugly malevolent smile. He pressed send again and quickly gave the instructions.

"Do you know what she looks like?" Al Rahman hissed in his ear while he was talking on the phone.

Devskoy blinked his eyes a couple of times trying to recall if he had met Donitz but then shook his head once vigorously.

"Ask her what she is wearing."

Devskoy asked the question, listened for a moment and hung up.

"There she is," Devskoy growled a moment later as a tall woman with bobbed blond hair came around the corner. She was wearing a blue summer dress and carrying a large handbag slung over her shoulder. They watched her as she stopped on the street corner, looked around for a moment and then stepped into the stationary store.

Devskoy glanced anxiously at the threesome at the café. They were still talking, making no sign they were about to leave but he was getting anxious. He reached for the cell phone again calling Donitz just as she exited the store.

Al Rahman watched her as she stood still listening attentively to the instructions he could hear Devskoy speak into the phone. He heard Devskoy terminate the call and then watched as the woman placed the phone back into her bag and begin to walk towards the café.

* * *

Vladimir was leaning forward in his seat. He was tired of the repetitious questions, but understood the need to sound and look convincing. He had to earn the trust of the two American agents. Without their resources, finding his quarry was almost impossible.

"You know Mr. Kosnar, I find this Al Qaeda link a bit unlikely," said David Green as he looked unblinking at the Russian. "I mean, how does a Russian agent just link up with Al Qaeda? Hell, we can barely find them with all our resources, how could he possibly do it. Could you?"

Vladimir said nothing for a moment and then shrugged his shoulders before replying. "I don't know that it is Al Qaeda, it's just a guess. But," he paused as he glanced at each special agent, "it is not such a stretch if you think about it. The Soviet Union had very good relations with Syria for many years. We had a lot of people operating in Damascus and in Beirut during the Lebanese civil war. I was there myself ..." his voice drifted off as an attractive blond woman walked towards them on the sidewalk momentarily catching his attention. He stared at her for a few seconds and then returned his gaze to David Green.

"So are you saying that Syrian intelligence is working with Al Qaeda?" David Green asked, the tenor of his voice both insistent and incredulous.

Vladimir sat back, his eyes drifting back to the blond woman on the sidewalk. As their eyes met, she returned his gaze with a smile. She was about twenty feet away now, striding confidently. Suddenly Vladimir sat upright. He recognized the woman! Donitz. Sasha Donitz. The name popped into his head. She was now only ten feet way. He stood up and raised his left hand, palm towards her, indicating for her to stop. David began to turn in his chair, looking for what was distracting the Russian. Casey also turned to look where he was looking, but David was obstructing her view.

* * *

The Russian woman strode purposefully towards the threesome. She had been instructed to make contact with the older man. "Pretend to recognize him," Devskoy had said. "Address him as Vladimir."

At twenty feet, Vladimir had looked over at her and she had immediately responded with a smile. "This is going to be easy," she thought.

Now she slowed down with some confusion. Vladimir had *recognized her*. He was holding his hand up, shouting in Russian. She continued to walk towards them, with less confidence, but with a smile still on her face.

"*Ostovani*!" he shouted out in Russian. "Stop."

David rose out of his chair, not knowing quite why, but responding to Vladimir's actions, treating her as a threat. Casey was stuck. Her chair was caught in a crack in the sidewalk and she could not quite push it back far enough to give her room to stand. Placing both hands on the arm rests, she dipped her head, trying to increase her leverage. She wanted to see what had caused Vladimir to rise and start shouting. David was up blocking her view. She gave her seat one last shove.

* * *

Sasha was within five feet of David Green, the closest to her. By now she was hardly moving, her smile gone, her face a mask of confusion. She had not expected to be recognized, but now her target was screaming at her in Russian to stop. Perhaps because it was so many years since she had been an active agent, she forgot her training and wandered what to do.

Across the road, Devskoy had stepped away from Al Rahman and was standing at the edge of the sidewalk, making certain he had a clear view of the café. As Donitz approached the threesome he pulled the activator out of his pocket and without taking his eyes off the woman, flipped off the safety switch and placed his thumb on top of the plunger.

She was close now. Devskoy's hand tensed on the plunger, but he forced himself to wait. Suddenly he saw Vladimir rise out of his seat, arm raised and he was shouting at Sasha, but Devskoy was too far away to hear. Sasha was still moving forward, but slowing. Devskoy starred at Sasha, urging her under his breath to keep moving, but she stopped completely. She was turning, looking around, uncertain what to do next. Devskoy pushed the plunger, turned and began to walk away. He heard the explosion, and almost immediately, the screaming that followed, but he kept on walking.

* * *

David Green absorbed most of the blast from the explosion as Sasha Donitz's tall body disintegrated in front of him. Shards of titanium and staples pierced his body and ripped at his face and neck as he fell backwards onto Casey. Vladimir also felt the sting of shrapnel as it struck him, but was too far away for it to cause him much harm. Momentarily dazed, he shook his head to clear it, and then quickly jumped over the flower boxes separating the café's tables from the sidewalk. There was chaos on the sidewalk just in front of the café and he was almost knocked down by a rush of people running away.

He glanced up and down the street trying to see a familiar face in the crowds and then began to run towards the park.

David Green was on top of Casey; the back of his head on her chest, arms dangling at his sides. His white dress shirt was now absorbing the blood that had already saturated his undershirt. Casey struggled to calm the panic threatening to overwhelm her. David's face was almost next to hers. She looked down and could barely recognize him. His face and neck were a pulpy mess, bloody and shredded. She could hear a gurgling sound emanating from his lips and throat.

"David," she said, almost whispering. "Oh David, please, no."

His body went limp in her arms. She knew he was dead. She looked over at Vladimir's seat, and realized he was gone.

* * *

Vladimir raced down the sidewalk as fast as he could. People were pouring out of restaurants and office buildings to see what the commotion was and he could already hear the sounds of police sirens in the distance. About fifty yards down the sidewalk, he slowed, looking up and down the street, trying to find Devskoy. He crossed the street, dogging traffic, trying desperately to find his quarry, but to no avail. This was the closest he had come to Devskoy, his best and perhaps only opportunity to find the man, but he was nowhere to be seen. Vladimir stayed on the sidewalk for another minute and then turned, crossed the street and began to run back to the restaurant. As he ran, a figure walking towards him caught his eye. He slowed down as their eyes locked for a second before the man quickly looked away and turned in to the crush of people gathering on the sidewalk and disappeared. Vladimir stared after the man for a moment with the strange and unsettling feeling of having seen him before, but the sound of police sirens drawing near caught his attention and he ran back to the restaurant. His mission had suddenly become even more urgent and now he had to finish telling his story.

CHAPTER 17

A T THE CAFÉ and on the sidewalk in front of it there was pandemonium. The shattered remains of Sasha Donitz's body lay on the sidewalk, her pelvis missing, lower legs crumpled beneath what remained of her chest and head. Next to her a man and a small boy lay dead, their clothes and bodies ripped apart. A small crowd had gathered around the grisly scene and one middle-aged woman stood over the remnants of the little boy's shattered body, screaming hysterically.

In the restaurant patio, some patrons remained immobile in their seats, two of them their faces peppered with staples. Others sat, too dazed by the shock of the explosion to move. A waitress lay on the ground in a fetal position, rocking herself and crying. A large fleshy piece of intestine from the murdered woman hung from her hair.

Vladimir jogged back to the ghastly scene. He looked over and saw Casey cradling the limp body of the FBI agent in her arms. Her hands and clothes were covered in David's blood, her face ashen. She looked up as Vladimir approached.

"Ms. Jennings," he said to her quickly, "we have to leave here now."

"Who's doing this?" she said to him softly. "Who is doing this?" she repeated, louder this time.

"I'll tell you everything I know, but we must leave here now. Please hurry," Vladimir said urgently. The wailing siren noises were close now; any minute some of the local foot patrol would arrive.

"What? I can't leave him," said Casey, looking down at the dead agent in her arms.

"No, Casey," said Vladimir, dropping the formal titles they used to address each other. "We must go. If I stay, the British police will arrest me. I have to leave, and I need your help to stop this madness."

Casey looked up at Vladimir and stared at him for what seemed like a long time. She felt so tired. She had not slept in almost twenty-four hours and now she was holding the battered remains of her colleague in her arms. A few feet from her lay the broken bodies of the Russian woman and the other victims. She closed her eyes, trying to steady herself. She looked back at Vladimir, trying to read his face, trying to determine if he was part of the problem or the solution, forcing herself to think clearly.

"Please, Casey," Vladimir said once more, only much more urgently.

Casey eased the limp body of David Green onto the ground and stood up. If Kosnar left right now without her, they might never find him again and he clearly had information that would be useful. On the other hand, her colleague, her friend was dead on the sidewalk and abandoning him seemed inappropriate. She almost stumbled as she stood, but Vladimir reached out and grabbed her arm to steady her.

The crowd around the restaurant was quite large now, people stepping forward to help the injured and Vladimir had to push his way through, pulling Casey behind him. He could hear the sounds of running footsteps as the first police officers began to arrive.

"This way," he said, still holding Casey's arm.

Casey allowed Vladimir to guide her away and they walked quickly down the sidewalk away from the approaching police. As soon as they had put a bit of distance between them and the restaurant, Vladimir looked for a cab. Casey had blood on her hands and clothes from her dead colleague and Vladimir's face and clothes were cut and ripped where the pieces of staples had caught him. They needed to get off the street quickly. When a black cab stopped in front of them, Vladimir opened the door and gently urged Casey through the door.

* * *

Abd Al Rahman and Michael Devskoy stood silently watching across the road from the bombed café where they had reunited after becoming briefly separated in the chaos as the area around it was flooded with police, ambulances and fire trucks. In the crush of the crowds and the wailing of sirens, both men lingered longer at the scene of the bombing longer than was prudent, trying to make out who had been killed. But, as they simultaneously caught sight of the American woman and the Russian climbing into a black cab, it was obvious they had missed their target.

Al Rahman was not completely disappointed by the result: he estimated at least three people were dead and many more wounded. If the goal was to create panic they had certainly succeeded. For a moment he imagined what would happen if ten of these bombings had occurred within minutes of each other in different parts of the city.

Kosnar was still a problem as the bomb had obviously missed him. Al Rahman wondered if Kosnar had recognized him during the fleeting moment their eyes had met just after the bombing. If Kosnar could recognize both him and Devskoy they would be vulnerable until they could neutralize him. However, today's failure would make him much more wary. Catching him in the open again would probably be impossible.

He glanced over at his companion and noticed that Devskoy was becoming unsettled and demonstrative as he swore loudly in Russian before his companion grabbed his arm above the elbow and directed him away from the bombing.

* * *

As Casey and Vladimir climbed into the cab, the driver turned to look back at them.

"Are you all right?" he asked, his concern for them genuine, but his concern for his clean seats perhaps greater. His next fare probably would not appreciate having to sit on blood.

"Yes, we're fine," answered Vladimir with a forced smile. "Could you please drive us around Hyde Park."

"You just want me to drive you around the park," said the cabby, growing less comfortable.

Vladimir dropped five twenty-pound notes onto the front seat. "Please," he said with a little more emphasis, "just drive us around Hyde Park for about thirty minutes. OK?"

The cabby looked down at the fives bills, put the cab into gear and turned into the street.

Vladimir closed the partition between the passenger cab and the driver's seat, sat back in his seat and turned to look at Casey. He pulled a clean handkerchief from his pocket and handed it to her. She took it in her hand but did nothing with it as she stared at him balefully, suspicious of his motives and uncomfortable at having left the scene of the crime and her dead colleague. The sound of police and ambulance sirens wailed behind them.

"Why are you hiding from the British police?" she asked pointedly.

"I'm not," Vladimir replied.

"It sure looks like you are," Casey retorted, her hand describing a sweeping motion to indicate the taxicab.

"Let me explain," said Vladimir, turning to face her. Casey just stared back at him, her expression a picture of increasing hostility.

"Just before the..uh ... explosion," Vladimir said, searching for the appropriate words to describe the woman's body blowing up in front of them. "Just before the explosion David asked me who was behind all this. I need to tell you that, and one other thing, before we talk to the British police. It is very important to me that you know everything first. Once the British police get hold of me — of us," he pointed at her, "we might get slowed down, interrogated, distracted. We don't have time. We don't have any time." His voice was urgent, his usually stoic demeanor unmasked.

"OK," said Casey, still unconvinced. "Who and why?"

The cab drove around Hyde Park at Speakers Corner, a famous London landmark. Every Sunday morning people gather there to speak freely, condemn the Queen, the Royal family, the British government, or any other target of concern. On clear days, large crowds often gathered to hear the speakers, but today, Speakers Corner was mostly empty. Even if it had been crowded and boisterous, however, Casey and Vladimir would not have noticed.

"The man originally behind all this is named Michael Devskoy," said Vladimir. "He is a low level former KGB operative who transitioned to the FSB which replaced the KGB."

"So this is a Russian operation then," Casey said bluntly.

"No, it is not a sanctioned operation, but yes, you are correct it is being carried about by a former agent using FSB assets." He needed Casey as an ally and did not want to argue any point with her too strongly.

"So this man, Devskoy, why is he doing this?"

Vladimir paused for a moment trying to collect his thoughts and speak clearly before the opportunity to speak with Casey alone was lost.

"I don't know the exact reason but as I said earlier he is probably working for another party or group to create terror."

"Why, I mean for what purpose?"

Vladimir shrugged and replied simply, "Money." He paused briefly and then added, "and because he probably likes doing it."

"What?"

"Devskoy had a special talent for extraction, the use of torture to gather information. He developed a reputation in the KGB for his success in getting good information despite the often unsavory way in which he did it."

Kosnar paused for a moment before continuing. "His main predilection seems to have been abusing and torturing women. He found any excuse to be involved in the interrogation of female prisoners. I am told he often interrogated women who needed no interrogation, if you know what I mean."

The Russian shook his head and grimaced slightly before he continued. "Until recently he was a fall down drunk just filling space in a small office until retirement when by some terrible mistake the entire classified folder on this assassination program was delivered to him. A few days later he disappeared completely. That was about nine months ago."

The taxi slowed in traffic and Vladimir looked up and out the back window of the cab. He could still hear the sound of sirens in the background and he knew the patrons at the cafe and other bystanders would have reported his and Casey's presence to the authorities. Their disappearance from the crime scene would be viewed as suspicious; the British Police would be frantically looking for him and Casey. Also, the FBI would be equally frantic about the well being of their agent after the death of Agent Green. Somebody had probably seen them get into a cab together and a manhunt would be underway. He would have to tell his story quickly. He looked back at Casey's bloodstained face.

"If he was, as you say, a fall down drunk, why wasn't he let go? It doesn't make any sense," she said.

Vladimir nodded as he glanced down at his hands. "Normally you would be correct. He was no longer useful in intelligence and probably a liability but he was protected by a few senior officers in the FSB."

"But why?" Casey asked. She had finally begun to use the handkerchief to wipe the blood off her hands and face.

"In the early nineteen eighties Devskoy became something of a hero in KGB. For a while he was quite notorious in the service."

"What did he do?"

"Do you remember in 1983, a number of Russians operating in Beirut were kidnapped and taken hostage?"

"Vaguely," said Casey. "As I recall, unlike the American hostages, the Russians were quickly released or rescued."

"Correct," Vladimir continued. "Soon after they were kidnapped, Devskoy was sent in to assist in his capacity as interrogator, although I have a feeling he arranged for himself to be sent. As it turns out, his skills came in very handy."

Vladimir paused for a moment as he again looked back through the rear window. The road behind them was full of the usual London traffic. He could not tell if they were being followed. He turned back to Casey.

"When Devskoy arrived in Beirut, he went directly to the Russian embassy. We had a large number of operatives already working there and our people put out the word that if our hostages were not returned alive and well very soon, all hell would break loose. We assumed the kidnappers were smart enough to know we would not be constrained from violence in the same way the Europeans and Americans were."

"What happened?"

"When Devskoy arrived, there were two young Muslim women who had just been picked up and brought in. Apparently, an informant had fingered them as being associated with the kidnappers. One of the women was quite attractive, and Devskoy took a fancy to her, in his own brutal way."

Casey sighed and lowered her eyes. She could easily imagine the rest of the story.

Vladimir continued speaking, his voice urgent but measured. "Devskoy had the two women put in adjoining rooms in the embassy basement. He made the good looking one undress in front of her jailers, a terrible humiliation, especially for a Muslim woman. Then, for the next couple of hours while she sat naked in this room, he put the word out on the street she was a captured Israeli spy, a Jew, and any of the young armed hoodlums who roamed Beirut in those days could come and see her."

Vladimir paused again and then looked directly at Casey. "For the next six days, the woman was raped repeatedly. We estimated later she was raped at least one hundred times that week."

Casey briefly closed her eyes for a moment but quickly reopened them as the Russian continued speaking.

"Devskoy watched every rape. Every few hours they would hose her down and clean her up and then more young men would come in, it would start again. Finally after six days, it stopped."

"Who stopped it?" asked Casey.

"The other Muslim woman in the next door room heard what was happening to her friend. After six days she broke down and asked to speak to Devskoy. She told him where the hostages were being held. Within two hours they were rescued."

"What happened to the two women?" Casey asked.

"After abusing them as we did, we could not return them to the street. Admittedly we had a reputation for being ruthless, but the gang rape of a Muslim woman would have made it more difficult for us to operate in Beirut."

"You have not answered my question," said Casey. "What happened to the two women?"

"They were killed and buried in the embassy grounds that night. Devskoy shot them himself."

Casey sat quietly for a few moments staring at the back of the driver's seat and then turned to look at Vladimir. "You were there, weren't you?" she said. "You were in Beirut."

"Yes," said Vladimir quietly.

For a few long seconds neither of them spoke. The only sound was the noise of the cab and the traffic. Finally, Vladimir turned to Casey and said: "I needed to tell you this story so you would know who you were dealing with."

"I do understand," said Casey. "I was at the coroner's office today; I think I understand something about this," Casey mumbled, her voice trailing off as she said it. She stared out of the window for a moment.

"Why are you here?" Casey asked as she turned back to face him. "My understanding is you're retired from the FSB."

"I am retired," Vladimir replied. "I was reactivated for this mission." He paused before continuing. "I'm here because it is personal."

"What do you mean personal?" Casey responded heatedly. "Is this some vendetta between you and Devskoy? Is that why he tried to kill you today and instead killed David?"

"No," Vladimir replied quietly. "It is personal because of the identity of one of the assassins."

"What about her?" Casey asked, shaking her head.

Vladimir looked at Casey, paused for a moment and replied, "One of the assassins is my sister."

CHAPTER 18

C ASEY SAID NOTHING but just stared at the Russian sitting next to her in the taxi. She was too tired, stunned, overwhelmed by the day's events to respond properly.

"What... Who's your sister?" she asked in a half whisper.

"Her name is Myda Konitska," he replied simply, not inclined to embellish his answer at this moment.

Casey sat forward in the cab, closed her eyes, and with the tips of her fingers, rubbed her temples. She was trying to organize her thoughts, put everything into context. She was an expert analyst, normally able to absorb and organize huge amounts of information, but now with everything that had just happened and what she had just heard made her head hurt. Fatigue swept over her again as she squeezed her eyes shut and tried to focus. This latest piece of information from the retired, but now activated, FSB officer was almost more than she could comprehend.

Kosnar sat quietly next to Casey, just watching her. After a few moments Casey put her hands down and looked up at him, all hostility and reserve she had displayed up to now, dissipated. Until that moment Casey had been quietly seething about the assassination program, upset at the injustice of it, the murderous abuse of women for financial and political purposes. But also up to that moment, the women had been faceless, unknown players in a long forgotten war. They had not been real in the sense connected them to families, children or brothers.

"How?" she asked. "How is that possible?"

"I don't have time to explain to you now," Vladimir replied, "but it is the reason I am here, the reason I was asked to come. He made an inflection on the word 'asked' indicating it really was not optional. "You can see I am personally motivated to stop it."

He was interrupted as the taxi suddenly swerved sharply out of traffic, the front wheel bouncing off the road and up onto the curb as the driver slammed on the brakes. Even before the car stopped moving, the driver shoved the gear stick into park throwing his passengers off their seats and into the partition separating them from the driver. The driver quickly opened his door and took off running, leaving the door open.

Picking themselves off the floor of the cab, the two agents glanced at each other for a second and then looked out the window. Two police cars had pulled in directly behind them and as Kosnar and Jennings peered out of the windows, two additional police cars squealed to a stop in front of them, lights flashing, sirens wailing. At each police car, officers took up defensive positions behind their open car doors, weapons pointed directly at the taxi. Two motorcycle mounted police roared up at high speed and quickly stopped all traffic passing in both directions past the awkwardly parked taxi.

The two agents sat immobile in back of the taxi waiting for instructions. They understood instinctively that climbing out of the car would probably make the police react violently, potentially with deadly force. They did not have to wait long for instructions.

"Passengers," an urgent and uncompromising male voice boomed out of a nearby loudspeaker. "Exit the vehicle from the right side door, hands in the air, one at a time. Do it slowly and do it now!"

Vladimir leaned forward to open the door but Casey quickly reached up to his jacket and pulled him back into his seat. She looked at him a bit ruefully and said, "I think its best that I get out first. They are less likely to shoot a woman than a man and it might defuse the situation if they see I am alright."

Vladimir nodded and sat back in his seat but as Casey slipped past him in the back of the cab he grabbed her arm.

"Please, what I have just told you. Please keep it secret for now," he said urgently.

Casey stared at the Russian for a moment, eyes narrowed and lips pursed. She could quickly think of many reasons why keeping this information secret was a bad idea but after a brief pause, she nodded sharply once and as he released his grip on her arm she opened the right side door and slowly stepped out in a crouched position, hands extended in front of her. As she straightened up she saw three policemen standing a few feet away in full urban combat gear pointing their rifles directly at her head. She was surprised to feel a light rain coming down; her last recollection was that it was a bright and sunny day.

A disembodied voice barked at her loudly. "Turn around and kneel down." Casey did as she was instructed feeling the damp sidewalk soak into her pants at the knees.

"Now place your hands behind your head and lock your fingers together."

Casey slowly lowered her arms placing her hands behind her head and interlocked her fingers as instructed.

"Next passenger," the voice ordered again. "Step out of the vehicle, arms raised high above your head."

Vladimir did as instructed except he was ordered to lay face down on the ground, arms extended straight from his sides. As soon as he was in the prescribed position, two officers rushed forward and pinned him roughly to the ground, quickly pulling his arms back and securing his wrists in handcuffs. Then the officers stepped back leaving him in the prone position on the wet ground and they turned their attention back to Casey. One officer pointed his weapon directly at her head while two others pulled her hands from behind her head and quickly snapped handcuffs on to her as well. As soon as she was cuffed, she was quickly pulled to her feet by two officers standing at her sides and half carried away from the taxi.

Despite the drama of the moment, Casey was calm and unafraid. Her stoicism was partly due to her complete exhaustion from the long flight, the trauma of the bombing and David Green's death in her arms and because she understood that the police probably had a report of her and Kosnar leaving the scene of the bombing. She was almost relieved to be physically supported by the two policemen and for a moment felt like she might pass out but quickly steadied herself.

Just then she heard shouting and glanced around to see Inspector Campbell running up and pushing himself through the cordon of police surrounding them and shouting out his identity. As he skidded to a stop on the wet sidewalk in front of Casey his eyes widened at her wet and bloody appearance, his breathing heavy as he tried to catch his breath.

"Jesus Christ Casey, are you alright?" he panted.

Before she could reply he noticed she was handcuffed.

"What the fuck?" He turned to one of the uniformed officers and barked out an order to remove the cuffs. The officer did not move but looked over at another more senior uniformed officer who was striding purposefully towards them.

Spotting the senior officer, Campbell demanded from him that the handcuffs be removed from Casey's arms.

"This woman is with me. She is in my..uh..custody," he said almost shouting.

The senior office ignored Campbell for a moment, glanced over the still prone prisoner on the ground and then looked directly at Casey.

"Madam, what is your name?"

"My name is Casey Jennings," she replied deliberately.

Campbell stepped forward again, trying to get between Casey and the police officer. "She is an American FBI agent and she is in my custody. Now take off these fucking handcuffs."

The two men stared at each other for a moment and then the senior office nodded to one of the men holding Casey to un-cuff her. Then he cocked his head in the direction of Vladimir Kosnar who was still lying prone on the ground.

"Do you know this man?"

Casey nodded. "His name is Vladimir Kosnar." She did not want to embellish her answer at this time.

"Was he involved in the bombing on Kensington Street? He was seen pushing you into this taxi. Did he kidnap you?

Casey quickly shook her head. "Can we discuss this somewhere else please? Mr. Kosnar did not cause the bombing and he did not kidnap me. In fact I think he is our best resource to stop the next bombing which might actually be imminent." She glanced around uncomfortably as she spoke.

"What do you mean? Why do you think another attack could be imminent?" the senior uniformed officer demanded quickly.

Casey looked around at the wide street, traffic backed up all around, crowds gathered nearby on the sidewalk to watch the action.

"They could be watching us right now, sending another bomber into the crowd over here or there," she indicated with her head. "The attack on Mr. Kosnar was not a coincidence. He was targeted." She paused for a second before continuing. "The longer we stand around here in the open, the more likely it is they will try to hit him again."

CHAPTER 19

WALKING AWAY FROM the chaotic bombing scene, Devskoy was in a foul mood. He was alternately demonstrative, shouting out expletives in Russian or despondent, walking with shoulders hunched forward, heels of his shoes scuffing the sidewalk at each step and muttering under his breath. Al Rahman walked beside him, growing increasingly worried about the man's state of mind, his ability to function. Despite his earlier concerns about Devskoy's constant consumption of alcohol, he steered the Russian away from the busy street to a quieter side street, in to a small but busy pub and quickly ordered him two vodkas. Devskoy drank them both in one quick swallow and the alcohol calmed him down somewhat.

Al Rahman was concerned about their situation as well. The failed attack on Kosnar was a serious problem. Worse yet, their eyes had met briefly right after the bomb blast and he had immediately recognized the man who had hunted him down, denying him his martyrdom so many years before. He was almost certain Kosnar had recognized him as well.

A television was playing in the bar and providing live coverage of the bomb blast they had just orchestrated. Devskoy's mouth curled into a happy sneer as the commentator relayed the deaths of four people and injury to a dozen more, some quite serious. Al Rahman was more interested to hear the comments from one police officer who stated in quite confident terms the bomb was probably planted in one of the flower boxes that rimmed the seating area of the restaurant or perhaps in a small satchel that had been planted close by. Asked about possible suspects he replied that while no suspects had been arrested, CCTV recordings were being carefully reviewed to see who might have planted the bomb.

"I think we will have some good results when we see who was acting suspiciously in that area earlier in the day," the officer stated confidently.

Al Rahman glanced back at Devskoy who was trying to attract the attention of the waitress.

"What is CCTV?" he asked.

"What?" the Russian replied, a dull expression on his face.

The waitress stopped at their table to take Devskoy's order. She turned to Al Rahman to get his order and he just asked for water but as she turned away he called out to her. "Miss, excuse me but what is CCTV? Do you know what that is?"

"CCTV, you don't know what that is," she answered with surprise. "It's the closed circuit television thing they have on every street corner. You know those little black or white cameras you see attached to buildings or lampposts all over the place."

Al Rahman shook his head in response, not recalling having noticed one.

"Who uses them? What are they for?"

"Security I guess," the waitress replied. "The police watch them to look for suspicious activity. Stuff like that."

After she walked away, the two men sat quietly, each alone in their thoughts. Devskoy continued to mumble into his drink while Al Rahman pondered their situation. They had made no attempt to hide during the set up before the attack and Devskoy had initiated the bomb quite openly. Even worse, they had stayed around the chaotic scene after the bombing for at least a few minutes, probably in full view of the cameras.

Devskoy interrupted Al Rahman's thoughts with another loud and bitter outburst. "That fucking bastard Kosnar is going to fuck this whole thing up you know."

Al Rahman indicated with his hand for Devskoy to both calm down and lower his voice but the admonishment only aggravated him more.

"You know what he's like. He's fucking crazy. When he starts after something he never stops until the end. He's like a fucking robot. He never ever gives up."

The words came out in a rush, spittle flying from his mouth as he angrily waved his hands in front of Abd Al Rahman's face.

The Arab said nothing but just stared back at his agitated companion. He needed a plan, a plan to deal with Devskoy, avoid Kosnar and execute the mission. Up to now their actions had been haphazard without any strategic purpose but as he sat in the bar he began to formulate a strategy. Most importantly, he had to get out of England before he was identified.

"How many do you have in America?" he asked quietly

Devskoy looked up from his drink and wiped his mouth with his sleeve before answering.

"Fifty-two."

"Where in America?"

"I was instructed to put half into New York and the rest are all in California, split between Los Angeles and San Francisco."

"Where are they staying?"

Devskoy shrugged. "Different hotels all over. Why?"

The Arab said nothing for a moment before replying. "I want you to give me the names and phone numbers of the all the women in America. I will pay you an extra fifty thousand for each one, one hundred and fifty thousand each."

Devskoy sat back in his chair and shook his head. "No, I'm not giving them all to you. I told you already. Ten at a time. That's it."

Al Rahman quickly responded with a more generous offer.

"Give me their names right now and I will give you two hundred thousand for each one." He held up his hand to stop Devskoy from responding before he finished. "You keep the money you already have, stay here and find Kosnar and use the women in London to kill him." He was playing to Devskoy's paranoia, using it to separate them, giving him an opportunity to work independently.

"Two hundred thousand each for fifty two?" Devskoy asked.

The Arab nodded. "That's right, over ten million dollars in your hands by tomorrow."

Devskoy licked his lips and stared at the Arab for a moment. "Alright," he replied, you transfer the ten million dollars to me and I will give you all the names in America."

Al Rahman shook his head firmly. "No, give me the names right now, and I will execute the transfer first thing tomorrow, but I want the names now."

Devskoy leaned forward in his chair and began to waive his finger in Al Rahman's face, shouting his response. "I told you the deal, money first then names."

In a quick move, Al Rahman slapped Devskoy's hand away from his face and thrust his own mangled right hand between them, holding it just inches from the Russian's face. The hand looked grotesque with small stumps where the fingers and thumb had been brutally cut off. Devskoy backed away but Al Rahman leaned forward across the table pressing his hand almost against the Russian's face.

"Do you remember this Devskoy? Huh? Do you remember?"

Devskoy dropped his eyes and looked down at the empty vodka glass in front of him and said nothing.

Al Rahman slowly retracted his mangled hand and placed it back on his lap out of view as he stared unblinking at the Russian. "For what you did to me I should stab you through the heart and feed your pathetic body to the dogs," he hissed angrily. "Instead I am offering you millions of dollars and you are arguing with me. You should be thanking Allah and begging my forgiveness."

Devskoy looked up at the Arab for a moment and then with a look of resignation, took his cell phone out of his pocket.

"You will transfer all the money tomorrow, two hundred thousand for each one?"

Al Rahman raised his left hand. "I swear it."

Devskoy blinked slowly back at him and then reluctantly began to pass on to Al Rahman the tools that would empower him to kill anonymously and remotely.

CHAPTER 20

THE BRITISH SECRET Service, better known colloquially as MI5 is housed in a building called Thames House, located just south of Westminster in London. Built in 1929, the building's old and austere façade hides an always busy and very sophisticated, highly experienced team of professionals dedicated to protecting the British homeland. Their emblem hanging proudly in the ornate lobby displays the lion, the enduring symbol of Great Britain and reads *Regnum Defende*, Defend the Kingdom. The men and women who serve at MI5 are on the forefront of Britain's war on terror, using a combination of technology, surveillance and dogged police work to preempt terror attacks on the British homeland. As the head of MI5 constantly reminds her dedicated team, theirs is a twenty-four hour a day job requiring no less than one hundred percent success. The bombings in the London subway and the subsequent failed attempts to detonate huge car bombs only reinforced the urgency of their assignments.

As the lead service providing both protective security and operating as Britain's leading anti-terrorism
organization, M15 immediately became involved in the
bombing site analysis and the interrogation of Vladimir
Kosnar. He was quickly transferred from police custody
to an MI5 case officer and transferred under full security
to Thames House for interrogation. Casey Jennings was
also transported to Thames House with Ian Campbell,
still her assigned escort, so she could also provide a full
accounting of what happened.

Sitting with a stenographer, Ian Campbell and two
MI5 case officers, Casey recounted in as much detail as
she could what had happened from the moment she and
David Green had left the hotel to walk through Hyde Park.
She was interrupted occasionally by one of the MI5 officers who asked her to confirm some fact or detail but for
the most part, she spoke without a break, concentrating
hard to provide all the information. As an experienced
agent she understood that any small detail, insignificant
though it might appear at the moment, might actually
become vitally important later on.

The deposition took about two hours and then after a
brief break Casey was asked to witness the interrogation
of Vladimir Kosnar. She sat in a small dark room with a
large flat panel television showing Kosnar's head and upper torso. Besides his voice, Casey could hear questions
from three other disembodied voices in the room, two
men and one woman and it was obvious they were treating him more as a suspect than a witness. Each answer
he gave was challenged, sometimes repeatedly as if they
were trying to inadvertently reveal some hidden detail.

A well dressed middle-aged man who had identified himself to her as Peter Boyle, but provided no title or position at MI5 sat next to Casey as she listened to the interrogation. Ian Campbell left to find out about the status of the closed circuit television recordings that had been collected soon after the bombing.

Casey paid close attention to Kosnar's description of events, but occasionally her mind wandered as she fought off a recurring urge to close her eyes and just sleep. Finally after an hour of sitting and listening, Peter Boyle asked Casey if she believed Kosnar's description of what had occurred was accurate.

"I think so," Casey replied.

"Are you sure?" Boyle replied with some insistence.

Casey nodded. She was so tired she could barely think clearly. "Yes, it seems quite accurate."

"Very well. I'm going to need to keep you around here for a while I'm afraid, in case we need you again. We do have a couple of bedroom suites located in the building you can rest in until we call you."

* * *

Casey Jennings lay on a bed in a small suite on the upper floor of the building trying to sleep. The suite had a small sitting area, bathroom and kitchen but once inside and alone, Casey had ignored everything and just fallen onto the bed, desperate for sleep. Despite her exhaustion and jet lag, her mind was still racing with the events of the prior day, the death in her arms of her friend and colleague, David Green and the revelation from the Russian that his sister was a member of the assassination team.

She sighed as she tried to calm her mind and rest for a couple of hours.

All too soon a knock at the door woke her out of a deep sleep. She sat up on the bed slightly disoriented, brushed the hair out of her eyes and invited the visitor to come in.

A familiar face appeared from around the partially opened door.

"Casey, its Ian Campbell. Can I come in? Did I wake you?"

"Yes," Casey replied glancing at her watch and clearing her throat. She glanced up at Campbell and back at her watch. Is it four o'clock AM or PM?"

Campbell laughed briefly as he stepped into the room. "AM I'm afraid. You've only had a couple of hours of sleep but I do have two pieces of good news for you. Firstly, they delivered your suitcase from the hotel so you can finally get changed."

She rewarded him with a wry smile as he placed the bag on the floor near the bed. "Thank you. And the other piece of good news?"

"We've found Devskoy."

"You're kidding. You found him already! That's incredible. Do you have him in custody? Is he talking?" Her questions came out in a rush.

Campbell held up his hands to her rapid set of questions. "Uh, well not exactly. Take a couple of minutes to freshen up and then I'll come back and get you. I'll fill you in as we go."

After a quick shower and a change into clean clothes, Casey felt a little more refreshed as she walked with Ian Campbell down one of the long corridors.

"Where are we going?" she asked

"To collect Kosnar. He's going to help us identify the body."

Casey stopped walking and turned to face the English detective who also stopped.

"Ian, don't keep me hanging. Do you have Devskoy or not?"

"We have a body and we are pretty sure it's Devskoy, but not certain."

They continued walking down the corridor. "What makes you think it's him?" Casey asked.

"Kosnar has provided us with pictures of all the women and Devskoy. Some are fairly current, many are not, but Devskoy's picture was quite recent. The onsite detectives ID'd him immediately."

As he finished talking, Campbell stopped in front of a dark heavy door marked 'Private' and knocked. After a moment the door opened and Pete Boyle stepped out, closing the door behind him. He got straight to the point.

"As best we can tell, Kosnar is telling the truth," he said. "Under normal circumstances we would keep at him for another day or two but I don't think it would change anything."

He glanced over at Ian Campbell before continuing. "I'm turning him over to you Campbell, at least for now, but I don't want him released yet. Do you understand? Keep him in your custody."

Campbell nodded and replied curtly.

"Understood."

Peter Boyle turned to open the door again and then just before he pushed it open he glanced back over his shoulder at the English detective and FBI agent with a wry smile. "I wouldn't stand to close too Kosnar if I were you. Whoever tried to kill him yesterday might try again."

* * *

Ten minutes later Campbell, Kosnar and Jennings were being driven at high speed through the mostly empty streets of London. Casey sat between the two men trying her best to keep her balance as the policeman drove fast, tires squealing as he negotiated the narrow roads and occasional late night traffic. She glanced at Kosnar who was just starring ahead with a blank expression on his face. She had been a bit shocked by his appearance as he came out of interrogation. He looked exhausted, dark shadows under his eyes, skin a slightly grayish pallor. She gently touched his arm to get his attention.

"Are you alright?"

Kosnar turned to her and nodded, flashing a quick and reassuring smile. It looked more like a grimace.

"It was a long night, but yes, thank you. I am fine." He turned to face forward again, his face once again an expressionless mask.

As the car turned into a narrow alley way, Casey could see flashing lights up ahead and then as they got closer, she could make out a number of police cars arrayed on the narrow sidewalk as the car slowed to drop them off. The threesome quickly climbed out of the back of the car and then followed the English detective as he walked towards a small knot of uniformed and plain clothed police officers up ahead standing next to a large and battered blue dumpster. It had been raining earlier in the evening and the light from the cars and street lamps was reflecting off the small puddles of water.

As they approached, one of the plain clothed officers turned towards them and waived them forward. He quickly shook hands with Ian Campbell and then turned to Vladimir.

"Mr. Kosnar?" he asked looking at the Russian.

Vladimir nodded in response and Campbell verbally confirmed his identity.

"Please step forward Mr. Kosnar and tell us if you recognize this man."

As the Russian stepped forward, Casey peered around him. She could see the outline of a body under a yellow plastic tarpaulin lying on the ground in the narrow space between the dumpster and the wall of the next door pub. Bulging trash bags overflowed the dumpster and lay in piles around it and underneath the body. Broken glass crunched underfoot as they approached the body. The detective stepped around the body and pulled the tarpaulin away from the face. The man's head was rolled unnaturally to the side as if he was looking at the wall and Casey could see that his mouth was agape, tongue protruding awkwardly from his mouth. A large piece of broken glass was sticking out of a jagged hole in his neck, coagulated blood pooled below his Adam's apple and on the ground directly below his head.

Vladimir Kosnar stood beside the body next to the head. Then he placed one foot on the other side of the dead man so he was straddling the body and bent over, staring hard at the face below him. As he straightened up, he turned and stepped back towards Ian Campbell.

"It's him, its Devskoy," he said.

"Are you quite certain Mr. Kosnar?" Campbell responded forcefully. "Are you sure it's him?"

Vladimir nodded vigorously for a moment and then repeated his statement.

"Yes, it's him, its Devskoy."

Kosnar looked over at the plain clothed officer who had directed them to the body. "Excuse me sir," he said formally. "Have you searched the body? Did you find anything on the body?"

The officer glanced at Campbell who just shrugged slightly before he turned back to Kosnar as he answered.

"No Mr. Kosnar, not a thing. Whoever did this to him cleaned him out. No identification, no money, not even loose change."

Kosnar glanced back at the body as he spoke. "Do you have a cause of death?"

The officer grunted slightly before he answered. "Whoever did this to him, really wanted to make sure he was dead. According to the coroner, first he snapped his neck and then he drove that broken piece of glass into the guy's throat."

The detective stepped around the body again and this time pulled the tarpaulin away from his torso so his entire upper body, arms and hands were showing.

"And take a look at this," he said as he grasped the dead man's right hand by the wrist and held it up.

All the fingers on the right hand bent backwards so they were perpendicular to the palm of the hand.

"All of the fingers on his right hand have been snapped back at the knuckle. The coroner said the killer most likely did this after the man was already dead."

The detective began to stand as he tossed the tarpaulin back over the body, but was almost knocked to the ground as Kosnar quickly stepped forward and whipped the tarpaulin away from the body and grabbed at the grotesquely mangled hand. He looked at the hand and then closed his eyes as his mind flashed back to the fleeting glance at the familiar but unrecognized face he had seen the day before. When he turned back to face the detectives and Casey Jennings they could see even in the washed out light his face was ashen.

CHAPTER 21

THE POLICE CAR threaded through the early morning traffic in the pre-dawn light with siren wailing and lights flashing. Sitting next to the driver, Detective Ian Campbell was dialing out on his cell phone as he urged the driver to speed up as they drove back to Thames House. As soon as his call connected he spoke urgently.

"We'll be there in about twenty minutes," he said. "When we get there I want all the CCTV tapes up and ready to go with a technician standing by." He was quiet for a moment before he continued. "Yes, that's right. Have the technician load the tapes that recorded across the street from the bombing. I don't want to see the bombing but I do want to see what happened starting about thirty minutes before the bombing but across the street. Do you understand?"

In the back seat, Casey was on the phone to her boss, Gordon Lewis. The connection was not very good and she covered her opposite ear with her hand in order to hear him over the sound of the siren.

"Yes, that's right," she was saying. "Abd Al Rahman. Mr. Kosnar is certain it is him but we are heading back to Thames House to check the video, see if we can get a confirmation."

Lewis asked for description of the Al Rahman and in the dim light Casey read from the notes she had hurriedly written before calling him.

"He's in his late forties, about five feet ten inches tall. According to Kosnar, he is lighter skinned than most Arabs."

She turned to Vladimir who was sitting beside her and said, "He wants to know what nationality he is?"

Kosnar paused for a moment before replying. "I think he might be Lebanese but I'm not sure."

Casey relayed the information and then said, "Gordon there is one more identifying item about him. He is missing all the fingers on his right hand."

She paused as Gordon Lewis responded and then said, "No, according to Mr. Kosnar, his fingers were cut off during interrogation. And Gordon, listen to this. The person who cut off his fingers was Devskoy."

She glanced over at Vladimir with eyebrows raised as she heard her boss' incredulous response on the phone.

"Right now we don't know if they were working together and then had a falling out or if Al Rahman just disposed of him because he didn't need him anymore. We just don't know." She paused as she listened to his response.

"OK, I'll call you if we have a confirmation from the video."

She hung up and glanced at her Russian companion who seemed to be quite agitated, clenching and unclenching his fists, his jaw tight. She reached over and touched his arm.

"You seem very upset suddenly, even more than yesterday after the bombing. Why are you more concerned now than before?"

Vladimir adjusted himself in the backseat to face her more directly before responding. "You need to understand this man, Al Rahman." He closed his eyes for a moment and pursed his lips.

"He is absolutely ruthless, but worse than that he won't stop, he never stops." His voice was agitated now. "When I chased him in Afghanistan he was so ruthless he would routinely take refuge with people in their homes and then kill them when he left so they couldn't give us any information about him. He would just shoot them, men, women and children. It meant nothing to him. And after we captured him and tortured him, cut off all his fingers, he gave us nothing, absolutely nothing. Most men would be begging for mercy after one finger but not Al Rahman. He shattered some of his of teeth he was clenching them so hard against the pain, but he never gave in."

Vladimir paused before he continued. "Devskoy was a fall down drunk. It was just a matter of time before he made a mistake and he was caught or killed."

He leaned closer to her as he spoke. "The worst mistake we can make is to underestimate Abd Al Rahman. He will do whatever it takes to complete this mission."

"You mean he will kill all these women if, he in fact, now has the means?"

His eyes remained fixed on hers as he nodded vigorously. "You must understand the difference between Devskoy and Al Rahman. I'm sure Devskoy was just in this for the money, but Al Rahman is a true believer, a ruthless jihadi and he will do anything to see it through."

As he finished speaking, he held his gaze on Casey's face for a moment, then turned away slowly and stared out the window.

* * *

"That's him right there." Vladimir Kosnar was out of his chair pointing at a figure on the large flat panel television screen.

The room was dark, illuminated mostly by the computer monitors arrayed around the room. The large plasma screen covered one wall and a small crowd was sitting on the few available chairs or standing behind them.

After rushing back to Thames House from the spot where Devskoy's body had been found, they had only been reviewing the CCTV tapes for a few minutes. Vladimir had suggested that instead of reviewing the tapes from thirty minutes before the bombing they should look from the moments just after the bombing when Kosnar thought he saw Abd Al Rahman. Campbell quickly agreed and the technician loaded the tape to the few seconds after the blast.

The technician froze the image and moved his mouse pointer the face of the man Kosnar was pointing to.

"This guy?" he asked.

"Yes," Vladimir replied.

The technician tapped on his keyboard and the image of the man expanded to fill the screen, blurring as it did so. A few more clicks on the keyboard and the image became more focused but not completely clear.

"That's the best I can do," he said.

Vladimir Kosnar stood up and stared at the screen. After a moment he turned back to face the crowded room and said, "That man is Abd Al Rahman."

Peter Boyle who had led Kosnar's interrogation spoke up. "Are you quite sure?"

"Absolutely," Vladimir responded. "It's him."

"Very well,' he said. "We need to confirm that Devskoy and Al Rahman were together. I want you to remain here, Mr. Kosnar, and assist us." He turned to Ian Campbell who was in the back of the room.

"I have to go and speak with the Director," he said referring to the head of MI5, the Director General of the Security service. "She is going to need to speak to the Prime Minister. In the meantime I suggest you start coordinating with your people to get a manhunt started for Al Rahman." He glanced back at the technicians before turning back to Campbell.

"We'll have these chaps find you the best set of images of Al Rahman from the CCTV tapes and get them over to you."

CHAPTER 22

N O LONGER ACCUSTOMED to rigorous physical activity, snapping Devskoy's neck and then mutilating the corpse had left Abd Al Rahman physically drained. Years away from the battlefield, middle-age and the limited use of his hands would normally have made the task of quickly killing Devskoy difficult, but a mad anger and hatred for the Russian overcame his physical limitations. Stabbing him in the neck with the broken glass was to just insure that he was dead but breaking the dead man's fingers was an impetuous action that gave him a brief measure of satisfaction. Staring down at the mutilated body he felt somewhat detached, his mind wandering back to the bitter suffering he had endured from Devskoy in the Afghan prison.

The sound of approaching footsteps snapped him out of his reverie and he quickly bent over the body to rifle through the dead man's pockets. He shoved the few items he found into his jacket pockets and then quickly checked his clothes to make sure they did not show any obvious evidence of the murder, and walked out of the alley.

He had to move fast. It was likely that his face, if not his identity, would soon be compromised. His anonymity, his ability to blend unnoticed and unsuspected in to western society was the reason they had selected him for this mission but the brief moment he and Kosnar had locked eyes might have been enough for Kosnar to recognize him and the security cameras were certain to have captured his image with Devskoy at the bombing. He had to get out of England quickly.

A sudden rain squall took him by surprise and he ducked into a small corner grocery store to find shelter. Looking around the shop he walked over to the magazine and newspaper rack, waiting for the rain to pass. Glancing at some of the English and European papers, he reached for the New York Times European Edition, pulled it from the stack and began to glance at the headlines. The edition was too late to have any information about the bombing earlier in the day and was mostly focused on the up coming American presidential elections. As he scanned the paper, one headline did catch his attention. 'Candidate Finalizing Convention Speech' the headline read. He quickly read the rest of the article and turned to walk out of the store with the paper.

"Hey. Hey you!" The sing song Pakistani accented voice rang out and drew his attention.

"Hey, you not pay for paper," the proprietor shouted as Al Rahman stood in the doorway.

"Oh yes," Al Rahman mumbled and quickly dropped a couple of pounds on the counter and turned to leave.

"Hey, you get change," the Pakistani sang out again, but Al Rahman was already gone, oblivious now to the heavy rain.

He squinted into the dark wet night as he looked up and down the street for the familiar site of an English public phone booth. He was reluctant to use his cell phone or Devskoy's, both of which he had in his pocket, but he needed to make his plane reservation right away. He spotted two phone booths up ahead and quickly walked towards them. One was occupied by a woman who was on her cell phone and just using the booth for shelter and the other was broken, the smashed receiver dangling from frayed wires.

Al Rahman stood outside the red phone booth and glanced at his watch. The woman inside the booth had her back towards him, still engaged in animated conversation. He looked back at his watch then tapped impatiently on the glass door. The woman glanced at him briefly then turned away, ignoring him.

Al Rahman looked up and down the now quiet and wet street. The heavy rain diminished the light coming from the over head street lights and he saw no one else around. He pushed open the glass door and grabbed the woman's wrist.

"Bloody hell-" the woman started to shout.

Shifting his weight and grip, he grabbed her collar, first pulling her and then pushing her of out of the booth. Standing for a moment in the rain, the woman screamed at him she tried to force her way back into the phone booth, still shouting at him.

"You stupid little fuck," she screamed, her mouth almost touching Al Rahman's ear. "Get the fuck out of there!"

Al Rahman turned to face her, his left arm driving into her neck, pushing her back against the glass wall. He said nothing, but stared into her eyes, his face inches from hers, his arm pushing hard against her neck.

She looked back, eyes wide at the menace in his face the fight gone out of her now. He slowly released the pressure on her neck and she stumbled from the booth, regaining her balance as she backed away.

"You fucking piece of shit," she shouted, keeping her distance. "I'm going to find a copper and have him thump you a few times, you big shit." She looked frantically up and down the street.

"Why is there never a fucking policeman when you need one?" she screemed into the rain. "I'll be back," she shouted at Al Rahman as she ran off.

But Al Rahman was not paying attention. He had to make reservations quickly and he had no time to worry about some hysterical English woman.

* * *

Ian Campbell, Vladimir Kosnar and Casey Jennings were sitting at a small sandwich shop near Thames House. Two uniformed policemen stood outside the shop and two more plain clothed security officers sat at a nearby table watching all the shop patrons with wary eyes. Their function was two fold – protect the three-some from an attack and secure Kosnar. His status was still a bit ambiguous and no-one in the police or MI5 was ready to release him.

Of the three, Casey was the only one to have had any sleep in the past twenty four hours and she still felt exhausted. Campbell seemed to be the least affected and was eating heartily while Casey and Kosnar just picked at their food. She kept glancing at Kosnar who had discarded his sandwich after just a few bites and was slumped back in his chair. He seemed detached and emotionally spent, his eyes hooded and face gray with exhaustion and sadness. She had a strong urge to encourage him, but given the circumstances, despair was probably the appropriate emotion. If his sister was at large as he believed, Al Rahman could dispatch her at any time. He could be anywhere plotting his next move and they were powerless to stop him. A massive manhunt was on throughout Great Britain but the expectation of finding him before the next attack was low.

"You know for a couple of seasoned agents you two seem to be taking this whole thing a bit personally, don't you think?" said Campbell glancing first at Vladimir and then Casey.

Casey shot a quick look at Vladimir who returned her look but said nothing. After a brief pause Casey said, "I think you need to tell him."

"Tell me what?" asked Campbell, a quizzical look on his face. "Tell me what?" he repeated.

Kosnar said nothing but he nodded at Casey.

"Look, what are you two hiding?" demanded Campbell, his voice getting agitated.

Casey leaned forward in her seat and spoke softly. "One of the women Al Rahman controls is Vladimir's sister."

Campbell sat up rigid in his chair, knife and fork suspended above his plate, color briefly draining from his face.

"What? I mean... your sister...Oh my god...." His voice trailed off.

Kosnar nodded briefly but did not speak.

"Are you quite certain about this?" Campbell asked as he noisily placed his knife and fork on his plate, his appetite suddenly diminished.

"Yes," Vladimir responded simply as if he was reluctant to be discussing the topic.

There was an awkward silence at the table as each person sat alone with their thoughts. After a few moments Campbell broke the silence. "There are some benefits to living on an island Mr. Kosnar. It's hard to leave without being noticed. If Al Rahman does try to leave I am sure we'll get him."

Kosnar said nothing but responded to the English detective's comments with a slight smile, but his expression quickly returned to its impassive and unhappy state, eyes staring at the ground. Campbell looked over at Casey and as she returned his look he grimaced slightly and slowly shook his head. Casey said nothing as she stared back at him.

CHAPTER 23

THE POUNDING ON the door startled Casey awake and left her momentarily disorientated. She pushed her hair out of her eyes, clicked on bedside lamp and rolled out of the bed reaching for the bathrobe she had flung over a nearby chair before she had collapsed asleep. The pounding on the door was more insistent.

"Hang on," she shouted. "I'm coming."

"Casey," a muffled voice answered through the door. "It's Ian Campbell."

She unlocked the door and opened it a couple of inches, peering through the gap at the English detective.

"What's up Ian? What's happened?"

"We found him. I mean we traced him to the US."

Casey swung the door open and pulled the bathrobe tight around her as she stood in the open doorway. "You found Al Rahman?"

"Well, we didn't exactly find him but we traced him to the United States. He boarded a flight to San Francisco yesterday morning. He landed there about eight hours ago."

There was a pause as if Casey expected to hear more information.

"Well, what happened? Was he arrested when he arrived?"

Campbell shook his head. "Nope. Apparently he made it through US Customs without issue."

The phone rang and Casey quickly walked over to answer it as the English detective followed her into the room, closing the door behind him.

"Casey Jennings," she answered.

"Casey, its Gordon Lewis."

"Hi Gordon-," she began to respond but he cut her off.

"We think Al Rahman might be here, in the US."

"Yes, I just heard so from Ian Campbell."

"Did he tell you he made it through Customs and disappeared?"

"Yes, he's right here with me now. He just told me Al Rahman was traced to a flight that landed in San Francisco about eight hours ago."

"That's right." Gordon Lewis continued to speak, but Casey closed her eyes as she tried to recall something about San Francisco that was suddenly important.

Then it hit her.

"The Democratic National Convention," she blurted out, cutting him off in mid-sentence.

"What?"

"I am sorry Gordon but aren't the Democrats holding their national convention in San Francisco this week or next. Actually, I think it's in a few days... I can't remember exactly."

"Oh Christ," Gordon said. "You're right. It is next week." Casey could hear the weariness in his voice.

There was a pause as both FBI agents contemplated the magnitude of their realization. Thousands of delegates, congressmen, governors and two ex-presidents, it was a potential security nightmare and extraordinary threat to the national elections.

"Listen Casey, Homeland Security is already deeply involved but I doubt they've made this connection. I am going to get the British police to turn Kosnar over to your custody. He is the only person who knows Al Rahman, how he thinks and operates and of course he can recognize him. I need him here right away. I'll take care of the authorization with the British and US Immigration, you take care of the logistics." There was a click as he hung up.

Casey sat down on the edge of the bed and looked up at Campbell.

"That was my boss Gordon Lewis. He wants me and Kosnar on a plane to the US right away. He is working to get the authorization from the British government to release Kosnar to my custody."

"Anything I can do to help?" Campbell responded.

"Where's Kosnar?"

"He is still being held by MI5."

"Do you think they will release him to my custody?"

Campbell shrugged his shoulders. "I don't know. I suppose it depends on the powers that be making the right phone calls."

"Ian, how do we know for sure Al Rahman boarded that flight?"

Campbell responded with a quick smile. "We had people checking all the airports, interviewing all the security staff doing carry-on baggage inspection. It took a long time because there are three shifts of people and someone decided it would be logistically easier to interview them all as they returned to duty. So it took a while." He paused before continuing. "As it happened Al Rahman was stopped at random just before boarding by a security officer who did one of those quick handheld metal detector checks. She found nothing on him but when she made him raise his arms from his sides she noticed that all the fingers on his right hand were missing. Apparently she is squeamish about these things so it stuck with her. We also pulled up the CCTV tapes from that terminal and Kosnar confirmed it."

Campbell grinned at Casey as he finished talking. "I told you and Kosnar we would find him. It's tough to leave an island without someone noticing."

"Have they traced his name? Do they know what name he is traveling under? Casey asked.

His cell phone rang before he could answer. He pulled it out of the belt holster and put it to his ear.

"Campbell."

He listened intently for a few moments and then muttered a few words of affirmation and then clicked the clam shelled phone shut.

"Well, I guess the powers that be are working overtime today. It seems the custody transfer has already been authorized and I am to take you directly to the airport. Kosnar is already on his way there with a police escort."

CHAPTER 24

CASEY WAS LEAFING distractedly through a magazine. She glanced over at Kosnar who was sitting, arms folded across his chest staring at the back of the seat in front of him.

"May I ask you some questions about your sister?" Casey asked turning in her seat to face him.

Vladimir discretely glanced around him before he answered. The flight to San Francisco was completely full, but the hum of the engines made it difficult to hear other people's conversations. No one seemed to be paying them any attention. Still, he kept his voice low as he spoke.

"Yes," Vladimir replied softly, "but I don't know if I will be able to answer them. I really don't know much about her."

"What do you mean?"

"Well, the last time I saw my sister was thirty eight years ago."

"Thirty eight years!" Casey exclaimed. "You must have been just children."

"I was about eight or nine years old and she was five or six. We were in an orphanage together. One day, they came and took her away. Until a few months ago, I was not sure if she was alive or dead." Vladimir looked down at his hands for a moment, then back at Casey with a pained expression. "Unfortunately, now that I have found her, she might be dead before I can see her again."

Casey dropped her eyes for a second then looked back directly at Vladimir. "I'm sorry. I wish I could offer you more encouragement."

Vladimir ran his hand through his hair and sighed. "Usually, my assignments left me quite cold," he said. "I was given a mission, I executed the mission. I returned to await orders for the next one. Mostly my job was quite boring, sometimes exciting, occasionally terrifying. But this…" He shook his head slowly and looked away from her as he spoke. "This is simply painful."

"How?" said Casey. "How did it happen that your sister ended up in this program?"

"Well, according to the documents the FSB used to get me to accept this assignment, my sister was taken from the orphanage because they believed she had unusual athletic ability. My memory of this is vague, but apparently some visitors did tests on all the children to determine athletic potential. The tests included running and jumping, but also more sophisticated blood and muscle response tests. My sister must have tested well because they came back for her a few weeks later. That was the last time I saw her."

"Do you know where they took her?" asked Casey.

"They sent all the other children selected from around the country to special training facilities. There they began a program of athletic training, trying to work out which sport suited each child. Some were assigned to swimming, others to track, and so on. Most were eventually rejected and sent back to their parents or orphanages or wherever they had been found."

"What was the purpose of this? To create super athletes?"

"I suppose so," Vladimir replied as he shrugged his shoulders. "You must remember this was just after the 1956 Olympics. The Soviet Government decided that we would prove the superiority of the Communist system by developing the world's best athletes. It makes sense when you think about it. Athletics were becoming a much more important part of the national pastime in Europe and America. The Olympics were a great stage to compete against each other as nations."

"Do you remember your sister from the orphanage?"

"Vaguely," said Vladimir. "Unfortunately, all I can really remember is her leaving. She kept saying my name over and over again when they took her away. I...I..." Vladimir's voice broke and he closed his eyes and laid his head back against the headrest, his jaw working, clenching and unclenching. Casey placed her hand on his arm and squeezed it firmly as she looked at his strained face. She held her grip for a few moments and then removed her hand.

"Had you ever tried to find her since then?" Casey asked, breaking the awkward silence.

"Many times. I tried when I became a junior officer in the Soviet army, but I was unsuccessful. The orphanage had long since closed and I was unable to find any record of her anywhere. Later on, when I was in the KGB,

I even enlisted the help of some of my superiors, but it was hopeless. I did locate one clue that she might still be alive, but was never able to confirm it."

"What was that?"

Vladimir reached into his wallet and pulled out a carefully folded newspaper clipping and handed it to Casey, who held it delicately with both hands. She looked carefully at the happy face in the picture for a few moments, then back at Vladimir. "Is this her? Is this your sister?"

"When I saw this picture in the paper, I was convinced it was her. I could not confirm it, you understand. The caption gives her name, but it was not the right last name. I just thought she looked very familiar. At the time, I tried to find out more about her, but I was unable to discover much. Even for a KGB officer, it was not good for me to ask too many questions in the Soviet Union. The woman in the picture was the national champion that year, but she never competed again after that, never made it to the Olympics. At the time I wondered why. Now I know."

"And you are quite sure she is definitely one of these women?" Casey asked, referring to the assassins.

"Oh, yes. The information I was given before I left Moscow was comprehensive. There were records on my sister going back to the day she was taken away from the orphanage. There was even a copy of her original birth certificate with her birth name."

"So you being selected for this mission was not coincidental?"

Vladimir looked over at Casey and smiled sadly. "It turns out my own last commanding officer, the one who asked me to take this mission, had known about her for years."

"Why didn't he tell you?"

Vladimir sighed. "I think we often to tend think people in high places are there because they are intelligent or capable. Unfortunately, something always comes along that demonstrates their human failings."

"What do you mean?" asked Casey, furrowing her brow.

Vladimir sighed before answering. "General Victor Siminov, former KGB general, today a senior officer in the new Federal Intelligence Service, had the opportunity eight years ago to have all the titanium hip replacements containing explosive material replaced again with normal regular ones."

"How could he have done that?" Casey asked

"Apparently hip replacements tend to loosen every ten or twelve years so the recipients need to be hospitalized so they can be tightened. There was some consternation in the KGB in 1989 when one of the athletes checked herself into a hospital because she was having trouble walking. Just in time, the KGB found out and quickly had her transferred to a KGB hospital. The orders were to remove the explosive hip joint and install a normal one but unfortunately, those orders were countermanded." Vladimir stopped speaking for a moment and slowly shook his head, still apparently not quite able to grasp what had transpired next. He looked back over at Casey and said, "Instead of removing the explosives, they had the battery system replaced with a new and much more sophisticated power system. Then they tracked down and called in all the remaining women and did the same to them."

"What was different about the new power system?"

"I don't know the details but the new system is biomechanical. It charges up automatically every time the women walk."

"You mean it never needs to be replaced?" Casey asked, incredulously. She continued without waiting for him to answer. "So how long will it work?"

Vladimir shrugged his shoulders. "Until they stop moving, I suppose."

Casey shook her head and swore under her breath. "You mean they are now basically perpetual time bombs that can never be turned off?"

He nodded before responding. "Yes, unless the hip joints are removed and replaced."

"And they reactivated the entire assassination group?"

"Yes," said Vladimir. He looked down at his hands, murmured "Stupid, stupid," under his breath a number of times.

"But surely it was recognized that these women were getting too old to be used as angels. They were in their late thirties by then."

Vladimir just shrugged. "They still seem to be quite effective now, twenty years later, wouldn't you agree?"

"That's true," said Casey, her mind flashing back to the headless body of Gerald Rifkin on the slab in the morgue and her dead colleague David Green lying in her arms.

"So, what you are telling me is the KGB had the opportunity to remove the explosive hip joints and replace them with normal ones, deactivate the assassination capability, and make this awful idea go away."

"No," said Vladimir, as he slowly shook his head. "It's worse than that. These women were already deactivated. The battery packs in the hip joints had a life span of about ten years, but by 1988, the batteries were dead or dying anyway. The group was being deactivated by default. If the KGB had not inserted biomechanical systems, this whole thing could not have happened."

Casey sat quietly for a moment, pondering what Vladimir has just said. Now she understood his comment about people in high places eventually demonstrating their failings.

"And the person who ordered the new power unit to be installed was General Siminov?"

Vladimir did not answer. He just looked at Casey with a sad smile on his face and nodded slowly. They sat quietly for a few minutes.

"What about you?" he asked. "Are you married? Do you have children?"

Casey looked away for a moment before turning back to him to answer the question.

"I was married but my husband died before we had any children," her voice breaking slightly as she spoke.

"I'm very sorry," Kosnar responded. "I did not mean to intrude."

Casey dismissed his concern with a wave of her hand. "That's alright," she said as she cleared her throat. "My husband died four years ago and I still miss him so much."

She looked away towards the window as she spoke, embarrassed that she could not control her emotions.

"What happened to him?

"He was killed by a drunk driver while out jogging. The guy just drove straight over him and kept on going. They told me he was killed on impact."

"I'm sorry," Kosnar said again.

The hum of the engines droned on behind them as they sat quietly, alone in their thoughts.

* * *

Abd Al Rahman sat on the king sized bed in the plain and dark hotel room with a map of San Francisco spread out in front of him. With a fine tipped felt pen he had drawn a circle around the Moscone Center, the site of the upcoming Democratic National Convention. He had already reconnoitered the area earlier in the day for hours and had familiarized himself with the different streets leading into and out of the convention area.

His arrival in San Francisco had been uneventful. The airport was very crowded and there were banners in the arrival terminal welcoming all the delegates to the convention. The immigration officer had glanced at his passport and then stamped it without saying a word.

Leaving the airport, Al Rahman deliberately avoided traveling to the City and instead took a shuttle bus to the East Bay in Oakland and rented a room in a small nondescript hotel in the downtown area. He was relieved when the desk clerk had not asked him for identification as is typical at European hotels when he filled out the registration form with a false name, but he had an anxious moment when the clerk asked for a credit card. He quickly solved the problem by paying in cash for a week in advance plus a couple of hundred dollars in deposit.

More then ever he intended to remain incognito. Traveling to the United States he had been forced to use his nom de guerre and name on his passport, Philippe Métier, but once in the country his plan was to disappear, using only cash to pay for everything and never declaring his name, real or otherwise. He assumed his real identity had already been compromised by Kosnar and it was just a matter of time before his false identity was also determined. In a country of three hundred million people he would become a ghost, only manifesting himself with his attacks on the infidels.

He reviewed the list of the women's names and locations Devskoy had given him. Half were split between New York and California. The ones in New York he would leave for phase two. Now he needed to concentrate all of the women based in California in the bay area. He was formulating a plan and he intended to use them all.

Having witnessed the bombing in London Al Rahman understood that used singly the women could cause limited destruction but could be very useful against a high profile target. But used as group, deployed throughout the City and exploded in a carefully crafted sequence, the affect would be devastating. The death toll might be relatively small but the chaos and terror that would follow would have the desired affect.

He pushed the map away and laid back on the bed running through the sequence of events in his mind's eye. The first explosion would take place as close to a high value target as possible. He would wait a few minutes as the first responders, police, fire and ambulance arrived to secure the area and treat the wounded. Then he would initiate the second attack with two to three women simultaneously all targeted at groups of police officers and firemen.

Then he would pause. In his mind he could see the events play out, dead bodies laying in the street, the wounded screaming and crying for help. Chaos would erupt as the police fought to maintain order, forcefully driving a larger a perimeter to secure the Moscone Center and themselves. They would be harsh and aggressive seeing themselves as the intended targets and exacerbating the situation while they acted to try and control it. The crowds would be pressed and confined in the narrow streets around the convention center and panic would ensue as people desperately sought safety.

Then he would strike again, maybe this time at the back of the crowds at the very periphery, pushing them back toward the police and forcing waves of panic to roll through the crowd as the terror ratcheted up.

A small smile crested Abd Al Rahman's lips as he intoned a supplication.

"Inshalla," he said and then repeated twice, "Inshalla, Inshalla."

Eyes still closed, he admonished himself to think carefully about the operation, to consider problems that might arise such as keeping the women sufficiently apart so that killing one would not kill them all. It was vital to stagger the attack, the maximum terror being the wave of small attacks instead of one large one.

Communication and identification would also be critical. He would have to be ready to call them at the right time to move them into place. It occurred to him he should have them wear shirts of different colors so each wave of attackers would be easier to spot in the crowds.

He stood up and placed the map on the small desk in the room. Leaning over it he carefully began to familiarize himself with street names, routes and distances and the best spot to place each woman. Then he began to meticulously go through the things he needed to do, jotting down notes in a small cryptic script. The first and most urgent task was to move the women from Los Angeles to the Bay area. Flying was not an option as security was so tight and because he was concerned the hip joints would set off the metal detectors. The women would have to travel by train or bus. The conference would begin in two days and it would take the women at least a day to arrive if he got them started right away.

He began to practice speaking in Russian, trying to imitate as best he could Devskoy's accent. He would keep the conversation with each woman very brief just providing the necessary instructions to get them all moved. Once they were in position in the next few days he would give them their final instructions.

Using one of the three pre-paid cell phones he had purchased at the airport he began to make his calls.

CHAPTER 25

ORDON LEWIS SLOWLY closed the binder holding the detailed security plan for the Democratic National Convention and took in a deep breath and slowly exhaled. He had spent the better part of the past two hours of the flight to San Francisco on an FBI executive jet carefully reading the plan and was pleased to see it was very well thought out. Close cooperation between all the relevant agencies – local police and fire, California Highway Patrol, the FBI, Secret Service and Homeland Security had been arranged. Common communication systems had been configured and a Command and Control Center had been set up at FBI headquarters in San Francisco.

Representatives from each agency had been working at the control center for three weeks conducting dry runs on various emergency scenarios including a major earthquake, anti-globalization riots and terrorist attacks. Lessons had been learned and they had improved the system to the point where he could find no significant fault with it.

And yet he knew that despite everyone's best efforts, meticulous planning could only go so far. If an attack happened, bombs exploding through the city as he now expected, he doubted the system could hold together with minimal casualties. A series of small seemingly random attacks were more of a concern to him than one big one. He knew from numerous studies conducted by the FBI and Homeland Security that a rapid series of sporadic violent attacks tended to be more destabilizing because panic tends to set in among the public and the authorities quickly lose control. Compounding the problem was Al Rahman's best advantage; the women under his control would easily blend in and be difficult to identify.

He reached for the secure phone on the console in front of him and placed a call to Lance Jessep, Special Agent in Charge or SAC at the San Francisco FBI office. He reached him on his cell phone near the Moscone Center where he was conducting another security check.

"Listen Lance, what are we doing about the search for these women?" he asked dispensing quickly with small talk. "I mean do we have their pictures posted with the police departments in the bay area?" he asked.

There was a slight delay before Jessep responded. "Uh no, Gordon our APB has been limited to Al Rahman. No-one has really suggested we do the same for all these women."

"I'm not suggesting an All Person Bulletin on each woman but I think at least we can get their pictures out there."

"Well that's a lot of pictures, and some, as you know, are pretty dated, but if you think it's a good idea I'll do it," Jessep responded sounding dubious about the idea.

"Yeah, go ahead," Gordon Lewis insisted. Limit the distribution to just San Francisco and the east bay – Berkeley, Oakland, San Jose... you know the area."

"OK Gordon, I'll get on it. Anything else?"

"No update on Al Rahman I take it?" Gordon asked, his voice conveying a lack of optimism.

"Sorry Gordon, nothing new. I think you already heard we found Al Rahman on a couple of video surveillance recordings in the arrival terminal and then leaving the airport terminal, but the range of the cameras did not extend beyond the drop off area. We have no record of how he left the airport although I am pretty sure he did not rent a car. We have checked every rental agency at or near the airport, spoken to every rental agent on duty when his flight arrived and no one recognized him. We have also spoken to a lot of taxi and shuttle van drivers but with no luck. They are a much harder group to chase down because they tend to work irregular hours so I doubt we have spoken with more than half of them by now."

The two men wrapped up their conversation and Gordon Lewis glanced at his watch. He should be arriving in San Francisco within the hour. Casey Jennings and Kosnar were due in at almost the same time. Perhaps there would be more information by then. He certainly hoped so.

* * *

As Casey Jennings stepped out of the jet way with Vladimir Kosnar at her side, she noticed Gordon Lewis in the arrival lounge and a small group of men clustered around him. Lewis was standing with his arms folded across his chest, his face set and expressionless but he smiled briefly and dropped his arms to his sides as he saw her approaching. Casey quickly introduced Vladimir to Gordon who in turn introduced them both to the rest of his group.

"Follow me please," Lewis said as the group finished shaking hands.

He lead them to a nearby small conference room where a uniformed immigration officer was seated at the conference table.

"Take a seat please, Mr. Kosnar." Lewis instructed.

Kosnar sat down and faced the Special Agent in Charge who sat across from him.

"This officer," said Lewis indicating the immigration officer with his hand "has the necessary documents allowing you to enter the country. You and I will each sign these documents which stipulate that you are entering the country in the custody of the United States Federal Bureau of Investigation." He paused before continuing.

"Mr. Kosnar, you are not under arrest. However, and let me be absolutely clear here, the conditions of your stay in the United States mandate that you remain in the custody of the FBI at all times. We will assign agents to accompany you. If at any time you try to evade their company, you will be arrested and deported. Do you have any questions?"

Kosnar shook his head.

"Do you accept these terms and conditions?"

"Yes I do."

"Very well," Lewis responded. "Now, as soon as you and I have both signed these documents my men will escort you to the FBI station in San Francisco. I understand that you are probably tired from your trip but I am afraid we need to get started right away."

"I'm not tired," Kosnar replied. "What do you need me to do?"

"We have flown in two FBI profilers and a psychiatrist who are waiting to meet with you. I want you to help them create a profile of Abd Al Rahman, as detailed as you can. We need to get to know this man, what he thinks, how he operates. OK?"

Vladimir nodded vigorously and quickly signed the documents placed in front of him by the immigration officer and rose to leave.

"One more thing Mr. Kosnar, does the name Philippe Métier mean anything to you?"

Kosnar said nothing for a moment then shook his head. "No, I'm sorry. I don't know anyone by that name."

"Well that's the name we believe Al Rahman used to board the flight and enter the country. We've checked almost every passenger on his flight and except for just a couple of men who are unaccounted for, his name popped up as the most likely."

"Was his nationality registered as French?" Casey asked.

"Yes, he arrived on a French passport."

"Any help from the French on his identity?" Casey asked.

"They're checking for us right now, but I don't expect much," Gordon replied. "We have found one former CIA officer who was stationed in Pakistan during the Soviet occupation of Afghanistan who claims to remember Abd Al Rahman. He says he never met him but he knows him by reputation. He described Al Rahman as an animal, ready to kill anyone at any time if it furthered his cause."

"That pretty much confirms what Vladi...uh... Mr. Kosnar has been saying," Casey said.

"Well, since then this guy seems to have been a ghost. He's not on any terrorist watch list anywhere. We've checked and rechecked since we got his name and found absolutely nothing about Abd Al Rahman for the past twenty years. He seemed to have disappeared from Afghanistan in the late 1980's and then just showed up in London this week," Lewis said shaking his head as he spoke. "Now he's arrived here and we have no idea where he is."

His words hung in the air for a moment and then he turned to the three agents with him.

"Alright, let's get moving. Mr. Kosnar you will travel with these men and Casey you ride with me."

CHAPTER 26

THE MEETING WAS not going well. Special Agent in Charge, Gordon Lewis and the local SAC, Lance Jessep were seated at the table in a small conference room facing Gavin Newhouse, the mayor of San Francisco and Richard Westly, the head of the Democratic National Committee. The tone of the meeting had quickly degenerated as Lewis tried to make the two politicians understand the gravity of the risk facing the City and the convention, but the conversation was not going well.

Rickard Westly, a large and boisterous man was getting demonstrative and red in the face as he spoke, hands gesturing almost wildly. He had personally orchestrated almost every facet of the convention from the length of each speaker's speech to the color and number of balloons that would fall when the Democratic party nominee finished his speech. He was absolutely determined that the nomination of the Democratic candidate would be executed perfectly.

"Look, you guys always exaggerate these threats every time we do one of these things. Personally I think it's some kind of stupid governmental conspiracy to perpetuate yourselves. Either that or it's just the Administration trying one more time to push us off the front pages." He stood up and angrily pushed his chair back against the wall with his legs and stood hovering over the two FBI agents, hands on his hips.

Gordon Lewis responded calmly but very deliberately.

"Mr. Westly, I can assure you we have absolutely no political bent here. We are simply trying to make you understand the nature of the threat we believe is potentially imminent. I would not be doing my job if I did not inform you that I strongly believe that we need to substantially increase the security for the convention."

The chairman of the DNC began to speak but the mayor cut him off. The youngest mayor in the City's history, he had achieved enormous wealth selling an internet based business in the late 1990's, and despite many peoples' reservations about him, had established himself as a popular and effective city leader.

"Mr. Lewis, I understand the kind of pressure you and your team are under and I appreciate your candor with us regarding this potential threat, but what you are asking me to do by shutting down Market Street during the convention is just not practical. Market Street is the principal thoroughfare through the heart of the city. The convention kicks off every day at three o'clock in afternoon so the important speeches coincide with prime time on the east coast. If we shut down Market Street and expand the cordon around the Moscone Center as you suggest, the City will cease to function."

Gordon started to respond but the mayor stopped him with a wave of his hand.

"And if we do push back the cordon around the Moscone Center, all the protest groups that have promised to remain peaceful in exchange for our agreement to allow them to congregate within an audible distance of the convention center will come unglued. You know what this city is like. We have anarchists, pro-lifers, pro-choice advocates, environmentalists, anti-globalization fanatics, hell I can't keep up with all the groups outside the convention center demanding to be heard."

The four men said nothing for a moment and then Gordon Lewis turned to Lance Jessep. "Lance, will you please bring Agent Jennings and Mr. Kosnar here."

Jessep quickly left the room and the three men remained silent, Richard Westly leaning his large frame against the wall, a look of disdain on his face.

A few minutes later Casey Jennings stepped through the open doorway quickly followed by Vladimir Kosnar and Lance Jessep.

Gordon Lewis made quick introductions. "This is Special Agent Casey Jennings and Vladimir Kosnar-"

Richard Westly cut him off before he could finish.

"Casey Jennings," he said as he came around the conference table with a huge smile on his face, his hand extended to shake her hand. "I read all about your exploits in Afghanistan. It's a real honor to meet a true American hero-"

Gordon Lewis, loud and insistent, cut him off. "We don't have time for this now. Mr. Westly, will you please sit down and listen to what these people have to say."

Westly glared at Gordon Lewis but grudgingly returned to his seat.

"Now as I was saying, Mr. Kosnar is a former Colonel in the Soviet and Russian security service. He knows a great deal about Mr. Abd Al Rahman. He personally chased him down and caught him during the Soviet occupation of Afghanistan. As I am sure you are both aware, Ms. Jennings and Mr. Kosnar were almost the victims of one of his attacks a few days ago in London that killed an FBI agent." He glanced at both the politicians before turning to face the Russian who had taken a seat beside him at the table.

"Mr. Kosnar, can you please provide some insight to Abd Al Rahman so these two gentlemen will understand the nature of the threat we are dealing with."

Vladimir sat silently for a moment as if he were collecting his thoughts. Then he leaned forward resting his forearms on the table as he began to speak, his voice was monotone, but his words were clear and distinct.

"At some point in the late 1980's the Mujihadin acquired some very high powered sniper rifles. They infiltrated Kabul, the capital of Afghanistan and began to methodically start shooting Soviet officers on the street, in their cars and eventually in their homes and barracks. It got so bad we had to brick up the windows in the embassy and officer's compounds to protect them. We lost a lot of people including some senior officers, but after a few weeks, the sniping stopped and things settled down."

He paused and looked at the men opposite him before continuing.

"The Soviet embassy in Kabul was the most secure building in the city. It had double blast walls, wire netting to catch mortars and a huge security team surrounding it at all times, something like the secure green zone today in Baghdad. Senior civilian and military officers lived at the embassy with their families and some never left. There was a school and outdoor playground for the children." He fixed his eyes at the mayor and held his gaze as he continued speaking.

"Al Rahman discovered a vulnerability to the compound. From a high point in the city, on the roof of a private house, the door leading to the children's playground was exposed. He set up a sniper team and for days they watched the buildings, learning the typical schedule of the school. Finally one morning as the children came out to play, they waited until the last child came out holding the teacher's hand and shot them both. Then as the other children tried to run back in to the building they cut them down as well."

"Oh my God," the mayor said as he slumped back in his chair, his face drained of color.

Kosnar continued speaking. "As security guards rushed in to the playground the snipers held their fire waiting for the children's parents, mostly mothers rushing to get their children."

He paused before he continued. "They shot four mothers, two embassy officials and nine children."

The room was silent as his words hung heavily in the air. Casey glanced at the mayor and she thought the man had visibly aged since she had entered the room. He seemed to be having trouble breathing. Even the head of the DNC seemed deflated.

Kosnar continued. "Later on we learned there were actually four snipers on the roof, but at the last minute one of them seemed to have a crisis of conscience and refused to fire at the children. Al Rahman dismissed him and the man eventually returned to his village. Six weeks later, Al Rahman showed up at the village with a truck full of Mujihadin and took the man, his two wives and all their children away. They drove them to a cliff and one by one, threw each child off the cliff, followed by their mothers. The man they left standing on the –"

"Stop, no more please," the mayor shouted out as he leaned forward on to the table and buried his head in his arms. He remained like that for almost a minute before he looked up and Casey could see his eyes were red and he was fighting to keep his composure.

"Please," he said. "no more.. no more."

"Well, you don't really think that can happen here do you? I mean I just find this story incredible," Richard Westly remarked, his voice less forceful than his earlier comments.

The mayor jumped up pushing his seat away from the table so hard it crashed in to the wall behind him.

"Dick, just shut up," he shouted waving a dismissive hand at the head of the DNC.

"But you don't really think-"

The mayor turned on him, his face red.

"Shut the fuck up. You just shut up." He took a deep breath before he continued, his voice getting softer as he gained control of his emotions. "I am the mayor of this city and I am responsible for the safety of its citizens and visitors."

He paused to collect himself and then turned to the Special Agent in Charge.

"Mr. Lewis, I am very certain you have the best interests of our city at heart and I do appreciate your candor in this matter. We are going to do everything within reason you suggest. Now, I cannot shut down Market Street for three days but I am authorizing you to expand the cordon around the Moscone Center by another one hundred yards. I will also immediately contact the governor and ask him for additional resources, state police and CHP to help us maintain security and if there is an attack, to maintain order."

Gordon Lewis nodded at the mayor. "Thank you sir, I appreciate your cooperation."

"No Mr. Lewis, I appreciate what you and your team are doing to protect us. I know you are doing your best. Now if you will all excuse me, I am going to find the nearest bathroom and throw up."

CHAPTER 27

"**L**OOK, IT SEEMS to me we are just playing defense here, waiting for something to happen."

Gordon Lewis was sitting in a small conference at the FBI building in San Francisco leaning forward in his seat so his face was close to the speaker phone in front of him. Seated next to him, Lance Jessep, Special Agent in Charge of the San Francisco office was leaning forward in his chair, his eyes focused on Lewis. This was the most senior meeting, or at least conference call, Jessep had ever participated in and he wanted to make sure he missed nothing. On the call was the head of Homeland Security, the President's National Security Advisor and the Director of the FBI.

"Well, what are you proposing Gordon?" his boss asked, his strong southern accent identifying his voice.

"Sir, I think we need to flush him out. If Al Rahman's target is in fact the convention, then he must be here somewhere in the bay area. My guess would be that he is not in San Francisco because all the hotels are completely sold out because of the convention, so he is probably staying either in the South Bay or East Bay somewhere. There are hundreds of hotels and motels available in those two areas and they also have the good transportation to the City."

He glanced over at Jessep before he continued.

"My recommendation is twofold. One, we immediately contact every police and sheriffs department in a fifty mile radius of San Francisco and have them deploy officers publicly at transportation hubs, particularly the subway system. We distribute the pictures of all the women Kosnar gave us and we have them actively look out for these women."

He paused again to see if there was a question and then continued.

"Second, I would like to bring in agents from every field office we have in the West to help search for Al Rahman. We'll set up a task force and put them on the street wearing FBI jackets and have them check every hotel in the same fifty mile radius. Somebody must have seen this man –."

He was interrupted by the Director.

"How many agents are you talking about Gordon?"

"Well sir, we think about five hundred will probably be enough." He glanced over at Jessep as he said the number expecting a strong response. He was not disappointed.

"Five hundred! Are you kidding Gordon?" The Director's voice boomed back through the speaker. "That would basically empty every FBI office between San Francisco and Utah?"

Another man's voice came on the line, Bob Taylor, the Presidents National Security Advisor.

"You do realize this is not the only potential terrorist threat we are dealing with right now. By my last count there were approximately fifty other substantial threats under investigation. Doing what you are asking will effectively reduce those efforts to nothing while everything is focused on San Francisco. Do you really think that is wise and really necessary?"

Gordon Lewis hesitated for a moment before he answered.

"Mr. Taylor, I understand what I am recommending is a massive undertaking with many cascading repercussions, but I have spent some of the last two days with the Russian, Mr. Kosnar, and if what he has told us about Abd Al Rahman is even half right we are dealing with a deadly and potentially massive threat. This man is a stone cold killer who, if he really is here in the US and we are certain he is, will not stop, will never stop until he has carried out a deadly terrorist attack. He has the means to kill upwards of hundreds of people and create massive panic in San Francisco, a city hemmed in on three sides by water with limited exit routes. If panic does take over the City, hundreds might die just in the chaos. And if we don't find Al Rahman now and he gets away, he will find other ways to strike. And he will never ever stop. If we miss him here, assuming this is his target, he will keep attacking and killing until we find him."

His words hung in the air and there was silence from the speaker for a few moments.

The Director's voice came through. "OK, listen up. We are going to call you back within the hour with our decision." The speaker phone clicked as it was disconnected.

Gordon Lewis slumped back in his chair and looked over Lance Jessep. "What's your guess Lance? Do you think they'll do it? Do you think they really understand what we are dealing with here?"

Jessep nodded for a moment. "I think so," he replied. "You were pretty convincing."

The two men chatted for a few more minutes and then the phone on the conference table rang. Jessep reached for it and answered. After a very brief exchange of pleasantries, he handed the phone to Gordon Lewis.

"It's the Director for you Gordon," he said.

"Yes, Sir," Lewis said into the mouthpiece.

He said nothing while he listened for about a minute and then he said yes one more time and hung up the phone.

"Well," said Jessep staring at him expectedly.

Lewis sighed. "OK, we got them. Five hundred agents will be directed here starting now. We have to take care of all their logistics when they get here."

He stood up. "Come on," he said wearily, "we have a lot of work to do."

CHAPTER 28

FLUENT IN GERMAN from her athletic training in East Germany, and comfortable in English, Natasha Mislov's athletic body, fair skin, blue eyes and blond hair made her a natural choice for a California assignment. Adding to her capabilities was a talent for mathematics and she had actually considered a degree in engineering while recovering from hip surgery. She never quite understood what had happened to her hip just before the Soviet Olympic trials, but she was so grateful to be walking normally again and without pain, she had put her athletic career out of her mind. The engineering option also went by the wayside when she was notified to appear at KGB headquarters in Moscow.

Arriving at the infamous building with some trepidation, she was glad to find out that rather than being in trouble, she had been selected to join the KGB and would be trained as a foreign operative. Natasha considered the opportunity to serve her country a great honor, and the idea of secret overseas spy mission excited her more than she wanted to admit. Soon after completing her physical rehabilitation, she entered into the KGB training program.

Her cover in California was of a German student studying abroad. She spent nine months being trained at Moscow University on the intricacies of microchip design and had enough superficial knowledge to convince most of the young computer designers and scientists she met that she was studying electrical engineering. One major benefit in her favor, as she sought to make contacts in the bars, coffee shops and clubs frequented by the technical elite in Palo Alto and San Jose, was that there were so few women in the computer business at that time. She was very unusual, a situation she exploited with her good looks.

Her handlers back in Moscow, operating through her local controllers in California, put enormous pressure on her to deliver. At that time they were most interested in acquiring the design of the high-end graphical engineering workstations being used for Computer Aided Design, known as CAD. There were three major developers of these systems operating in the Bay Area, any of which could be used to design highly sophisticated weapon systems. The sale of these computers to foreign companies was restricted, and by the time the Russians acquired a few, they were already outdated. The idea was that if they could get access to actual chip designs, they could build their own systems and leapfrog the American's technical advantage.

After three months of networking, Natasha's break came at the huge computer exposition held each year in Las Vegas. Tens of thousands of software and hardware engineers gathered in Las Vegas to see the latest products and to brainstorm new ideas and concepts. A highly intelligent group, they tended to keep away from the gaming tables, entertaining themselves instead with lavish parties and trips to the nudie bars on the Vegas strip. It was at one of these parties Natasha met and seduced a young engineer employed at BRSV Graphics, one of the top three CAD systems companies. She had been following him for several weeks after inadvertently discovering he was a senior chip designer.

His name was Dr. Walter Walker, and he was smitten by her. At thirty-three, he had a doctorate in physics, but had had only one real, albeit brief relationship before meeting Natasha. He could not believe his good fortune. She was really cute, laughed at his jokes, and seemed really interested in his engineering work. After they quickly established a relationship, she gladly washed his greasy hair and cleaned up his expensive, but disorderly house. She helped him buy a new wardrobe and made him actually look quite dapper.

The best part was when he took her to the annual company picnic, which was held soon after they met. All the guys in his design team stood with their mouths agape as he and Natasha walked in holding hands. Natasha charmed them as well, but made sure she never left Walter alone or made him feel jealous for a moment. She was constantly aware of his emotional fragility and did not want to jeopardize her opportunity to drain him of detailed technical information.

He was more than willing and loved the fact she was really interested in his work. They would spend hours together going over the intricacies and specifications of new chips his team was working on. He began to bring home design blueprints to show her, on more than one occasion even took her into his office, all of which he knew was prohibited.

For five months, Natasha put up with Walter, his strange personality, his bizarre and weird predilections in bed. She felt like an actor, living a role rather than playing it, but it was working. Her first report on BRSV Graphics' new chip design reached Moscow about a month after she met Walter and she was given more specific instructions about information to gather and told to make information drops every week. Her handlers were elated and told her so. The praise and the success of her mission inspired her to continue the relationship, but after five months, he was becoming more than she could bear.

He began to take her for granted, ordering her about his house, which they now shared, and occasionally becoming verbally abusive. He worked tremendous hours, was under enormous pressure to deliver better and faster designs and finally he grew tired of her incessant questions. Finally, one day, he pushed her hard, knocking her to the ground. He did not scare her, and she felt more than able to take care of herself, but after the fall, her right hip began to hurt. She mentioned this in her last drop and quickly received a response that she was to leave immediately and make her way back to Moscow through the prearranged circuitous route.

Natasha was surprised to be recalled so soon. She had mixed feelings about leaving California. The people had seemed so nice, so free, with money and time for pleasures unknown to most Russians, but she was glad to be going home. She was tired of the stress of spying and playing the adoring girlfriend. Upon her arrival in Moscow on a flight from Germany, she was surprised to be met by an ambulance and rushed to the hospital. Her hip still hurt, but she did not believe she had suffered any major damage. She was X-rayed and examined repeatedly for a few days, then informed she would need surgery almost immediately. Her recovery took months but eventually the pain subsided and she got on with her with new assignments.

So many years later, Natasha was surprised when she was contacted and immediately scheduled to leave for Europe, so many years after her last and only foreign assignment. She had become used to her research job in the FSB, which changed little for her when the service was renamed and reorganized.

Since her quick departure to America on this new assignment, her stay had been mostly lonely. She was really excited when the caller gave her instructions to fly to San Francisco. She looked forward to seeing the beautiful bay area again, to visiting some of her old haunts. But now, as she lay on the bed in a modest motel room in downtown Oakland on the East Bay she was frustrated. For weeks, she waited for her cell phone to ring, changing motels every few days to avoid drawing too much attention as a long time resident, visiting the City and on one occasion even some of her old haunts.

That had been a mistake because she was sure someone had recognized her. She had been having a coffee in one of the numerous Starbucks in Palo Alto, a very upscale town located near Stanford University where she had spent a lot of time. The man had stared at her and tried to make eye contact but she kept looking away and finally left the coffee shop, taking a circuitous route back to her hotel just in case the man tried to follow her. From then on she kept to the East Bay, staying away from San Francisco and the South Bay.

Finally, the call came. The caller spoke in Russian but his accent sounded different from the man who had first called. He gave her detailed instructions which he made her repeat back to him twice in confirmation.

"Take the BART to San Francisco from the station nearest to her hotel, the Lake Merritt station and ride it all the way to the Montgomery Street station," he said. From there she was to walk to the corner of 4th and Howard and stand near the Carousel building. She was to remain in place until he called and altered her instructions. She was to wear comfortable clothes and an orange shirt.

Two hours later, Natasha Mislov stepped out of her hotel for the short walk to the Lake Merritt BART Station.

CHAPTER 29

S PECIAL AGENT ADAM Marks wiped his mouth, tossed the napkin onto the remains of his half eaten sandwich and sighed.

"You ready to get back to it?" he said to his colleague sitting opposite him in the brightly lit fast food restaurant.

Special Agent Michael Ginella nodded slowly in response. He was exhausted. In the last two days they had slept less than eight hours and the work was a grind. They had finally stopped in downtown Oakland in the early afternoon to take a break and grab a quick meal. Thirty six hours earlier, they had been working on a field assignment in Reno, their regular jurisdiction, when a call had come in from the Reno SAC instructing them to immediately go home, pack some clothes for a few days, specifically including their FBI windbreakers and drive to the San Francisco regional office for an emergency assignment.

As seasoned agents they were both used to unusual schedules and assignments, but it was orders like these that wreaked havoc on their family life. Agent Marks was working on his second marriage and his new bride was already complaining about his long work hours and erratic schedule.

Within two hours they were heading west on Interstate 80 to San Francisco. The SAC called them again with new instructions to head to the Holiday Inn Hotel in Walnut Creek where they were to spend the night. Marks tried to find out from him what was going on but all he was told was that hundreds of FBI agents were being sent to San Francisco from all over the Western United States on an emergency basis, but he had no idea why.

Marks and Ginella had arrived at the Holiday Inn to find a number of other agents checking in. There had been some grumbling about having to double up in rooms, but the hotel lacked sufficient rooms for all the agents checking in so they the ended up sharing.

They had finally gotten to bed around midnight and were woken up by a call just after five in the morning with instructions to meet in the lobby within one hour. When they had reached the lobby they were directed to a large conference room already almost filled with at least one hundred agents.

The presentation had begun almost immediately.

"Ladies and Gentlemen, my name is Lance Jessep and I am the Special Agent in Charge of the San Francisco regional office." He looked around the room as the noise died down and made sure he had everyone's attention.

"I know many of you have traveled a long way to get here and did not get much sleep last night, but I need you to pay very close attention to everything I have to say."

He paused and glanced around the room as his audience quickly quieted down.

"Five days ago as you all know, a colleague of ours, David Green was killed by an explosion at a restaurant in London." He reached down and uncapped the lens of the projector on the table in front of him and a large image popped up on the white screen behind him. The image was slightly indistinct, clearly taken from a video feed but the face was clear and recognizable.

"This man is Abd Al Rahman. It is believed he was either directly, or at a minimum, indirectly involved in Agent Green's murder."

He clicked the mouse pad on his computer and another similar image of the same man's face appeared on the screen.

"This picture was taken four days ago at passport control at San Francisco International Airport. This man's passport identified him as a French Citizen named Philippe Métier." Jessep clicked through a few more images of the same face.

"As you can clearly see, Métier and Abd Al Rahman are one and the same."

The presentation went on for another hour with Jessep providing detailed background information about Al Rahman, his past as a Mujihadin fighter in Afghanistan against the Soviets and his reputation as an absolutely ruthless killer, making sure all the agents understood the nature of the threat.

Finally, he paused again placing his hands on his hips as he looked around the room. "I have one more picture to show you and its not pleasant so be prepared."

A moment later the shattered body of Sasha Donitz filled the screen. There was an audible gasp in the room.

"This woman," said Jessep, "was carrying the bomb that killed Agent Green. Now, the British police have managed to keep this information suppressed from the public at least for now, but the bomb was not in her handbag or wrapped around her body in a typical suicide bomb vest as the British press has speculated. This bomb was inside her body, encased in a titanium hip joint."

He held up his hand as the room erupted in quick exchanges of comments between the seated agents.

"Listen up. Listen please." The room quickly quieted down again as all eyes focused back on Jessep. "I am not going into deep background of how and why this device was installed in her body. However," he continued as he lifted up between his thumb and forefinger a set of five pages stapled at one corner, "these five sheets of paper each contain pictures of twenty women, all of whom we believe have been similarly armed and deployed here in the United States."

The room stayed silent as all agents remained focused on Jessep. "We believe Al Rahman's target is the Democratic National Convention starting tomorrow in San Francisco. We have no idea where Al Rahman is right now and as we speak I have agents checking every hotel, motel and B&B in San Francisco. However, we believe he is most likely in the East or South Bay somewhere, staying out of sight until he is ready to deploy and activate the women. Your job," he continued as he pointed his finger towards the crowed room, "is to flush him out, put him back on the streets and make him aware we are looking for him. Right now there are four other meetings just like this one going on around the Bay area and within about two hours, almost five hundred agents will be hunting for this man. You will operate in two man teams and you can expect to be working all day and into the night."

The meeting had wrapped up with folders containing numerous pictures of Al Rahman taken from the video surveillance tapes, being handed out to each team of agents. Each team was assigned a grid and tasked with checking every hotel in their assigned area at least twice to make sure that all the day and night clerks were shown pictures of Al Rahman and questioned about any suspicious guests.

Marks and Ginella had been assigned a grid in the East Bay including Oakland and parts of Berkeley. They had alternated between walking and driving between hotels and motels and so far had nothing to show for their efforts.

"Ok, so what's next?" Marks asked Ginella as the two stood up and walked out of the fast food restaurant.

"I think we can walk to the next one," Ginella replied as he scanned the list of hotels they had not yet covered. "It's called The Civic Center Lodge Motel and it looks like it's up the street here and around the corner."

The two agents shook off their lethargy and strode purposefully to the motel.

* * *

Abd Al Rahman stared at himself in the mirror. The reflection back was odd but yet somehow convincing.

He gently touched the full toupee covering his head and turned his face from side to side to see if his disguise was obvious.

He had made the decision a day earlier to change his appearance. If Kosnar had recognized him, the British police had most likely pulled his picture from one of the CCTV cameras and now his face would be easy to recognize. He had found the name of a wig store not far from the motel and had convinced the proprietor with a substantial cash over payment, to prepare and sell him a new wig that same day, a process that usually took about a week. The wig maker had shown him how to fit the wig and take care of it and when Al Rahman had declined to wear the wig out of the store, had placed it in a small square box.

Finally convinced his appearance had been sufficiently altered, Al Rahman gathered his cell phone, the bomb activation device, and a casual jacket and left his hotel room. He pulled the door shut behind him, checking once to make sure it was locked, and walked along the open passageway and down the stairs to the hotel parking lot. He glanced around and then, seeing only the old Indian man working in the front office, walked as quickly as he could with his awkward gait to the Lake Merritt Bart Station.

* * *

Agent Marks and Ginella walked through the mostly empty parking lot of The Civic Center Lodge Motel towards the small front office. Marks pushed open the door and held it as Ginella walked in past him.

A middle-aged dark skinned man who appeared to be Indian rose up from his chair behind the counter and welcomed the two agents.

"Good afternoon gentlemen," he said in a slightly sing song voice. "Are you looking for a room?"

"My name is Special Agent Adam Marks and this is Special Agent Michael Ginella," said Marks as he indicated to his partner with a toss of his head. "We are with the FBI and we are trying to find someone we believe might be checked into your motel."

The Indian's eyes widened with surprise.

"Do you have anyone registered here by the name of Philippe Métier?"

"Umm.. I don't think so," the Indian replied. "Let me check the roster." He ran his finger down a list of names and shook his head. "No. No-one by that name."

"Do you have any guests who paid with cash or travelers checks?" Marks asked.

The desk clerk said nothing for a moment and then answered in the affirmative. "We did have one gentleman check in two nights ago who paid in cash for the whole week. Not very common these days," he said with a quick laugh. "Everybody uses credit cards now, but cash is cash so we are happy to take it," he continued with a shrug of his shoulders.

"What did he look like, this gentleman?" Agent Ginella asked.

The Indian shrugged. "I don't know. I did not check him in. I work here during the day and then my son comes in the afternoon from Berkeley where he is studying to be a lawyer. He works here for a few hours so I can take a break and then my wife and my daughter take turns in the evening, but they are away in India visiting relatives so it's just me and my boy right now."

"Is this your establishment?" Marks asked.

"Yes, I bought it ten years ago and now my family runs it."

"So you have not seen this man, the one who paid cash?"

The Indian just shook his head in response.

"Do you have the registration card he signed when he checked in?"

The Indian picked up a small wire tray and placed it on the counter. He pulled out a small stack of about ten registration cards and carefully looked at each one before setting it back into the tray.

"Let's see," he said as he peered at the last card. "I think it is this one." He placed it on the counter and turned it around so the agents could look at it.

"Can you read that?" Marks said to Ginella as the two men looked at the card.

"Geez," Ginella responded. "Each line just looks like a scrawl. I don't think I can make out any of the letters."

"When people fill out these cards, don't you pay attention to what they write?"

The Indian shrugged. "Not really. As long as they initial next to the price, we don't really care what they write down. Collecting that information is just a…a… formality," he said as he struggled to find the right word.

"When will your son be back here?" Marks asked.

The Indian glanced at his watch. "He should be here soon because he promised me to come early today to help out because my wife is away."

The two agents glanced at each other but said nothing.

"Do you mind if we stay here and wait for him. We would like to ask him about this man who paid cash."

"Of course, of course. Wait, wait," he quickly exclaimed. "I think I see him coming now."

The two agents turned to look out to the parking lot and saw a young man with a helmet on his head riding a bicycle up to the office, hopping off just as he got to the door. He pushed the door open and wheeled the bike in looking up quizzically at the two men with FBI jackets standing in the small lobby.

"What's going on?" he asked in clear unaccented English as he unclipped the helmet and pulled it off his head.

"These two men are from the FBI," his father replied. "They are looking for someone and need your help."

A third year law student, the young man already had a natural instinct to be wary of police officers and federal agents. He wheeled his bicycle behind the counter and carefully propped it against the wall. Then he slipped a small backpack off his back and dropped it onto a near by chair. He stepped behind the counter and looked at the two FBI agents.

"Gentlemen, what can I do for you?" he asked.

Marks identified himself and Ginella to the young Indian who responded by extending his hand and identifying himself.

"My name is Bhim Naidu and my father's name is Chadran. Now, how can we help you?"

"Your father says you checked in a gentleman two nights ago who paid in cash for the whole week?"

The son nodded but did not say anything.

"Is this his registration card?" Ginella asked as he turned the card around to face the young man.

"Yeah, I think so but it looks pretty illegible. We don't really pay much attention to those things."

"So we understand. If you saw a picture of him would you recognize him?"

"I guess," the young man replied. "We have a lot of people come through here but I might recognize him."

Ginella placed two pictures of Abd Al Rahman on the counter facing the young man. Bhim picked one of them up and stared at it for a few moments and nodded his head.

"Yeah, this is the guy. I am pretty sure it was him."

"Are you sure about this? Marks asked. "As you say, you get a lot of people through this place."

"No, I am pretty sure. This is the guy."

There was silence for a moment as two agents glanced at each other.

"What room number is he in?" Marks asked as his partner moved towards the door and scanned the parking lot.

"Uh...let me see....he is in room 203, on the other side of the parking lot on the second floor."

"So we can't see his room from here?" Marks asked.

"No. His room is on the other side. You have to walk through the passage way over there to see him."

Agent Ginella was holding the door open as he kept glancing around the parking lot. "Did you happen to notice anything unusual about his hands?" Marks asked.

The young man slowly shook his head. "Nope, I don't think so. I was pretty distracted that night studying for an exam so I checked him in pretty quickly and just gave him his key. I have not seen him since then."

"Did he have a car? Do you see it in the parking lot?"

"No, I am pretty sure he came here on foot. I don't think he drove here."

The two agents stepped out of the office for a minute and then Agent Ginella walked through the passageway and disappeared from view. Agent Marks came back into the office and looking at the younger man said, "I want you to call his room and ask him if the maid service was satisfactory. Can you do that? Just ask him if the room has been made up already."

The father and son exchanged looks as the younger man reached for the phone. He dialed the room number and held the phone to his ear. The phone rang six times before he replaced the handset.

"I don't think he is there."

"Let's wait about two minutes and then try again."

The three men stood in silence as the time slowly passed until Agent Marks indicated for the young man to place the call. This time he let the phone ring at least ten times before he hung up.

Agent Ginella walked back to the office and beckoned to his colleague to join him outside. "The curtains are drawn shut in his room and the light appears to be off," he said as the door to the office closed behind Marks.

"Yeah, we just called his room twice and no-one picked up."

"OK, we better call this in right away," said Ginella. "We have a positive visual I.D and they are going to want know about it."

CHAPTER 30

A BD AL RAHMAN raised the hot cup of black coffee to his lips and sipped it slowly. Nothing about his demeanor as he sat at a small coffee table about one hundred yards from the Lake Merritt BART station indicated his state of vigilance. He had worked hard for two days to choreograph the placement of each woman in just the right location in San Francisco and now the plan was unfolding before him.

So far he had spotted eight of the women, three wearing orange shirts, two in blue shirts and one in red, who had already walked past him and into the BART station in the last hour. He did not know what they looked like but each one was wearing the colors he had assigned them and appeared to be of the right age and appearance as Devskoy had described them. He was waiting for one more in orange who he would follow to the City. The remaining women were approaching from different locations throughout the Bay Area, but it had been satisfying to see these eight do as instructed.

He glanced at his watch and looked up to see a woman in an orange shirt and knee length skirt cross the road near him and walk into the station. He watched her until she disappeared from view and then he stood up and followed her.

* * *

Officer Peter Pallard was bored. He had only been on duty since lunch, but hated this kind of assignment. It reminded him of guard duty during his Marine Corps service: standing around for hours and hours, with nothing to do to make the time go by. He did not even have his partner with him, admittedly not a great conversationalist, but at least it would have been easier if they were together.

Leaning up against a pole at the entrance to the Lake Merritt BART station, watching the occasional young coed go by, he reminisced about the previous year, his rookie year on the Oakland City Police Department, possibly the best of his young life. He had been named Rookie of the Year and received a special commendation from the mayor. Fifty stolen cars recovered in one year, his rookie year. Most cops wouldn't find that many in a lifetime but for him it had been easy. It had always been easy for him to quickly memorize things, even something he saw just once and briefly. His high school counselor told him he had a photographic memory and his friends in high school hated him for it. He would study for exams in the hallway outside the classroom, five minutes before the exams began, and still ace the test. It never helped much in Math and Science but it was great in all his social studies.

At roll call each morning before he and his partner set out on patrol, he would scan the list of license plates of stolen cars reported the day before and memorize the list. Then, as they were driving around Oakland, he would watch the cars and glance over at their license plates. He got his first one his first day out. After that he was racking up one a week, except for the day when he nabbed three, one still occupied by the thief.

Now, he was out of his patrol car again for another day stuck at the BART station for his shift. At the morning roll call the day before, there had been two FBI agents handing out pictures of women, some clear and in color, others in black and white. Apparently, these ladies were trouble, big trouble, enough to have every police department in the Bay Area on the look out for them, enough that the Oakland and other Bay Area police departments had been requested by the BART Police to provide additional resources. It was even decided to increase the density of officers on the street, so most officers were reassigned, one to a patrol car instead of two, the second officer being added to foot patrol or sent to guard transit points. But the weird part was that they were specifically ordered not to try and arrest the women. The FBI agent said it twice: "If you see any of these women, do not, I repeat, do not apprehend them. In fact do not make any sort of contact. Just call it in. That's all."

He sighed and adjusted his position against the post. He looked up and watched a couple of young college girls bounce down the stairs to the station. Oh, those light summer dresses. He smiled at the girls and they both smiled back. He caught himself blushing as they walked by.

A moment later, he noticed another woman walking towards the station. She was tall, slender, much older than a coed, but she had an attractive, athletic body. She was wearing a patterned skirt and an orange shirt and as his eyes ran up and down her, he caught himself thinking about what she must look like naked. She was about ten feet away as his eyes left her breasts and sought out her face, trying to make out if she was pretty.

It took a second for it to sink in. Her face was older than he expected, still very pretty, but more lined. But the photograph he had seen that morning, my God, she looked like one of the women the FBI was after. It was her, he knew it was her. He stared, mouth open, and heart pounding.

She walked by him and he stood there for a second, not sure what to do. He started to approach her, and then backed off slightly, remembering the instructions not to make contact.

Wait a second, he thought, this lady can't be a terror-ist or something. No fucking way. But the face. *It's her. It's fucking her!*

He was about twenty feet behind her now, follow-ing her as she walked. As he entered the big glass dome above the station entrance, he keyed the microphone to his two-way radio.

* * *

Abd Al Rahman watched with alarm as the policeman turned and followed the woman in the orange shirt into the station. He stopped and glanced around to make sure no one was following him and he briefly thought about leaving but, reassured his own identity had not been compromised, he followed the policeman into the station to see why he was following the woman. It seemed impossible he had somehow recognized her but Al Rahman had a clear view of his face when he had seen her and by his expression, he had clearly recognized her.

* * *

Special Agent Marks snapped shut his cell phone and turned to his colleague, Special Agent Ginella. "That was Jessep," he said, referring to the Special Agent in Charge of the San Francisco FBI office. "He said they are working fifteen other positive IDs on Al Rahman and he needs more confirmation."

"What's he want us to do?" Ginella asked.

"He wants us to do a quick check of the guy's room to try and find anything confirming his identity."

"OK, I'll go wait by the room and you get what's his name... Bhim to come up and unlock the door."

A few minutes later the two FBI agents and the young Indian were standing outside room 203 on the second floor of the motel. Both agents were standing to the right of the door and had their weapons drawn. Agent Ginella nodded to the young man and with his left hand simulated a knock on the door. Bhim glanced at him and then nervously stepped forward and rapped on the door three times.

A few seconds passed and Ginella indicated for him to knock again, and again, there was no response.

"Ok," he said, "open it and then step away. As soon as we go in you go right back to the office and wait for us there."

Bhim nodded vigorously and leaned forward to unlock the door. His hands were shaking slightly but within a few seconds the lock opened and he pushed the door open. Agent Ginella quickly stepped forward and pushed Bhim out of the doorway as he entered the room, his weapon pointed directly in front of him. The room was dark and it took a second for his eyes to adjust but he quickly confirmed the room was empty.

Agent Marks followed him in, closing the door behind him as he holstered his weapon. The two agents quickly began to search the room. They checked every drawer, every article of clothing, under the bed and small suitcase in the closet and found nothing. No receipts, plane tickets or even a luggage tag on the suitcase.

"Place looks almost sanitized doesn't it?" said Marks.

"I don't keep my room this clean when I travel," Ginella responded.

His partner laughed. "I know. I roomed with you for the last two nights."

Ginella said nothing for a moment as he stood in front of the small closet. The closet was dark and he bent down as he stepped inside and looked around making sure he had not missed anything. A small box in the far corner on the floor caught his eye. Reaching down he picked it up and brought it out into the light.

"What did you find?" his partner asked.

"It looks like a wig storage box," he replied pointing at the label on the front of the box. The label listed the name of the store, its address and phone number.

"That address is not far from here. I wonder if this guy has purchased himself a disguise."

The two agents exchanged a glance and then Marks quickly jotted down the particulars of the wig store. They replaced the box and, after one more quick sweep of the room, they stepped out and locked the door behind them.

* * *

Officer Peter Pallard knew his radio would not work so he tried repeatedly to call in to dispatch on his cell phone as he followed the woman down the long escalator into the BART station, but the signal was weak in the subterranean station and he could not get through. He stopped trying, and, as nonchalantly as possible, followed his target through the turnstile. She chose the westbound platform, servicing trains to San Francisco.

Noticing a pay phone on the platform he quickly walked up to it, dialed the emergency number, and, as the dispatcher answered, identified himself and told her whom he had seen. She asked a couple of questions and then put him on hold. A moment later a new voice came over the phone.

"Pallard, is that you?"

Pallard immediately recognized the voice of the Chief of Police.

"Yes, Sir, it's me," he said in a low voice, alternately turning towards the phone and casting glances over at the tall woman. "I'm at the Lake Merritt BART station Chief -."

"I know where you're at, Pallard," said the Chief, cutting him off. "Quickly, tell me what you saw."

"One of the women they were looking for at roll call yesterday morning, Chief. She's right here." His was trying to keep his voice low, cupping the mouthpiece with his hand.

They showed us about one hundred pictures," the chief responded, with some incredulity in his tone. Do you really thing you recognized one of them?"

"Ah.., yes Sir. I'd say I'm pretty sure."

"Pallard," said the Chief loudly. "Give me a straight answer. Is it her or not?"

Pallard stole a quick glance at the woman again, trying desperately to match her face to the photograph he had seen the day before. He could feel his heart pounding, and his hand was clammy as he gripped the receiver. He took a deep breath and spoke more firmly into the phone.

"Chief, as best as I can tell, it's her. She is one of the women we were shown at roll call yesterday morning."

"OK, stay on the line, Pallard. Don't go away."

Pallard turned to look back toward the woman. At first he panicked when he did not immediately see her, but then he noticed her studying the map of the BART system.

"The next train to San Francisco will be arriving in two minutes, two minutes for the next train to San Francisco," a dull metallic voice intoned over the loud speaker.

"Oh, shit," said Pallard out loud. "Hello, hello," he said quickly into the phone, but there was no response. The Chief had put him on hold.

"Shit, shit, shit," he repeated under his breath. He could see people on the platform gathering themselves, getting ready for the train's arrival. He pressed the phone to his ear again, hoping to hear from someone, anyone on what to do.

"The next train to San Francisco will be arriving in one minute. One minute for the next train to San Francisco," the voice on the loudspeaker intoned again.

Pallard hung up the phone and quickly dialed the emergency number again. He got a different dispatcher this time. Quickly he identified himself and asked to be patched through to the Chief.

"Why do you need the Chief?" the dispatcher responded.

"Come on, please, it's urgent. I was just talking to him a minute ago." He felt a blast of wind strike his back as the train rolled into the station.

"The Chief's line is busy. Please hold."

"No, no..." Pallard begged, but she was gone. There was silence on the phone. He looked back and saw the woman board the train. The platform was clearing. Almost everybody had boarded. A beeping noise sounded across the platform signaling the doors were about to close. Pressing his ear to the phone one more time, Pallard listened to the silence, hung up the phone, and ran towards the train, quickly stepping into the same car as his target.

Further down the platform, the doors were closing as Al Rahman forced them back open and pushed his way into the car directly behind the one Officer Pallard had just jumped into. The train began to pull out of the station.

* * *

"What do you have?" Gordon Lewis asked as he responded to the urgent summons from Lance Jessep. They were standing in the hastily arranged command center that had been setup in the largest conference room available in the San Francisco FBI office. The room was warm and noisy with about twenty agents alternately clicking away at computers or talking on the phone as they worked to coordinate and collect information from all the extra agents that had been put in the field to hunt for Abd Al Rahman.

Jessep quickly relayed the information about the confirmation of Al Rahman in the motel in downtown Oakland.

"I instructed the onsite agents to search the room to try and confirm the ID and they found a box from a wig store," Jessep replied as pushed the key on a speaker phone next to him.

"Marks, are you there?" he said as he directed his voice towards the speaker phone.

"Yes Sir," Marks replied over the speaker.

"I have Gordon Lewis, the EAD for intelligence and counter intelligence with me. I want to you to tell him what you just told me."

"Yes, Sir. Well, as I told you we got a visual ID from the night clerk at the motel on Al Rahman but he did not see the man's hands or see his limp so we weren't sure of the ID. However, after we entered his room we found a box from a wig maker located here in Oakland and we just talked to him and told us he sold a full hairpiece to a man yesterday who demanded the wig on the same day and paid in cash."

"Did he ID the picture?" Lewis asked.

"Well sir, we haven't shown him the picture yet because we are both still at the motel, but I spoke with him and he absolutely confirmed that the man who bought the wig was missing all the fingers on his right hand. He said it was an issue because the man struggled to attach the wig with only one good hand."

"Holy crap!" Lewis exclaimed glancing at Lance Jessep. "That's confirmed." He turned back to face the speaker phone.

"You stay there at the motel but get out of sight. If Al Rahman comes back and sees you he will run and we'll be back to square one. We're going get you some help to setup an around clock stakeout on the motel. Do you understand?"

"Yes Sir," Marks responded.

"Good job Marks. Now let's hope we find the bastard."

He turned back to face the San Francisco SAC when he was interrupted by a shout from one of the agents across the room. He was standing, holding the phone to his chest.

"Mr. Jessep," he yelled across the hum in the room. "There is an urgent call for you from the Oakland Chief of Police. He is demanding to speak to the SAC right away."

Jessep and Lewis exchanged glances.

"Did he say what it was about?" Jessep shouted back, anticipating a complaint about jurisdictional issues with so many FBI agents in Oakland.

The agent placed the phone to his ear again and engaged in a brief conversation before turning back to the SAC. "He claims one of his officers just saw one of the women we are looking for at the Lake Merritt station in downtown Oakland."

CHAPTER 31

"QUIET! EVERYBODY BE quiet." Lance Jessep, SAC of the San Francisco office was standing next to Gordon Lewis in the makeshift command center. The urgency in his voice got everybody's attention and the room quickly quieted down. Only the low hiss and squawk of the police monitors filled the void. All the faces in the room turned to look at the two senior agents.

"This is Lance Jessep," he said into the phone. He listened for a moment then hit the speaker button on the desk in front of him. As he replaced the handset, the Oakland Chief of Police's voice filled the room.

"- saw the woman at the Lake Merritt station about ten minutes ago. She was waiting on the platform for a westbound train."

"Where's your man now, Chief?" asked Gordon.

"I put him on hold in order to contact you, but he's not responding. I have officers on their way to the station right now."

"What's their ETA at the station, Chief?"

"Just a moment." The sound of background murmurs filled the room as they could hear the Chief checking on his men.

The Chief's voice came back.   "They've arrived. They're there now."

There were more sounds of muffled voices and murmurs in the background. Then the Chief's voice returned, carrying a lot more tension this time.

"Apparently he boarded the train."

"Who boarded the train?"

"Pallard, Officer Pallard. He was seen boarding the train."

There was a brief moment of silence as both men contemplated the situation.

Lewis glanced over at Jessep, then back at the speaker.

"Chief, how far is the Lake Merritt station from the uh…" he glanced over at Jessep and asked, "where was Marks calling from?"

"The Civic Center Lodge Motel," Jessep replied. He repeated it louder into the speakerphone.

"Uh… just a couple of blocks," the Chief replied. "Why, what's at the motel."

Gordon Lewis stared at his colleague and said in a low voice that did not carry to the speakerphone. "Jesus, Al Rahman could be on that train. We've got to stop that train."

"Where's the train heading?" he asked in a louder voice. "Can your men stop it at the next station?"

"I don't think so," the Chief responded. Background murmurs again came out of the speakerphone as the Chief turned to get more information.

"Look," said the Chief, "there is only one stop before that train goes under the bay to San Francisco. My guess is it has already passed the West Oakland Station by now so we are probably too late to stop it." He paused. "It looks like it's coming your way."

As Gordon Lewis stared down at the map for a moment, Lance Jessep leaned over and drew a large X, glancing over at Lewis.

"It's the Embarcadero station," said Jessep. "The first stop from the East Bay in San Francisco is the Embarcadero."

"All right, Chief," said Gordon, looking back at the speakerphone, "thanks for your help."

Lance Jessep leaned forward and clicked the speaker phone button and disconnected. Then, looking at a list of emergency numbers, he quickly dialed the BART Operations and Control Center. The phone rang three times before the call was picked up.

"BART OCC."

"This is Gordon Lewis," he announced into the phone, calmly and clearly. "I am the FBI's Assistant Director for Domestic Terrorism." Experience had taught him that titles count. His usually got people's attention. "With whom am I speaking, please?"

"This is Jeremy Brown," a nasally voice responded.

"Jeremy, are you the supervisor over there."

"No, just a sec." They could hear mumblings in the background.

"Uh, this is Gus Collins, shift manager at the BART OCC."

Lewis repeated his title and continued without pausing. "Mr. Collins, you have a train heading to San Francisco from the uh... Lake Merritt station. I need that train stopped and stopped immediately so we can detain some of the passengers. Can you do that for me right away please." As Gordon finished, he cocked his head to the side, listening for the response.

There was a long pause and Gordon almost asked the question again, but as he leaned forward, Collins spoke up.

"Yes, I can stop your train. It will be at the Embarcadero station in about four minutes. We can stop it there."

"No!" Gordon responded emphatically. "I need you to stop it before it gets to San Francisco."

There was another pause before Gus Collins spoke up again. "I'm afraid it's too late Mr. Lewis. The train just went under the bay, about thirty seconds ago. Unless you know something I don't, I have absolutely no intention of stopping that train while it's under the Bay. We will stop it at the Embarcadero. You can meet it there."

CHAPTER 32

AT ITS DEEPEST point, the Transbay Tube, which runs from Oakland to San Francisco, is one hundred and thirty feet below the bottom of the Bay. It consists of fifty-seven binocular-shaped sections of steel and reinforced concrete, each about three hundred and fifty feet long by forty-eight feet wide by twenty-four feet high. Constructed by the Bethlehem Steel Company, at three and six tenths of a mile, and six miles overall including approaches, at the time of its construction it was the largest underwater transit tube in the world.

Natasha Mislov was not aware of the moment the train began the quick subterranean portion of its journey. The decent underground was so gradual it was imperceptible and as she sat in the middle of the car in one of the four chairs that faced inward, she was paying too much attention to the policeman at the end of the car who was stealing quick and furtive glances at her to really care about the precise location of the train.

She had seen the policeman almost as soon as he followed her into the station, then watched him board the train at the last moment. Now he was in the doorway at the end of car as far away from her as he could be, but looking at her. She was very uncomfortable. She had not played the role of *femme fatale* for almost ten years and was not quite sure what to do. Her training and professionalism helped her maintain an aura of disinterest, similar to the few other passengers in the car, but internally she was churning. The policeman had obviously recognized her, but why? What had she done to get his attention? She had committed no crime and had not even received a target from her handler. In all her previous assignments, she had never been followed or tailed, at least that she knew of. There was something really strange going on and she did not like it.

* * *

Officer Pallard held on to one of the four shiny metal poles framing the doorway at the end of the rail car. He tried to act as nonchalant as possible, not wanting the woman to notice him, but in spite of himself he kept stealing glances at her. She did not appear to notice, although once she did catch him looking at her. He thought about putting his sunglasses back on, but realized that would look pretty silly in a subway.

He fiddled with his cell phone, partly to distract himself, but also because he hoped it would work as soon as the train arrived in San Francisco. At some point the woman would get off the train and he would have to follow her to maintain contact.

Oh shit he thought. *I hope I haven't fucked this up.* He wiped his brow and ran his hand through his short hair. Leaving his post and following the woman onto the train meant leaving the Oakland jurisdiction. If he'd followed the wrong woman, the Chief would eat him for breakfast. He looked back at the woman. Even in profile, he was sure. *It's her. I know it's fucking her.* He straightened up, bracing against the rocking of the train as it slowed. We must be approaching the Embarcadero station, he thought as he glanced out of the window but saw only his reflection against the tunnel's dark background. He glanced over at the woman trying to see if she was getting ready to get off. His thoughts were interrupted by an announcement over the loud speaker.

"This train will be going out of service at the Embarcadero Station," the voice intoned. "All passengers will disembark at the Embarcadero." The announcer repeated his message.

"OK," Pallard thought to himself, "if she leaves the station, I'll follow her. I'll follow her until she gets above ground and then I'll try to call it in. If that doesn't work, I'll just find a BART policeman or a City cop and have them call it in. Just keep her in view, that's all I've got to do. *Just keep my distance and keep her in view.*"

* * *

The Embarcadero station was not Natasha Mislov's scheduled stop. She was supposed to get off at the next one, Union Station. That would put her in close walking distance to Moscone Center. However, she knew she needed get away from the policeman, or actually just confirm he was following her. If she got off the train at the Embarcadero, she had a lot further to walk to Moscone

Center, but it would allow more opportunity to get away from him. But now with the train going out of service, the decision had been made and perhaps to her advantage. With everyone getting off the train at the same station she would have a better chance of losing him in the crowd. She glanced back over at the policeman, catching him again as he quickly tried to avert his gaze. He was following her, she was certain of it.

* * *

"Lance," Gordon Lewis, his voice urgent, "we have to stop that train and check everyone on board. We might have Al Rahman trapped right now."

"BART police might already be onsite. If we can get them to-." He was interrupted by a young agent yelling his name.

"Mr. Jessep, the Assistant Chief of the BART police is on the phone. She wants to know why you instructed BART OCC to stop the train at the Embarcadero."

Jessep quickly maneuvered through the crowded room and grabbed the receiver.

"This is Lance Jessep, Special Agent in Charge of the San Francisco FBI office." He did not wait for a response. "Please listen. I need you to close the Embarcadero Station right away. Can you do that?"

There was a brief pause before a women's voice responded.

"Yeah, I can but why?"

"Please, I can't explain it right now. Can you just give the order and dispatch officers there right now to close the station. This is really urgent."

There was another brief pause.

"OK Mr. Jessep. Stand by."

Jessep handed the phone back to the young agent and told him to stay on the line with the Assistant Chief then he turned to Gordon Lewis.

"Gordon, we've got to get down there right away. For all we know there could be ten of these women on the train. If we trap them all below ground and Al Rahman activates them we could have a lot of casualties down there."

"You're right," Lewis answered back quickly. "Grab a bunch of agents and let's get down there."

* * *

As the train slowed and pulled into the station, Natasha Mislov stayed in her seat, studying the reflection of the officer in the window. He was still watching her. He looked tense, nervous, ill at ease, as if unsure what to do. She casually disembarked, began to walk with the crowd along the platform. Out of the corner of her eye, she could see the young officer almost hop off the train as she stepped onto the platform.

By now she had no doubt. He was definitely following her. He was being so obvious, frantically trying to keep her in view. She saw his reflection in the train windows as his head bobbed up and down in the crowd behind her.

The trick now was to lose him either here in the station or on the way to Moscone Center. She began walking slowly along the platform toward the escalators. She took her time, stopping to look at a poster advertising a movie and glancing back at the policeman. He stopped as well, at first seeming a bit confused, and then he began to look around anxiously. As she stepped away from the poster, she saw him jog towards a pay phone and pick up the handset but when she stepped onto the escalator, he quickly replaced the handset without having made a call and followed her.

* * *

Abd Al Rahman watched the entire interaction between the nervous policeman and the woman in the orange shirt and decided it would be better to watch Mislov from outside the confines of the underground station. He hurried past her and walked as quickly as he could, pushing through the crowd up the escalator. As he stepped into the open, he saw a number of police officers running towards the station and he turned away from their direction, joining the crowd on the sidewalk. As he looked around for a convenient location to watch the station, more police began to arrive on foot and by car. As he turned, he was bumped by a young man in a suit who was breathing hard. The man grunted an apology as he ran past Al Rahman down the steps into the station, taking two steps in every stride. As Abd Al Rahman stared after him, two more men came running up and hurried down the steps into the station without breaking stride. Abd Al Rahman quickly moved away from the station entrance and found a good vantage point about thirty yards away. He glanced around furtively, anxious that Kosnar might also be around, but as he delicately touched the toupee, he reassured himself it was unlikely he would be identified. Things were obviously going to get interesting. He tensed slightly in anticipation.

CHAPTER 33

MOLLY ROBBINS WAS feeling dejected and somewhat irrelevant. This morning she had found out there were as many accredited journalists in town to report on the Democratic National Convention as delegates. Local TV reporters like her were unable to get to any of the major figures and the only stories they managed to report on were all fluff and nonsense. It was frustrating, so bad that last night her producer had her do a story on the other journalists. She and her cameraman, Sammy, had taken some great shots of a sweaty horde of reporters asking the same inane questions of some pontificating minor politician. They had put her segment in the middle of the late night news and that felt pretty good. Still, she wanted a real story, not this crap.

Now she and Sammy were in downtown San Francisco doing a 'man on the streets' piece, again for the evening news.

"Get me some Republican responses to the Democratic Convention," her producer had intoned. "Two minutes. I don't want to see you and Sammy back here until you've gotten me two good minutes."

So far they didn't have two good seconds. Finding a Republican in San Francisco was a bit like trying to find a gopher in your garden: you know they existed, but you had to look in just the right spot. After ten tries, they had struck out every time.

"Sammy, let's go over to the financial district," Molly said to her cameraman. "This area is too full of graphic artists, web page designers and other artsy folks. We need a couple of bankers who can rail against the liberals and give us something half decent for tonight."

Sammy smiled back at her, peering around the video camera hoisted on his shoulder. "OK, boss," he said. "Whatever you say."

Sammy was Molly's favorite cameraman. He was a small Filipino American with a big smile and an agreeable personality. Unlike the other cameramen she had to work with, he never complained about their assignments or having to carry the gear. He always just smiled at her and said "OK boss." Also, he never hit on her like the others, which also made him even more pleasant to be around.

"Come on," she said. "We can cross Market Street over here and then walk over to California Street. We're more likely to find a couple of Republicans there."

"Whoa, what's that all about?" she said as she and Sammy simultaneously noticed three big black but unmarked SUVs driving fast through traffic, swerving in and out of lanes and at one point, even driving on wrong side of the road. Suddenly, as traffic forced them to slow down, the doors of the first SUV, and then all of them, popped open and men and women jumped out and started running. Some were wearing suits and ties but a number were in casual clothes and windbreakers emblazed with the letters FBI on their backs.

Molly looked over at Sammy. "What do think?" she asked, her reporter's instinct surfacing.

"I don't know. It's the FBI. They must have some emergency on Market Street somewhere." He grinned. "Let's check it out."

"Ah, I don't know, Sammy. We haven't gotten shit yet for tonight."

"Don't worry," he said, still grinning. "We'll get something. Hey, maybe this will be better. Maybe we can get a scoop."

Molly eyed him balefully, torn by her assignment and the chance to film a breaking story. "OK, come on," she said. "Let's go take a look. It's probably nothing, though."

They quickly crossed the street and began to jog in the same direction the men were running. They were only about fifty yards behind them, and although they were not running as fast, it was still easy to keep them in sight. Molly was glad she had decided to wear slacks and her running shoes while doing an on-the-street assignment, a trick she had learned from a mentor a few years back. She glanced over at Sammy to make sure he was all right with the heavy camera on his shoulder.

"No problem," he said. "We'll catch them in a minute."

Molly looked ahead at the running men just as they began to dash down the entrance to the Embarcadero station.

"Shit," she thought to herself. "I hope we aren't chasing a bunch of guys late for a train."

Molly's fears were quickly put to rest. As she and Sammy jogged up to the entrance to the station, three BART police cars pulled up, sirens blazing. The cops quickly jumped out, most of them running directly into the station, one of them moving immediately to stop anyone else from entering or leaving. Sammy began filming and Molly stood behind him, directing him towards certain shots. She could hear more sirens as additional police cars roared up. Two more men in suits came running down the sidewalk towards the station. One of them was slightly older and out of breath. He stopped and talked briefly to the policeman guarding the entrance, and then he also disappeared down the stairs and out of view. Molly pulled out her cell phone and pressed the speed dial to her producer. Something was definitely going on at the Embarcadero Station and she was on site to report it.

* * *

Officer Peter Pallard decided it was time to act. He had no guidance or authority, but if this lady was as dangerous as the FBI claimed, it was his duty to stop her before she started walking around the streets of San Francisco. His heart was pounding in his chest as he jogged up past her, taking a wide berth as he ran around her. When he was about twenty feet past, he abruptly stopped, turned and faced her. He put his left hand up, palm facing directly towards her and placed his right hand on his gun without removing it from its holster.

"Stop!" he said loudly. "Stop right there!"

The woman looked at him, her face questioning and surprised. She slowed, but did not stop completely.

Pallard took two steps backward and then yelled "Stop," again, louder, more firmly. The woman stopped. Pallard could feel people staring at him and felt uncomfortable being so far from the woman. Normally, he would be in her face, quickly making sure she was not armed, and then equally quickly handcuffing her to ensure compliance. But now, he was at a loss.

"Uh...put the bag down at your feet. Yes you, I'm talking to you."

Natasha Mislov looked around trying to act as if she was unaware the policeman was talking to her.

"Put the bag down *now*!" Pallard shouted as he pulled his weapon from its holster and pointed it at her. The woman dropped the bag. "Now take two steps to your left away from the bag and keep your hands by your side. Do it!" He was shouting out the instructions over the noise of the station to make sure she could hear him. Again, she complied.

Just then, he heard a commotion behind him. He could hear running feet and shouting, but he kept his gaze firmly on the woman. Then he heard his name.

"Officer Pallard? Peter Pallard?"

Keeping his gun pointed at the woman, Pallard raised his left arm and waved it above his head. "Right here," he shouted, turning his head slightly and trying to project his voice behind him without actually turning around. Two men in suits skidded up next to him, both breathing heavily.

"Lance Jessep," said one of the men, between big gulps of air. "Lance Jessep," he repeated. "FBI."

He looked over at the woman and then back at Pallard.

"Is this her?" he asked as he gulped in air. "Is this the woman?"

"Yes, Sir," said Pallard, as he holstered his weapon, his heart skipping a beat as the thought crossed his mind he might be wrong.

Jessep stared at the woman, not recognizing her himself, but automatically assuming she was a suspect. That's how he was going to treat her until he was told differently. He took a clean white handkerchief out of his trouser pocket and began to wipe down his sweaty face as he looked around the station. It was mostly empty with only a few clearly confused Japanese tourists milling.

"Shit," he said out loud to no-one in particular, "where is everybody?"

As he turned around he could hear more people running up. Five BART policemen came running over. He swallowed hard, thinking briefly about his authority and jurisdiction, and then immediately put it out of his mind. He was dealing with an imminent threat requiring the deployment of all available resources. He put his hands up as the men came charging over, indicating to them to slow down.

"Lance Jessep, Special Agent in Charge, San Francisco," he said breathlessly. "Is the station closed?" Do you know if they closed the station?" he demanded, his eyes darting from officer to officer as he waited for an answer.

"Yeah, yeah, it's closed," one of the Officers replied. "We've got people at every exit. No-one is getting in or out."

"Good, good," he replied as he tried to quickly think through the best course of action.

"Listen, it looks like a lot of people got out of here before we were able to close the station. I want you to assemble everyone left in the station and place them uh... over there," he said as he pointed to a row of narrow seats. "Just have them gather over there. OK?"

As the BART policemen walked off, Jessep turned to Pallard and said, "Good work, son. Well done. Now, you can assist these officers in securing the station.

Pallard looked over at him. "Sir, I'm not sure I can do that. I'm just an Oakland police officer. I'm way outside my jurisdiction, Sir."

Jessep patted Pallard on the back. "Don't worry, son," he said. "With what you just did, I think you're entitled to work in any jurisdiction."

Pallard blinked quickly a couple times and smiled briefly. The tension suddenly ebbed from his body, relieved that someone else had taken over and was making all decisions.

"Yes, Sir," he said simply, and walked over to help the other officers.

* * *

Gordon Lewis arrived at the Embarcadero station just as BART Police Chief John Gonzalez was pulling up in his car. Gonzalez had been on his way to a meeting with the deputy Mayor to review security issues related to the Democratic Convention when he was called about the FBI's request to close the Embarcadero Station. He quickly changed his plans and drove to the station.

The two men introduced themselves as they jogged down the stairs into the station. In the middle of the station he could see two men in suits and about twenty feet away from them was a women standing alone and quite still, hands by her sides, a small bag on the ground a couple of feet away from her.

"All right,' he said looking over at Gordon Lewis. "It looks like we've averted disaster. The area appears secure."

Lewis glanced around at the mostly empty station, shaking his head and swearing under his breath. "We were hoping to catch someone on the train or in the station but it looks like most of the passengers left before we got here."

He paused before continuing. "We still have a big problem. If the ID the officer made is confirmed, we are still going to have a difficult time getting her out of here."

By now they had walked up to Lance Jessep and another agent keeping a close watch on the woman. Gordon Lewis made a quick introduction.

"I don't understand," said the Chief. "Why can't we have her disarm the bomb and then take her into custody?"

"Well, unfortunately it's not that simple. She's not even aware of the bomb, Chief. She doesn't even know she has it and even if she did know, she is unable to disarm it or even arm it for that matter."

"What do you mean-"

Gordon Lewis interrupted him. He did not have time now for long explanations. "It's a long story," he said. "Trust me on this. The bomb is controlled remotely. For all we know, the controller could be standing outside the station ready to arm the bomb at any time. We have to extricate her and take her to a safe and remote location where we can be sure the bomb cannot be activated. Then and only then can we allow someone to approach her and disarm it."

"Jesus H. Christ," said the Chief. "How the hell are we going to do that? If she is that dangerous, we can't even put her in a car and drive her. Hell, she could blow up and kill the driver!"

Lewis ran his hand through his thinning hair. He had not really thought about that. Until now he had just been concerned with stopping the woman before she could be killed and kill others. The Chief was right. Extricating this woman was going to be difficult and dangerous. He looked over at Lance Jessep.

"Anyone got any ideas?"

"Hey, why not put her back on to the BART and send her back to the East Bay?" Gonzalez asked. "It would probably be a lot less crowded in the East Bay than it is here in the City."

Gordon Lewis scratched his head as he considered his options. "That's not a bad idea," he said after reflecting for a moment, "but I'm not sure." He was quiet for a minute before he continued. "We'd have to clear every station between here and the station we pick as the final destination, which would basically shut down BART. She'd also have to travel alone in one train car while we rode in another and I don't like the idea of her being out of our direct custody." He grimaced as he continued. "Look, there are no good options, but I don't think going back to the East Bay is any more practical than extracting her right here and right now."

"Uh...well we know the lethal range of the bomb is about fifteen feet," Jessep replied. "If we can find some way to separate her from the driver in a large vehicle somehow, we can get her out of here."

"What do you mean? Put her in the back of a bus or something?" Lewis responded.

"How about we attach a police car to a tow truck and have her sit in the empty police car and have it towed to a safe place. That way she will be completely separated from the driver and will have no opportunity of approaching him," Lance responded.

"Good idea," said the Chief. "I can have a tow truck brought up. We can have it hooked up to a car and have her out of here pretty quickly.

"What then?" said Lance. "Once we have her secured, where do we take her?"

"The most secure place will probably be an army or air force base. Some place with a hospital sophisticated enough to perform surgery on her," Lewis replied.

"Surgery!" Chief Gonzalez exclaimed. "You mean the bomb is inside her, inside her body?"

Just then Gordon Lewis caught Natasha Mislov's gaze. John Ganzalez's exclamation had been almost shouted and his voice echoed through the empty station. He could tell the woman had heard exactly what the Chief had said. He held her gaze for a second and then looked away, unable to respond to the look of fear and confusion on her face. The Chief realized what he had done and became uncomfortable.

"I'll..uh…go and arrange for the tow truck," he mumbled. "We will have it outside for you and ready to go in about twenty minutes." He walked away quickly, anxious to distance himself from the uncomfortable group.

CHAPTER 34

MOLLY HAD TO give her producer credit. Within just a few minutes after calling to tell her what had happened, she was called back and told a mobile broadcasting van was on its way down to the Embarcadero station. Apparently the news studio had been monitoring the police radio traffic and Molly's producer had quickly determined she was onto a good story and instructed Molly to stand by to do a live broadcast.

As soon as the mobile van arrived, Molly and Sammy quickly set up in a location giving them clear view of the station entrance and surrounding area. The police had moved everybody well back from the entrance to the station, but they were still close enough to film whatever happened. Right now, that was nothing much, except more and more police were arriving. A large crowd was gathering outside the station, beginning to press the police's ability to contain them.

Molly was talking to her producer on the phone, trying to coordinate a live broadcast in the next few minutes. While they talked, Molly scribbled notes furiously in her notebook and then hung up.

"Sammy, you ready to go live?" she asked.

"Ready, Molly." he replied. By now he was wearing a set of headphones connecting him directly back to the local broadcast studio. "I'll cue you in as soon as they let me know."

Molly grabbed a small mirror out of her bag and checked her makeup. Her face looked fine, but her hair was a little mussed from the run. She quickly ran a brush through it.

"Thirty seconds, Molly," Sammy shouted.

Molly tossed her bag towards Sammy's feet and then stood facing the camera licking her lips, trying to keep them moist as she prepared to ad-lib her live report.

"Ten seconds, Molly," said Sammy.

He held up his free hand, palm open and fingers spread out and began to count down with each digit, finally he gave her the go signal, pointing at her.

"This is Molly Robbins reporting live from the Embarcadero station in the financial district of San Francisco...."

* * *

The rapid departure of most of the agents from the FBI Command Center had quickly transformed the conference room from a cacophony of noise and drama to an almost unnatural quiet. The few technicians who were left began speaking in low voices, just loud enough to be heard over the squawking, crackling police radios.

"Hey, look, it's the Embarcadero on CNN," shouted one of the technicians, pointing at the TV.

"Quick, turn up the volume," said Casey.

"...we are now monitoring a breaking story from San Francisco," the voice of the CNN newscaster intoned. The camera was slowly panning over the scene, showing the haphazardly parked police cars and groups of police officers trying to hold back a large crowd. The camera stopped panning as it focused on the face of young woman.

"The film you are seeing is from KRON TV in San Francisco," the CNN newscaster continued. "Let's listen in to their broadcast."

"...repeating again. About thirty minutes ago, a number of men thought to be federal agents...uh...FBI agents, were seen running down Market street directly towards the Embarcadero Station. A number of them rushed into the station while the local police kept anyone else from entering. Shortly after that the station was evacuated and since then there has been little visible action. We do know there are a number of agents still in the station. I was told just a few minutes ago by someone who claimed to be in the station when it was evacuated, a woman was arrested there. We have no official confirmation, but I was told by a witness the police had detained the woman inside the station. Now...oh." Molly stopped speaking for a moment as the camera panned to the left.

"Right now as you can see, a tow truck has just arrived. It seems to be backing up to a police car. Uh... uh...I'm not sure why." Molly went silent for a moment. "OK, the tow truck operator appears to be fixing a tow bar to the police car. I have no idea if this activity has anything to do with the activities in the station or what…. now the police seem to be moving the other police cars away from the one going to be towed. Again, we don't know the significance of these actions, but since there is no indication the police car you are looking at has broken down I think we can assume this must have something to do with the person being held in the station."

The camera panned back over to the entrance to the station. Four men, two in uniform and two in suits, were huddled in a tight conference just beyond the entrance. Molly Robbins continued to keep up her play-by-play.

"…what you are looking at again is the entrance to the Embarcadero Station. We don't know the identities of all four men in the picture, but I'm sure that one of them, the one on the left of your picture, is John Gonzalez, Chief of BART Police. The other uniformed officer is Deputy San Francisco Police Chief Dan Willmot. We think, but we are not sure, one of the men in the suits is Lance Jessep, Special Agent in Charge of the local FBI office, but that has not been confirmed. We don't know the identity of the fourth man, although he does appear to be the one directing the operation."

* * *

Gordon Lewis was talking earnestly to the senior police officers and to the local SAC, Lance Jessep, concerned about extracting the woman from the station over open ground with so many people around. She might try to run into the crowd, or Al Rahman might just decide to blow her up.

"Look," he said to the two senior police officers. "I want us to move very slowly and carefully as we bring her out. Dan," he said looking over at the Deputy Chief, "Put two sharpshooters on that roof," pointing to a mid-sized building with a clear view of the BART Station and its surroundings. "You instruct them that if, and only if she starts to run, they should take her out. OK?" The Deputy Chief nodded, and then jogged over to the Special Weapons and Tactics truck that had just driven up.

"Now," Gordon continued to the others, "we still haven't worked out what to do with her. My suggestion is we get her out of the City as soon as possible. Lance," he said turning to the SAC, "what do you think?"

"Well, I don't recommend we take her out on either the Bay Bridge or the Golden Gate. We are going to have to drive her down the peninsula, and then get her to a safe place where the bomb can be removed."

"Hell," said Gordon, "that'll cause a logistical nightmare. We will have to clear the roads and freeways along the route. It's going to be rush hour soon. Is there no other way out of the City?"

"What about a helicopter?" suggested John Gonzalez. "We can have one land right on top of the one of these high-rises."

"Uh, I don't know," said Gordon. "What if Al Rahman sets off the bomb while the helicopter is just taking off. No, I don't like that one."

"Well, what about moving her to a secure location here in the City where we can put her on a chopper," the chief countered.

"Yeah, we could take her out to the Polo Fields in Golden Gate Park. The chopper could land there and we can secure the park to be sure that Al Rahman is not in range," Lance Jessep responded.

"That sounds better," said Gordon Lewis. "We run the tow truck with the car behind down to the park, then the chopper takes her out and over the Bay to a secure location. That sounds good. OK, Dan, can you have a police helicopter meet us in San Francisco at Golden Gate Park?" Gordon asked.

"Do you have a destination in mind?" the police officer responded.

"I'm working on it. By the time you have the chopper in place, we'll have a destination. All right," he said looking at the two men, "let's get to it. We'll bring her out now, nice and easy."

* * *

Casey's cell phone rang. "Casey Jennings," she said absently as she stared at the television.

"Casey, its Gordon. Listen, I need you to do something for me. We have the woman in custody. We are about to evacuate her, but we have to find a military base nearby with a hospital equipped to handle her."

"OK, Gordon," said Casey. "I'll get on it right away."

"Call me back as soon as you have a location. Don't try for permission. Just find it. I'll get the clearance."

"No problem. Oh, Gordon," Casey continued quickly before he hung up, "I'm not sure if you are aware of this, but we are watching the whole scene on CNN. It's being broadcast live."

"Oh crap," said Gordon. "Price of a free country etceteras..." He paused, then said, "Say, Casey, you know what...if you're watching this on CNN, then we can try to ID her as we bring her out. Is the FRS up and running yet?" he asked referring to the Face Recognition Software the FBI had tried to deploy to find all the assassins.

"Hold on," Casey replied, "I'll check."

She called out to one of the technicians in the room and he just shook his head with a disgusted look. She knew they had been trying to make the software work all day but it had been generating so many false positives it had to be shut down. Casey turned back to the phone.

"No luck I'm afraid. The FRS is still not working."

She could hear Gordon Lewis swear under his breath. "Ok. Well, when she comes out of the station I will have her pause for a moment. I am sure the camera will zoom in on her. I want everyone in the control room to look at her face and compare it to the pictures Kosnar gave us." He paused very briefly before continuing. "Get Kosnar as well. He might have some special insight into what she looks like. Do it now and I will call you back in about three minutes."

Casey quickly relayed Gordon Lewis' instructions to the small group of agents still in the room and then hurried out of the conference room to get Vladimir Kosnar.

After completing his seemingly endless interview with the profilers, Vladimir had asked permission to sit with the agents monitoring the closed circuit television system that had been set up at the FBI headquarters to monitor crowds and traffic around the Moscone Center. The initial plan had been to use the FRS software to identify the women Al Rahman had potentially deployed around the Moscone Center, but when the software failed to work, the value of the video surveillance had diminished. The two agents who had been manning the surveillance monitors were pulled out onto other more pressing assignments and Vladimir Kosnar had been left in the room alone. Casey had dropped into the control room a couple of times and the first time she had sat with him briefly, watching as the images from thirty cameras were rotated through eight different screens. She had tried to speak with him each time she visited but he always seemed completely intent on looking at each camera shot and so after that she had left him alone.

He was still alone at the monitors, hand on the camera control lever when she walked in and seemed to catch him by surprise. He quickly recovered and seemed pleased to see her but his face darkened as she quickly relayed what was happening at the Embarcadero station. He followed her out the surveillance room with one quick glance back at the monitors as she led him back to the command center.

Her phone rang again as she walked back in. "They're bringing her up the steps right now," Lewis said as soon as she answered. "We're going to walk her over to a police car, which will be towed away by a truck. Stand by."

He was back on the phone a few seconds later.

"Casey, are you there? Is everyone ready to make the ID? We are bringing her out now."

"We're ready Gordon," she replied. "Go ahead."

* * *

Natasha Mislov was so afraid she was shaking. She had been standing for almost fifteen minutes until one of the men finally told her to sit down. She did as instructed, knees pulled to her chest, arms wrapped around her legs, head resting on her knees. She could not understand what the man had meant when he said there was a bomb inside her body. That was ridiculous. How could that even be possible? But why was nobody coming close to her? Everybody was keeping their distance, treating her as if she was a dangerous criminal, as if she had some strange disease.

How did they even know who she was? She wasn't here to spy on anyone. That wasn't her job any more. Actually, she did not even know what her job was. All she had been told to do was stand outside Moscone Center and try to shake hands with important people. What was the crime in that? Was it possible they were arresting her for the industrial espionage she'd done all those years ago? Maybe they knew about it then, but were just making the arrest now. But the bomb. That didn't explain what the man said about the bomb. One of the men had asked her name and a couple of other questions, and she had given him her pseudonym, but when he asked where she lived, she decided it was better not to answer any more questions.

* * *

Lance Jessep looked over at the woman on the floor. She looked scared, which made him feel uncomfortable.

If she had been correctly identified, he realized, he probably knew more about her predicament than she did. He felt sorry for her, tried to ask her a couple of questions, but all she would tell him was her name. His instincts told him Officer Pallard had done a good job, an amazing job, actually, in noticing her. Anyway, they would know in a few minutes, when they took her out. If they could not confirm the ID, then they might have lots of explaining to do. However, if experience and instinct counted for anything, he was pretty sure he knew she was one of the women even without the formal confirmation.

"OK, Lance," one of the special agents said as he walked towards his boss. "The car is ready. Mr. Lewis wants us to move her out now."

"All right," said Lance, "let's do it just like we discussed. I want four agents in front of her, four behind. I will walk with the forward team. As soon as my team gets to the exit, we will stop and wait until I give you all the all clear sign. Then, and only then, we will bring her out directly to the car. Does anybody have any questions?"

There were no questions, so Lance looked over at Natasha and began to give her instructions.

"Ma'am," he said. "We are going to move you out now. We are going to do this very slowly and carefully. Do you understand?" He was speaking loudly, his voice echoing through the large nearly empty station.

Natasha looked up at him and nodded.

"OK, I want you to stand up and walk slowly towards me."

Natasha stood and moved to pick up her bag but Lance Jessep quickly dissuaded her of that notion.

"Leave the bag," he shouted. Natasha straightened up, looked at him, and then began to walk slowly.

"OK, very good. Just keep coming. Just like that."

Jessep and his team walked in front of her, keeping about fifteen feet from her. Behind her, the rear team stepped into place, following from a similar distance. She was boxed in by the narrow walls of the passageway and by the teams of men. As Jessep adopted a sideways gait so he could keep his eyes on her and still navigate the stairway, the group moved slowly through the deserted station.

Suddenly, Natasha stumbled, her foot snagging on a piece of broken tile. One of the agents next to Jessep let out a loud gasp as she struggled to recover balance, but she found her footing, and then continued to move forward. Now they were close to the stairway. As he glanced forward, Lance could see sunlight striking the stairs.

"OK, lets stop right here. Ma'am," he said to Natasha, "I want you to sit down again. That's right, just sit down with your back to the wall."

He watched her until she complied, then ran up the steps, taking them two at a time. As he got to the top, he saw Gordon Lewis and waved him over.

"Where is she?" Gordon asked.

"Right at the bottom of the stairs. We can bring her out any time."

"OK. Let's do it, then walk her over to the car." Gordon paused and looked around at the gathering crowd. "This part is tricky," he said to Lance, with a frown on his face. "She'll be in the open now. For all we know, the guy with the remote control could be, in fact is, in the crowd right now." He shook his head and grimaced and then turned back to Lance.

"Listen, go back down and tell her we are going to take her out of the station and to some place safe nearby. Tell her when she gets to the top of the stairs, you want her to pause for a few seconds. That'll give the TV crews time to film her and hopefully give us time to confirm her ID. Tell her after that she is to walk directly to the car behind the tow truck. Got it?"

Lance nodded in affirmation. Gordon Lewis gave him a slap on the back and said, "OK, let's do it. Let's bring her out." Lance turned and hurried back down the stairs into the station.

* * *

The camera was directly focused on the exit to the station. Molly Robbins's voice continued to give a running commentary, although very little appeared to be happening.

"...OK we think they are about to bring the woman out of the station. The police and the FBI have all backed away from the entrance. OK here comes someone now."

On the screen, Casey could see Lance Jessep and three other men emerge from the station. As the camera panned back slightly, she could see them begin to take up positions on either side of the pathway to the car. Lance had his back to the camera and was looking directly back at the station entrance. Suddenly, the camera zoomed back to the station entrance as a woman emerged and focused on her face.

A technician quickly typed some commands onto his keyboard and the woman's face was quickly frozen and projected onto a number of computer monitors in the room. Casey stared for a moment at the woman's face and then glanced down at the sheets of pictures in her hand, trying to find a match.

"Mislov," one of the agents shouted out as he waved a sheet of pictures in the air. "I think its Natasha Mislov from page three, uh…. second row, third picture."

Casey and the other agents quickly flipped to that page and tried to make the match. Casey quickly found the picture which was clear and in color but it was also dated, of a woman much younger than the one on the monitor. Casey glanced back and forth between the two trying to confirm the woman's identification when she felt Kosnar at her side.

"It's her," he said in almost a whisper as he stood close to her. "It's Mislov."

She turned to look at him and urgently asked, "Are you sure?"

Kosnar just nodded in response.

By now most of the remaining agents were also confirming the woman's identification as Casey glanced between the picture on the monitor and on the paper. She hesitated for a second and then shouted into the phone.

"Gordon, are you there?"

"Yes," he replied quickly. "Did you find a match?"

"Yes, we are quite sure her name is Natasha Mislov. Vladimir also thinks it's her."

Gordon Lewis did not even bother to respond. Before he had even disconnected the phone, Casey could hear him shouting for them to get moving. Watching the TV, she could see Gordon waving at the woman, encouraging her to move towards the police car. Casey watched as Mislov walked slowly but deliberately towards the car.

Casey felt like she was holding her breath. It was a moment of agony. She knew Al Rahman could be lurking nearby. This might be exactly what he wanted: to create a spectacle in the middle of San Francisco by executing the poor woman right there on national television as she walked towards the waiting police car. Casey could barely watch.

* * *

Abd Al Rahman was less then fifty yards away. He had found a good location next to a large concrete flowerpot with a clear view of the entrance to the station. In front of him was a heavy decorative chain that ran from flower box to flower box along the street for about one hundred yards. The police were using the chain as a barrier to control the crowd and to keep it away from the station. In front of Al Rahman, just beyond the chain, two policemen faced towards him and the rest of the crowd, trying to make sure no one crossed the line. They paid no particular attention to him and seemed quite ignorant of the significance of the proceedings behind them.

The crowd around Al Rahman had become quite large. Occasionally, as the crush would ebb and flow, it would push him up against the concrete flower box, and he would have to work hard to maintain his position. He was afraid not of getting trampled, but of missing his opportunity. Every few moments he would pat his left jacket pocket, reassured by the presence of the remote control.

"He heard a rumble from the crowd as Natasha emerged from the station and then stopped and stood still, right in the entrance. As the press of the crowd against his back threatened to move him away from his vantage point, he grabbed the heavy chain with both hands, hanging on as tightly as he could to anchor himself. An FBI agent momentarily obscured his view of Natasha, but then he saw someone waving her on and watched her as she began to walk towards the police car attached to the tow truck. His eyes darted back and forth between her and the men guarding her. They were standing too far away from her to be hurt by the blast. He swore under his breath. This was a perfect opportunity, out in the open. Nobody could deny it or pretend it didn't happen. But he was reluctant to act. It would be a waste, really, he thought, to activate her now and simply have her die alone. No, he had to wait until she was closer to some of the policemen or even some of the citizens watching with him. He patted the remote control again, counseling himself to be patient.

* * *

By now Natasha had reached the police car. The rear right side door was wide open, but before she stepped into it, she turned and looked back at Gordon Lewis. He had been waving her forward as she moved towards the car and she wanted to be sure he really wanted her to get in.

Lewis tensed slightly as the woman turned away from the open door and looked directly at him. He gave her an encouraging nod and motioned to her with his hand, feeling a surge of relief as she turned back to the car and climbed in, pulling the door shut behind her.

* * *

It is human nature to anthropomorphize the machines that surround us, do our bidding, obey our instructions, but the receiver embedded in Natasha Mislov's titanium hip had no self-awareness, no patience, and no forbearance. Its design was ingenious, brilliant even, but its logic was hard-wired and limited. As long as its power source was available, it remained in a state of readiness, digesting the electronic signals it received.

It was actually quite a simple device, requiring a four-digit activation code out of six possible numbers. Occasionally in the past, it had received two of the four numbers necessary for activation, but when the subsequent digits had not immediately followed, it had quickly erased its tiny memory and returned to its state of readiness. Twice in 1989, it had received three of the four numbers, but again, without the fourth digit activation had not occurred. Then, early in 1990, the power source had died and the receiver's vigilance ended. For almost three years, nothing was processed; all the radio noise present in the ether passed by unnoticed.

Late in 1992, power was restored, and once again the device methodically digested the information it received. Now, however, its minute circuitry was busier than ever. Every day, often more then once a day, two of the required four digits were received, and at least once a month, three of the digits were detected. Now, on a late summer's day in the center of San Francisco, while Natasha Mislov sat uncomfortably in the back of the police car, the four digit code came out of the ether and was detected by the device. Immediately, a single electronic switch was turned on and the activator at the base of the receiver drained the battery, drawing the energy necessary for its mission. In a millisecond, the activator reached critical mass and sent its entire charge directly into the explosive material surrounding it.

* * *

Lewis moved quickly towards the front of the tow truck. There were two motorcycle policemen in front of the truck, already mounted, engines running. Gordon shouted for them to go, and as the motorcyclists began to move forward slowly, he looked back at the tow truck and began to twirl his right arm above his head in a signal for the small convoy to get moving. He watched the truck jerk forward as the driver put it into gear. And then, just as he was turning back to look at the woman, he saw the flash and almost instantly felt the heat as she exploded.

* * *

Casey gasped. The camera was on the police car, but the explosion caused the cameraman to momentarily lose the shot. He quickly regained it, focusing directly onto the car. For a few seconds, it was lost in a haze of smoke and flying glass, and then Casey watched in horror as the right rear door of the police car, its hinges severed, crashed heavily onto the pavement. She held her breath as the upper body of Natasha Mislov fell, as if in slow motion, out of the shattered car and on to the car door.

In the conference room, one of the technicians screamed as Casey put her hand to her mouth and struggled to stifle her own voice. In spite of herself, she looked back at the television and watched as the cameraman pulled back from the shot, showing the police car, the woman's shattered body, and the policemen and FBI agents lying where they had taken cover.

She felt a hand touch her arm and glanced back to see Vladimir Kosnar standing behind her and then turned quickly to face him.

"Oh my God, that wasn't your sister....?" Casey started to ask as she saw him.

"No," he replied with a quick shake of his head.

He glanced around and then, his hand firmly on her arm, led her out of the conference room back into the room with the surveillance monitors.

"What is it?" she asked.

"We have to leave here right now," he whispered urgently.

"What?" Casey hissed back at him. "You can't leave. You know–."

Kosnar cut her off. "Look," he said as he adjusted the camera control lever. The image on the monitor blurred momentarily as it zoomed in on a woman sitting on a low wall. He pointed at the monitor as the image came in to focus and said, "That's my sister. I know where she is and we have to get her right now."

Casey's eyes widened as she looked at him.

"Are you sure?" she asked.

"Yes, I was watching her a few minutes ago when you came to get me. We have to go to her now."

"But you can't leave here. You're in FBI custody."

"You come with me. I'll be in your custody," he replied, his words coming quickly, urgently.

"Let me call Gordon and arrange-"

He cut her off again. "You just saw what happened to that woman. All those cops and FBI agents around her and they still couldn't protect her. If you call for help, Al Rahman will see the cops and he will kill her just like he killed Mislov. We have to go now before he can get to her."

CHAPTER 35

THE SUDDEN EXPLOSION caused the crowd surrounding the Embarcadero station to surge back and forth in chaotic waves, as people reacted first to the explosion and then to the sight of the woman's fractured body falling out of the police car. Al Rahman struggled to retain his balance as the crush pressed him hard against the heavy metal chain in front of him. He still held both hands on the chain, in a losing battle to support himself as he was almost doubled over, the crush of people pressing against his legs, driving them into the chain a couple of inches above his knees. He bit his lip in pain as one of the links bore into the old wound in his thigh.

Finally the crush eased and Al Rahman regained his balance. He was breathing quick, sharp shallow breaths as his old wound throbbed. He looked up, momentarily confused by the scene in front of him — the damaged police car, the body of Natasha Mislov lying on top of the car door, the FBI agents and policemen, coming to their feet. A rush of shock and anger flashed over him.

Someone in the crowd next to him or behind him had activated the bomb! Still favoring his injured leg, he reached into his jacket pocket, withdrawing the activator. He looked at it carefully, turning it over in his hand, trying to understand what had happened. The safety switch was still engaged. He disengaged it and then reset it. With the safety switch engaged, he pressed down on the plunger and, as he expected, it did not move. He glanced around him, trying to find an answer in the surrounding faces, but saw nothing untoward.

"Kosnar," he muttered. Al Rahman tried to scan the crowd, looking for a familiar face, but was still penned in by the mass of people. He looked down at the activator in his hand, checked once more the safety switch was engaged, and jammed it back into his pocket. Then he turned into the crowd and began to push his way through. He had to hurry. His carefully orchestrated plan to create chaos and panic had been compromised. Now everyone would be on alert. If he wanted to do something dramatic, he would have to do it now. His leg ached as he pushed his way forward head down and limping as he bumped and squeezed his way through the crowd. He had to get to Moscone Center as quickly as possible.

* * *

Myda Karrina was not sure what she was supposed to do. She had rushed from Los Angeles to Oakland as instructed, taking the train instead of flying, again as instructed. Once in Oakland, soon after she had checked into the hotel he had designated, he called again. His instructions had been simple but clear; purchase a blue shirt, wear comfortable clothes and travel to the area of the Moscone Center at two o'clock the next day. She was to go to the corner of Howard and 3rd Street and stand near a multi-colored statue of three dancers. She was to wait there for further instructions.

"Don't leave that location or try to make contact with me or anyone else," he admonished her. "I will contact you with instructions."

She had followed her orders precisely, traveling to her assigned location first by BART from Oakland and then a quick walk to the statue. But now, as she spotted her assigned location, she could see that getting next to the statue was not an option. Wooden police barricades blocked access to the sidewalk within one hundred yards of the statue and uniformed officers made sure no-one ventured beyond the barricade.

She wondered what do. Glancing around, she saw a low wall further up Howard Street across the street from a bank branch that would at least give her a clear view of the statue. Since her assignment had already been com-promised, she drew on her training and adapted to the circumstances, sitting down on the wall to wait for fur-ther orders.

As she sat down she confirmed her cell phone was still on and fully charged and then glanced around trying to familiarize herself with her surroundings, but she did not notice the security camera on the Wells Fargo Bank building across the street as it slowly swiveled on its axis and pointed directly at her.

* * *

Al Rahman hobbled down the crowded sidewalk. His leg was throbbing; he could barely put any weight on it as he walked. He was not sure how to get to Moscone Center, but thought he was going in the right direction. He stopped to ask a woman for directions, but she gave him a strange look and hurried away. Just ahead he saw a young black man and asked him for directions. The man looked at him with a funny expression on his face, but pointed him in the direction of the Moscone Center. Al Rahman walked on as best he could, despite pain in his leg. He noticed, or at least he thought he noticed, people staring at him, but he ignored them until he caught a glance of himself in a shop window.

He stared at his reflection, taken aback by what he saw. His toupee was completely awry. It must have been knocked loose in the crowd and now was turned almost ninety degrees, putting the part just above his brow. He looked ridiculous. Stepping closer to the window, he tried to reset the toupee with his one good hand, using his reflection as a mirror. He moved and shifted the wig, but the adhesive had worn out; the wig would not lie on his head properly. He re-seated it as best he could, then with an unhappy grunt, turned and continued his painful shuffle towards Moscone Center.

* * *

Casey and Vladimir managed to exit the local FBI headquarters building without attracting any attention. By leaving the FBI building with the Russian, she guessed she was committing about fifteen different felonies, but she tried to put the thought out of her mind as she and Vladimir ran towards Moscone Center.

As they ran down the street, she realized they, or at least she, had no plan. They were going to go and find a woman carrying a bomb that could not be disarmed and could be activated remotely by a man nobody could recognize. This was crazy. She slowed to a walk as she called to him.

"Wait," she called to Vladimir, who had continued a few steps beyond until he realized she had slowed down. He walked back towards her.

"What? What is it?"

"Do you have an action plan here? If we find this woman, your sister, what are you going to do?"

"Take her to a hospital. Have them remove the titanium hip joint and the bomb."

"Are you kidding?" Casey was almost laughing. "We are just going to walk into a hospital with this woman and tell the admitting nurse our friend has a bomb in her hip and can they admit her and remove it please."

"Do you have a better idea? Look, I'm not sure what to do. We'll play it by ear, as you Americans like to say. But ultimately, yes, we will have to take her a hospital and have them remove the device. But whatever happens, we have to keep her away from Al Rahman. If he gets within fifty feet of her, she's dead."

Vladimir was already striding away as he finished speaking. Casey just shook her head a couple of times, then trotted after him until she caught up. They walked in silence for a couple of minutes until they were less than half a mile from Moscone Center, and then Vladimir began to slow down.

"What is it?" Casey asked.

"If Al Rahman is here, he will recognize me. I don't want to help by making myself obvious, moving too quickly. Also, my sister might be gone from the place I last spotted her. We need to watch out for her."

The two agents began to look carefully at the faces passing them. They were just a few hundred yards from Moscone Center now, across the street from the Wells Fargo Bank building. Stopping at the corner, Vladimir looked around, trying to find his bearings. Gazing up, he spotted the surveillance video camera attached to the building just behind them. Looking in the direction the camera was aimed, he stared for a few moments, then grabbed Casey's arm.

"There she is," he hissed at her.

Casey looked at Vladimir to see where he was looking. "Which one is she? Casey asked, unable to distinguish their target from the rest of the milling crowd.

"Blue shirt, light pants, big sunglasses."

"OK, I've got her," said Casey.

"I suggest we approach her slowly and as soon as we are close enough, I will talk to her in Russian. You stand on her left side and I'll be on her right. If she starts to move away, identify yourself as an FBI agent so you get her attention. OK?"

They cautiously stepped into the street, dodging the slow moving traffic that was becoming increasingly congested as the police were closing other routes, preparing for the President's arrival. As they reached the other side of the street, Vladimir paused, looking up and down the sidewalk, checking to see if Al Rahman was visible but, there was no sign of him.

They were about ten feet away from her now. As they strode towards her it was obvious she had spotted them moving towards her and she turned her head away, trying to act as nonchalant as possible.

"Myda Kosnar." Vladimir addressed her using her birth name, hoping it would spark a memory.

She slowly turned back towards them, trying to keep calm, but inwardly fighting panic welling up inside. The man knew her first name, but he used a last name that was not hers. Still, it sounded familiar, but she was not sure why. As planned, Vladimir and Casey took up positions on either side of her. Casey, fighting her own nervousness, smiled at the woman, trying not to look threatening. Vladimir spoke in Russian.

"My name is Vladimir Kosnar," he said slowly, deliberately, gently. "Your name was Myda Kosnar, but now it is Myda Karrina. In 1959, when you were about six years old, you were taken from Orphanage 132. Do you remember?"

The woman maintained her composure but her eyes were wide with confusion and fear. She had not expected to be approached, let alone by a man who spoke Russian and seemed to know as much, maybe even more, about her childhood than she did. She turned away from him and started to walk up the sidewalk. Vladimir jogged past her and stood in front her, partly blocking her way.

"Who are you?" she asked in slightly accented English.

"Vladimir," he replied. "Vladimir Kosnar. Do you remember being in the orphanage?" He was still speaking Russian. "Do you remember being taken away? Perhaps you remember a small boy who was with you when you left." Vladimir paused. "I was that small boy. I am your brother."

Myda looked over at Casey, then back at Vladimir.

"What are you talking about?" she said, struggling with confused memories and the disconcerting juxtaposition of her location, her mission, and this strangely familiar man standing in front of her.

Vladimir made a gesture towards Casey and said in English, "This is Casey. She has been assisting me in my search for you."

Casey stepped forward and extended her hand towards Myda but the Russian ignored and it and Casey dropped her hand.

"Who are you?" Myda asked Casey in Russian, her face a mask of confusion and doubt.

"I'm sorry," said Casey, "I don't speak Russian. My name is Casey Jennings." It did not feel like the right time to mention she was an FBI agent.

As Casey introduced herself, Vladimir stepped a couple of feet away from the two women, scanning the sidewalks in both directions. They were in an incredibly vulnerable position and he was concerned it would take some time to convince his sister of their veracity. He was about to rejoin the two women when he saw something that held his gaze. About fifty feet away he could see a man hobbling towards them. He was looking down at the ground as he walked, in a slow painful shuffle that appeared to cause him great discomfort every time he put weight on his left leg. Vladimir squinted, trying to get a clearer view. The limp looked so familiar, but there was something else. The hair, the man's hair looked out of place, unnatural.

Vladimir stepped away from Casey and his sister and he slowly started to walk towards the man. It had been a long time since he had seen Al Rahman, but he remembered the limp and that Al Rahman had purchased a toupee. The two men were about twenty-five feet apart now.

Suddenly the man looked up and at that moment, their eyes met. A look of anger flashed across Al Rahman's face. He saw his former nemesis just in front of him, and just beyond him he could see Karrina and another woman who also looked familiar. He stopped, and for a second considered turning and walking away, but instead he started to fumble in his jacket, reaching for the activator.

As Al Rahman stopped, Vladimir broke into a run and then a sprint, dodging pedestrians as he strove to get to Al Rahman. Al Rahman found the activator in his pocket and tried to pull it out, but it was stuck in the seam in his pocket. He fumbled for another second trying to use the stump of his right hand to hold his jacket and finally managed to free the device just as Vladimir's shoulder drove hard into to his solar plexus. With a grunt, Al Rahman fell backwards, the activator sailing out of his hands in a broad arc towards the street.

Vladimir's diving tackle caused him to fall to the ground almost on top of Al Rahman. As he fell, he was unaware of the location of the activator. He rolled onto his back and as he began to sit up, he could see Casey running towards him, drawing her weapon as she ran. Scrambling to his feet, he waved her off with his hand.

"Go!" he shouted, finding his voice. "Get her away from here," he screamed. "Take her to the hospital."

Just then Vladimir caught sight of Al Rahman scurrying toward the street. For a second he thought Al Rahman was trying to get away, but then he saw the object of Al Rahman's frantic scramble.

"Go! Go!" Vladimir shouted again at Casey, then turned and in one fluid motion stepped directly onto Al Rahman's back and then dove hard into the street, stretching out to reach the activator. He did not hear the squeal of brakes as the approaching taxi driver tried desperately, but unsuccessfully to stop before hitting him. The congested traffic and the driver's fast reaction meant the blow to Vladimir's head was not as bad as it could have been. Still, he was struck hard, already unconscious by the time his body fell to the ground, his head just inches from the taxi's front wheels.

CHAPTER 36

C ASEY ONLY REALIZED Vladimir was moving away from them when she saw Myda become distracted, turning just as Vladimir broke into a sprint. As he tackled his quarry, Casey ran towards him drawing her weapon and roughly pushing through the crowd gathering on the sidewalk. She slowed as Vladimir rolled to his feet and shouted to her to go. His words were unclear, but Casey thought she heard him say the word 'hospital'. She stopped and looked back at Myda and then back to Vladimir just as she saw him step onto a man lying on the ground and dive into the street. She cringed as she saw the taxi hit him and began to move towards him, but stopped again, turning back to Myda. She felt a moment of a panic when she did not see her, but then, just as quickly, was relieved when she realized Myda had moved towards her, was almost beside her. She grabbed Myda by the arm and pulled her away from the two men, one picking himself up from the sidewalk, the other lying still on the street.

"Come on," she shouted, "we've got to get you out of here." Myda resisted, shaking off Casey's hand, turning back to the small crowd quickly gathering around Vladimir. Casey grabbed her by the wrist more firmly this time, and pulled her down the sidewalk until Myda stopped resisting and the two women began to run down the street. Casey saw some passengers disembarking from a taxi near them and she dashed up to it, pushing Myda ahead of her into the back seat.

"Uh...Uh....San Francisco General Hospital, please, driver. Quick as you can."

As soon as the cab pulled out onto the street, Casey turned and looked through the rear window, trying to see either Vladimir or the man she assumed to be Al Rahman but the small crowd gathering at the accident obscured her view. As the taxi sped up, the scene receded and she reached for her cell phone. As she pushed the buttons to call Gordon Lewis, Myda demanded her attention.

"Who are you?" the Russian woman shouted. "Where are you taking me?"

"Hold on a moment," Casey replied looking down her phone, still trying to get a call out to her boss.

She glanced up as the taxi slowed in traffic, and then almost dove across the back seat as Myda started to open the door.

"No, please. You must stay with me," she yelled as the two women wrestled with the door. After a moment, Myda let go of the door handle and sat back in her seat, glaring at Casey.

"What's going on back there?" the taxi driver shouted as he turned to look over his shoulder. "What are you doing?"

Casey leaned forward in her seat and held her Bureau identification inches from his face. "FBI," she said as firmly as she could. "You just keep your eyes forward and drive." She held her position next to his head for a few more seconds before sitting back in her seat and looking at the Russian woman. She desperately wanted to call her boss, let him know what had happened, but first she had to get her to calm down.

"Ms. Karrina, I'm sorry. I know this must be confusing. Please listen very carefully. What I am about to tell you is disturbing, but I do believe it can be ...uh... resolved."

Casey closed her eyes for a second, sighed again and began a careful explanation of who she was, who she worked for, who Al Rahman was. She explained that the trip she had been sent on was a rogue mission, unauthorized by her own government, and that Vladimir, her brother, had been sent to stop it. She did not mention the other women or the murders in Europe.

"Ms. Karrina, I have to ask you a personal question," she said as the taxi fought the traffic. "Do you have a scar on either hip, a scar from an operation?"

Myda's eye's widened. How could this woman, a person she had just met, know that?

"Why?" Myda asked.

"Do you?" Casey repeated. "Do you have a surgical scar on your hip?"

"Yes, I do," Myda responded, "But why are you asking me this? What does this have to do with anything?"

Casey reached down and took one of the Russian woman's hands in her own. "Ms. Karrina, Myda, many years ago, your hip joint was replaced, but they did not install a normal joint. They put in one containing a small amount of explosive, enough to kill you and somebody you are with or who is nearby."

Just then the taxi driver hit his brakes and Casey and Myda fell hard against the front seats. "Lady, do you have a bomb in my cab?" the driver shouted as he turned almost completely around in his seat. "Are you fucking crazy?"

Pushing back on to the edge of her seat, Casey leaned over to the taxi driver and said, "I told you to shut up and drive. Now stop eavesdropping on our conversation and just get us to the hospital. There is nothing to worry about. Just drive." Her voice was calm but resolute.

"But-"

Casey cut him off before he could continue. "Face forward and put both hands on the wheel. Now, just drive us to hospital and everything will be fine."

As the taxi driver drove on casting anxious glances in his review mirror, Casey turned back to the Russian woman beside her. Myda's eyes were wide with fright but she said nothing.

"Please," Casey said. "You must believe me. The man your brother tackled was carrying the activator that would explode the bomb in your body. He has already killed women like you, one of them today, right here in San Francisco. We believe he was going to use you to kill other people at the Convention." She stopped speaking and her words hung in the air.

"I...how can this be possible...?" Myda replied, struggling to express herself.

"I understand you don't believe me," said Casey, with a shake of her head. I wouldn't believe it either, if I had not seen what I have seen the past few weeks. But you must believe me. What I'm telling you is true."

"I don't understand. What have you seen?"

"I've seen women just like you, athletic, attractive, former Soviet Olympic hopefuls, all about the same age. All murdered, murdered in hotel rooms or on the streets of London and San Francisco."

The Russian woman's face was pale. She had moved as far away from Casey as possible in the back seat of the taxi, her back up against the door. "But what does that have to do with me? How do you know I am involved with that?" She was indignant, defensive. Afraid she might try and open the door again and jump out when the taxi slowed, Casey wanted to keep her engaged in the conversation.

"Were you on assignment here today?" she asked.

Myda did not answer. The FBI agent was asking her about an assignment, a tactical mission. She was not ready to answer such a question.

"What were you doing outside Moscone Center," said Casey again, pressing her. "Did you have a specific assignment?" Casey realized she was on dangerous ground making assumptions about what Al Rahman had told Myda to do but she had to gain this woman's trust quickly.

Myda looked over at Casey and then dropped her eyes. She was trying desperately to reconcile what she was hearing and what had just happened. A stranger walks up to her and claims to be her brother, but now he is apparently hurt and abandoned in the streets of San Francisco. A woman with him claims to be an FBI agent and forces her into a taxi. And the stupid assignment, standing on the street corner waiting for the phone to ring. She looked back at Casey.

"My assignment did seem unusual," said Myda, "but that doesn't mean I am carrying a bomb or that…uh…uh I have a bomb inside my body."

Casey looked back at her with an encouraging expression. She could understand the woman's suspicion. She was sure she would feel the same. The information was so unacceptable, so out of the realm of comprehension, it required a suspension of disbelief to accept. Casey could see from Myda's face, however that she was starting to trust her, that perhaps the strange nature of her assignment was convincing her she was caught up in something she did not understand.

"Please, you must believe me. I want to help you. We need to have the device removed from your body."

"San Francisco General Hospital," the taxi driver called out at as the car squealed to a hard stop in the parking lot.

Casey looked out the windows to get her bearings. "There," she said, pointing past the driver. "Pull up at the Emergency Room drop off."

* * *

Abd Al Rahman saw the front of the taxi strike Kosnar's head and watched his adversary fall hard onto the street. As he stumbled awkwardly to his feet, he could see the activator just beyond the Russian's prone body. Standing up, Al Rahman stepped around Vladimir and the nervous taxi driver hovering over him. He scooped up the activator and then, still bent over, pulled the wig off his head and shoved it into his pocket. Then he turned to look down at Vladimir, saw the blood on his head, heard him utter a low groan.

The taxi driver was almost dancing a jig of panic as he looked down at the man he had struck.

"Did you see him?" the taxi driver yelled to the gathering crowd. "He just jumped right in front of my cab. No way I could stop in time. The man just jumped in front of me. Motherfucker, my boss is going to fucking kill me. I can't believe this bullshit. What am I supposed to do?"

Abd Al Rahman had to think quickly. As the crowd gathered near Vladimir and he could see a policewoman running towards them. Clearly his plan for the day had been compromised but he was ready to adapt. Killing Kosnar would revenge an old debt. He would reassemble the women at another place and another time but now he had to eliminate Kosnar.

"Is he all right?" Al Rahman asked the policewoman, speaking with Russian accented English.

"I think he was just knocked unconscious," said the officer.

Al Rahman reached out and gently stroked Vladimir's brow, mumbling a few words to him in Russian.

"Do you know this man?" asked the policewoman.

"Yes," said Al Rahman, still stroking Vladimir's brow. "We are friends traveling together in United States," he continued, his voice breaking just slightly.

"Well, your friend needs to go the hospital right away. I'm going to call an ambulance."

Reaching for the microphone to her radio, the police-woman began giving information to her dispatcher. As soon as she was done, she looked back down at Vladimir and then over at Al Rahman.

"Where are you from?" she asked him.

"Russia. We are Russians traveling here on business," Al Rahman replied. "I am here to help my friend with English. He has no English."

"Oh boy," said the officer. "In that case, I suggest when the ambulance arrives, you better go with him. You understand?"

"Yes," Al Rahman replied, still caressing Vladimir's brow. With his fingerless right hand, he reached up and patted his pocket, reassured again by what it contained.

* * *

As Casey and Myda walked into the emergency room, Casey's cell phone was ringing.

"Casey, we are getting reports of an incident near the Moscone Center. Was that you and where are you and where the hell is Kosnar?" Gordon Lewis demanded as soon as she answered.

"I'm at San Francisco General Hospital. I'm with Kosnar's sister. I…uh, we managed to find her and I brought her here. We've just arrived. I'm going to try and find the hospital administrator and have her admitted for surgery right away."

"What? How did you... never mind that now. Is she disarmed? Did you secure the activator?" His words ran together.

"No, she is not disarmed and Al Rahman is still at large. I saw him but, it seemed more prudent to separate her from him." As she stood talking on the phone Casey started to feel she had made wrong decision. Al Rahman had been a hard target on the ground not far from her. She could have shot him on the spot, taken the risk despite the fact there were crowds of people gathering.

"So is she still lethal or not?"

"I..uh...I guess you would have to call her lethal. But if they do surgery now, quickly, they can remove the device and disarm it." Her last few words came out in a jumble.

"Jesus Christ, Casey. You are going to try and convince the hospital and a couple doctors to operate on a woman with a bomb inside her?"

Casey closed her eyes and grimaced slightly as she responded. "Well, that was my plan. Yes, Sir."

There was a pause as neither party spoke. Casey looked over at Myda and tried to flash a reassuring smile, but it came across as more like a grimace.

"Casey, look, I'll be right there." Gordon's voice had softened slightly. "Identify yourself to the hospital, have them summon the chief administrator, tell them your story. Tell them I'm on my way. And Casey, please, put that woman somewhere secluded. We've already had one woman explode on us in a public place. Let's try and avoid a second occurrence."

CHAPTER 37

V LADIMIR'S HEAD HURT. He tried to open his eyes, but the effort was too great. He could hear people talking, but the voices were a jumble, occasionally clear, mostly just noise. He felt removed from his own condition, aware and yet somehow detached. He heard counting and then felt himself being lifted onto a bed or a gurney. Then he felt a pat on the shoulder and someone talking to him.

"Hey buddy, are you OK? Can you hear me?"

He couldn't answer, but he thought he heard a voice, a woman's voice say, "Don't bother asking him any questions. He doesn't speak English. He's a Russian. If you have any questions, you'll have to ask his pal over there."

Then he felt a mask being placed over his mouth, a tug as straps pinned his arms. He wanted to say something, but no words came out. He lay still, breathing deeply, trying to collect his thoughts. He heard a door slam. In the distance he heard a siren and wondered if there was a fire.

* * *

Vladimir heard a voice that sounded familiar, but couldn't place it.

"Which hospital are we going to?" the voice asked.

"SF Gen."

"Is that San Francisco General Hospital?" The familiar voice again.

"Yup, that's the one."

"Is that the closest one?"

"Hey, don't worry, man. We gonna get your buddy there in just a few minutes. He's going to be just fine."

Vladimir groaned. He opened his eyes and then quickly closed them again. He lay still for a few moments, then again slowly opened his eyes, blinking rapidly, but this time was able to keep them open. His vision was blurred. At first, he just looked up at the EMT, but then became aware of another man in the ambulance and turned towards him. His eyes widened then closed, shut hard as if he was trying to reset his focus. Opening his eyes again, this time he looked directly at Al Rahman. He stared for about ten seconds, and then tried to reach up to his face to remove the oxygen mask, but the straps on his arms stopped him. He groaned, trying to speak, but nothing came out.

"Can't you give him something for the pain?" Al Rahman asked the EMT. "That's my plan, Jack," said the EMT. "Give me a second." Vladimir looked up and saw the EMT drawing a clear liquid from a bottle with a syringe. When the syringe was half full, he removed the needle from the bottle, squirted out a tiny amount, and reached down to administer the shot. Vladimir tried to move away, but the EMT quickly found a spot and injected the sedative. Vladimir reluctantly closed his eyes, but could still hear the voices around him.

"OK, that should feel a little more comfortable. Anyway, we should be there soon. Don't worry. The docs will take care of him in a few minutes. He'll be fine."

* * *

Dr. Judith Frank had been Chief Administrator at San Francisco General Hospital for almost ten years. Her arrival in San Francisco had been celebrated; she was the first woman to lead a major American hospital, but to her it was no big deal. She had absolutely no doubt about her abilities to manage the large and complex medical center. She understood her mission, never wavered from her dedication both to serve people and to keep the large and sensitive egos of the doctors sufficiently in check. There had been a few extraordinary management challenges during the past five years, but she had to admit the woman in front of her was describing something quite bizarre. The FBI agent had insisted that her companion, another woman, be secured alone in a large room. With some reluctance, Dr. Frank had placed the woman in her own office. Now she and Casey stood just outside its door.

"Ms. Jennings, let me repeat what you have told me. The woman in my office is a Russian agent of some kind. I believe you mentioned the acronym FSB. You are telling me that against her will and without her knowledge, an explosive device has been placed inside a titanium hip joint used to replace her own natural hip. Am I summing up the situation correctly?"

Casey nodded vigorously.

"You also said the only way to activate this uh...uh... device is by remote control from a short distance away."

"Yes, Doctor, exactly right." This was going better than Casey had hoped.

"And this remote activating device is where, exactly?"

"Well, I'm not sure. I did see it last in the possession of the man who wanted to use it, but I believe he lost it." Casey did not want to go into an explanation of who Vladimir and Al Rahman were, and what role they played in all this. The last time she saw them Al Rahman was flat on his back on the sidewalk and Vladimir was diving into the street. She had seen something fly out of Al Rahman's hand, but she was not even sure if it was the remote device, and if so, where it was now. She assumed Vladimir had secured it, but could not be sure.

"So it's possible the device is right here in my hospital."

Casey shook her head. "No, I'm pretty sure it is not here."

Casey was interrupted by the figure of Gordon Lewis rushing through the door. She was relieved both to see him and for the interruption. She did not want to stand around answering questions while the threat to Myda persisted. She just wanted them to get that god-awful thing out of her as soon as possible.

"Dr. Franks, I'm Gordon Lewis, Assistant Director in Charge of Domestic Terrorism. I'm very sorry for the trouble we have caused you. I understand the uh...uh... victim is in your office."

Mr. Lewis, I'm pleased to meet you," said Dr. Frank as she held out her hand, "although I wish we could have met under better circumstances. Yes, the woman is in my office. I understand she needs to be operated on immediately. I believe, however, we will need the services of the bomb squad to assist in the surgery."

"Yes, Doctor," said Gordon, "that's correct. I'll make the arrangements to take care of the disposal if you can assist us with extraction."

Dr. Franks stared for a moment at the two agents and Casey was briefly worried she would deny them, but the hospital administrator quickly put her at ease.

"I will arrange for a volunteer surgical team," Franks said. "As it happens, we do have one orthopedic surgeon who has recently returned from duty in Iraq. Perhaps he will have some insight into these kinds of things. I will see if he is available." Dr. Frank turned and walked over to her secretary's desk, quickly giving her instructions.

"Casey," said her boss, turning to her, "I hate to interrupt this unfortunate woman's reunion with her brother, but let's go in and talk to her for a moment." Before Casey could say anything, he pushed open the door to Dr. Frank's office and stepped inside. Before he had passed the doorway, however, he stopped and turned back to Casey.

"Where's Kosnar?"

"I don't know," said Casey.

"What do you mean, you don't know?" said Gordon speaking louder than he intended. "I thought he was with you."

Casey took her boss's arm, moving him out of the doorway and away from Dr. Frank, who was now on the phone. Once out of earshot, she rapidly brought him up to speed on the events that had transpired, starting with Vladimir recognizing his sister on the video monitor. Gordon Lewis stood impassively listening to her explanation and when she finished, he stared at her for a few seconds. Then, shaking his head he said, "I'm not sure I approve of your actions, Casey, but then again, I'm not sure I would have done it differently myself." He paused.

"Ok look, you get on the horn to the local police bomb disposal unit and have them get up here right away. Also, alert hospital security. Have them be on the lookout for anyone suspicious. This hospital is going to be in a very vulnerable position until we get that thing out of her body. If your boy Kosnar is who he says he is, then I expect he will try to make contact. I just hope he and Al Rahman are not cooking up some scheme right now. You and I have gone out on a limb for that fellow. I hope he is on the up and up."

*　*　*

Dr. Zack Powell had just finished a long day at the hospital and was glad to be going home. Having spent most of the past year in Iraq performing countless surgeries on gravely injured American and Iraqi soldiers, he was still trying to get back into his regular home routine with his wife and two young daughters. His wife had strongly supported his decision to volunteer his medical expertise to the army, but her joy and relief at his return had been stronger then either of them had expected. As he strode towards his car he was looking forward to a quiet dinner and some play time with his girls. He clicked the remote to unlock the car as his beeper went off.

Tossing his backpack onto the front seat, he pulled the beeper off his belt and glanced at the message. The numbers 911 quickly got his attention and he reluctantly jogged back into the hospital as he heard his name over the hospital's public address system, asking him to immediately contact Dr. Franks, the hospital administrator. Grabbing the nearest phone, he dialed the number, and Dr. Franks' assistant put him through immediately. Dr. Powell listened for about a minute and then exclaimed," You're kidding." He listened for a few more seconds and then said, "I'm on my way," as he quickly hung up the phone and ran, towards the elevators. Given what he had just heard, he was anticipating a long and difficult evening at the hospital more reminiscent of his time in Iraq instead of dinner and playtime with his family.

* * *

Gordon Lewis was desperate to get his hands back on Vladimir Kosnar. He was very worried now that both Kosnar and Al Rahman were out there on the loose, perhaps working together. Perhaps everything that had transpired so far had been a ruse to distract the FBI from their real purpose. Maybe something else was going on. He had trusted Kosnar, assumed the man was telling the truth, still he instinctively believed the man was honest, but years of adversarial combat with the KGB, and more recently the FSB, predisposed him to doubt. Even if Kosnar was telling the truth, if Al Rahman was still on the loose, the doctors and nurses operating on the unfortunate Russian woman would be in danger. He would have to find a way to protect them. He immediately arranged for additional security at the hospital.

CHAPTER 38

C ASEY WAS EXHAUSTED. The last seventy-two hours had left her emotionally and physically spent. Her trip to London felt like it was weeks ago, rather than just two days before. Dr. Franks suggested Myda be kept in her office while the surgical team was assembled, and Gordon Lewis instructed Casey to remain with her. There had been a quick debate about evacuating the hospital or at least an area near where Myda would be located, but they decided an evacuation would be too disruptive for the patients. The real threat was only to people who were close to her, the doctors and nurses who would be doing the actual operation. That was of much larger concern to Dr. Franks, and she had quickly engaged Dr. Powell in conversation as soon as he arrived at her office.

Casey and Myda sat together uncomfortably for almost forty-five minutes, waiting for the surgical team to get ready. They talked briefly a few times, but they could never get the conversation going. Casey noticed Myda seemed at once both distracted and stoic. She sat quietly on the couch in Dr. Frank's office, her shoes off, legs pulled up close to her chest. Casey was about five feet away from her in a large comfortable chair. The moment she sat down, she realized she had picked an unwise location if the bomb in Myda's hip was detonated. She closed her eyes briefly at the thought and then put it out of her mind; they were in this together. She had put so many people at risk by bringing the Russian woman to the hospital in the first place, it seemed only right she share in the danger. The two women sat quietly, the minutes passing slowly.

Finally, there was a knock at the door and Dr. Powell walked in without waiting for a response. He quickly introduced himself and told Myda he would need to do a physical examination before they began surgery. Casey got up to leave, but Dr. Powell stopped her.

"Ms. Jennings," he said, "normally when I examine a woman, a female nurse is present. However, under the circumstances, I don't want to endanger more people than necessary. Please stay with us while I conduct the examination. Come on over here and stand next to me, please." Casey nodded and walked over to the spot he indicated.

The doctor turned back to Myda and directed her to lie flat on her back on the couch. Kneeling down on the floor beside her, he gently pulled her dress up above her waist, and then pulled her panties down away from her hips so both hip joints and her pubic hair were exposed. Casey remained standing above and just to the left of doctor and his patient. She felt uncomfortable at the sight of the exposed woman in front of her, but was quickly distracted, surprised by the scars on Myda's hips. Both hips. Two sets of long, thin scars ran for about six inches, almost parallel to each other, along both her hips. Dr. Powell looked up at Casey and said, "I thought we were dealing with just one hip replacement. There appear to be two."

Casey just shook her head and shrugged her shoulders. Dr. Powell turned back to Myda. "Did you have both your hip joints replaced?" he asked his voice even and soothing.

"I'm not sure," Myda responded. "They never really told us what they were doing. I had very bad pain in my left hip, although after my first surgery, I had scars on both sides. I asked why, but they just said it was necessary," she said, shrugging.

"And then you had surgery again more recently?" asked Dr. Powell.

"Yes, they contacted me and told me I had to come back for corrective surgery." She shrugged again. "I did what I was told. When I woke up from my second surgery, there were two more scars, again one on each side."

Dr. Powell gently ran his fingers along each scar. Then he had Myda move her legs up and down and side to side.

"OK. Very good," said Dr. Powell. He gently pulled Myda's panties back up and then pulled her dress back down. Flashing Myda a reassuring smile, he took her left hand in both of his as he stood up.

"We're going to have you X-rayed now and then you will be brought to the surgery. This is going to be a long process, so we need to get started. Do you have any questions for me about the procedure?"

Myda, still on her back on the couch, looked up at him and began to open her mouth to say something, then stopped, just shook her head and then looked away.

"Ms. Jennings," said Dr. Powell looking over at her. "There is an orderly outside with a wheelchair. Please tell him to come in."

The orderly pushed the wheelchair into the room and Dr. Powell, still holding Myda's hand, gently helped her up onto her feet. He directed her into the wheelchair, watching as the orderly knelt down to adjust the footrests.

"There are two gentlemen outside who are with the FBI," said Dr. Powell. "They will be escorting you to the X-ray facility and then back the surgical theatre as soon as the X-rays are done."

He patted Myda on the shoulder. "I'll see you in the operating room in a few minutes." Then he looked up at the orderly and said to him, "Quick as you can. I want pictures of both hips. The moment you're done, bring her to us. Don't wait for the picture. Got it?"

The orderly nodded and pushed the wheelchair through the open door. The two FBI agents quickly took up their positions, one in front of the wheelchair, and one behind the orderly. Casey started to follow, but before she could leave the office, Dr. Powell called her back.

"I was hoping we could have the hip replaced in about ninety minutes, but it looks like she has had both joints replaced. Is there any way of knowing which is the lethal one?"

Casey shook her head. "I don't know. Maybe something will show up in the x-ray," she said hopefully.

"Hmm, maybe," Dr. Powell replied with a long sigh. "I suppose we could do an MRI, but that will take a lot more time. This is going to be a longer ordeal than we planned so we just need to get started. I'm going right up to the OR right now. Would you find Dr. Franks and update her please."

As Casey watched Dr. Powell walk down the hallway, she wished she had said something to Myda before they had wheeled her away, something encouraging, but nothing had come to mind. She pushed the hair back from her forehead and rubbed her eyes. She was desperate to sleep but did not anticipate an opportunity to relax for quite sometime. This was going to be a long night, much longer than anyone had anticipated.

* * *

Abd Al Rahman sat in the small cramped emergency room waiting area feeling uncomfortably exposed. An armed security guard stood at the entrance to the waiting room and an assortment of injured and sick people sat or lay about on the plastic chairs clearly designed to prevent anyone from getting too comfortable. The incongruous site of a large man with a bloody face and wearing a blood splattered dress and high heels sitting opposite him drew his gaze, but he quickly looked away and he picked up a magazine, trying to look inconspicuous.

Soon after he had followed Kosnar's gurney into the emergency room, he had been ushered into the waiting area as they took the injured man for X-rays. Now, as he sat waiting, he pondered his options. He was certain he had heard Kosnar shout to the American woman something about taking the woman to the hospital. It made sense. If they knew, and Kosnar certainly did know, then they would try to get her to a hospital to have the replacement hip joint removed somehow. But which hospital? Was it possible the ambulance had taken Kosnar to the same one the American woman had taken his *shaheed*? Was she here now, in the same building undergoing surgery?

The image of doctors and nurses bent over a patient who suddenly exploded, sending body parts and shrapnel from surgical instruments across the room flashed in his mind. He glanced around, put his hand into his jacket pocket, carefully slipped the safety switch off and with one more glance around him, pressed the plunger. He involuntarily tensed, waiting for the sound of an explosion, but there was nothing. He waited for a few more seconds, and then reset the safety switch. Maybe it was too much to expect that Kosnar would have been taken to the same hospital as his *shaheed*. Still, he reassured himself, maybe this was a big hospital and she could be in a different part of the building, too far away to activate the bomb.

Just then the door to the emergency room opened and young male nurse stepped out. He beckoned to Al Rahman, who quickly rose from his seat.

"Your buddy is back from X-ray," the young man said brightly. "No fractures or any serious damage. Just a nasty cut on the head and probably a really bad headache. We sutured the cut and bandaged him and he'll probably be discharged in a few hours, after he has had some time to rest."

Al Rahman did his best to the show the man a happy, relieved smile. "Thank you very much," he said.

"You can go back there to sit with him if you like," the nurse said as he pushed the door open wider to let Al Rahman through.

For a moment Al Rahman panicked. It had not occurred to him he would be put into a room with Kosnar and even with the Russian in a weakened condition, he had no desire to see or confront him. He felt no fear of the Russian, only a loathing that he had denied him his martyrdom in Afghanistan and now interrupted his carefully made plans to attack San Francisco. But a confrontation with Kosnar would expose his cover and for a moment he stood still, not quite sure how to respond, but as he glanced at the nurse, he realized he was expected to go in. Not doing so would arouse suspicion.

As Al Rahman followed the nurse through the emergency room he was not sure what to do. If he walked in to Kosnar's room and Kosnar was awake, there would be a confrontation. Even if Kosnar was injured and debilitated, he would still probably react violently and quickly at the sight of Al Rahman.

The nurse walked quickly down the corridor, turning into a room with two beds separated by a green curtain. A young man with his leg in a cast laid uncomfortably on one bed, an older man sitting on the bed next to him trying to comfort him. The nurse pushed aside the curtain blocking the view to the second bed and exclaimed, "What the f…"

Al Rahman glanced around the nurse's back and, noticing the empty bed, quickly looked behind him, tensing for an attack from Kosnar. The nurse turned back to face him.

"He's not here. He must have gone to the bathroom. Stay here while I go find him. He's not supposed to be walking around unaided."

The nurse walked off shaking his head, muttering something about patients who don't listen as Al Rahman stood in the doorway watching him go. He stayed there until the nurse disappeared from view and then stepped into the corridor. Up ahead, he could see a large double door. He was not sure where the doorway led, but he knew he had to get out of the emergency ward. With a quick glance over his shoulder, he walked as quickly as he could on his still painful leg and pushed his way through the double door.

* * *

"I want everyone to stop what they're doing for just one moment, please," Dr. Powell said to the small surgical team working feverishly to get ready. From behind masks and protective eye shields, the anesthesiologist and surgical nurses turned to look at him.

He paused for a moment to make sure he had everybody's attention. "I want to reiterate that your assistance in this procedure is voluntary," he said, his bright eyes accentuated by the mask covering his mouth and nose, his voice carrying over the low hum of a machine in the background.

"Just to repeat and update you on what I think you have already been told. The FBI has informed us that the woman upon whom we are about to operate has a small explosive device inside the titanium hip joint in her left hip. I have just completed an examination of this woman and have discovered she appears to have had both hip joints replaced. It is therefore possible she has two explosive devices in her. These devices can be activated remotely. Apparently as you all probably heard already, that happened to a woman right here, today, in San Francisco." He paused and glanced around at the faces surrounding him. "The person or persons who are able to remotely activate the bomb are still at large. The FBI and police are doing their best to secure the hospital, but they cannot guarantee our safety. I had estimated we could be done with the extraction of the old hip joint in about ninety minutes, limiting our exposure as much as possible, but now with this new information, this will probably take about three hours." Powell paused for a moment, letting the information sink in. "If you feel uncomfortable or unwilling to participate, please step outside now. You are absolutely under no obligation to assist if you do not want to."

Powell stood quietly for a moment and then looked around the room making eye contact with everyone. Nobody moved.

"All right team," he said. "Let's get to work. Our patient will be arriving at any moment."

* * *

The darkness gave Vladimir some comfort. The only light coming in to the storeroom was through the bottom of the door. He lay back on the small bed of towels he had thrown together, eyes closed, breathing shallow, but steady. The throbbing in his head seemed to be ebbing and he was beginning to feel a little better. Not strong, but less weak and vulnerable than before.

It was an old agent's trick he had used: if disabled or incapacitated, find a hole or some place to hide to reduce your exposure. And with Al Rahman in the hospital, Vladimir knew that in his debilitated state, he was very exposed. Al Rahman regarded him as a threat, justifiably so, and would kill him in an instant if he had the opportunity. It was probably only the presence of all the medical personal that had kept him at bay so far.

Slipping out of the emergency ward had been quite simple. Even with the bandage wrapped around his head no one had noticed or challenged him. There were so many people coming and going, he had simply put on his clothes and walked into the main part of the hospital through a set of double doors. It had been an effort to maintain a normal gait, the pain in his head still making him disoriented. He looked for a safe spot in which to hide and was lucky to find a large linen storage room. The light was off as he walked in, but he could tell that the room was filled with large metal-framed shelves, each stacked with sheets and towels and other supplies. He had quickly made a bed for himself in a corner furthest from the door. He guessed that as night fell, the hospital staff would be reduced to a skeleton crew; the storage area might not be used until morning. He just needed a couple of hours to rest and clear his head.

* * *

As soon as Al Rahman walked out of the emergency ward into the hospital, he realized he needed to find some cover. There was a lot of police activity; uniformed officers, and men and women with green jackets with the acronym FBI emblazoned on the back milling about. Despite the threat of their presence, it reassured him to see them because he assumed that the FBI and police would not be around unless they had something to protect. He was increasingly confident Myda was in the building, perhaps undergoing surgery right now. All he had to do was walk through the hospital activating the remote. If she was in the building, eventually he would get close enough to her that the activator would work.

Up ahead of him in the corridor, a group of policemen were talking to two FBI agents. They had not seen him yet, but he did not want to walk past them. As nonchalantly as possible, he turned down a side corridor and began to look for cover.

As he walked through the wide hospital corridors, he saw an old man shuffling towards him dressed in a long bathrobe tied loosely around his waist. Under the robe, Al Rahman could see a well-washed hospital gown. With his left hand, the old man was pushing a tall metal pole supported by a four-way frame of small black wheels. Hanging from a small hook on top of the pole was an intravenous drip bag, with a thin pipe running from the bag until it disappeared into the left sleeve of the old man's gown. Al Rahman stopped and turned as the old man slowly passed him. He waited until the old man was about ten feet away, then he turned around to follow him.

* * *

Casey found Gordon Lewis in a room next to the hospital receptionist's desk. He had set up his command post there, and was standing over a map of the hospital when Casey walked in. He looked up at her and gave her a perfunctory smile.

"I take it the young lady is now in surgery." It was more a statement than a question.

"Yes," said Casey, "although we have a new complication."

"What now?"

"It appears she has had both hip joints replaced."

"What?" said Gordon, a look of astonishment on his face. "Is this what the doctor told you?"

"I saw it myself. The doctor had me watch the examination. She has two sets of scars on both hips. It looks like both were replaced in 1981 and both were updated at a later date."

"Oh, hell," said Gordon. "What does this mean? Are they going to remove them both?"

"Dr. Powell asked me to tell you that the window of vulnerability has gone from about ninety minutes to three hours."

Gordon glanced down at his wristwatch. "OK," he said, "this changes nothing. It's almost eight o'clock right now. That means we will be clear by about eleven, baring any new complications. We've already decided we can't evacuate the hospital, so we'll just have to maintain our security curtain a bit longer. Does Dr. Franks know about this?"

Casey shook her head. "I was going to tell her after I had updated you."

"I'll update her right now," said Gordon as he reached for the phone. "Then you and I can go round and review the security arrangements."

"OK," said Casey, "I'll wait for you in the lobby."

Casey stepped out into the lobby as Gordon Lewis asked the hospital receptionist to page Dr. Franks. She was desperate for a cup of coffee. She couldn't remember the last time she had eaten anything, and the idea of coffee seemed enticing. She wandered over to the receptionist's counter and casually leaned up against it. There were two women behind the desk, one of whom had her back to Casey and appeared to be organizing some files. The second was in a conversation with an agitated male nurse also standing at the counter.

"What do you mean, you can't find him? He can't just have walked out," said the receptionist.

"Well, I'm telling you I can't find him anywhere. I've looked in every room in the emergency ward and he just isn't there. He's gone, skedaddled, checked out, left."

"He was a head case, wasn't he?" said the receptionist looking down at a file. "Hit by a car. Wasn't he brought here with somebody?"

"Yes," said the male nurse. "That's what I'm telling you. They're both gone. I took his buddy in to see him and found the empty bed. Then I went to look for him. When I came back the buddy was gone. Couple of foreigners," said the nurse, shaking his head. "Don't know how to follow the rules, always screwing things up."

"Excuse me."

The receptionist and the nurse both turned to look at Casey.

"Did you say there were a couple of foreigners in the emergency room? Do you know where they were from?"

"Who are you?" said the nurse looking over at Casey.

"Casey Jennings, FBI," said Casey, flashing her badge.

"Russians," the nurse said, quickly becoming accommodating. "They were both Russians."

"Are you sure?" said Casey. "How do know they were Russians?"

"They said so. Actually, the guy who was injured didn't say anything. His buddy told us they were visiting Russian businessmen."

Casey put her right hand on the nurse's arm, just above the elbow. "The injured man, what happened to him? Was he badly hurt?"

Before the nurse could answer, Casey heard Gordon Lewis' voice behind her. She turned to look at him and noticed he was talking to a couple of FBI agents just outside his office.

"Gordon," she said loudly. "Gordon," she repeated her voice insistent.

Gordon Lewis quickly broke off his conversation and strode over to her.

"What's up?"

"I think they are both here, in the building."

"Who?" said Gordon, narrowing his eyes.

"Kosnar and Al Rahman. I'm pretty sure they are both in the hospital somewhere."

CHAPTER 39

MICHAEL FREED WAS laughing at his younger colleague. "It's not fucking funny," said the younger man. "You don't understand, this chick is a babe, a fucking babe. Tonight was our third date, you know, the big one. We were finally going to do it." He made a phallic gesture.

At four o'clock that afternoon after the explosion outside the Embarcadero Station the Mayor had declared a citywide tactical alert. The partial shutdown of the BART system, the presence of thousands of convention delegates and arrival of the presidential candidate had made rush hour in San Francisco unbearable. The city was in gridlock. Even with additional resources sent in by the Governor to help the city prevent a terrorist attack and maintain order, there were simply not enough officers on duty to manage traffic and the extra security required by the convention. With the tactical alert authorization in hand, the Chief of Police directed all officers to remain on duty after their shifts ended. He further ordered all off-duty officers to report in immediately. He put out the word that only a doctor's note stating they were near death would excuse any officer. He needed every available resource if public order and safety were to be maintained.

Michael Freed and his younger colleague, Peter Chin, had been about to go off duty at four that afternoon when they were ordered to stand by. After sitting around for a while with nothing to do, they had been dispatched to the San Francisco General Hospital and temporarily assigned to the FBI to assist with search and security. Soon after their arrival and a quick briefing, they were directed to the hospital's third floor.

"What about you, man? Didn't you have any plans this evening?" Chin asked.

"Nothing special," his partner replied. "With a kid in college and one graduating from high school, I'll take all the overtime I can get. Anyway, my wife is working tonight too, so I'm not being missed at home or anything."

"Shit, well I'm being missed, or I hope I am. She was pretty pissed off when I cancelled."

"Man, you're so damn horny, I better tell all the nurses to watch out. In fact, I don't plan to turn my back on you myself the rest of this evening." Chin gave Freed a good-natured punch on the shoulder and said, "Come on. Let's check all the rooms on this corridor and then go and get some coffee."

The two policemen walked down the long passageway, methodically checking each room as they went.

* * *

Vladimir rolled slowly onto his back and opened his eyes. He felt a lot better but his head still hurt, but not nearly as badly. He lay still for a moment, and then tried to stand, but he moved too quickly. A wave of nausea swept over him. He sat back down and rested his head between his knees, waiting for the nausea to dissipate. Grabbing hold of a metal shelf he pulled himself up, slower this time, much more deliberately. He reached up and gingerly touched the bandage wrapped around his head, testing to see if blood was seeping from the sutured cut. He felt nothing on his fingers. He could not walk out with the bandage on so he carefully unwrapped it, again gently touching the stitches in his forehead to make sure there was no blood. He wished he could put a small bandage over the cut making it less conspicuous but the storeroom only seemed to contain linen.

Feeling much steadier on his feet he made his way through the storeroom and stood behind the door. He looked down at his watch. The glass face was cracked, but the watch appeared to be working. Almost nine o'clock. He closed his eyes, tried to work out how long it had been since he had seen Abd Al Rahman, since the accident.

Five hours, it must be at least five hours. If Casey had brought Myda here, then he was probably already too late. Al Rahman would have had ample time to activate the bomb. Vladimir pursed his lips and closed his eyes briefly, then reached down for the door handle. It was stuck. He pushed, but it remained closed. Then he put his shoulder against the door. It gave way and he stumbled out into the passageway, directly in front of officers Peter Chin and Michael Freed.

* * *

"He's right here, Sir. Third floor, on the West Side of the building. We found him just as he stepped out of a linen storeroom," Peter Chin said into his portable radio.

"You sure it's Kosnar?" Gordon Lewis asked.

"Yes, Sir," Peter Chin responded. "He confirmed his identity to us. He also matches the description."

"Anyone with him?" Gordon asked. "Any sign of Abd Al Rahman?"

"No, Sir. He's all alone. We checked the storeroom. It's clean."

"OK," said Gordon. "I'll send people up to get him. Walk him over to the elevators on the third floor and meet them there."

"FBI is on the way," Peter Chin said to his partner. "We'll meet them at the elevators."

"Yeah, I heard," Freed responded. "Come on, Mr. Kosnar. This way please."

Peter Chin took up a position on Vladimir's right side, holding him firmly with one hand just above Vladimir's right elbow. Michael Freed placed both his hands on Vladimir's left arm, his right hand just above Vladimir's elbow, his left hand on Vladimir's wrist. Walking slowly, the three men proceeded down the corridor.

The route to the elevators was down one short corridor and then down a second long corridor to the right. The corridors were mostly empty. A couple of nurses passed as they walked, giving them quizzical looks but saying nothing. The three men turned the corner and continued towards the elevators, now about forty yards away at the far end of the corridor. A doctor in a white coat was walking towards them, but he stopped before he reached them and went into a room, closing the door behind him.

Vladimir's eyes were hooded, half closed as he walked with his escorts. His head still hurt, although being up and walking made him feel better physically, but emotionally he was drained. He had failed. He had come so close, actually making brief contact with his sister, but now he was sure she was dead. Too much time had passed since he and Al Rahman had arrived at the hospital. He felt almost relieved to be in the FBI's custody, tired of the chase, but mostly just sad. To have come so far and gotten so close, only to lose her at the end was cruel irony.

* * *

The hospital layout was a bit confusing. Al Rahman was trying to be methodical, slowly walking the same route on each floor, pressing the remote every few seconds, but the floors were not all the same. He had gotten lost on the second floor and had to retrace his steps to make sure he covered it completely. Once a nurse asked him what he was doing wandering around, but he just mumbled something unintelligible to her as he shuffled away. She stared after him for a few seconds, and then shrugged and walked off in the other direction.

He was sure it was just a matter of time. If she was here, he'd get her. He just had to get close enough. He shuffled over to the elevator, hesitated briefly at the sight of a policeman inside, and then continued forward as the officer held the door open for him. He pushed the button for the third floor and again the policemen held the door for him when the elevator stopped. He grunted a thank you as he awkwardly pushed the ungainly intravenous holder in front of him with the palm of his mutilated hand, breathing a small sigh of relief when the policeman did not follow him. Then, looking up, his heart jumped when he saw Kosnar and two policemen turn into the corridor walking towards him. He briefly considered getting back on the elevator, but decided to keep going. Tucking his chin as far into his chest as he could, he slowly shuffled forward.

* * *

Vladimir looked up and glanced at the old man coming towards them. Something about the old man made him look more closely. He was dressed in a long bathrobe that ran down to his ankles and was tied tightly around his waist. He was pushing a wheeled intravenous stand with his right hand. A plastic tube from the IV bag looped down below his arm and disappeared back into his right sleeve. His left hand was tucked firmly inside his pocket. A large woolen cap covered his head and he was walking with his eyes downcast, in a slow and what looked like a painful shuffle. But there was something oddly familiar about him.

The policemen and their charge were now about ten feet away from the approaching patient. Vladimir looked him up and down and then noticed the intravenous bag was empty, completely drained. Vladimir tried to look at the man's face, but his head was down almost to his chest so it was not possible to make out his features. As they were about to pass in the passageway, Vladimir noticed the man's hand on the intravenous bag holder. All the fingers were just stubs and he was pushing the pole with the palm of his hand. Vladimir's first reaction to seeing Al Rahman was intense anger followed almost immediately by relief. If Al Rahman was still in the hospital wandering about dressed like a patient, he must have failed to detonate the device. Vladimir was tempted to look back over his shoulder, but did not want to alarm his escort. He kept in step with them for a few more paces, until he estimated Al Rahman was about ten feet behind them, and then he acted.

Peter Chin, the officer on his right was holding him with just one hand, so Vladimir dealt with him first. Using a short, sharp jab, Vladimir drove the side of his hand into the man's groin, eliciting a painful grunt and momentarily immobilizing the man. The second officer responded quickly and appropriately. As Vladimir attacked his partner, Freed twisted Vladimir's left arm up and behind his back, using his leverage to try and control his prisoner. It was a good move, one that would have worked on most people, but not the former KGB officer. Instead of trying to counter the policeman's painful grip, Vladimir moved with him, pulling the policeman towards him and off balance. Then he turned from right to left and hit Officer Freed with two quick and hard blows directly on his temple with the point of his elbow. Freed cried out and dropped down to one knee. When Vladimir hit him again, this time on the back of the neck and Freed went down.

Vladimir quickly turned his attention back to Peter Chin, who was recovering from the blow to his testicles. He was at once pulling himself up using the wall for support and reaching for his weapon. His hand was already on the gun's grip when Vladimir hit him again, driving his knee into Chin's head. Chin grunted and fell forward against the Russian, releasing his hand from his weapon. In one smooth movement, Vladimir pulled Chin's weapon from its holster, cocked it and then turned to face his nemesis.

Al Rahman was running as fast as he could on his lame leg. He had heard the commotion behind him and after a moment's hesitation abandoned the intravenous stand and took off down the long corridor. The bathrobe was constricting his movement and he struggled to untie it as he ran. As he reached the end of the corridor, he turned left, placing his left hand on the wall to help him make the turn. Vladimir fired a single shot before his target disappeared down around the corner.

* * *

In the elevator, the sound of the single gunshot was clearly audible followed almost instantly by the bell indicating their arrival on the third floor. Casey Jennings and the two young FBI agents with her quickly drew their weapons and took up defensive positions on either side of the elevator doors. Casey braced herself against the doorway, slightly crouched, gun held in both hands, pointed down and in front of her. Across from her, the two agents had assumed the same position.

The elevator jerked to a stop. After what felt like an eternity, the doors slid open. Weapon held out in front of her, Casey peered into the corridor just as a loud scream echoed down the hallway.

* * *

Vladimir wasn't sure if he had hit him, but he heard a scream and then the sound of metal and glass crashing to the ground. Running down the corridor, he skidded around the corner, gun in front of him. A nurse was lying on the floor, a metal tray and broken glass around her. Al Rahman had disappeared.

"Which way?" Vladimir shouted. "Which way did he go?"

"Uh…I don't know," the nurse answered as she rolled onto her knees." I didn't see what happened. Someone just came around the corner and crashed into me. I don't know…"

Vladimir looked down the corridor and saw a door swing slowly back and forth on its hinge. Walking towards the room, he stopped outside. He listened for a moment and then pushed the door open and stepped in. A woman lay on the single bed occupying the center of the room, sheet pulled up to her nose, eyes wide with fright. Al Rahman was on the far side of the bed, his left arm dangling uselessly, blood running down his arm and dripping onto the floor. Vladimir's single shot had shattered his left elbow but he still managed to hold the detonator in his hand.

The two men stared at each other across the bed. Vladimir's face was inscrutable, only his unblinking, cold gray eyes providing any clue to his emotions. He was even oblivious to the small trickle of blood oozing out of the wound in his head and running down his face. Al Rahman was breathing hard, trying to catch his breath and ignore the pain in the shattered arm. His eyes were closed and with lips barely moving, he muttered a prayer.

Opening his eyes he stared at Kosnar and then tried to turn off the safety switch with his right hand, but without a thumb, he couldn't move it. Grunting, he tried unsuccessfully to use his wounded arm and howled in pain and frustration as the activator fell to the floor. He stomped on it once and then stopped and stared at Vladimir Kosnar. He blinked once slowly. His face was gray and he was unsteady, rocking back and forth on his heels. Then he dropped his arms by his side leaned his head back and looked up as if in supplication and began to chant "Allahu Akbar, Allahu Akbar." God is great, God is great.

Vladimir's eyes narrowed as he stared at Al Rahman. He thought he heard his name shouted out, but he wasn't sure. A strange memory of a cold, harsh, unforgiving place briefly entered his consciousness, and just as quickly the sensation was gone. Slowly, he raised his weapon and pointed it directly at the other man's head. Sighting down the short barrel, he fired.

CHAPTER 40

ONE OF THE FBI agents started to step out of the elevator but Casey grabbed the back of his jacket and yanked him back in. She looked at the two young agent's faces. They were wide eyed and pumped full of adrenalin, just itching for their first take down. The last thing she needed was a couple of rookies charging down the corridor and getting themselves shot or shooting a patient.

"I'll lead," she hissed at them both. "You follow and cover me and for Christ's sake hold your fire. Remember, we're in a hospital."

Without waiting for a response, Casey stepped cautiously out of the elevator. A few feet in front of her she could see one policeman lying prone and motionless. Next to him another policeman was slowly pulling himself into a sitting position, his back against the wall. He was obviously in a lot of pain. A couple of people had come out of their rooms into the corridor.

"FBI. This is the FBI," Casey shouted, her voice echoing down the corridor. "Please return to your rooms and close the doors. You Sir, yes you." She gestured at a man peering from a nearby doorway. "Step back into your room, please. Everybody get back into your rooms."

After making a quick sweep of the corridor with her eyes, Casey ran over to the injured policemen. She knelt down next to the one who was sitting up and asked him if he was all right.

"Yeah," he grunted. "I'm OK, I'll be OK."

"What happened?" Casey asked.

"Uh...I don't know," the man said as he grimaced and clenched his teeth against the pain in his groin. "He... uh...just attacked us, got my weapon, uh...he took my weapon."

"Which way did he go?"

"I'm not sure." The policeman grunted again. I heard a shot, but I didn't see who he shot or where he went. I'm sorry...sorry..."

"That's OK. Take it easy, you'll be OK."

Casey looked over at one of her young colleagues who was checking on the still prone and motionless police- man on the floor. "Man, this guy is out cold..." he started to say before Casey cut him off.

"He's taken this guy's gun. He's got his gun."

"Kosnar?"

"Yes, he must have fired the shot. He must have seen Al Rahman."

Casey stood up and waved over a couple of nurses hovering nearby in a half-open doorway. "Did you see which way he went?" One of them shook her head, but the other pointed left.

"He went that way. I saw the guy fire and run over there."

"OK, come over here please and take care of these guys."

As the nurses stepped forward, Casey and the two agents ran toward the end of the corridor then stopped, peering carefully around the corner. Casey shouted out Vladimir's name.

"Vladimir," she shouted. "Vladimir Kosnar, can you hear me?"

Just then the explosive sound of a single shot fired nearby echoed and reverberated harshly through the hospital corridor.

"Over there," Casey shouted, pointing with her weapon to a door three rooms down the corridor. She hesitated for a second, then kicked the door open and stepped in. The two young agents followed her in.

Vladimir had his back towards them, his weapon still pointed out in front of him as if he was aiming at some object on the wall.

"Secure him," Casey ordered the agent behind her, indicating Kosnar with a flick of her head.

One of the two agents stepped around Casey and placed the barrel of his gun firmly on the back of Vladimir's head. "Drop your weapon, Mr. Kosnar," he said. "Do it now, please."

Vladimir let out a long breath that whistled through his lips, and then slowly raised his arms over his head, gun dangling in his right hand. The agent quickly took it from him and handed it his colleague who checked the safety and then shoved the weapon into his pants.

"Hands behind your back please, Mr. Kosnar," the young agent said as he tapped the Russian on the shoulder with the barrel of his gun. He quickly snapped handcuffs onto Vladimir's arms and holstered his weapon. He paused a second and then drove the heel of his foot into the back of Kosnar's knee forcing him harshly to the ground.

"Hey," Casey snapped at the agent, flashing him a dirty look. "That's not necessary."

She glanced at Vladimir's head, noticed the blood oozing from the wound in his head and running down his face.

"Stand him up and get him to a doctor right away."

As the agent led Kosnar away Casey looked down at the woman in the bed. She was clasping the sheet over her head, only her fingers exposed, bright red fingernails in stark contrast to her white hands and white sheet. Casey pulled the sheet away and stared down at her. "Are you all right?" Casey asked her.

The woman said nothing but nodded vigorously. Then she grabbed the sheet from Casey's hand and pulled it back over her head. Casey patted her briefly on the shoulder, and then leaned over the bed to look at the man on the floor. He was obviously dead. There was small hole in the center of his forehead and he was lying flat on his back, dark red blood pooling near his shoulders and neck. His arms were flung out from his body and Casey could see a long thin tube near his right hand. She holstered her weapon, quickly moved around the bed, and stepped over the body. Then she knelt down and slowly, carefully, she picked up the tube with just her forefinger and her thumb and held it up. The sound of running feet drew her attention as Gordon Lewis burst in followed by two more FBI agent all with guns drawn.

"All clear, all clear," Casey shouted. "It's OK. It's all over."

"Where's Al Rahman?" Gordon Lewis asked urgently.

Casey waived him over to the far side of the bed and Gordon Lewis stared at him for a minute.

"Alright," he said after a moment, "it's over.

Just then the door burst open again as the hospital administrator Dr. Franks came rushing in.

"Did you stop him, did you get him?" she shouted. Casey held up the remote activator and showed it to her. "This is it," she said. "He's right here-he's dead."

"Here, in this room," Dr. Franks exclaimed as she looked over the bed at the body. She stepped back placing her hand over her heart. "My God, do you know where we are, where we're standing?" She pointed up to the ceiling. "The operating theater they're working in is just one floor above and two doors down. We're less than fifty feet from that woman."

Gordon Lewis and Casey Jennings glanced at each other for a moment. Gordon raised his eyebrows and said, "Casey, let's get that thing out of this building and away from here right now."

Casey nodded, quickly walked out of the room and started to run towards the elevators. Then she stopped and turned to the doorway for the stairs. Taking the steps two at a time, she dashed towards the hospital entrance and handed the activator to a member of the police bomb squad. Within ten minutes it had been placed in a secure portable trailer and was a mile from the hospital.

* * *

Casey found a quiet room near the nurse's station to wait until the surgery ended. After the gunfire, Dr. Franks, the hospital administrator, had declared a state of emergency at the hospital and had closed it for all new patients. Non critical emergencies were directed to other hospitals. Two surgeries had been scheduled for the evening, but she had them postponed until the next day. All visitors, except for parents and guardians in the pediatric ward, were sent home. Dr. Franks had had enough excitement for one day. The coroner had already removed Al Rahman's body from the third floor, and the two injured policemen were resting comfortably. Casey had checked on Vladimir who had been treated by a doctor and was being held in a conference room. He asked about his sister and she told him what she knew and then he asked about the two policemen he had attacked. She smiled wryly as she responded.

"They're a bit bruised and battered but they'll be alright."

She had wanted to sit with him but Gordon Lewis had ordered him to be held in a small conference room for a thorough debriefing on what had just occurred while his memory was still fresh. Gordon had ordered the handcuffs to be removed as FBI agents debriefed him.

Casey was exhausted. Gordon had tried to send her off to her hotel, but she insisted on waiting until the surgery ended. She lay down on a sofa and quickly fell asleep.

"Casey Jennings."

It took a few seconds for her to realize her name was being called. A nurse was shaking her shoulder.

"Are you Casey Jennings?"

"What? Oh yes, I'm sorry. I'm Casey." She sat up, pushing her hair away from her eyes, blinking rapidly at the woman above her.

"There's a call for you from England. Gentleman says it's urgent. He says he needs to talk to you immediately."

"From England? Did he say his name?"

"Yes, I think it was a Campbell, Alex or Ian. Something like that. I told him you were resting but he insisted on speaking to you right away."

* * *

Casey Jennings, Gordon Lewis, and Dr. Franks were standing inside Dr Frank's office, all staring down at the black speaker box on her desk.

"Ian, it's over," Casey was saying, her voice carrying just a hint of frustration at Ian's insistence the call was urgent. "Al Rahman is dead. The remote has been secured. Myda Kosnar or whatever her name is being operated on as we speak. The second uh...surgery should be completed in about an hour." Casey glanced over at Dr. Franks, who nodded once in confirmation.

"You say they are still operating on her now?" Ian Campbell said, his accent sounding a lot thicker to Casey over the phone. "Well, if that's the case, then I'm afraid it's not over. Let me introduce you to Dr. Paul Thompson, Professor of Telecommunications at Sussex University. He's the gentleman who has been studying the remains of the receiver we found. Dr. Thompson, please go ahead."

The sound of a man clearing his throat came over the speaker.

"Yes, good morning or should I say good evening to you over there in California. Um..uh...the device Inspector Campbell sent to me was very interesting. It's an old analog receiver built in 1978 or '79. Japanese made, quite ingenious for its time, but highly unsophisticated by today's standards."

"That's very interesting professor," Gordon Lewis interrupted, "but I'm afraid I don't understand the relevance-"

The professor continued speaking over the interruption. "This type of receiver was built long before the wide distribution of cellular phones, portable computers, or hand-held video game units. It was built when there was very little competition for radio frequency, so it does not have any kind of built-in encryption." There was a pause as the professor stopped speaking.

"So," said Ian Campbell encouraging the professor to continue.

"So," the professor said slowly, "the receiver simply needs to receive a very basic message to be activated. The sequence of codes required to activate it is only four digits long."

"I still don't understand what-." Gordon Lewis began before Dr. Franks cut him off.

"Professor Thompson, are you saying the code necessary to activate the receiver simply requires a sequence of four numbers to be generated, in other words, the number of possible codes is four numbers out of ten?"

"No, it's worse than that I'm afraid. It's four out of six. The code is as simple as one two three four, or three five two six," the professor responded.

Dr. Franks' eyes widened. Her undergraduate degree had been in mathematics. She quickly guessed where the professor was heading.

"I still don't get it. What does this mean?" Gordon Lewis insisted his voice agitated.

"Well," the professor continued, "every electronic device broadcasts electronic noise in a certain frequency range. Even devices not designed to produce a signal do so anyway. That's why when you fly they always make passengers turn off their portable computers and video games during take off and landing. There has been some evidence electronic noise produced by portable computers and iPods and other devices can affect the plane's navigation system."

"But what does that have to do with the four digit code in this receiver-?"

"Mr. Lewis," said Dr. Franks, cutting him off, "I think what the professor is telling us is that the number of permutations or sequences of numbers required to activate the receiver is very small. Apparently, when they built the receiver, they did not expect it to compete with the millions of additional signals broadcast by all these new devices."

"You mean something else could activate the bombs? Gordon Lewis asked. "But," he continued before the professor could answer, "it must still be unlikely the receiver would pick up exactly the right signal, wouldn't it?"

"I can't give you the odds," said Professor Thompson. "It would depend on the number of electronic devices being used and their proximity to the receiver. However, I would guess in a densely populated urban area, the odds are quite high. Inspector Campbell told me almost half of these women have died since 1992. I think this might explain why. That time frame would coincide with the huge new deployment of cellular phones in Russia."

There was a pause in the room while everyone digested what they had just heard. The professor started up his explanation again, thinking perhaps he had not been completely understood.

"Look," he said. "It's a bit like automatic garage door openers. They all operate on frequencies of 290 to 440 megahertz. Thousands of them are on the same frequency and yet the odds are that your door and your neighbor's door are on different frequencies so you won't be accidentally opening up each others door when you activate the remote. However, I am sure you have all heard of garage doors just seeming to open and close spontaneously."

He was getting a little breathless, speaking more quickly now, excited to be sharing his considerable expertise.

"Just like the analog device you gave me, that part of the spectrum isn't uniquely assigned to garage doors, so people with powerful radio-controlled model airplanes have been known to send the neighbor's door flapping up and down. For that matter, garages on the flight paths of airports have been subject to fits of spontaneous opening. Normally the devices operate properly, ignoring extraneous signals. The incoming waves must be of the right frequency, arriving in the proper direction, and strong enough to trigger the radio-controlled switch. That's usually sufficient to guarantee proper operation, but not when the ionosphere is wobbling about severely. Then there are the radio-propagation games played by the troposphere, the breathable layer of the atmosphere." The professor realized his information was probably getting more detailed than his audience cared to hear at this time.

"Uh, look, uh, when it's cold and a strong inversion layer develops so the hills are much warmer than the valleys, other local signals operating near garage-door frequencies can be bent or bounced from their path. Garage doors then can receive stray radar signals, military communications, all manner of normally unnoticed broadcasts. If I correctly recall my visit to San Francisco many years ago, it's a very hilly city with wide temperature changes."

The professor stopped speaking and his words hung in the air for a few seconds. Dr. Franks' eyes narrowed for a moment and then she pushed the intercom on her desk.

"This is Dr. Franks. Connect me to OR four," she barked into the receiver as soon as she heard the receptionist.

While waiting for someone in the operating room to answer, Dr. Franks glanced at Gordon and Casey. Both

FBI agents were looking at her expectantly, but other than slightly narrowed eyes, Dr. Franks' face did not reveal her level of stress.

She spoke into the phone again. "This is Dr. Franks. Can you put Dr. Powell on the phone please." After another pause, she said, "Dr. Powell, this is Dr. Franks. I'm sorry to disturb you, but I need another estimate of how much longer the surgery will take?" Dr. Franks was quiet for a moment, and then said, "Thank you doctor. Please listen carefully. I need you to turn off every non-essential electronic device in the operating room. It is imperative that only the equipment essential to completing the surgery be maintained. Everything else in the OR must be turned off. I'll explain why later but, please do it right away."

There was a pause as Dr. Franks listened to the surgeon's response. He did not appear to be arguing. Then she said, "I'd admonish you to work faster if I thought you could, but I know you are doing your best." She hung up the phone and said simply, "about forty minutes, another forty minutes." She glanced down at her wristwatch and then hurried out of her office.

Gordon Lewis quickly thanked Ian Campbell for the information and hung up the phone, turning to Casey as he did so. "Get upstairs. Have our people turn off their portable radios and cell phones. Better yet, collect them and get them off the hospital grounds. I'll go outside and get the cops to turn off their portable radios and car radios–"

He was interrupted by Dr. Franks' voice over the loudspeaker.

"This is Dr. Franks. I am the Hospital Administrator. I am sorry to disturb you, but I have an important announcement to make. First of all, I want to assure you the hospital is secure. The noise you heard earlier was gunfire, but the police and FBI have completely secured the building." She paused before continuing.

"Now please do exactly as I say. If you are watching TV or listening to the radio, please immediately turn them off. If you are wearing a pager or using a cell phone, please turn off those devices as well. Please do not be alarmed. You are not in any danger. This is purely a protective measure we are taking. This will last for about forty-five minutes. I repeat. Please turn off all television sets, radios, pagers, portable phones, and computers and any other non-essential electronic devices. Nurses, all ward nurses please immediately check each room in your area and ensure these devices are turned off. Nurses, please collect all remote controls for the televisions and bring them back to your stations. I repeat I want the nurses on each floor to collect all TV remotes. I apologize to everyone for the inconvenience, but I must insist you comply immediately. Thank you for your cooperation."

Casey followed her boss out of the executive offices and turned to run towards the elevators. She almost knocked over Dr. Franks, who was coming out of a side office just in front of her, also running towards the elevators. The two women looked at each other as they reached the elevator bank, but said nothing. Casey glanced at her watch. She looked up at the elevator floor indicator lights and impatiently pushed the button again to summon the elevators. "Come on, come on," she said under breath.

A bell sounded and the elevator doors slid silently open. Both women dashed inside and Dr. Franks pressed the button for the forth floor, then pressed and held the door-close button. As soon as they stepped off the elevator, Casey realized that Dr. Franks' broadcast message had been effective. Nurses were scurrying about, some struggling with handfuls of TV remote controls. A couple of patients were standing in the hallways in their hospital gowns or pajamas looking confused, trying unsuccessfully to get someone's attention. The sound of an argument echoed down the hallway from one of the rooms. As Dr. Franks hurried off in the direction of the argument, Casey ran towards the operating room.

* * *

"We're ready for them now," Dr. Powell called out, Myda's second titanium hip joint held securely in both hands. Two members of the San Francisco bomb squad stepped into the operating room, stopping at the entrance as instructed. They were covered from head to toe in bulky body armor. Between them was a small but heavily reinforced steel drum they had wheeled in with them. As Dr. Powell walked towards them carrying the device, the policemen unsnapped four heavy bolts securing the lid of the steel drum. Together, they lifted the heavy lid and waited while Dr. Powell, slowly and very carefully, placed the hip joint inside. The first time they had done it with the first hip joint, Dr. Powell had let the device bump against the side of the drum as he lowered it in, making everyone jump slightly. This time he had no trouble, and was already turning back to his patient while the officers were securing the lid on the steel drum. Slowly, they wheeled it out of the operating room and back into the corridor. Dr. Franks, Gordon Lewis, Casey Jennings and a few other FBI agents and policemen watched as the two men maneuvered their heavy load toward a freight elevator. Then they were gone.

CHAPTER 41

H OURS AFTER AL RAHMAN was killed, a raging
debate broke out in the upper echelons of
the national security apparatus about what
to do about the Russian women with the bombs still
implanted and at large. Some members of Homeland
Security wanted the FBI to launch a massive manhunt
to find, capture and disarm them while others in the
Administration wanted to get the story off the front
pages of the newspapers as soon as possible. With a
presidential election coming up, the threat of randomly
exploding women was a tough topic to counter.

The National Security Advisor, a man known and
well respected for his blunt assessments, summed up the
situation before the President and a few of his political
and security advisors in his typical way.

"Mr. President," he said, "about two million Americans die each year, the vast majority from natural causes.
However," he continued as he looked around the room,
"thousands, in fact tens of thousands of Americans die
from unnatural causes in car accidents, fires, shootings,

stabbings, drug overdoses and yes, even explosions. We have gas explosions, accidental dynamite explosions, and methamphetamine lab explosions. The list is simply endless." He paused before he continued. "As long as the public believes these deaths to be part of our culture, part of our status quo, no-one really cares. Just the threat of a foreign terrorist attack strikes fear, probably irrational fear into our society, but an ex-husband stabbing his wife to death or setting her on fire, or a teenage gangster shooting another teenager to death because he was wearing the wrong colored outfit in the wrong part of town is just part of our daily noise. It comes and it goes." He gazed around the room once more before continuing.

"Should we make every effort to find these women and secure them? Of course we should. But if we don't find them all and some just explode spontaneously without being specifically targeted by a terrorist handler will it matter? Statistically not a whit, and politically and socially it will matter even less."

There was silence in the room when he finished speaking until the President uttered a short, sharp laugh. "Well, I suppose the National Security Advisor won't be competing for the national humanitarian award any time soon," he said with a smile as he glanced around the room.

"I know its harsh and cold Mr. President," the man, continued as he spoke over the laughter following the President's comment, "but it's also realistic. Now that Devskoy and Abd Al Rahman are dead and cannot manipulate these women, cannot use them for their own ends, these women are no longer terrorists, they are just victims."

As is typical in Washington, a compromise was reached and a task force was established to quietly identify and find each woman. No national bulletins were issued but the FBI team worked diligently to find each woman. They focused their search in the San Francisco Bay area assuming that Al Rahman had positioned more than just two women there. A rigorous check of most of the hotels in the bay area turned up numerous leads but nothing concrete. Two women died alone in hotel rooms in the east bay in spontaneous explosions that were confirmed to come from hip replacements and another woman died in the back of taxi in Manhattan also killing the driver but after that the leads dried up and the task force made no further progress. By then the story had dropped off the front pages as the country geared up for the national election and then Christmas. The public's initial fascination with the story ebbed and the talking heads on television found something else to talk about. Members of the task began to be reassigned to other more pressing issues.

Myda Kosnar's dual surgeries left her quite weak but her naturally athletic body responded well to the physical therapy that began almost immediately. She was released from the hospital after six days and deemed ready to fly back to Washington in a FBI corporate jet reconfigured so she could lay prone the entire trip. In Washington, Myda and her brother were set up in a small but comfortable apartment near the FBI headquarters where she could convalesce and he could help the FBI track down the still missing women. He spent hours in meetings, reviewing pictures and providing background, as much as he knew about the operation. He resisted firmly when asked to provide details on the new Russian Security Service reminding his interviewers he was still a loyal Russian citizen and had no intention of being disloyal to his country.

After a few days, requests started to come in from the CIA, NSA, NATO and Military Intelligence to speak with him about his experience fighting the Afghan Mujahideen during the Soviet occupation of Afghanistan. The war against the Taliban in Afghanistan was not going well and Kosnar's success there, despite the overall Soviet failure to suppress the Mujahideen was well regarded. Gordon Lewis arranged a few meetings with intelligence operatives and then decided they were beginning to take undue advantage of Vladimir's knowledge and experience. He suggested the government offer Kosnar a consulting job in return for his advice and analysis. He spoke about this with Vladimir at a private lunch meeting.

"They are prepared to offer you a contract for at least one year," he said. "It's a good offer, a substantial hourly rate. More than I make in a year," he said as he laughed.

Vladimir was appreciative but non-committal. He asked about the status of his sister, if she could stay in America with him and Gordon Lewis suggested that could probably be arranged but he would confirm that for certain.

"What about after the first year?" Vladimir asked. "What if my services are no longer needed after that?"

Gordon Lewis smiled and laughed again. "I can think of fifty US based multi-national companies who would pay very handsomely for your knowledge and experience. Companies doing business in Russia and the Middle East need people like you desperately. I can barely hang on to experienced career officers in the FBI with much less depth of knowledge than you who are hired away from us each year."

Vladimir remained non-committal but he promised to consider the offer.

Casey Jennings went through her own rigorous debriefing processes upon her return to Washington. There was some debate about some of the decisions she had made, specifically about first agreeing to meet in the open with Kosnar and then later leaving the scene of David Green's murder. Casey participated openly in these conversations, confident in her decisions which she felt were vindicated by the outcome.

She had not seen either Kosnar nor his sister since a couple of days after Myda had been flown to Washington and so, early one Sunday morning, she purchased some pastries and three cups of coffee and drove to their apartment. She was a little apprehensive about the unannounced visit but she was warmly welcomed especially by Mdya who beckoned her over to the couch where she was resting so she could give Casey a hug.

They sat and chatted awkwardly at first as they nibbled on the pastries but the conversation quickly warmed up as they talked about their lives and experiences. Casey was quite amazed by the difference in Vladimir's demeanor. He had gone from appearing almost resolutely expressionless to happy, smiling easily and breaking in to a shy laugh she found very disarming. Casey particularly liked the tender way in which he treated his sister, not fussing over her but always making sure she was comfortable. Hours passed before Casey finally rose to leave but Myda grabbed her hand and asked her to come back for dinner later that week. Casey agreed and she followed up by offering to take the brother and sister out into the Maryland countryside for a drive and a picnic. Myda was still hobbled, awkwardly moving on crutches but they managed to ease her in to the back of Casey's car and take a drive on a beautiful fall day. When Casey returned them to their apartment she hugged them both before she left.

Her visits became more frequent and on a number of occasions, at Myda's instance, she and Vladimir had gone out for dinner or early morning walks. The conversation between them had come easily, but they said little about the events that had brought them together.

Almost five weeks to the day after the double hip replacement surgery, Casey rode with Myda and Vladimir to the airport. Myda was quite chatty on the ride, but Casey and Vladimir said very little. At the airport, a Red Cross official met them to assist Myda onto the plane. Working with the Red Cross, the FBI had arranged for Myda to travel in first class in order to minimize her discomfort on the long flight back to Moscow. Vladimir was not so fortunate and had to look forward to a long flight in the economy class.

After hugging Casey goodbye and thanking her profusely Myda switched her crutches for a wheelchair, and was pushed into the terminal by the Red Cross official.

Casey and Vladimir faced each other on the sidewalk.

"Thank you," he said. "Thank you for everything."

Casey smiled and thanked him in return and then stepped forward to give him a hug. They held each other for a moment and as she drew away, Vladimir pulled her back to him and kissed her on the mouth, gently at first and then passionately. Casey closed her eyes and reached behind his head with her arm and pulled him close.

After a few moments, Vladimir pulled his head back, his eyes wide and face blushing.

"Excuse me," he mumbled. I'm sorry."

Casey smiled at him as she gently touched his lips with the tips of her fingers and then took his hand in hers.

"Don't be sorry," she said.

Vladimir pulled her close again and then kissed her tenderly on the forehead.

"Can you get a message to Gordon Lewis for me please?" he asked her.

"Sure, what is it?"

"Tell him I accept the job."

"Does that mean you will be coming back to Washington?" she asked.

He smiled as he answered. "Yes, as soon as possible."

Casey leaned forward, kissed him again on the lips and then said, "You had better go. You don't want to miss your flight."

They had one more quick embrace and then Vladimir walked through the automatic double doors into the terminal, turning back just once to glance at Casey who waved and smiled.

* * *

Miriam Konitska was almost out of money. It had been almost eight weeks since she arrived in Washington DC from London after receiving instruction to travel to the US Capitol and wait there for further instructions. Since then there had been no communication. She kept her cell phone charged and with her at all times but as always, there were no calls. She had arrived in Manhattan with just over ten thousand dollars, but after eight weeks, the cost of the hotel and meals, had depleted most of her funds.

At the beginning of the sixth week she twice approached the Russian Embassy, tempted to make contact. But each time she walked by, her controller's admonishment never to make contact rang in her ears. Finally she was down to just enough money to change her plane ticket, settle the hotel bill, and pay for transportation to the airport. She was nervous about leaving without authorization, but felt she had no choice. Also, she was tired of being away for so long without contact with friends or family. On her last morning, she was conflicted between wanting the phone to ring and at the same time wanting so badly to go home, so she left the hotel and boarded the shuttle to the airport.

* * *

Vladimir eased his seat back, stretched out his legs as much as possible in the narrow economy seat and sighed deeply. He had surprised himself when he kissed Casey but was very glad he had. He smiled at the thought of her, and could still feel the taste of her lips on his. For the first time in a long time, perhaps ever, he felt a sense of ease and peacefulness. The reunification with his sister, despite the difficult circumstances in which it had occurred, was bittersweet. He had always felt so guilty when she had been dragged away from him at the orphanage and then never really got used to the permanent emptiness that stayed with him, never knowing what had happened to her and reluctant to put himself or her at risk in the old Soviet regime by using his rank to try and find her. For years he had borne the guilt of their cruel separation.

Myda had asked to see him as soon as she came out of surgery and he had approached her bed nervously, not sure what to expect from her. She was lying on her side, eyes closed, her blond hair spread across the white pillow.

As he stood beside the bed, she opened her eyes, slowly adjusting to the light and peering around the room without moving her head. Looking up, she saw Vladimir and with lips barely parted she whispered his name.

"Vladi."

"Yes," he answered quietly. "It's me."

She pulled her hand from under the sheet and said softly, "Give me your hand." Vladimir gently placed his hand in hers, and lifting her head just slightly, Myda placed the palm of his hand under her face so it cupped her cheek on the pillow and then closed her eyes, a small smile etched on her face as she drifted back to sleep. He had stayed like that for an hour holding her face in his hand, gently caressing her cheek with his free hand. It was only the need for the nurses to provide additional postoperative care that had forced him to leave her again, but just briefly.

Sitting on the plane as it reached cruising altitude he wondered how she was doing in first class, disappointed not to be sitting with her. Glancing up the aisle he saw the flight attendants beginning the beverage service so he decided to wait before moving forward to check on her. Finally, about three hours into flight, he unbuckled his seat belt and stood up and started to make his way to the first class cabin. He stopped to help a woman who was struggling to pull her computer bag out of the overhead bin. A few rows ahead, a couple of boys were already fighting over a hand held video game despite the best effort of their mother to get them to share.

The business class cabin was separated from economy class by a curtain drawn across the isle. He drew the curtain back and stepped through.

"Excuse me, Sir," said a flight attendant serving drinks to the business class passengers, "you can't come through. This cabin is reserved."

"Yes, I know. I just wanted to check on my sister to make sure she's all right."

"Oh, I'm sorry," said the attendant, her tone softening, "you mean the Red Cross passenger in first class. She's towards the front on the right hand side. Please, go ahead."

Vladimir thanked the woman and walked in to the first class cabin to his sister's seat. She had the chair fully reclined, a blanket wrapped around her body.

She saw him and smiled at him as he bent down to kiss her.

"How are you?" Vladimir asked. "Are you comfortable?"

"Yes, I 'm fine. In fact I think I could get used to this, just lying here, having people bring me food and drinks. Not a bad way to live."

"Can I get you anything, something to read, perhaps?"

She reached over and caressed his cheek with the back of her hand and shook her head.

"No, Vladi, I'm fine, thank you. I just wish you could sit with me."

"Me too," he responded with a smile. "I don't think I am going to eat as well as you tonight."

"I'll save you something. Come back later; we can share my dinner."

"You eat everything they give you," he admonished her gently. "You need to build up your strength."

They chatted for a few more minutes then Vladimir leaned forward and kissed her on the forehead.

"I'll come back to check on you later."

He walked out of the first class cabin through business class and back into the economy section. Flight attendants were serving dinner, the carts blocking both passageways. He declined the attendant's offer to try to squeeze past, happy to remain standing for a while. Stepping back towards the plane's center doorway, he leaned down to look out the small window. There appeared to be cloud cover as far as the eye could see. He stepped back into the aisle and slowly followed the flight attendants, casually glancing at the faces of his fellow passengers. His eyes moved indiscriminately, stopping briefly at the sight of a man wearing a very obvious toupee. Something else made him linger and take a second look at a woman about three rows back who was thumbing through a magazine. Even with her head turned slightly down, he could tell she was quite pretty. His stared at her for a moment until she lifted her head and gazed straight at him. Then she dropped her eyes and looked back at her magazine.

Vladimir felt himself take a step back. Reaching out, he steadied himself against the seat next to him, closed his eyes, and shook his head just slightly. Then he looked at the woman again. Miriam Konitska. He was certain it was her. He had been studying the pictures of all the women in the assassin program for days with the FBI task force and had practically memorized each woman's face. Miriam Konitska was sitting almost directly over the wing in a window seat. Vladimir glanced back at the front of the aircraft and for a moment, thought about approaching the pilot. He looked at his wristwatch. They had been airborne almost four hours. The flight was scheduled to take nine hours. If they turned around now, it would still take them at least three hours to land at the nearest airport. He glanced over at the woman again. She had put her magazine down and was staring out of the window. He closed his eyes briefly, and then with one last look at the woman continued towards his seat. It was going to be a long flight home, he thought to himself, a long flight home.

ABOUT THE AUTHOR

R OY BERELOWITZ WAS born in South Africa in 1960. As a young man, Roy served as a paratrooper in the Israeli Army and later immigrated to the United States. After graduating from college, his professional career has focused on computer software in the banking industry, but his avocation has always been writing stories and poems, as well as storytelling. He lives in Orange County, California with his wife and two sons.

Made in the USA
Las Vegas, NV
03 July 2022

51048150R00246